THE
SECRET
MEMOIRS
OF
LORD BYRON

THE
SECRET
MEMOIRS
OF
LORD BYRON

Christopher Nicole

J. B. LIPPINCOTT COMPANY
Philadelphia and New York

U.S. Library of Congress Cataloging in Publication Data

Nicole, Christopher.
 The secret memoirs of Lord Byron.

 1. Byron, George Gordon Noel Byron, Baron,
1788-1824, in fiction, drama, poetry, etc. I. Title.
PZ4.N6425Sd 1978 [PR9320.9.N5] 813 78-14395
ISBN-0-397-01290-X

TABLE OF CONTENTS

THE TALE OF
A MANUSCRIPT

Cruising is my hobby. Every June my wife and I shut up our house and take to the sea in our fifty ton motor yacht, and for three months become carefree nomads. I write about the sea, to a large extent, and so it is all useful background material, but more than that, it is an essential exchange of the make-believe world of the novelist for the realities of nature. You do not wish a storm away by ending a chapter.

Our playground is Western Europe, our favourite sea the Mediterranean, our destination whenever possible the islands of Greece. No doubt, like Byron himself, we are drawn by the mountains, the wine dark sea, the thought that we are sailing where Odysseus went before.

But neither Byron nor the glory that was Greece was in my mind on a stormy June evening two years ago, when we approached Zante on a passage from Valetta, and came upon a fishing boat in trouble. Her engine had broken down and she was being battered by quite large waves. With some difficulty, we managed to pass her a line, and took her in tow, and next morning, when the wind and the seas had eased, and Zante was rising out of the eastern horizon, we discovered that she was crewed by a father and son. Our conversation had to be conducted mainly by signs, as they spoke no English and our Greek is very limited, but with the aid of a chart they were able to show me where they wished to be taken, and so it was that about noon I steered *Sprayline* into a tiny little creek, and peered at the half dozen houses which clung to the shores of the inlet, above which the cliffs rose sheer. There was one other boat moored in the centre of the little harbour, and clearly the pair were the village's entire fishing fleet, for at the sight of *Sprayline* nosing her way into their kingdom the waterfront was suddenly crowded with men and women and children, all chattering, all pointing, all highly excited.

By now I was realising that the place was so very small, at least when it came to adequate water, that there was no hope of turning the yacht; I would have to back the whole way out. Nor could I see that I could possibly anchor, without immediately swinging into either the moored fishing boat or the shore.

I need not have worried. As I brought the ship to a stop we were surrounded by rowing vessels, and boarded in a manner which made me think of West Indian pirates. My own warps were carried out, two from the bow and two from the stern, until *Sprayline* was secured so firmly that she could not drift an inch in any direction. By now Papa had taken control of the situation, was giving orders, and inviting his friends into the wheelhouse to show them the wonders of modern science, Jean's galley, the armchairs in the saloon, and even taking them below to illustrate the double bed in the master stateroom.

Jean and I wondered what was going to happen next, for so far not a word of English had been spoken, when, happiest of sounds, a voice said: "We are very grateful to you, sir."

The speaker was a woman, tall and black haired, with handsome rather than pretty features, and a good deal of strength of will evident in her long jaw. "I am the schoolmistress," she said. "And on behalf of my friend, Nicolo Chalandritsanos, I wish to thank you for saving his life."

"We happened to be there," I pointed out, embarrassed.

"Nevertheless, we would like to entertain your wife and yourself," she said. "It is the least we can do."

Of course we accepted, exhausted as we were, and were treated to an afternoon of *garides* and *calamari*, *hirino* and *nefro*, gallons of *ouzo*, and a good deal of singing and dancing and handclapping. Not all of which could be appreciated, as our constantly closing eyes were concentrating on gaining the quiet of that double bed. But it was impossible to stay sober, especially as none of our hosts or hostesses were doing so, and so it was that around dusk I found myself sitting next to Papa, who was weeping into his *ouzo* and muttering beneath his moustache.

"Nicolo is sad," said the schoolmistress. "He is a poor man, and he can see that you are a rich man. How can he reward you for saving his life?"

"I do not wish a reward," I explained. "But I'd like to point out that I am not a rich man. I wish I were. I'm a reasonably successful writer who has tied up his every last penny in a boat. It's a way of life."

"A writer," she said. "You are a writer." And she immediately began to tell her friends. A reaction one gets used to, even when it is invariably accompanied by the remark: "I am afraid I have never read one of your books."

"My dearest wish is to meet someone who has," I agreed. "They must be there, somewhere."

She ignored my attempt at humour. "Nicolo has something he would like you to see."

My heart sank all the way down to my boots. I suppose the biggest hazard to which any writer is exposed is the desire of everyone he meets to trot out a dog-eared manuscript for criticism and help in placing. But Nicolo was already on his feet, as was the schoolmistress. I gave Jean a hopeless look and followed, up the street and into a little cottage at the top. Half the village crowded in behind me, into a small but delightfully neat living-room. Here I was seated before the table, while Nicolo went upstairs, accompanied by his son and his wife.

"I'm afraid I do not read Greek," I said to the schoolmistress. "But I suppose I could take the manuscript to someone in Athens."

She smiled, archly. "This is Nicolo's dearest possession," she said. "He inherited it from his father."

Which roused my interest at least a little, although I could see even less chance of finding a publisher for a Greek novel written perhaps in the nineteen thirties, even supposing it was well written. But before I could think of any more platitudes, Nicolo was back, and with a vast parcel, which sent my heart plummeting once again.

The parcel was placed on my lap, and the family stood around, expectantly.

"He wishes you to open it," the schoolmistress explained. "This is a great honour. I do not think even Nicolo has ever opened that parcel."

"I hope it doesn't contain a bomb," I muttered, and released the string. To discover another layer of brown paper. The old box joke, perhaps, I thought hopefully, and undid this in turn. I was right. Yet another layer of brown paper. But this was very old. My heart began to rise again, and even to pound a little. I had certainly never come across anything like this.

The fourth layer was oilcloth, and the knots were beyond even a seaman. I was strangely reluctant to cut them. "Has he no idea what is inside?" I asked the schoolmistress.

"He has never opened the parcel," she said. "It is a family, how do you say? Treasure?"

"Heirloom," I said.

"That is it," she agreed. "No one knows when it came into

possession of the family. But it has been here for years and years. More than a hundred years. It was left here, so it is said, by an Englishman. When we were fighting the Turks. . . ." She paused as if she would have liked to spit on the floor, but apparently changed her mind.

By now my heart was thumping quite a bit. "Then I cannot possibly take it," I said. "It may be very valuable."

"But you have saved his life," she said. "And his boat, which is equally important. Believe me, sir, he would be offended were you to refuse his offer. He can pay you nothing."

"I do not wish, or require payment," I insisted.

"The debt is one of honour," she pointed out, equally adamant.

I took the manuscript, saying that I would at least have a look at it, rescued Jean from the attentions of the dancing villagers, and regained the privacy of *Sprayline*'s stateroom. I had not slept at all the previous night, and it was again dusk, but I no longer felt in the least tired.

Yet I was still reluctant to cut the cords holding the inner parcel. I assaulted the knots with a marlinspike, and after several minutes worked them loose. The oilcloth opened, and out spilled an avalanche of sheets of paper, all covered in an extremely well-formed, almost copperplate handwriting in *English*, although in many places the ink was so faded as to be almost illegible. Nor were the sheets in any order, suggesting that the parcel had been opened at some time in the past, perhaps more than once, and an attempt made at deciphering the contents. But they were numbered, which made the task of restoring them to coherence merely tedious. Not that I would have cared if it had required a year of work, for while the sheets of the manuscript itself were flat, there was a folded letter tucked in the centre, and one look at this convinced me that I had come upon perhaps the greatest literary discovery of all time.

I would not, then, have termed myself a Byron scholar. I knew a great deal about him, of course, and had read most of his poetry. I was familiar with the disastrous course of his life, of his marriage, and I knew the famous story of how his Memoirs, given to Thomas Moore in 1819, had been burned in the presence of Moore himself, Hobhouse, and Murray the publisher, soon after Byron's death, an act of quite unbelievable literary vandalism. I find it difficult to express my feelings as I turned page after page, and realised that not only was this a first draft of the original Memoir, and in Byron's own handwriting, but that it had been brought up to date, and to within a few days of his death, just across the water from Zante, in the town now known as Missolonghion.

How did such a treasure come into the hands of a Greek fisherman who did not even know what it was? You may choose to draw your own conclusions from the letter, but it seems fairly obvious to me that either the boy Lukas or someone else removed it from the dying poet's bedchamber, almost certainly under instruction from Byron himself. Perhaps at that time it was the intention to obey his last wish, and send the manuscript to Augusta Leigh, but for some reason this was never done. In the excitement and grief of Byron's death it may have been overlooked. More likely it is that it was secured by our friend Nicolo's ancestor, anxious for some souvenir of the great man who was the hope of Greece. We know there was such a scramble for souvenirs amongst even the so-called gentlemen who were attending him. And of course, *no one knew of the existence of such a memoir*, so it was not missed.

The question must immediately be asked, is this work a forgery? Perhaps it may be thought rather odd that anyone prepared to undertake such a mammoth task would have suffered it to sit in a chest in a remote Greek village for over a hundred and fifty years. More important is the content. This is certainly a Byron who, if known to his friends, as his letters prove, has been forgotten by the public at large, who see only the poet, the lecher, and the would-be hero. He is all of those things, if in a slightly different sense to the generally accepted judgements. His poetry he regarded as an affliction. He wrote it whenever in the grip of an extreme passion, as a lesser man might have got drunk, and although he never underestimated his own genius, he regarded the muse as merely the least important of his talents. And if he was perhaps more lecherous than has even been suspected by his worst enemy, at least after he had overcome his Calvinist scruples, this can not only at least partially be excused by the events of his childhood, but also by his own personality. To say that he was over-sexed is like saying that the moon is a long way away. The desire to *know* people, of either sex, was the overwhelming passion of his mind, and he assumed that everyone would be equally anxious to *know* him, and so spent his life shocking friend and foe alike by the remarkable candour of his words, his letters, and his poems. And finally, if he certainly set out to be a hero, this was because he felt it his duty to be one. He *knew* he was born to greatness, but being the man he was he could not believe such greatness would be nothing more than literary. The

11

opportunity to lead a people he in any event loved more than his own appeared to him an act of God.

More than any of these, however, the Byron revealed by these Memoirs is a man forever seeking to realise true happiness. The misanthropy of his poems and some of his actions only rarely comes through; he is a man of moods, but the vivacious, fascinating Byron of after-dinner conversation is present too. He is a man for whom life is a gigantic adventure, for whom tomorrow is never as important as today, and yesterday is only to be savoured by what has been accomplished. To read this autobiography is to be shocked, but it is also to enter the mind, and the body, of one of the most vibrant personalities ever to walk the stage of history.

The original Memoir given to Moore was written soon after Byron left England in 1816 upon the break-up of his marriage, and included the chapters on that marriage. It did not, as stated by Byron himself, and confirmed from the various references to it made by Moore, include any mention of his love for his sister, which at that time was a tremendous scandal, and one to which Byron was not inclined to add. It would seem that he wrote the chapter on his relationship with Augusta at a later date, no doubt for his own gratification, as he realised that he would never be allowed to see her again. Similarly, there are portions of this draft, enclosed in brackets, which I assume were deleted when the fair copy, given to Moore, was made. In view of their content, one would like to *believe* they were omitted. Why he chose to continue the autobiography is amply explained in the Letter. But it will be seen that the work naturally lends itself to three divisions. For the sake of continuity I have inserted the sections on Augusta where they belong, immediately before his marriage to Anna Isabella Milbanke, and that portion written after 1816 comprises the third and final section. I have also further subdivided the work into chapters, again for readability, and wherever it appears that Byron himself broke the narrative, for whatever reason.

This arrangement apart, editorial comment has been kept to a minimum and is used only to identify the characters to whom he refers so familiarly, and also to overcome the odd place where the writing has defeated the best efforts to decipher it. I have added some essential punctuation, and I have altered spellings, especially of names, to maintain consistency, just as I have reduced his underlinings [here reproduced in italics] – to which he was very partial – for the sake of readability. There are also several pages missing, no doubt lost on previous openings of the manuscript, when it was allowed to fall on the floor or table, and attain the state of remarkable disorder in which I found it. These missing pages are a tragic loss, but they do not in any way spoil the narrative, or the overall impression of energy, or perhaps grandeur, which accompanies it.

And so, ladies and gentlemen, I give you, George Gordon Noel Byron, 6th Lord Byron.

THE LETTER

Missolonghi,
Greece.
12 April 1824

My Dearest Guss, (i)

Should you read this, I shall be dead. No melancholy. I doubt it *will* ever be read, by you or anyone.

Yet a man must prepare. The truth of the matter is, I have suffered from a fever these last few days, brought on at least as much by frustration as by miasmic swamp vapours, and am feeling uncommonly low. I shall be well, and soon. I can say this with confidence, as these confounded leeches will soon leave me with no blood on which they can feed, and must then necessarily give up their assaults. (ii) But once I *am* well again, I propose to embark upon our first military campaign, and seize the port of Lepanto, which I am informed is but scantily defended. We shall triumph, to be sure, but who can tell where a stray bullet might find its lodgement?

I offer you here no more scurrilous poetry. *Don Juan*, to be sure, is several cantos advanced, and will no doubt raise his usual scream of protest from the enlightened English public, but that is a matter for the devious Hunt. (iii) Here we have nothing more important, or less so, than my life.

I do not imagine you are acquainted with Tom Moore. Lucky Sis. He is a most charming fellow and at one time, but so long ago, the writer of equally charming verses. When I was a lad, and how long ago *that* seems, they quite turned my head. Now he is grown altogether too sober to be contemplated, save from a safe distance. But to him, in my unwisdom, I consigned the first half of this laborious love, when it was completed, in 1819. My instructions were for him to obtain the best possible price for it, from that scoundrel Murray, but

15

to delay publication until after my death. It contained a faithful, no doubt too faithful, account of my peccadilloes, as well as my triumphs, such as they were, and my disasters, such as certainly were, and was intended, I suspect – it is difficult to be sure of one's moods at a distance of eight years – to justify my side of the marriage bed. I do assure you, Sweet Sis, that not a word was written which indicated anything more than my utter and consuming love for you, which I have never dared deny, but pursued in the light of a lord and a *brother*.

Moore having obtained the advantage, this pile of paper is worthless to you, alas. Nor would I have it otherwise. Let him publish what he wills. The enclosed is for your eyes *alone*. The original is here. You may contend his omissions, or more important, perhaps, any *submissions* that may creep in. But the added material is of an altogether personal nature. I have written of you and me, that you may for a moment relive that rapture we once found for so brief a time. I have written of Teresa. Who knows, you may meet her one day.(iv) Only you could understand how much we shared, because we *shared*, as two people ought, as two people once did.

And I have written of Shiloh.(v) We never loved each other. We merely loved, and that is perhaps the most sublime of all emotions.

You will ask yourself, why write a Memoir at all? And I will reply from the grave, how else may a man know himself? Save in recalling the events, and more important, the people, who made him what he is. A new-born babe is to my mind like a square stone boulder, set to face the winds and the rain and the lightning. Over the years these forces, in the form of those people and those events which affect him deeply, eat away at the rock, and uncover what lies beneath. It is possible that the erosive process will reveal nothing more than soft clay, ever crumbling into dust. It is possible that the outer stone may disappear to leave only granite, hard and unyielding. And very rarely it happens that the covering rock, as it dwindles, exposes a vein of purest gold running through the whole. It is at least interesting to watch this process at work.

So read it, Guss, and lock it away. Or read it, and burn it. I am entrusting it to a faithful lad, Lukas Chalandritsanos, who has been serving me as best he is able, and who is well connected in these parts, and thus able to insure that the manuscript reaches you in safety. To such lengths am I reduced. Stanhope(vi) would surely burn it, and Parry(vii), if not so critical, would most certainly read it first, while the thought of its falling into the hands of someone like Trelawny(viii) quite makes me shiver. Pietro(ix) would be a safe courier, but I write of his sister, and of you, and only *you* can understand.

So fare thee well, dearest Sis. I swear you shall never want.(x) And when you think of me, of the good times no less than the bad, remember only this: I loved, *you*. What a triumph we would have enjoyed had I been born a Pharaoh.(xi)

Ever thine,
Byron (+ + +)(xii)

BOOK THE FIRST

MAY

A man's first example should be his father. Mine disappeared from my life before I was three years old, and died a year later, alone and friendless, without, by all accounts, a shirt to his back, in a France already seething with anger, already embarked upon the road to Robespierre.(i)

Yet his influence has been profound. Consider that he bore one of the oldest names in the realm; there was a Byron at Great William's elbow when he struck Harold to the dust.(ii) Consider that he was surrounded within his family by wealth and position, an uncle who was a baron,(iii) a father who was a famous admiral,(iv) and yet possessed none of the worldly goods necessary to sustain such rank; his own father, Foulweather Jack himself, performed the act of disinheritance. And consider finally that, by the most prejudiced account, he was a handsome and dashing fellow, then we must conclude, as I early did, that the world was fortunate he did not turn his *mis*fortunes to piracy or highway robbery, but instead sought only to live, and laugh, and love.

In which last capacity he was prodigiously successful, thus leaving his two children an example upon which they could only hope to build. That we have done so is surely to our credit. His first wife, the Countess of Carmarthen,(v) was extracted from her own first husband's bedchamber, and became three times a mother for dear Dad. Of these adulterous offspring only one survived, but that was my sister Augusta. Had the fair Countess lived, while *I* would never have been born, Papa would have prospered, for she was also possessed of a large personal income as well as a humour to match his own. Unluckily for him, she died as Augusta was born, and with her, her fortune.

Which left Papa with no alternative but to seek a successor, and this time he was less discerning. I intend no disrespect to my mother. The facts are there. Her family was every bit as old and even better connected than the Byrons; one of her ancestors was conceived within a royal bed. (vi) But they were *Scots*. I am proud of my Scottish blood. It is wild and untamed. It is also uncouth. And Mama's family, the Gordons of Gight, were renowned for their savagery even amongst their savage peers. (vii) Add to which the unfortunate fact that Mama was fat and by no means handsome, where the Countess had been slender and by all accounts a rare beauty – which I can believe when I consider her daughter – and that her speech was all but unintelligible with its "'twas" and "gaes" and "bonnies" and "braes", and it will be appreciated that Papa must have been desperate.

For money. But even in this respect Mama was a total failure. For where the Countess had possessed four thousand a year, Mama possessed twenty thousand in all.

What then was left for this unhappy person to do, save bear her lord a son, handsome and strong and able and ambitious, to wipe the spectre of failure and of poverty from his father's anguished brow? Alas for poor Mama. She fulfilled her duty to the best of her ability, but the result was a sad thing, a creature deformed in body, and some would say, my own dearest wife to the fore, (viii) in mind as well.

My earliest memories, therefore, are of Papa shouting at Mama, of Mama shouting at Papa, and of pain. This is not intended as a plea for pity. Far from it. Rather do *I* pity *those* who spend their childhood in dull contemplation of their navels. *If* I remember Papa, and I am sure I do, my senses were alive and functioning well before the age of three, and if a certain amount of discomfort is necessary to such precocity, then I welcome it, and would recommend it to my friends.

In itself of course my right foot did not ache. What did cause me intense discomfort were the efforts of my mother and the various quacks to whom she turned for help, to correct the deformity, which was nothing more than a turning in of the toes, so that I walked on the very outside of the foot, and awkwardly. Thus special boots and iron braces were the order of the day, together with even more horrid medical remedies, such as hot wax. No doubt early considerations, in which I shared, that I should one day rival Sheridan, (ix) were based entirely upon the strength of my overtrained lungs.

Far harder to bear than any physical pain was the pity of all around me, headed by my mother. And hers was the worst, for she varied moments of maudlin anguish over my misfortune with others of foaming anger over *hers*, in bearing such a Caliban. And I undoubtedly added to her nature by displaying my own. Aware that *something* was wrong with me, if perhaps unable to be sure of what, I found my pleasures in driving her to distraction, and achieved my greatest coup when throwing a dummy made up of bed-clothes from my window and past a lower one at which I knew she was sitting, thus leading her to suppose for an hysterical moment, that her son had left to join his father.

She loved me, I have no doubt, especially in retrospect. But it was difficult to be aware of it at the time. Thus lacking all pleasure in my intimate surroundings, I sought it outside. We lived in Aberdeen, a place of granite and grey skies, but beyond the town there was beauty enough for those who sought it. The Bridge of Balgounie, with its splendid curve and the dark waters flowing beneath. And the mountains of the Highlands. Here was a strength and a nobility I doubted I would ever possess. My happiest childhood days were spent at Ballaterich, which was farmed by the Duffs, cousins of Mama's, and from whose pastures I could climb, slowly and painfully but the more enjoying my exertions, over crags and along ledges, to feel like an eagle, to understand the deathless beauty of nature, to allow my lungs and my heart to fill, with a sense of space, and grandeur.

It was at the farm that I fell in love, for the first time in my life, with my cousin, Mary Duff. I suppose I was six, she perhaps a year or so older. A mystifying experience, even now. I knew nothing of man's desires, nor woman's, nor even that either sex possessed them. I was not even sure of the Difference. I knew only that here was a fabulous creature, with long, floating dark hair, and huge blue eyes, who, no doubt carefully coached by her parents, was happy to see me, to walk with me and talk with me, childish things but not less valuable for that, and of whom I was happy to dream.

Did she love as well? Does she ever, now, remember that crook-legged little fellow, already with a reputation for deviltry, and surely with no looks then visible, who followed her around like a devoted dog? Or was her motive entirely sinister? For by the time I met her I was a changed being. The laws of heredity move in a mysterious way. Thus my great uncle, the 5th Lord Byron, had never borne any love for old Admiral Foulweather his brother, had not even communed with him over thirty years, and lived alone and bitter in his crumbling abbey at Newstead. The two branches of the family had split asunder, a split which was accentuated when milord's heir, William, eloped with his cousin Juliana, Papa's sister, and was promptly disinherited, to die young. His brother-in-law was proud only to be known as Mad Jack, and also suffered disinheritance. But the third William, who succeeded his father as heir to the title, was a perfect model of duty. And England's duty, as so well explained by the noble Horatio, (x) is to suffer shot and shell that the Tory landowners may sleep easy in their beds.(xi) Thus cousin William, at that same siege of Calvi where our great admiral lost his eye, contrived to stand even closer to an exploding shell. Far more disastrous, the poor fool had *not even managed to marry and beget.* Well, Mad Jack had already perished in his Parisian garret, Foulweather had long been in his grave, so to the total scandal of the entire Byron family, and they were sufficiently numerous, even then, to deserve the appellation of clan, the "lame brat" became heir to a barony.

Mama was not, of course, informed. The news reached her by various circuitous routes, but I shall never forget the day it arrived. "Geordie," she screamed, making the rafters ring. "Geordie. Ye're to be a lor'. Ye're to be a lor'." She burst into my room, seized me by the shoulders and shook me as if I were a delinquent dog. "Ye're to be a lor'. Whadye think of that? A lor'." She sank on my bed, and remarked, quite irrelevantly I then thought, but most ominously: "Lor's canna be gaoled for debt."

Having never met a lord, my concern was to study myself in the glass, to note the change which would surely set me aside from all other men, and was disturbed to note not a one. I was then six years old.

So dearest Mary *may* have been told to be nice to her cousin because he would, eventually, be the 6th Lord Byron. Which no doubt accounted for the very brief nature of our acquaintance. Lords might not be capable of going to prison for debt, but their heirs were not necessarily wealthy.

Papa, as was his wont, had squandered every penny of Mama's money that he could discover, and from the wreck she had rescued an income of roughly a hundred and fifty pounds a year. Well, it may be said, many people live well upon a great deal less, and Mama was not an extravagant person. Far from it. Yet was she a great lady, and she required a certain style. There was nothing to spare for my education, and even she was capable of understanding that the 6th Lord Byron could not be a broad-accented Scots yokel. But her pleas for assistance went unanswered. My great uncle might have been the great god Baal for all the notice he took of anything save his own pleasures. And so I

24

was despatched to the local grammar school, to become at least acquainted with *amo* and *amas*, although most of my time was spent in learning to write this lamentable hand.

When I was not fighting. For to my schoolfellows I was an object of derision. They ran and I hobbled. Yet where one limb is weak another invariably compensates. From the waist up I had the physique of a Jackson,(xii) even at that early age, and once let an adversary come within reach of my fingers the difference of opinion was as good as settled.

But here again I would describe my misfortune in being friendless at school as a blessing. Deprived of companions eager to share my leisure hours, I began to read. History in the main. I devoured every fact known about the past, and managed to remember most of them. There was also time for books on travel, and works of fiction. I remember especially Gessner's *Death of Abel*; and *Zeluco*, by John Moore, a character with whom, as I grew to know more of the history of my family, I could not help but find much in common. But my favourite work of all was Knolles' *Turkish History*. My interest in the Levant was thus early aroused.

So what have we here? A confused callow cripple, aware by the age of nine that life was an uphill business, knowing only that he was certain to become one of the leaders of the nation, rendered by his circumstances aggressive and impulsive, but made by his nature able to understand and appreciate beauty.

And as yet, as is everyone at that age, unaware of the vital spark that makes him a *man*. Although the moment was at hand, for in 1797, soon after my ninth birthday, my nurse, Alice Gray, wished to marry, and thus to leave my mother's employ, and in her place recommended to dear Mama her sister, a girl named May.

My first impression of May Gray was one of extreme pleasure, and it would be false of me to pretend that I do not still enjoy a thrill of delight when I think of her, for all the pain she later caused me. She is not alone, God knows, in accomplishing that.

Her sister Alice had always seemed to me to be a rather remote figure. She was *over twenty*, and she was, in addition, the most rampant Calvinist that ever walked the earth, or so I supposed at that time. An extra helping of jam for tea was evidence of that yielding to temptation which ensured me a place in the fiery furnace, and her choice for my reading consisted of the *Psalms* with which I thus obtained an intimate acquaintance. She even conceived of my mother, the most femininely inept of persons, as being a succubus in disguise merely by possessing the odd piece of jewellery, not to mention a ball gown which revealed the bulging tops of her breasts. I fancy Mama was quite pleased to see Alice go, and perhaps a little uneasy at the thought of replacing her with another from the same stable.

But May put us all at ease with a single smile. She was a remarkably pretty girl, as I remember, with somewhat small, pert features, and a mass of light brown hair which took on a reddish tinge when the sun struck it. In this lies my predilection for auburn hair, which to this moment has landed me in nothing but trouble. (xiii)

I met her for the first time upon my return from school one afternoon, with my red pantaloons split at the knee where I had fallen in the course of a set-to with one of my fellows, while my cheeks also carried evidence of the conflict. Mama promptly flew into a rage, occasioned as I now know by the thought of having to replace a pair of costly trousers, but seeming to me at the time quite lacking in sympathy. "Geordie," she squawled. "Ye are naught but a guttersnipe, and the son o' a guttersnipe. Brawling. I'll take ma stick to ye."

"If I'm the son of a guttersnipe," I pointed out, equally loudly, "then you must be the creature herself."

Which earned me a swipe across the head. I staggered across the room, seized the first object which came to hand, a silver picture frame containing the likeness of one of Mama's Gordon ancestors, and hurled it at her. She ducked and the missile removed a windowpane, which in turn earned me another blow.

A common enough scene in our happy home. Imagine my delight when on evading yet a third swing of Mama's fists I stumbled through the doorway and into the arms of this splendid creature, all starched white apron from neck to ankle, but all bubbling vivacity above.

"Hold him there," Mama bawled, now in full chase. "Hold the rascal, May. I'm not done."

"But he's hurt, ma'am," the gallant girl replied, clutching me against her starch.

"He'll be hurt more," Mama growled, delivering two more slaps on my defenceless bottom.

"Ah, ma'am, 'tis no business for a lady," May protested. "The lad needs a whipping to be sure. Can I no do it for ye?"

"See that ye do," Mama agreed, already out of breath. "I'll hear him bawl, mind. See to it."

"Upstairs wi' ye," May commanded, while I looked around for a suitable weapon with which to defend myself. But there was none to be had, and I was immediately made aware that she was an extraordinarily strong girl; when she gripped my arm and urged me forward there was nothing I could do save go. "Now," she said, having closed my bedroom door behind us. "Down wi' your breeks, and kneel at the bed." She rumpled my hair. "I'll not use a stick."

The whole thing smacked of a conspiracy, in which I suddenly longed to be a partner. I obligingly dropped my breeches, being at that time not aware that there might be anything unseemly about such an action in the private company of a woman only nine years my senior, and knelt by the bed.

"Now be sure ye bawl," she reminded me, and a moment later her hand crashed into my buttocks with a formidable force. In fact there was very little play acting in my utterance, which grew in volume as she hit me several times more. "Now ye can rise," she said, panting delicately.

Which I did, feeling sore, to be sure, but quite delighted, a sensation which was evidenced in a strange way to me, as my cocker had suddenly assumed a horizontal posture. Now this had happened before, usually in my bath, when I was wont to finger it and enjoy the sensation which followed, a pastime which had invariably earned me a bat around the ears from Alice. But I could not recall it happening of its own accord, and was at once bewildered and a little embarrassed.

While May appeared pleased. "Ye're a de'il, Master Geordie. Oh, nay doot of that." She smiled at me. "Maybe ye've no idea what it's about, ye poor lad." She swept me from the floor in a vast hug, completing the penetration of the starch to reach something much warmer and softer. "Maybe I should tell ye. Ye're too pretty a lad not to be at the girlies, soon enough."

A prospect I found entrancing, quite without understanding why. Suffice that I waited with impatience for my nurse to undress, for she shared a bed in my very room. As had her sister. But never had I been the slightest bit interested in Alice's pre-slumber machinations. May I watched with total absorption, marvelling at the prim way in which she folded her uniform, the grace with which she stepped out of her shift, observing, for the very first time in my life the quiver of a female bottom as she stooped away from me, the swell of her already heavy

27

breasts, deliciously upturned and dotted with a protruding nipple as large as my fingernail.

I say observed, because I remember these things as if they were yesterday, but yet without at the time any sense of appreciation, of wishing to possess those attributes of feminine delight. I was waiting for something to happen to *me*. And soon enough it did, for stretching me upon my back in my bed she proceeded to slide the forefinger of her right hand up my penis, from ball to tip, inducing a quite magnificent sensation of abandon into my brain at the same time as she brought the little chap hard as a ramrod.

"Procreation," she said sombrely. "Aye, 'tis a terrible thing, Master Geordie, in which a man inflicts his worst upon some poor girl, and she is done with, save he marries her, and even then 'tis naught but a bed of nails for the rest of her life. And here is the weapon himself," she whispered, kissing me on the lips as she did so. "And ready for a man's work, if ever I saw one."

I felt her hand close on me, even as something else quite remarkable happened. For the splendid feeling of abandonment which had seized hold of my being had swollen into a whirlpool of desire, for what I had no idea, accompanied always by a similar swelling in my groin and into her hand, which as suddenly exploded into a surge of the purest delight followed by a feeling of total contentment, coupled with amazement and just a little disgust as I observed that I had filled the dear girl's palm with a thick white liquid.

Which did not seem to distress her unduly. "The de'il himself," she remarked, and left the bed to wash.

My first ejaculation. And into the hands of my nurse at the age of nine. Precocity run riot. As far as I can ascertain, most lads reach manhood in a midnight turmoil which soaks the sheets and leaves them uncertain as to whether they have been in heaven or in hell, and at this moment it may be appropriate to ask what a great lout like myself was doing in the company of a nurse in any case. I should of course have already had a tutor, who would no doubt have performed a similar task to May, but possibly with a different result. But Mama could not rise to such an expense. Ours was an entirely female household, save for myself, and that such an existence could lead to anything other than perfect gentleness in me never crossed the dear old soul's mind.

But May was not a gentle person. To the instincts of a whore she added the very spirit of Calvin, and within moments of my initiation into the mysteries of the flesh we were on our knees together, praying for forgiveness, I am uncertain whether it was mine or hers.

Not that this seemed important at the time, to me. I lived only for the touch of that powerful right hand. Indeed I have no doubt at all that my seniors, and more especially Mama herself, saw in me a magnificent change for the better. The pain caused by the wearing of my hideous irons, the shame of it, the tantrums to which I had always been subject, now became entirely bearable. Each day was but a purgatory which had to be traversed to reach the privacy of my bedchamber, and the cool joy of those fingers. The very sight of May, standing in the doorway to summon me to my bath, could turn me into an angel. On his way to hell.

And what did she ask in return? What did she *seek*? I gave this not a thought at the time, but a great deal of thought in recent years. I can only suppose power. It is inconceivable that she could have found any physical attraction in me, nor did she ever require any reciprocal action. And yet every night she was at my body. Not always to my own delight. *Her* delight was everything carnal. My baths became slow and detailed affairs. Should I be constipated for a day, there was recourse to the enema. And sometimes her assaults on my poor penis were made in a quite uncharitable spirit, which however enjoyable during the moments of arousal would leave me distinctly sore, while she knelt beside me and wallowed in self abasement, calling upon her God to save her from herself, and from the machinations of the wicked young man into whose custody she had been placed.

Such confusion would have inspired an older and wiser man with a suspicion of disaster. I knew only that I was her contented slave, and could envisage no change at all in our existence. Because I did not suspect that a change, an improvement, was possible. So we were both on the road to catastrophe. The gates to hell were opened wide on 21 May 1798, when my great uncle, known as the Wicked Lord Byron, died.

THE 6TH LORD BYRON

Doctor Bowers must have his say, and at roll call the day after the momentous news arrived the entire class was struck dumb by his requesting an aye from someone called *"Dominus de* Byron". Several seconds of silence followed, while every head turned in my direction, an embarrassment which, I am ashamed to say, caused me to burst into tears. But after all, I was now very much the Lord Byron, and such pin pricks became irrelevant in the excitement of selling up our modest home to make our assault upon the splendid acres which were now mine.

I must confess that in my innocence of financial matters, I assumed that the day my great uncle died our floors would immediately become paved with gold. On the contrary, not a thing happened beyond the announcement of the event. Mama had to place all our goods at auction to raise sufficient money to transfer us south. But even she was in the best of humours. Shortage of cash could be no more than a nuisance. Newstead, situated in the county of Nottingham, mustered over three thousand acres of prime parkland, while in the county of Lancashire I apparently owned some additional property, containing coal mines of enormous wealth.

I could hardly wait to be there, and in fact soon enough we were off, following the coast road to Arbroath before turning in for Dundee and Perth, threading our way along the valleys to Stirling and Falkirk, rattling through Edinburgh before rejoining the coast to Dunbar, and crossing the border at Berwick upon Tweed. I may say that this was not the first time I had been in England, as I had actually been born in London, on 22 January 1788. But as I was almost immediately removed north of the border, I was *looking* at England for the first time.

The three of us, for Mama and I were accompanied only by the faithful May, our excitement increasing with every night and indeed with every rumble of the coachwheels beneath us, made our way down to Newcastle upon Tyne, past the lofty battlements of Durham Cathedral, and on to Darlington and the cloisters of York, thence to Doncaster and at last Mansfield. Four miles south of Mansfield, and still some ten north of the city of Nottingham itself, we arrived at the Newstead Tollgate.

Mama must now roll down the window. "And wha's estate may this be?" she demanded of the bewildered gatekeeper.

"Why, it was Lord Byron's, ma'am," the worthy fellow replied. "But he is lately dead."

"Then who is the heir?" Mama inquired, her voice rising higher yet.

The worthy scratched his head. "Ah, well, ma'am, they do say 'tis a Scot. A little boy what lives in Aberdeen, may God bless his soul."

Mama gave a peal of laughter, while May threw both arms around my neck and kissed me on the lips. "This is him," she cried. "God bless him."

Which left the poor fellow confounded and me wondering if perhaps neither Mama nor May had actually believed in my inheritance until they had heard the words spoken by a stranger.

In any event we were soon rolling down the drive to the Abbey, for Newstead had originally been a religious foundation and had been bestowed upon my ancestors by Great Harry when he was in the course of dispossessing all those God ridden priests who were seeking to interfere with his pleasures. Our emotions were decidedly mixed, for to begin with, the carriage drive was a most peculiar one, as it was bordered not by great trees, but by the *stumps* of great trees, while beyond, when we might have expected to see a small forest, there was nothing but more stumps, and in the distance, we could make out the farms upon which my income depended, but standing in a state of disrepair, for roofs had fallen in and palings were gaping, and indeed the whole countryside presented a picture of wanton neglect.

Nor was the Abbey itself, upon which we came after a drive of some two miles, in much better condition. Here again we saw the collapsed roof, a gaping empty wall, a pile of rubbled stone. But at least the house attached to it retained some semblance of a civilised dwelling while immediately beyond the house there glinted the waters of a lake, and beyond this acres of rolling land, although the whole continued to be strangely denuded of trees.

The carriage came to a halt before a fountain which decorated the forecourt immediately in front of the main doorway, and here we discovered several servants, and a lady and a gentleman, waiting to greet us. The servants meant very little to me at the time, although several of them were to mean a great deal in later years, but the lady and gentleman were to rank high in my life from the moment of this very first meeting, for they were a Mr and Mrs John Hanson, and Mr Hanson had been my late uncle's solicitor.

He was a stout, pleasant looking fellow. Reflection in later years convinces me that all men of affairs should avoid stout solicitors, as the question may well be asked, if he *is* a successful lawyer, with a large and businesslike clientele, how did he manage to become stout in the first place? This applies very strongly to dear Hanson, but I do not withdraw my adjective, for if he was certainly the most dilatory of men, whose sins of neglect and omission kept me in poverty for much longer than was necessary and surely assisted Mama into her early grave; he was also one of the most faithful, who when it came to a pinch stood at my side throughout the worst of my afflictions. (i)

On the occasion of this first meeting, however, he was all efficiency. "My lord," he said, taking my hand as gravely as if I had been thirty instead of approaching eleven. "I have awaited this meeting with impatience. I trust you had a pleasant journey."

"Tedious, man," Mama explained. "Tedious. And now. . . ." She looked around her with an expression of bewilderment. "There are no trees."

Hanson gave a gentle cough, with which I was to become well acquainted in later years. "His lordship . . . ahem . . . I mean his *late* lordship, was in the habit of cutting them down. Debts, you understand."

Inside the house things were as bad. A lord may not be liable to imprisonment for his debts, but there is no law to prevent his creditors seizing whatever they might, as I was to discover only too well a few years later. No sooner had my great uncle breathed his last than these vultures had descended upon his home and removed almost everything that was not a part of the building itself.

And yet it was a dream come true. Because of the space. Our entire miserable Aberdonian abode could have been fitted within one of the Newstead sculleries, while to know that all around me, whatever its state of delapidation, was mine for as far as I could see or indeed as far as I could ride at that tender age, was to feel my breast swelling to match its surroundings. And because of its responsibility. Our family motto, which I had never heard before, was "*Crede* Byron", and if this may well be considered a satire upon previous holders of the title, and their various relatives, I at least determined there and then that no one should have occasion to *dis*trust the 6th Lord.

But my love for Newstead was aroused, perhaps most of all, by the *sinister* air which overhung the entire property. My great uncle, as was soon to be whispered to me by servants and relatives alike, had been a dark figure, once arraigned before his peers on a charge of murder, following a somewhat irregular duel, a tyrant to his servants and his wife – he was even supposed once to have pitched her into the pond in a burst of rage – so that she eventually preferred to live and die apart, and at the end a mean tempered and lonely recluse, who sat to dinner with loaded pistols beside his cutlery, taking as his only friends a colony of crickets, which busy insects he had trained to crawl all over his dwindling body, and who were still very much in evidence, in secluded nook and cranny.

What impressions such tales might have made upon me as a *man* it is hard to say. But Great Uncle William was presented to me, in legend, when I was still a boy, and far from finding him a repulsive figure I was entranced, at once with the omnipotence he seemed to have enjoyed, and which I surely had now inherited, as well as the suggestion that he was a lonely, savage, defiant and above all *wicked* figure. A perfect *Zeluco* (ii) in the flesh, it seemed. As Mama had often suggested Papa had been. And as therefore it seemed more than likely I should also be. I adored Newstead, and everything I could learn about it, good or bad, at first sight, and was only regretful that after a brief inspection we were whisked away to Nottingham where our relatives were waiting to meet us, and more particularly their new lord.

What a crew. There was Aunt Fanny, (iii) who had spent some time in France living alone with Papa – now what does *that* suggest? – and her son George, (iv) a gangling young man already embarked upon a military career; there was Aunt Juliana Wilmot, (v) she being on her second husband, as she had earlier married Great Uncle William's son, causing that first explosion within the ranks of the family, and her son Robert, (vi) a lout some four years older than myself who sniffed all the time; there was Aunt Augusta Parker, (vii) married to a vice-admiral, no less, and her two children, Peter (viii) and Margaret; (ix) there was Aunt Sophia Byron, (x) the spinster to end all spinsters; there was George Byron, (xi) my cousin, and his uncle, Robert Dallas, (xii) his mother's brother, as well as his sister Julia;(xiii) and there was, at the very end of the list, a tall girl of fourteen, all bones and teeth and pimples, who to my utter consternation turned out to be my sister Augusta,(xiv) Papa's daughter by his fair countess, and who had been brought up by her mother's family in conditions of considerably greater affluence than had been *my* lot. I'm afraid on this occasion I took my cue from Mama, who obviously disliked this stepchild, and rebuffed her earnest efforts to be pleasant. I was far more interested in Margaret Parker, who was an absolutely beautiful girl and more my own age.

But in reality my thoughts remained centred on Newstead, as I believed were Mama's, because we both reacted with astonishment to Hanson's arrangements for us to live in Nottingham while our affairs were settled. "Newstead," I insisted. "I will live in my own home."

"Debts," said that lugubrious fellow. "Holes in the roof. No furniture. And besides, my lord, you cannot possibly live there until you are of age. It will be my business to find you a suitable tenant, who will pay a handsome rent and keep the estate in good repair until you are ready for it yourself."

"But you have not yet done so," I said triumphantly. "Hanson, I will live in my own house, at least until this paragon appears."

He looked somewhat taken aback, no doubt never having previously encountered a ten-year-old boy with such determination to have his own way, but as I was supported by Mama we duly took up residence.

And enjoyed one of the happiest autumns of my life. First of all there was the estate itself, and if I had fallen in love with the house on first beholding it, I find it difficult to recapture my feelings as I explored my kingdom. My great uncle may have been a bad man, but he also enjoyed a great many simple if expensive pleasures. Having had an abortive naval career when a young man he had never lost his love for the sea, and on the shores of our lake he had built a folly, as turreted and battlemented as any castle of legend, which overlooked the waters and from which he could watch his serfs fight mock battles in their little sailing boats. For his son's twenty-first birthday, indeed, this being before the rift, he had commanded an entire full-rigged ship, with guns blazing from time to time, to be brought overland from the sea to his own lake, and Nottingham, it will be understood from a glance at a map, is situated in the very heart of England. So down had come a few more oaks to pay the cost.

Then there were the servants. No doubt they found any change from the Wicked Lord for the better, but they seemed delighted to have me living amongst them, excepting perhaps old Mealey, who had been my uncle's bailiff, and who regarded inquisitive young masters as a colossal nuisance. It was at this time, I may say, that I first made the acquaintance of dear deceitful Fletcher, then a lad only a little older than myself, who came to us as groom.

Because above all there were the animals. I had never been allowed to have a pet – it really would not have done very well in our previous cramped conditions – while the expense of a horse had been out of the question. But here there were all the horses I could wish, and even more important, my uncle's surviving dog, a large hound of the wolf variety aptly called Woolly, who became my favourite companion, although he was given to outrageous behaviour and once even attempted to bite me so that I remember I was so angered I clapped my pistol to his head and considered blowing out his brains, from which I was dissuaded by the faithful Hanson.

For here was another cause for joy. In addition to servants, pets, and space, I now possessed all the weapons I could desire, and what young lad of spirit does not find his principal delight in the arms he may be called upon to use in manhood? Newstead was a perfect arsenal; I could play with the very sword which had figured in the famous duel, or shoot with the very pistols which Great Uncle William had nightly taken to dinner, a habit I cultivated myself.

But perhaps better than any of these pleasures was the joy of being a man of property, a host, a leader in the neighbourhood. People came to call, and I welcomed them with all my heart. Margaret and her mother spent some time with us, causing such a flutter in my heart that I actually dashed off some lines of verse to her while in the grips of a powerful emotion, setting a sad pattern from which I have never been able to free myself. Then there were our neighbours, the Chaworths, descendants of the very fellow Uncle William had run through in that darkened room.(xv) They seemed to have forgiven the murder, for it was probably that, but I felt the strangest sensation when sitting to table with them, especially as the daughter of the house, a girl called Mary Ann who like my sister was some years my elder and at what can best be described as the awkward age, was seated on my right. "A pretty child," Hanson remarked afterwards. "What a triumph it would be were you and she to marry, my lord. Annesley and Newstead united in one vast property, and two equivalent families bound together once again." Because there had at one time been an intermarriage, and this girl was in fact a distant cousin.

But the idea seemed abominable. "What, my dear Hanson?" I was forced to remark. "The Montagues and the Capulets marry?"

Happy days. I wonder if I have ever been so happy since? I have scaled greater heights of ecstasy, to be sure, than in my then ignorance I supposed to exist. But I have also fallen into deeper pits of misery. Newstead towards the end of 1798 seemed to me to be a paradise, in which I occupied myself entirely as I thought fit, rode and shot and played and commanded . . . and returned home every evening to my splendid bedchamber and my equally splendid nurse, who was more than ever anxious to satisfy my every longing in the glory of my ancestral home, to which she no doubt now considered herself an eternal appendage.

Alas, man is not really born for happiness. Christmas at Newstead was a great occasion, the first real Christmas I had ever enjoyed, surrounded by my mother and my servants, my dog and my weapons, with my own logs sizzling in the grate. But when it was over, this happy world almost immediately fell apart.

To begin with, Mama found it necessary to journey to London, in search of funds. She had already written in every direction, because to her disagreeable surprise, our rents from Newstead amounted to very little because of the neglect into which the farms had been allowed to fall. Worse, there was nothing at all to be had from my Lancashire coal mines, by far the richest part of my inheritance, at least potentially, because Uncle William had sold them off, which he was not entitled to do, by the terms of *his* father's will. Hanson was quite sure I would get them back, but only after lengthy litigation. So Mama found it impossible to provide for a peer of the realm, and more particularly his education, on her own meagre income, and was forced to appeal to the House of Lords for a pension from the Crown. This she duly obtained, from the Great William (xvi) himself, but for the moment we were separated for a good deal of the time.

In these circumstances it was felt that I could not continue at Newstead by myself, and so I was removed to a family called Parkyns in Nottingham, distant cousins, where I was to lodge until the immediate future could be discovered. This would have been bad in itself, as it was a severe blow for me to give up the broad acres of my own home and all the pleasures that had attended it, but far worse,

Mama now determined to make another effort to correct my uncorrectable lameness, and delivered me into the hands of a medieval torturer named Lavender, who would bathe my unhappy limb in oil, and then incase it in an instrument straight from the dungeons of Genghis Khan and twist and crush the miserable object until I was beside myself with pain.

The fellow was not only a failure as a doctor, but he made himself the more obnoxious by pretending to a learning and a wisdom he quite lacked. At the least I was able to puncture this particular bubble to my own satisfaction. I one day filled a sheet of paper with miscellaneous characters, arranged in the forms of words, but entirely meaningless, showed it to my faithful quack and inquired his opinion as to the language in which this strange document was written.

"Italian," he answered without a moment's hesitation.

Which afforded some amusement to myself and my tutor, a young man called Rogers, one of those unhappy beings who had happened to remain loyal to the Farmer (xvii) when the Americans were seeking their own destiny, and had thus been forced to flee his native New York amidst a hail of tar and feathers, and was now ekeing out a precarious livelihood by attending to the intellectual needs of impoverished lordlings. He was a *friend*, who seemed to suffer as much as I did from the agony which attended my foot at all times, and indeed remarked with tears in his eyes that he did not see how I could stand it.

"I do assure you, Rogers," I said with as much composure as I could manage, "that if you can manage to bear it, so shall I."

But the principal cause of my misery in that winter following my eleventh birthday was my betrayal by May.

Perhaps I have written enough already to indicate that even now I am confused and uncertain as to my real feelings for the red-headed succubus who haunted and delighted my youthful nights. But at the time she was all I desired. May could discipline me better than any virago with a whip merely by saying, "Ye have been a naughty boy, my lord. I'll not come to your bed this night."

Imagine then my feelings when I awoke one night to the opening of my bedroom door in the Parkyns's *ménage*, and saw by the light of a flickering candle, May enter the room, together with a *man*.

"We'll be well here," she whispered, closing the door behind the fellow, and even in the uncertain light cast by the one candle I could tell he was a common labouring type, while both from May's pronunciation and the manner in which the room suddenly filled with the stench of stale beer, I could further tell that they had both been at the inn.

"But the lad?" whispered Lothario.

"A heavy sleeper," May promised, putting both arms around the fellow's neck and kissing him on the lips, the while working her body against his in a most lascivious manner.

"At least douse the candle," the swain begged, having freed himself.

"It'll no' disturb him," she insisted. "Do ye no' wish to look at me, man? I wish to look at *you*."

She was already undressing, and with some haste, allowing her clothes to lie on the floor. But so was he, and I had seen my nurse naked before. Here was a creature like myself, although considerably larger in every possible way, for when his breeches reached his ankles his cocker positively leapt out, elevated like the most deadly howitzer, and very nearly as fat. I almost sat up in my delight, because I *was* delighted, but apparently I was not half so delighted as May, who gave a squeak of purest pleasure, fell on her knees, and began to kiss and suck the object, something she had never done to me, adding insult to injury, when she could spare the time to raise her head, by saying; "Oh, man, man, if ye knew for how long I've been starving on half rations."

He was meanwhile equally busy, running his fingers into her hair, reaching down to hold her breasts and bring her titties up harder than I had ever seen, the while grunting his pleasure. "Ease up, girl," he said. "Ease up. You'll have me away."

"I won't," she promised, and released the treasured object, sliding her body up his so that he could hold on to her hams, and truth to say of all the amazing and exciting sights I saw that night none quite filled me with such delight as to watch him squeezing those great soft mounds and pulling them apart so that I could see right through to her hair. By this time my own weapon was ready for any combat that might be offered to it, and I was so excited that I sat up, but neither noticed for the moment, he having fallen or been pushed back across the bed, she lying on top of him, her legs spread even wider now, while that entrancing backside rose and fell, clearly sliding up and down that splendid pole, giving off the while a series of ecstatic squeals and squeaks, until on a sudden she sighed, and lay still on his chest, while her legs slowly came together.

38

"Oh, girl, girl," the fellow muttered – their conversation had by now caused me to wonder if they had even troubled to be introduced – "but you're a darling. That you are. A. . . ." He looked past her and saw me, as I had by now almost left my bed in my desire to see more of what was happening. "The lad," he squawked, sitting up, and throwing poor May off his belly and off the bed so that she struck the floor with a noise that made the rafters tremble.

"In the name of God," she bawled, but her erstwhile lover was treading on her stomach in his haste to be away.

"The lad," he explained, dragging on his breeches.

"The lad?" she demanded, at the same time crawling away from his thumping feet, an entrancing sight being mainly composed of trembling breast and quivering buttock. "Geordie," she said, in a tone I had not heard before and did not much care for.

I retreated to my bed. "I wanted to watch."

"Ye wanted . . . where are ye going?" she inquired of the fellow.

"Away," he announced, and closed the door behind him, again with sufficient force to rattle a frame or two.

"Ye wanted to watch," May growled, getting to her feet, and suddenly I realised that she was angry. "Ye wanted to watch," she breathed again, looking from left to right and seizing upon my riding crop. "Ye wanted to watch." She moved with such speed I was taken by surprise, and the crop had cracked itself around my thighs before I could move.

"Ow," I bawled.

"Hush your trap," she commanded, striking me again. I howled with pain, and kept endeavouring to get up, only to be thrust down again by her strong left arm, while her right arm continued to hurl the strap against my backside.

How long this might have continued I would not like to say, but we were interrupted by a banging on the door, the unholy row having alerted Mistress Parkyns. "Miss Gray," she shouted. "Whatever is happening?"

The blows ceased, and I turned my head to see, though my tears, May hastily pulling on an undressing robe to hide her nakedness. "The wretch," she declared, opening the door. "Ma'am, he has assaulted me in my bed."

"My *lord*," Mistress Parkyns declared, going very red in the face.

"I . . . I . . . I. . . ." I was so surprised, I could only yammer.

"'Tis all of a man, he is," May cried, entering upon a bit of sobbing

39

herself. "All of a man, ma'am. Why, I thought the de'il himself was with me."

"My *lord*," Mistress Parkyns said again. "You deserve to be whipped."

I opened my mouth to inform her that this had already happened, but May beat me to it. "I've seen to that," she said. "Oh, I've taught him a lesson."

"Nevertheless," Mistress Parkyns said. "You'll not share this room any more, Miss Gray. My word, no. Come along now. We'll make you up a bed."

"The lad's me charge," May said.

"And you are both *my* charges," Mistress Parkyns pointed out. "Come along. Oh, dear, dear me, whatever will Mrs Byron say? The lad is a reincarnation of the Wicked Lord. Oh, dear me."

From that dreadful night the rapport which had existed between my nurse and myself was ended. I was deeply angry, at once at my beating and my humiliation, and at her having, to my mind, betrayed our friendship with another. She was equally affected by what had happened, for, speaking now with the benefit of hindsight, I have no doubt at all that she was a virgin before the appearance of her "man, man", that her religious beliefs had encouraged her to remain in that state until marriage, and that her surrender to her passions – for there can be no doubt that she had been the instigator of the event – had been a result of an over indulgence in ale acting upon senses which had been as inflamed as my own by our evening revelries. The result was that she now considered herself damned, and that I was the agent of the devil sent for the express purpose of securing her soul for eternity. It was even possible for her to see in my twisted foot the demon's cloven hoof.

Thus my few stolen moments of happiness came to an end, and within a month I was turned into the most miserable lad on this earth, and the most resentful, and not only against May. For naturally when I realised that our friendship was finished forever I endeavoured to speak to Mama about her. Alas, May and the dreadful Parkyns had been there before me, and my accusation was turned into a suit against me, accompanied by another belting.

But it turned out that I possessed a *friend*, and if often enough in later years it has been pointed out to me how slothful and indeed at times dishonest an attorney Hanson has proved – he has on occasion even driven *me* nearly mad with his delays and procrastinations – I can only say, in defence of my continued employment of the fellow, no one save he and I know from what he eventually extricated me.

His occupation with my affairs brought him often to Nottingham, where, although I have no doubt Mama regaled him as best she could with the horrific tales of my misdeeds, he was shrewd enough to observe that the faults might not all be on one side, and in any event, as he later told me, he was convinced that for any young man to grow up entirely surrounded by female companionship was a sad mistake. In July of 1799 he at last persuaded Mama to allow him to take me with him to London, for a variety of reasons, the most pressing being that he wished me to meet the Earl of Carlisle, a distant cousin who was being persuaded, reluctantly, to become my guardian, and also that he wished my foot to be seen by a proper London surgeon. To my horror Mama, while agreeing to these important steps, insisted that May come along with us, she having completely believed my nurse's version of the event. But as it happened the tyrant's days were numbered. My nurse she might be, but Hanson felt that at the age of eleven and a half my affairs were those of a man, and she was relegated very much into the background.

Thus on 12 July 1799 I re-entered London for the first time since a few days after my birth, and was agreeably delighted. In Nottingham, or at Newstead, or for that matter at almost any country seat you could mention, life proceeded in a backwater. It was difficult to realise that Great Britain was in the midst of a life and death struggle with the French. But in London one immediately felt the weight of great events. It was still possible to purchase broadsheets with descriptions of the Battle of the Nile, with hideous caricatures of the great Napoleon, with pronunciamentos by the implacable Pitt, with exhortations to young men of health and spirit to join the colours, or at least to take their places in the ranks of the militia, a path to glory which would never be opened to me, as I was rapidly made aware when I arrived at Hanson's quite palatial town house, to be introduced to the collection of boys and girls who were his children, all of whom had clearly been informed that I was a cripple, for they every one stared at my legs before my face, nor was my embarrassment relieved when the seven-year-old daughter, having carried out this inspection, remarked; "Well he is a pretty boy, however."

Hanson's plans not only included some proper medical treatment for my foot, and a meeting with Carlisle, but were also intended to free me as much as possible from Mama's influence by sending me to a proper school. And to this end. . . .(xviii)

. . . believe I wept? *She* was gone, and for ever. Yet her memory remained, and in more than her mere presence. For where was my nightly stimulation to arise in her absence? The early months of my life in London, on my introduction to Dr Glennie's school in Dulwich, and perhaps my own relief at escaping her anger, had for a while left me as chaste as a nun. But gradually the demands of my ever rising cocker made themselves imperative. Class work, at best the most boring of occupations, became a positive torture as I thought of those quivering mounds, coming towards me in vicious vengeance, as I longed to find myself alone in the most dismal of closets so long as I could drop my breeches and relieve myself with my own fingers.

But a school, alas, is not the place for privacy. Glennie soon enough discovered my secret – it is of course possible he had been forewarned by Hanson, following my confession to that worthy – and promptly gave me a bed in his own quarters, taking the precaution of securing my wrists to each other before blowing out the candle. He was in his own way a kind fellow, and perhaps had suffered some such an affliction in his own youth, for on the terrible occasion when he first discovered me with weapon in hand he did not flog me, as I supposed inevitable, but rather explained that such temptations were merely manifestations of the devil attempting to enter my soul, that they were common enough in defenceless young boys, and that they had to be combated by every possible means, as apart from the risk to my immortality there was the far more immediate danger of premature baldness and also of my going blind, should I continue to spill my seed upon the ground. The good doctor's words, so very close to May's although lacking so violent an accompaniment, completed my conviction that I was already breached by the foul Lucifer, that there was little left for me but to prepare myself for the fiery furnace and that as quickly as possible.

I can safely say that I have never encountered nor heard of a more miserable twelve year old, a situation compounded by the gyrations of Mama. I am forced to believe that Hanson, for all his vow, divulged my secret in that direction as well, perhaps as a means of finally persuading her that May had to go. In any event, from regarding me with suspicious loathing, she suddenly reached heights of maternal affection I had never suspected to exist. Apart from seizing me and pressing me to her bosom, quite without warning, she now adopted the policy, having so misjudged me in the past, of humouring my every whim. Should I declare a headache, then it was so, and I must be protected, and kept at home, while she was even in the habit of descending upon unhappy Dulwich at odd times during the week, and if dissatisfied with my appearance or my manner taking me back to her lodgings at Sloane Terrace with her. A situation which I naturally used to my best advantage, for in the privacy of my own bedchamber there was no Glennie to restrain my hands, and if such bouts invariably left me utterly depressed and intensely irritable, as I supposed another faggot thrown on the fire waiting to claim me, as I was in any event certain there was no escaping I soon recovered into a mood of defiant anger, against everyone within reach, which but the more convinced them that I was a true heir of the Wicked Lord and doomed to a lifetime of misanthropic misery. A view I held myself.

Mama's actions in keeping me from school were, however, apparently disturbing at once to Glennie, to Hanson, and to the noble lord who was my guardian. Here was no preparation for a member of the ruling class to take his place amongst his peers and dazzle them with the force and power of his learning and oratory. Many secret meetings must have taken place between these three worthies, and no doubt others, for the decision when put to my mother was unanimous: I was to be removed from Dulwich and sent to a school called Harrow, situated at some distance from London and therefore, it was piously hoped, more difficult of access to Mama. *I* was overjoyed, conceiving that nowhere could be quite as boring or as restrictive as Dulwich, and being as anxious as any of the gentlemen who were overseeing my career to escape the clutches of Mama. And so therefore on an April day in 1801, when I was approaching thirteen and a half, Hanson and I rode up the hill towards the high, small-windowed stone building, surmounted by remarkably sharp gables, which was to be my home for the next four years.

And entered a greater misery than ever human beings were meant to bear. For as I dismounted from the carriage it could be seen that my right leg was encased in a special boot from which an iron frame extended up my calf, and worse, I was that most despicable and unlamented of creatures, a *new boy*. I was not alone in this unhappy state, for dear Ted Long (xix) was also presented for torture on this occasion, but our mutual plight was not one from which either could draw any comfort.

The headmaster at that time, Drury, was a pleasant fellow, obviously well forearmed with knowledge concerning myself, and sufficiently interested to place me under the care of his son Henry, who was one of the masters, and was not quite so pleasant, being brisk and efficient and totally lacking in sympathy. I understand at this distance of time, indeed I came to understand it while still at school, that he was *not* lacking in understanding, and was indeed a very good fellow, but he conceived it as part of his duty to make us into men as rapidly as possible, and the more so on the part of a youth he had undoubtedly been informed was a mother's boy.

However, while I instinctively felt that there was no friendship here, my opening hours at Harrow were reassuring enough. Alas, with the approach of dusk Hanson departed back to happy London. Long and I were shown to our dormitory, and left to "make the acquaintance of our chums".

Now it may well be that Glennie had despaired of ever himself curing me of my affliction, as had Hanson, and thus they had decided to leave the task to others. If this is so they made a grave misapprehension of the situation; our early experiences at Harrow were designed to make us the most confirmed of Onanists rather than the reverse. We were, as I have said, deposited in this long narrow room, lined with iron bedsteads, and filled with boys of approximately our own ages, who ignored Long entirely in favour of making fun of my leg, attempting to trip me up and succeeding too often for comfort. They were already in the process of undressing, waving their all around and in a state of high excitement, apparently at being graced with our presence, although we found this hard to understand, as both Long and myself, being unused to undressing in public, were reluctant to display ourselves.

We soon learned the reason for their anticipatory joy. The door to the dormitory was thrown in, and we were joined by half a dozen fellows from the upper school, great louts of eighteen and better, sporting moustaches and one even hanging a thin beard from his chin. We goggled at them, for it had occurred to me that every bed was filled and I wondered where these newcomers proposed to sleep, while they regarded us as the Cyclops must have considered Ulysses and his merry men. "What a pretty pair," one said.

"And gammy to boot," said another, pointing to my leg.

44

"Then he'll not be able to run," said a third.

I was by now quite angry with my situation and their ribaldry, coming as it did on top of so much already. "And pray, sir," I demanded in my most cutting tone, "why should I run from you?"

Which earned me a clip over the ear. "Because I'm going to pull your tail for you," he said.

I had no idea what he meant, but the blow was enough to set me off, and I leapt at him, for while I might not be able to run I was certainly able to leap a few feet, seized him by the shirt front with my left hand, and struck him as hard as I could on the face with my right. He lost his balance and fell over, giving a gasp of pain and surprise, and I of course fell with him, completing his discomfort by inserting my knee into his stomach.

"Bravo," someone shouted. "There's a lad with spirit."

Two other of the big fellows however hauled me off my victim, who regained his feet, positively seething. "I'll skin his arse," he vowed.

"You'll not," said the fellow who had congratulated me. "He's got spunk."

"He'll still have to pull his tail," said another. "No favouritism."

"Oh, indeed," agreed my defender. "You'll drop your breeks, my lord."

"And you," Long was informed, and to my concern I saw that he was bent on complying as quickly as possible.

"*I* will not," I declared, and once again doubled my fists.

To no avail. "Then we'll pull it for you," someone decided, and before I could identify an adversary I was seized, one to each arm and one to each leg, deposited on the nearest bed, and stripped as expertly as the veriest Tartar might have vented his lust upon some beautiful maiden. The event had its effect and they were delighted with what they saw, but while poor Long was commanded to seize himself and fire away with the utmost possible rapidity, I was held down while a variety of nauseous substances, including tooth powder and boot blacking, were smeared over my unhappy cocker, all with loving care which raised me to a pinnacle, and which resulted in an explosion which again seemed to please them enormously, and which quite put poor Long into the shade.

The humiliation was the most complete I had ever undergone. I did not see how I could ever face anyone again, much less spend my entire time in their company. My mingled rage and disgust seemed to take entire hold of my being, and they having made the mistake of releasing my arms in their pleasure at having completed their sport, I laid about me with all the energy at my command, and had the satisfaction of landing one in the eye with a blow which made him squawk. They did not retaliate, but merely bundled me into the sheet, causing a sad mess, and left the room in peals of laughter, in which my sleeping companions joined, following which the candles were doused and I was left to very unfortunate reflections.

Over the next two years at Harrow it were better to draw a veil. To be sure my courage and my willingness to use my fists whenever I could saved me from a good deal of ill-treatment, although not from a succession of black eyes and bloody noses, but at the same time my determination not to sink into the slough of boyhood earned me few friends, and none at all in my first year. My dormitory companions, if having no desire to come within reach of my strength, were entirely against me, and played upon me the most diabolical of tricks, as for instance, whenever I was in a deep slumber, placing my afflicted leg in a tub of water, so that I awoke shivering and uncomfortable.

This sense of isolation, which necessarily had to be supported by an aggressive determination, naturally also affected my relations with my masters, and most immediately my tutor, Henry Drury. *His* disapproval of my often tart replies, and my readiness to take offence at the smallest cause, added to my misery when in the company of my fellows, combined to make the coming holidays the dream of my every moment, and once having reached Bath, where Mama, in the first flush of her improved circumstances, Newstead having at last been rented and her income as regards me having been increased to meet my school fees, decided to go, (xx) this having been the unhappy city where she had been courted by Mad Jack, I was totally opposed to returning to the horrors of Harrow, and indeed persuaded her to allow me to remain a while longer after term had begun, another event which did not endear me to the Drury *ménage*.

In fact things improved after a year in hell. Not only was I growing bigger and stronger with every day, and, dare I admit it, a trifle stout as well, and thus my multitude of enemies were even less anxious to tangle with my fists, but I was no longer a new boy. Indeed, I was now able to look to the latest comers for my friends, as, being a total outcast myself, I assumed the leadership of those others in my unhappy position, fought for them with my ever ready knuckles, and even made a friend or two, especially a dear lad called Harness, who suffered as I did from lameness.

And yet, such is the working of Fate, that those utterly miserable two years were perhaps the most important of my life, for two reasons. In the first place, such was the horror instilled in my breast by the circumstances of my initiation into Harrow, that my masturbatory and indeed my entire sexual instincts became atrophied, and I scarce wished to pee for fear of having to behold that object which was the reason for all my misery.

The second reason gives less cause for congratulation, and yet, who am I to cavil? Had I never written a word of poetry, I might have been a happier man, a more successful one, certainly. On the other hand, while I would have avoided the notoriety which has clung to me like a curse, I would also have avoided the fame, and undoubtedly this aspect of life is sweet. Be that as it may, left to myself with naught to do but either reflect or compose, I began to spend a great deal of my time in writing.

I would lie on a tombstone, believe it or not – for our school adjoined the churchyard of St Mary's – belonging to a gentleman by name of Peachey, one of those West Indian nabobs who all but ruled the world at that time with the wealth gained from their enormous sugar plantations, his being in St Kitts, but reduced, as are we all at the end, to clogging dust. Here I wrote, of things seen and unseen, of people known and imagined. I wrote of sweet Margaret, and here, with great tears dropping from my eyes, I wrote of her death, for the dear girl fell from her horse in the summer of 1802 and perished as a result, and left me desolate. For I could still love, supposing that affairs of the heart and affairs of the penis were entirely divorced one from the other. And here I even composed an opera, which I called *Ulric and Ilvina,* but which I had the good sense to burn upon completion.

MARY ANN

The rigours of school life were of course tempered by the vacations, although these in turn meant enduring the company of dear Mama. For with every month that passed she seemed at once to grow fatter and more irritable. I now know she had ample cause, as the more that she and Hanson delved into my affairs the more they discovered that while there was certainly a great deal of *potential* wealth in the Byron inheritance, it was so surrounded in misappropriation and litigation that the prospect of my ever seeing any of it was remote. But to me she merely became more and more of a virago, fond when enraged of calling me a "lame brat".

In the summer of 1802 she at least took me down to Bath, as I have related, and there I managed to amuse myself.(i) I recall attending a masquerade dressed as a Turkish boy, the first result of my extensive knowledge of Turkish history and custom. But the following year Mama elected to return to the vicinity of Newstead, and she rented Burgage Manor in the village of Southwell. This was quite intolerable. Southwell itself appeared to me as the most boring place on earth, for I had not yet made the acquaintance of dear Lizzy Pigot,(ii) while it was too close to my home, and left me a prey to the most disturbing emotions.

As a result I very soon after my arrival rode over to Newstead, where I was made welcome by old Mealey, in the absence of our tenant, Lord Grey de Ruthven. Grey had in fact left instructions that I was to be given the run of the place, should I choose, and I did choose, finding it far preferable to live with Mealey in the gate house, from whence I could ramble the estate, visit the house, use its library, and in general act the lord of the manor even if I had six years to survive before the play became fact.

It was still a lonely existence, however, and made more so because Mealey himself was not exactly pleased to have me on his hands on a permanent basis, as naturally he was required to attend to my wants, to wait on me at table, and in general to fulfill the duties of a steward, which after all is what he was. (iii) I thus soon tired of my own company, or of his grumbles, and one August morning I rode across to the neighbouring estate of Annesley. Hanson and I had visited here during my brief sojourn at Newstead, five years earlier, and so I anticipated nothing more than a pleasant journey, a welcome at the end of it, some gossip with the Clarkes, and a gallop home in the cool of the evening. To my distress, however, on arriving before the hall, I was informed by the butler that as my coming had not been expected, the senior members of the family had taken themselves into Nottingham for the day, and in fact there was no one at home at all saving Miss Mary Ann. (iv)

"Then let me at least pay my respects to her," I said, recalling the pimpled twelve year old who had sat beside me one evening at dinner, and wishing to impress *her* with how I had grown and matured.

The portly fellow bowed and escorted me through the hall to a withdrawing room which faced west and therefore the afternoon sun, and in the great bay window of which a young woman sat reading a book. The butler cleared his throat and announced: "Lord Byron to call, Miss Mary Ann." Mary Ann Chaworth raised her head as a shaft of sunlight entered the window to play on her features, and Lord Byron fell in love.

I had been in love before. I could still remember – I can still remember – Mary Duff as if I had seen her yesterday. Margaret Parker is all too likely to stalk through my dreams, dark hair flying, mouth smiling. But these had been at a very early age. Now I was fifteen, and I was beholding a girl of seventeen, and looking upon a woman for the first time with the eyes of a man.

The emotion was the more consuming because I had not anticipated it. To me Mary Chaworth was the pimpled girl I had met but once. I had assumed that *she* would start in amazed pleasure at the sight of *me*. What then did I behold, as she slipped from her perch and stood up to greet me? She was not tall, and if slender by no means thin; the high waistline of her white house gown allowed a delightful bulge above, and clung softly – the material must have been muslin, I suppose – to the contours of her hips. But her real beauty lay in her face, which was a perfect oval, dominated by large dark eyes and a most splendidly straight nose. Her mouth was wide, and deliciously firm in its setting, her complexion – which was all I had remembered about her to her disadvantage – quite flawless. Her dark brown hair was worn short, only just covering her ears, and was a positive mass of curls. She seemed, in that brief moment, to be every pretty woman I had beheld come together in one angelic being.

And what then, did *she* see? At fifteen I was not greatly taller than herself, and I am ashamed to say I already had that slight tendency to corpulence against which I have had to fight all of my life. On the other hand, I flatter myself that my face had already all but assumed its mature beauty; my features were not less regular than her own, and were no doubt already enshrined in that consciousness of superiority which is the birthright of our nobility. My hair had assumed its auburn colouring, but I was less inclined to allow it to wander and indeed as I recall wore it well plastered down on my forehead. That she did notice my limp is obvious, but at the moment it did not seem to concern her in the least, and I had some hopes that she might consider it the result of an accident, for such are the wonders of modern science that I was no longer bedevilled by an iron brace, but wore a cunningly devised *inner* boot, outside of which a normal shoe disguised my ailment.

"My lord," she said, her voice utter music. "An honour."

"For me, Miss Chaworth," I protested, allowing myself to be guided to the seat beside her, and discovering to my joy that the butler had departed and we were alone. To talk, to reminisce, to laugh over our previous meeting. And for me to make a most disagreeable discovery, for on the third finger of her left hand she wore a ring.

"I am betrothed," she explained. "You will have met John Musters?"

Possibly I had, but if so he had made no impression upon me. Yet, in his absence, he made a considerable impression upon me at that moment. Never have I so instantly disliked any human being.

Her parents returned from their expedition, we drank tea, I talked at my best, keeping them smiling with anecdotes of Harrow, of Hanson, of Scotland, and of Mama, impressing them with my knowledge as I called upon my remembered reading to supply me with worldly aplomb, and in general, I suppose, acting a role which those used to my more sullen moods would never have recognised. In fact I was as if in an euphoria, the cause of which I only understood as I made my lonely way back to Newstead in the dusk.

For here was an utterly new emotion. My thought for Mary Duff and cousin Margaret had been on a quite Dantesque plain. My consideration of their beauty ceased at their necks. That beneath their childish gowns there might lurk muscles and veins and odours and desires never crossed my mind for an instant. And then, with May, there had been no proper emotion at all, merely a physical desire which had grown and consumed, as one may play with a scratch, constantly touching the new formed skin, pulling at the scabs, ever renewing the injury in the compulsion to feel the sensation, however painful it often might be.

But as that night I lay awake in Mealey's uncomfortable bed I for the first time felt the two aspects of femininity come together. Uncertainly and indeed distressingly, yet it was there. I could think of nothing more delightful than to spend the rest of my life seated in that window with Mary Ann, laughing and conversing, for never had I found a human being easier to talk with. But at the same time I was aware of feeling how magnificent it might be if that rounded softness could find itself in my arms. I did not have the courage to suppose such a splendid body naked, I was too afraid of reawakening my old curse. But when I dreamed, it was of Mary, her head on my shoulder while I stroked that lovely hair, and I awoke in a tremble and a state of total disarray, having had the orgasm of a voluptuous dream.

Nor, on due reflection, was I disposed to be too concerned about her engagement. I soon made the acquaintance of this fellow Musters, as I began to ride across to Annesley every day. To be sure he was handsome, well built, a magnificent horseman whose sole interest in life was to ride to hounds, an amazing preoccupation when you consider that the arms of his betrothed were waiting for him should he ever choose to dismount. But obviously he possessed not a brain in his entire head. I could hardly consider such a man as a serious rival.

Especially as with every day, and every visit, Mary seemed the more pleased to see me. It was one of those good Augusts, when the sun shone and there was enough breeze for coolness. A lazy time of the year, and there is none to equal it. We rode together, often in a pony and trap, or we talked together, either in the spacious garden seated beneath a great oak, or in her favourite bay window on the occasions when clouds did interfere with our pleasures. We discussed every subject under the sun, save the one which was uppermost in my mind, and perhaps in hers as well, but that problem I cunningly circumnavigated by reading to her from Tom Moore's volume *The*

Poetical Works of the Late Thomas Little, a decidedly erotic accomplishment which included such suggestive phrases as "my Julia's burning kiss", which brought a pretty blush to the cheeks of my beloved, but seemed to make her even more anxious to be in my company.

Love is of course never a contented emotion. I was jealous. When once the Clarke family attended a dance I was forced to sit and glower at my dream disporting herself on the arm of sundry louts not fit to brush my shoes, and with every evidence of enjoyment, a purgatory which I could relieve by next day emptying my pistols time and again into an inoffensive door. While to watch her playing the adoring fiancée to the detestable Musters was more than I could bear. But all of these crosses disappeared beneath the warmth of her smile, her evident and growing pleasure at my company.

My progress into her esteem was therefore sure if slow. Accidental brushings of our fingers, touchings of our knees, the half embrace of leaning over her shoulder to look at some illustration in a book, soon developed into a frank holding of hands as we walked, or sat for hours with our thighs touching while all manner of desires lurked around the edges of my innocuous words, and I supposed, dominated her thoughts as well. I spent that August in a fine state of elation, concerned only with the devilish Musters, but taking heart from the knowledge that the wedding was not scheduled for another two years, a long time in which a great deal could happen, and would, I swore.

My happiness reached its zenith towards the end of the month. I had by now accomplished a scheme to which I had been bending my concentration, that of removing myself from Newstead – blasphemous thought indeed – entirely to Annesley. This had *seemed* to be a problem, as during the early weeks of my courtship I had returned to Mealey's modest roof every night, regardless of the weather, and thereby set a pattern. How then to wish myself upon my future relatives, for as such I was already considering them, without giving away the secret of my love, which to this moment I had not even revealed to its object. In reality the solution was simplicity itself. One thundery evening, as August drew to a close, I was making my way back to my ancestral home, my mind as usual ranging over a variety of subjects, all containing the magic name Chaworth, when I fell to thinking about the infamous duel which had driven the families apart for so long, and as a flash of lightning cracked across the gloom of the evening my answer presented itself. Next day I told the twittering family how I had been beset on my homeward journey by a demon, hell bent upon avenging himself upon me for his unhappy demise so long ago. Naturally Mrs Clarke absolutely refused to allow me to risk the dangers of another encounter with the spectre, especially as the evening was again lowering, and I had the delicious experience of wishing good night to my beloved when she was already clad in a nightgown and about to regain the safety of her bedchamber.

But how puerile such a delight was to seem with what occurred immediately after. For with an improvement in the weather, the Clarkes decided upon an expedition to the peak district of Derbyshire, and their guest was of course included. We picnicked and then decided to explore, in particular a famous cavern in which a subterranean stream found its way, winding through the darkness for some time before emerging into the light once again.

"Ah, 'tis a great adventure," declared Mr Clarke. "Why, at one point the roof is so low that you have to lie down in the bottom of the boat, and the boatman himself – he pushes, you know, from the stern – is forced to bend double. Now, who'll be first for the adventure?"

"I will," decided his wife. "And you will accompany me." For the boat held but two people at a time. Now you may imagine how my heart was thumping. I need not have feared.

"I shall be next," Mary declared.

"And who will accompany you into the darkness?"

"Why. . . ." She looked around her in pretended uncertainty, while I all but screamed my anxiety. "His lordship, to be sure. Could I have a more suitable protector?"

How I survived the tedious half hour while the Clarkes disappeared into the cave I shall never know, for it was necessary to laugh and joke, as they had come to expect of me, and appear quite nonchalant at the prospect of lying down next to my darling in the darkness. But at last my future parents – as I anticipated – re-emerged, pink cheeked and laughing to suggest that even after several years of marriage they had found occasion for dalliance in the gloom, and Mary and I took our places in the boat while our Charon once again entered the thigh deep water astern and commenced to push.

Perchance I should have studied the cavern, which I am told is a thing of great beauty and mystery. I had no idea it existed. Mary and I were already lying, on our backs on the cushioned seat, or bed would be a more appropriate description, while the light gradually faded, and the roof gradually lowered. Our hands lay beside each other, and a moment later our fingers were intertwined. Our shoulders pressed together, and I could hear her breathe, or perhaps sigh, as the roof all but brushed those delicious nipples which lay concealed beneath her bodice. Certainly I could not ask for a better cue. I sighed myself, and whispered, as to myself, "Oh, Mary, Mary, how I love you."

With an emotion for which the word delight is perfectly inadequate I felt her breath upon my cheek. "You darling boy," she said. I turned my head, and our lips touched, and more, for just a second our tongues brushed each other. Then she was gone, and it was again commencing to lighten. But still she smiled. "You *are* a darling boy," she said.

The rest of that day is quite lost to me. I had risked all, and I had conquered. There is no feeling to equal that. Mary was mine. Upon what had happened in the cavern we could only build, and as for fox hunting Musters, his days were already numbered. Our hands touched on the ride back to Annesley. My mind soared to heights it had never previously attained. I found myself composing epic verses which would send Marlowe tumbling to the dust in disarray. We reached the hall and a cold collation. I drank too much wine and delighted the company with my speeches. "The Lords will never have known your like," declared Mr Clarke, and Mary, having also indulged, smiled upon us with pink cheeks and sparkling eyes.

Our nightly farewell was by now a ritual for which the entire day was a preparation. I encountered her at her door, seized her hands and kissed them, longing to do the same to those magnificent lips, but knowing it was now only a matter of time before they were mine. She smiled at me, and entered the chamber, closing the door behind her, while I leaned against the wood, quite unable to understand how I should sleep that night.

I was not to sleep that night. For while in my advantageous position, my ear inadvertently pressed against her door, I could hear what was said within.

"Why, ma'am," declared my charmer's maid. "You *have* had a busy day. Willie the coachman has whispered that he believes you and the lord are truly in love, and wonders when the engagement will be broken."

There was a peal of laughter which was certainly Mary's but which I personally had never heard her utter before. "Silly wretch," she cried. "You know naught of the matter at all. Do you seriously suppose I could ever love a stupid *little boy*, and lame with it?"

My first impulse was to throw open the door and demand she say the horrid words to my own face. My second was never to speak with her again, or even to see her again. I ran to my room, seized my belongings, was at the stable within five minutes, and at Newstead by dawn.

But Fate, when once it has sunk its talons into the neck of a hapless human, does not relinquish its grasp until it has satisfied its uttermost savage delight. Newstead was not to be the refuge I had always considered it. For all unknown to myself, the tenant had returned.

"His lordship invites you to the hall, my lord," Mealey said as I awoke from a fitful daytime slumber. "Insistent, he is."

Not that it would have crossed my mind for a moment to refuse him. He was a man, older than myself, to whom perhaps I might be able to turn for comfort and advice, and besides, I had made very free with his absent hospitality over the previous months; the least I could do was thank him.

And in fact I found Lord Grey de Ruthven a very charming fellow, but twenty-three years old, splendidly acquainted with all the great world that lay beyond the narrow confines of Harrow. "My dear Lord Byron," he remarked. "Or should I say, my dear *land*lord? I am so pleased to make your acquaintance, having heard a great deal about you. Although no rumour can possibly have done you justice."

We dined, splendidly, and drank Madeira wine, which had a considerable effect upon my head, I having slept but little the previous night, with the result that after the meal, as we lingered over our glasses, I unburdened myself to him, and found him a ready and discerning listener, entirely sympathetic to my cause. When finally we staggered to bed, his last act was to throw an arm around my shoulders and give me an affectionate hug, and I deemed myself fortunate to have found so faithful a friend after the emotional storms of the previous two days.

Next morning he made it plain that he expected me to stay at Newstead as long as I desired, which was going to be for a very long time, I resolved, for the thought of returning to hated Harrow, where the autumn term was soon to commence, filled me with horror. I did not confide this determination to Grey, but accepted his invitation for the time being, and he despatched a note to Southwell to inform Mama that her son was in good hands.

The next few days we shot over Newstead itself, for the pheasants and partridges had lain largely untouched, save for the depredations of

Mealey himself, since my great uncle's death. We did very well, and returned in the afternoons pleased with ourselves, if comfortably tired and anxious to renew our acquaintance with the Madeira bottle. In the evenings it was his turn to regale me with tales of the adventures of his early manhood, a state of affairs to which I eagerly looked forward as an opportunity to rid myself of any dependence whatsoever upon perfidious femininity. A point of view with which he entirely agreed.

"For consider," he expounded on my third night at his table, "what can a female, any female, have to offer? Conversation? There is no such thing, in feminine company. It is entirely gossip. Humour? The dear creatures have none at all. The companionship of a bottle? A single glass and they are ready for bed. Well, then, what *of* bed? Beautiful hair? You possess that, Byron. Kissable lips? Are not a man's lips entirely kissable? Ballooning breasts? Well, there they have us. But what is a breast, my dear boy? A lump of flesh useless to all save a new born babe. And even he is solely interested in the tit, which is the source of sensation, and which we also possess in abundance. Ah, but you'll say there is the point of entry. Well, indeed, a female possesses two such orifices, but from the point of view of sensation, one will suffice, and who is to say ours is not the better?"

To all of which I nodded with owlish wisdom.

"So, fie to them all," he decided, rising to his feet. "They give us birth and in that capacity also provide us with heirs. They keep our houses in reasonable order. Let them confine themselves to those two aspects of human existence, and leave the business of *being* to their betters!"

"You are right, of course," I agreed, throwing *my* arm around *his* shoulder as we mounted the stairs. "Entirely right." And felt only contempt for myself for thinking at that moment, how pleasant it would be if Mary Ann Chaworth could be performing either of those womanly duties for me, on a permanent basis.

To my surprise, but not my concern, Lord Grey did not bid me good night at my chamber door, as he had on the previous evening, but came into the room, threw himself into a chair, and continued his diatribe. While I, tired and somewhat befuddled, threw off my jacket and continued to undress. It is a measure of the confidence I placed in him that I did not even fear to remove my boots, knowing instinctively that he would neither comment nor criticise.

As indeed he did not. His flow of conversation never altered, and I was constrained to complete my undressing, and reach for my nightshirt, when suddenly I discovered that he had left his chair, and was in fact standing immediately behind me.

"Oh, Byron, Byron," he whispered in my ear.

I turned in surprise, and found that not only was he standing against me, but that he had removed his own breeches, and his cocker, at that moment coming into contact with mine, was hard as a rod. I opened my mouth to protest, and he took this as the invitation he had been seeking, held me close, and planted the most passionate kiss upon my lips, involving tongue and teeth and saliva all at once. At the same instant he pushed me back so that my legs touched the bed, I overbalanced, and there he was lying on my belly.

It would be idle to protest that I felt only disgust, at that moment. I was a full-grown man, my cocker had risen to match his, and these two magnificent blood-filled sensors were bouncing against each other with as much eager violence as were our tongues. In similar circumstances I would defy *any* man not to feel the wildest and most consuming of emotions, a certainty that he was about to scale heights of the uttermost pleasure, a determination to reach those heights, come what may.

Yet I was at the same time aware of a feeling of acute embarrassment, and when he suddenly abandoned me, and regained his feet with the intention of divesting himself of the rest of his clothing, at the same time smiling at me in a most lascivious fashion, I felt I could no longer meet his gaze and instead rolled on to my face.

Which but proves my innocence. Being thus presented with the target he sought the poor fellow could not but suppose that I was as experienced in sodomy as himself, gave a whoop of the purest delight, and once again threw himself upon me, his cocker sliding over my buttocks to seek its way between, while his hand came round the front of my thighs to fondle my own.

Here he made his mistake. Left to myself, my entire body, my entire mind, a perfect volcano of seething desire, being constantly renewed by the gentle rubbing of my penis on the bedclothes, he might well have achieved his ambition and I might have been damned far sooner than eventually was the case. But the touch of his fingers on my already inflamed cocker was too much for the poor thing. I ejaculated immediately, flooding the bed, and while the event delighted him, my own passion immediately dwindled, as is the curse of the male sex, in this case to nothing at all, leaving me aware only of a total disgust akin to that I felt for my schoolmates.

"Dear Byron," he murmured, now jamming his rod into my backside as hard as he could, but still unable to make an entry as I had tightened my buttocks. "You are a *passionate* fellow. Byron?" This last comment because I had thrust my elbow into his ribs, an event which winded him and caused him to fall across the bed in turn, enabling me to wriggle free and reach my feet.

"Byron?" He sat up, his face purple at once with passion and uncertainty.

"Touch me again," I growled, "and . . . I'll kill you."

"Byron," he wailed. "Do not treat me so."

"Treat you so?" I shouted. "Why, my lord, I have not treated you at all, for which you may be grateful. Or I would certainly have broken your jaw."

He goggled at me, while I began to dress.

"Where are you going?" he asked at last.

"Away," I said.

"But. . . ." He licked his lips. "My dear boy," he said, "if I hurt you. . . ."

"You did not," I told him. "Nor will you." By now I was sufficiently recovered to feel more in command of myself. "You mistook my inclinations, that is all. We'll speak no more of it. Indeed, sir, we'll speak no more. Bear that in mind."

I buttoned my jacket, reached the door.

"You'll not repeat this," begged the stricken fellow, almost seeming to place his hands together in prayer as he asked my indulgence.

I permitted myself a sneer. "Are you then, so ashamed of your proclivities?"

"Ashamed?" he said. "Ashamed? My God, that I should be ashamed. 'Tis a hanging matter, did you not know? Sodomy is a hanging affair."

4

THYRZA

It is surely arguable that the true test of quality in any man is his ability to survive disaster, to play the phoenix, to triumph after all. Consider poor Byron. My sensibilities had been brutally assaulted in two directions at the same time; my unrequited love for Mary Ann on the one hand and the only too carnal love of Grey de Ruthven on the other. Had I been totally shattered and left a mumbling wreck no one could have blamed me. And as it was I could do no more than crawl back in abject defeat to Mama's boisterous bullying, and thence once again to Harrow on the Hill, prepared for another term of misery.

And found that I was but playing the pessimist. My last two years at Harrow were amongst the happiest I have known, at least in a physical sense. Make no mistake about it, emotionally I was ruined. I had loved, I did love, I would always love. Every time I remembered the touch of Mary Ann's tongue on mine I became quite giddy. But in my determination to put her, and all thoughts of the flesh, behind me, I discovered an entirely new world, of manly pursuits. I had always enjoyed swimming. Now I embarked upon it with great endeavour, for in the water no man could be my physical master.

I was equally determined that no man should be my physical master even on land. I had made myself a good pistol shot by constant practice at Newstead. Now I took advantage of a visit to the school of Angelo (i) to become a fencer as well.

Even on the intellectual side I made a great advance, as it was about now that I first opened a volume of poems written by Alexander Pope. I was amazed, elated. Here was a man whose point of view seemed to echo mine, and who had the power of conveying his opinions in the most delightful metre. From that moment, childish scribblings forgotten, I began to follow his example whenever the mood called me to verse, which was often enough. For it was at this age that I began to turn to poetry as an older man might turn to his bottle; whenever I felt the throb of emotion threatening to choke me, I sat at my desk and converted my madness into rhyme. My pen would fly across the page, and I would collapse into bed, hours later, exhausted and even sated.

But my new found enjoyment of life arose principally from the fact that I was now approaching sixteen, and manhood. I was no longer a new boy, and I was no longer in a junior form. I remained a notorious figure, to be sure, at once for my pranks, my refusal to study – my reading was a very private matter – my physical strength and capability, and my defiance of authority. And thus more then ever was I the natural leader of those boys who like myself would not immediately bend their backs before the outrageous behaviour to which they were subjected.

My closest friend at the beginning of this tumultuous period was Delawarr, (ii) like myself destined to become a peer of the realm the moment he attained his majority. Two years my junior, he had been one of the first I attempted to rescue from the slough, and in his defence my fists were often bloodied, while as he was as mischievous as myself I even found it necessary to intercede on his behalf from time to time with Authority, in the person of Tom Wildman, (iii) who was then a monitor. We were very close, in an entirely proper fashion, for in the misery of my return to school I saw in the noble lord the only true friend I possessed in all the world.

But he was soon to be replaced by another, even more dear. For this term the Earl of Clare (iv) arrived to take his place in the long line of distinguished Harrovians.

Clare was but eleven when he climbed the hill, really far too young to be exposed to the iniquities of initiation. He was also quite delightfully beautiful. Many young boys are, and lose their looks in grossness within half a dozen years. Clare remains as he was then, a perfect Adonis. Being privileged to witness the excesses of his first night at Harrow, I fell in love with him immediately.

The word I use advisedly, and with the advantage of hindsight. For there is a quality in mankind – perhaps the *best* quality in mankind – which demands that we respond without hesitation to those creatures who turn to us in their darkest hours. Clare, confused and miserable, as I had been, sought me as a shipmaster will seek a saving beacon on a stormy night. Following upon Mary Ann's rejection and Grey's lust he was as a cool wind coming at the end of an intolerably hot summer's day. My heart went out to him without restraint. He became my inseparable companion, to the exclusion of most others, to the dismay and indeed anger of Delawarr. Our love was so consuming it threatened to consume itself, for such was our jealousy, of look or even glance, of careless expression or worse, careless lack of expression in our correspondence, for we wrote to each other even while living in the same building, that some of our tiffs were bitter in the extreme.

And did we never wish more than the joy of our companionship, the pleasure of our mutual dreams, mutual plans for the future? Or rather it should be said, did *I* never wish to reach for more, for he was too young and too innocent. Of course I did. The opportunities were there. Swimming was my greatest pleasure, and he was happy to accompany me. Clothes were absent as we sported in the water, close together, inadvertently, and even advertently brushing against each other, on occasion laughing at each other's erection and holding our cockers to raise them higher yet. But I never touched him.

Sodomy is a hanging matter. Can that have been it? Somehow I doubt it. Rather was it a horror of playing Grey, a horror of what might follow, a horror of seeing my love for him dissipate itself in disgust, a horror of doing to him what May had done to me. A horror of entering our Eden in the guise of the Serpent. It was not easy. My reputation for misanthropy, for sullen self contemplation, for ill-temper and savage speech, grew with every week, and was regarded as but the natural concomitant of my lameness, for schools then, as no doubt now, believed that only in a healthy body could a healthy mind be found. Even Clare regarded me as a very dour fellow, even if *he* was always sure of bringing a smile to my lips. He never understood, he does not yet know, that it was suppressed desire for *him* made me so. He will know of it, should these words ever be published, but by then I shall be dead, and he will be allowed to smile to himself.

To be truly in love then is to be miserable. And yet, once again that fortune which has never utterly deserted me came to my rescue in my hour of need. To resist temptation by myself would have been ultimately impossible. But it was at this moment that I realised I possessed the truest friend any man could every dream of owning. When I was going half mad with frustrated desire for Mary Ann, with repressed desire for Clare, and with all too often yielded desire for myself, and feeling quite at the end of my tether, I received a letter from my sister.

I had met Augusta only twice in my life. Once when I had first visited Newstead, as a boy of ten, and once in the winter of 1802, when I had spent the holidays with the Hansons, and she had come to visit, entirely out of curiosity to see me, it later transpired. I had liked her much better on this second occasion. Four years make a great difference in the appearance of a girl; the pimpled fourteen year old had turned into a graceful and lovely eighteen year old, possessed of impeccable manners, a haughty awareness of her rank, this slight suggestion of reserve being tempered and made delightful by a ready and infectious sense of humour which made her more eager to smile than to frown. And she was beautiful. I have oft been accused of such a virtue myself, and I have had to contend with the disability of being Mama's son, although happily this has attended me more in a tendency to corpulence, which can be combated, than in any failure of feature. Augusta was my sister, but her mother had been as lovely as my father had been handsome, and slender with it.

Yet I remained beneath the influence of Mama's reasoning, that Augusta was a creature apart, a natural enemy. The fault was my own parent's. She had had the upbringing of the little girl, when I was born, and had decided the burden, emotional and financial, of caring for her predecessor's offspring was more than she could support. Augusta had thus been returned to the care of her grandmother, and where we had struggled along in penury for ten years, she, if a poor relation, had lived in surroundings of the greatest luxury, and amidst the very highest in the land, not excluding the royal family. Naturally generous and impulsive, I believe she from time to time attempted to correspond with Mama, and was regularly rebuffed. Thus she was the more anxious to establish friendship with her brother.

She seems to have followed my scholastic career through the medium of Hanson, and with his encouragement was at last inspired to write to me, letters I was the more eager to answer in my spiritual loneliness. For consider, here was my own sister, and yet a total stranger. I dared not of course reveal all, but I could reveal my own inner turmoils, sure in the knowledge that back would come a charming and warming epistle, assuring me of her interest and her sympathy at all times.

Her task was the more difficult as she even attempted to intercede for Grey. The circumstances were unusual. Considering me escaped his clutches, but anxious at once to have me back and to insure I spread no criminal tales about him, that viper had actually had the temerity to pay court to Mama, and she, poor middle-aged matron of fading charm, had conceived herself about to embark upon a new lease of life.

She was ever passionate – she was my mother. Delicacy forbids me to enlarge upon the dreadful business with the Frenchman, (v) but the thought of her becoming intimate with a man like Grey, which could lead to the ultimate catastrophe of my inheriting him as a stepfather, was too much. And yet, I would not betray him, nor myself. I suspect poor Augusta must have been sorely puzzled, and tempted to agree in the world's concept of my misanthropy, by the strong terms in which I expressed my loathing for the man without ever offering a shred of reason.

But she remained my friend, then and always. Which was as well, for soon there was another summer vacation to be endured, and this time there was nowhere to go but Southwell.

In fact Southwell was not quite the purgatory I had anticipated during that summer of 1804. With Mama there was of course the usual continual warfare, exacerbated on this occasion by her doting on the ghastly Grey, but there was Augusta to write to, and even more important, I made the acquaintance of a brother and sister, John and Elizabeth Pigot, with whom I was to become close friends, although both were somewhat older than myself. But for Elizabeth, indeed, I do believe I would that summer have either gone mad or committed suicide, for fool that I was, I could not return to Harrow before taking a ride, across the broad acres of Newstead, and into the hallowed borders of Annesley. And there, as fortune would decree, whom should I see taking an afternoon constitutional but the Dream (vi) herself.

"My dear Lord Byron," she remarked, coldly but politely. "It scarce seems a year since you so abruptly abandoned my father's roof, and my company."

She was more beautiful than ever. And for that reason more obnoxious to me, who had dreamed of her every night for a year. "I trust I have the manners, Miss Chaworth, to know where I am not wanted."

"Indeed, sir, you were always welcome at Annesley," she pointed out, her tone slightly softening.

"Extra boot and all?"

She flushed and frowned. "I had not supposed you so conscious of it," she said, suggesting a shallowness I had not previously observed. "Certainly *we* are not." Adding mendacity to her crimes. "I do assure you that we would much enjoy another visit."

"Perhaps," I said. "Perhaps in a year. Or will you not then be Mrs Musters?"

"I hope to be, certainly," said the heartless creature.

I bowed, and returned to my home, my heart a raging tumult of anger and despair. Elizabeth had recently left Southwell for an extended visit to the south, and in my abjection I spent the next few days at home, and even endeavoured to be pleasant to Mama.

Another example of the innocence of youth. No doubt Mama *was* pleased to have me around the house, but she was not disposed to show it, deeming that I required to be punished for spending so much time away during earlier holidays. She was cold, and two days later perpetrated a most hideous revenge, for as I sat at a window gazing at the lawn without and endeavouring to prevent my daily inundation of tears at the catastrophe which had overtaken me, she bustled into the room in apparent high good humour, shouting: "Wha' Geordie, 'tis a report I ha'e for ye. Ye'll remember wee Mary Duff?"

I almost fell from my perch. Mary Duff. Perhaps, my leaping brain seemed to say, all that has happened is but a play on the part of Fate. Mary Duff. Of all the women I had known here was the only one worthy of the title noble. And how could I ever have looked upon her with satisfactory adoration had my mind still been filled with thoughts of the disgusting Chaworth?

"She's to visit?" I begged.

Mama gave a peal of merry laughter. "Nay, nay, ye silly lad. She's wed. Would ye believe it, a lass o' sixteen? Wed to a Cockburn. Och aye, there's a good marriage. 'Tis to be hoped ye do as well."

I scarce heard the last two sentences. I stared at my mother in the most utter consternation, while my heart seemed to explode in a gush of blood which made me quite unsteady, so that I flopped on to the seat, unable to utter a sound.

While Mama at last noticed my condition. "Wha' Geordie," she cried. "Did ye love her still?" Another shriek of laughter. "Ye love her still," she bellowed. "Ye love her still."

That mothers manage to survive the adolescence of their sons is indeed an indication of the strength of filial piety. I could have strangled mine there and then, and gone to the gallows without a doubt that I had done the right thing. Instead I merely fled to my room, and prepared myself for what was to be my last year at Harrow.

*   *   *

Which had an odd flavour to it. For at the end of the Michaelmas Term, when I departed for my usual Christmas festivities with the Hansons, a bolt from the blue arrived in the form of a suggestion from Drury, the Headmaster rather than the tutor, that I not return.

He can hardly have supposed my scholastic needs fulfilled, as so far as he was aware they had made no progress whatsoever during my sojourn in his establishment. Which may suggest a reason for his peculiar attitude. Far more likely it is that he felt I was becoming too successful a leader of my band of rebels. My emotional experiences had served only to convince me that there was a great deal wrong with the world, and with human beliefs. It was, I think, Lord Calthorpe who gave me the appellation, "Atheist", which was not then, and is not now, true. Deist I would have accepted, and even today I find it difficult to suppose that God permits any appendages but the awful power of His name.

No doubt this tale, amongst others, got back to Drury. But he was also not insensible to the fact that I did possess certain qualities, public speaking being one of them, for I had taken some passages from the *Aeneid* to declame at our previous Speech Day, and he had been warm in his praise. Thus he was eventually able to relent, and permit me to complete the year, which ended with two great triumphs for me. One was at Speech Day, when I chose to recite Zanga,(vii) and was a tremendous success, and the other was at the very end of all, when the school had already broken up for the holidays, I was chosen to play cricket against Eton, crippled leg and all.

This match, the second and last ever played between the two schools,(viii) took place actually in London, at the ground owned by Thomas Lord and used as a headquarters by the Marylebone Cricket Club,(ix) which in recent years has replaced Hambledon as the premier club of All England. It required a great deal of organisation, as may be imagined, in which I was not involved, but I do recall our dismay on arriving at the ground to find that the Etonians were as a side bigger and stronger and somewhat obviously older than any of our people; it was difficult not to form the impression that some of them might already have attended university, or even completed their under-graduate studies. And so it proved in the match itself. They batted but once, we completed *two* innings, and yet the margin was still two runs in their favour.

Not that this disaster could be laid at my door. Despite having to have someone to run my runs for me. I notched eleven in the first

innings, and seven in the second, (x) figures which could be bested by
only two of our players, Brockman and Ipswich. I enjoyed my
moment of fame enormously, and indeed the evening following the
match was convivial in the extreme, as we attended the Haymarket,
got decidedly tipsy, both teams mixed up together, if I recall correctly
there being four Etonians and three Harrovians in a single hackney.
The evening also affords a measure of my growing poetical reputation, for the Etonians, scribbling away over dinner, came up with a
taunt:

> Adventurous *boys* of Harrow School,
> Of cricket you've no knowledge.
> You play not cricket, but the fool,
> With *men* of Eton College.

Which almost served to confirm our suspicions. But my school-
mates immediately turned to me for their rescue. "You are a poet,
Byron," they declared. "Answer them in style."
Which I did, after no more than a moment's composition:

> Ye Eton wits, to play the fool,
> Is not the boast of Harrow School.
> No wonder then at our defeat
> Folly like yours could ne'er be beat.

But the very day following this splendid and unforgettable occasion, I was on my way to Southwell, my boyhood days at an end for ever.

And was promptly assailed by the most profound melancholy. For
reflection assured me that nothing had changed, save that I had lost the
company of my schoolfellows. With whom were they to be replaced?
I was destined, in the autumn, for Cambridge. I wished to attend
Oxford, where my Harrow chums were headed, but there was no
suitable accommodation to be found at Christ Church, and so it was
Trinity-ho and the fens, and not a friend in sight.
Nor were any to be found closer at home. I had invited Augusta to
hear me speak at Speech Day, and she had not come. I was, after all, as
I imagined, not the highest in her esteem. In fact she was engaged in
the business of *becoming* engaged to gormless George, and the *happy*
couple were suffering from the opposition of Aunt Fanny to the
project, she having known dear Papa too well to wish her darling boy
to become closely involved with such a madcap's daughter.

And Southwell, of course, was where Mama maintained her lair, which was sufficiently distressing a prospect. Nor had she changed in the slightest save for the worse, as she soon illustrated, choosing a moment when we were in company to say: "Byron, I have some news for you."

"Indeed, Mother?" I replied, with total indifference.

"You will not like it. You had best take out your handkerchief before I speak."

"I do assure you, Mother. . . ."

"Nay, nay. Not a word will I say, until you have kerchief in hand."

I humoured her, and pulled out my handkerchief, whereupon she gave one of her great peals of laughter. "Miss Chaworth is married. Aye, married. To John Musters. Will ye no weep, Byron?"

I merely turned and left the room, for by now I was made of sterner stuff, as all who had watched me over the years came to understand. Augusta indeed was distressed at the change in my personality, from the eager, passionate boy to the cold, cynical man.

I found my solace in writing. Every day and all day. And I sat with Lizzie Pigot, and talked. My poems were frankly erotic. I *imagined* myself into a great lover, making do with words where the deeds were lacking. I out-Keated that lamentable boy in mental masturbation. And was silly enough to suppose it was all very good stuff. And so it will be understood that I attended Cambridge, with the bells still ringing in my ears to celebrate the glories of Trafalgar, in a very sorry state of mind.

I had been provided with a suitable allowance, on the surface, having regard to my station. I was enabled to obtain good rooms, in the south-east corner of the Great Court of Trinity. They opened on to a splendid wide staircase, and were surmounted by a tower, which proved handy in later years. True I was *surrounded* by authority, in the persons of my tutor on one side, the Reverend Thomas Jones, and by an old Fellow on the other, but I conceived this no disadvantage. I ordered furniture where I chose, laid in a stock of choice wines, stabled my horses, and lacked only my dog Boatswain, whom I for the moment abandoned at Southwell.

And if all my noble friends had betaken themselves elsewhere, I was not entirely bereft, for who should come to call upon my first evening but dear Ted Long, who had shared with me that first experience at Harrow. While my open house soon added more. Our Master of Ceremonies was Billy Bankes, a very wild fellow, who was concerned with every prank he could devise. In their own way these were harmless enough, but when they concerned a lonely cripple they could become dangerous indeed. I speak nothing of our drinking. In my first week at Cambridge I never attended bed sober, and I never attended any lectures at all, and not only from an aching head. No one else seemed to study either. And the Fellows did not seem to care. Had it not been for the efforts of Tommy Jones I would not even have read a book. Because here again was a quite forgotten practice in this seat of learning. If I formed a very adverse opinion of my fellows, which only grew the longer I stayed in their company, it is hardly to be wondered at.

Yet solitary studies, and at my own behest rather than others, was nothing new to me. I could carouse with the best of them and have no greater head next morning. But a young gentleman at Cambridge was not supposed to confine his leisure activities to drinking and playing at cards. He must also prove himself a *man*.

"A lord," madame remarked, sizing me up, for I wore the very best. (xi) She was a roguish creature, clearly past her first youth, to be sure, but all heaving bosom and heavy perfume, like the crowd of eager votaries who hovered at her elbow, but far less inclined to giggle than they. "Why, my lord, will I not suffice myself?"

I supposed this an honour, which it was, and a very sensible point of view, which possibly it also was. I knew aught, she knew all. I had secrets, she would have unearthed a great many, amongst which mine would be nothing remarkable. Had I been older and more acquainted with myself, I would have preferred one of the younger, giggling variety already being escorted to chosen chambers by Bankes and Long, but I opted for security.

And to do her justice, Jeanette, for such was her name, at least in business, had no cause to blame herself for what happened. "My lord," she said, escorting me behind my friends. "You are a handsome fellow." Which was stretching the truth some, as although my face had already assumed the noble contours it has preserved, I had put on weight during the summer, and was decidedly plump. And she gave me a hug.

"And you, Jeanette, are a beautiful woman," I said with equal gallantry, really stretching the matter this time.

"Flatterer," she admitted, and sat me on the bed while she eased my coat from my shoulders. "But I can see you are a man of the world."

Another obvious lie, as I was sweating like a pig. But at least my cocker was bulging, as she had already ascertained, being practised in these matters, and indeed she was unfastening my trousers with delicate haste, easing them down my thighs and returning a moment later to do the same for my drawers, removing them most eagerly, pausing to admire and to smile, before folding my garments over a chair. I felt exhilarated as I also regarded the proud, blood crimsoned fellow, all ready to honour the name of Byron, and any slight fear I might have felt that she would comment upon my leg as she drew off my boots were immediately dismissed, for she was a mistress of tact and never hesitated for even a moment.

I completed the destruction of my upper garments, and was then ready for the fray, as she eased me back upon the pillows before straightening to undress herself. Unhappy Byron. I had ever in my life observed but two women naked. May had been approximately the age I now approached, young and eager and firm. Upon her splendidly muscular body I had grafted my midnight dreams of Mary Ann. The other had been Mama, fat and flouncing and forty. Jeanette was not flouncing. But the breasts which had appeared so firm and so large and so inviting when confined and projected by her gown were now only large; they wobbled like blancmanges. Her belly, which was now revealed, was no better, and her thighs distinctly worse. While between was a yawning and forested cavern, into which it seemed I should disappear, never to be seen again.

These unfortunately imaginative thoughts acted as had once May's crop, and from six inches I dwindled in the space of a second to less than one, a retreat beside which Napoleon's later effort on his way home from Moscow pales into insignificance. Madame, having already relieved me of my guinea (xii) and having in addition her reputation at stake, was alarmed. I dismissed the matter as of no consequence, blamed it upon an obscure fever I had contracted while a child at my father's side during his sojourn in deepest Patagonia, a fictional coup de grace which left her gasping, and withdrew, to surrender to tears in the privacy of my own chambers.

Next day, a prey of the saddest considerations, for I could not tell if she would break the news of my catastrophe to my friends, I attended chapel, and heard a choirboy sing.

He performed a solo, at one stage, but it cannot have been the music attracted me. His voice was beautiful, but so were the voices of most of the Cambridge choristers. And to say that he was a handsome, nay a *pretty* young man would be superfluous. There was something deeper which drew me to him as the pole draws the compass needle, forced me to seek him out at the earliest opportunity.

His name was John Edleston. There can be no harm in making that secret public now, as we shall both have been long dead by the time these words reach print. He was but fifteen years of age, approaching sixteen, as I was seventeen approaching eighteen, for strangest of events, we shared the same birthday, even to the very hour. Never then can two human beings have been so selected by Fate to meet, even if set by that fickle jade in so different stations. He was the son of a respectable Suffolk tradesman, attending school in the university town, and I was the 6th Lord Byron. He was overwhelmed that so august a being should condescend to choose him for a friend, I was overwhelmed that so splendid a likeness of myself in another form should be willing to reciprocate my consideration, my affection, and my love.

Because we did love, jointly and fervently. The course of our romance was as brief as that of a shooting star, for upon that hallowed sixteenth birthday, his parents lacking the wherewithal to send him to university, he was intended to leave school and commence a mercantile career in the city. Thus we enjoyed scarce more than a month, yet in that time we saw each other every day, meeting in secluded places, touching each other's hands, walking together, knowing nothing save the pleasure of each other's company.

But the vast cloud which overhung my existence overhung his as well. As with Clare, I was the senior. My desires would count in the end. And my desires were manifold. But with Clare it had all been on my side. He had known nothing of what a man might wish, never having had the misfortune to encounter a Grey. He had, besides, been younger. Whether or not Edleston had already been seduced, or whether, being so close to me in everything else he was my twin in passion as well, there can be no doubt he *felt* as did I, and *wanted*, as did I, and hinted, on sufficient occasions, that his body was at my disposal.

And I did not take advantage of his offer. It may be believed that I have spent some time since in wondering why. I may say in the first place that both of us did not consider that fateful January day as the end of the matter. It would involve no more than a temporary separation, of that we were sure. Thus the future, which we should perhaps be

70

able to share without inhibition or interruption, seemed more secure than the present, when our every meeting was stolen.

But more important than that were my own feelings. I reasoned, at great length and at the cost of much mental agony. I was not a pervert. Of that I was sure. I was but consumed with a *passion*, physical, mental and spiritual, which I wished to share, and which I wished to have shared with me. My first choice had been Mary Ann Chaworth-Musters, and she had scornfully rejected me. Worse, in her rejection, in her reasons for rejecting me, she had seemed to sum up the probable feelings of the entire female sex.

Augusta has since told me that my letters of this period are amongst the most disturbing I have ever written, in that I constantly hint at some great and overburdening weight lying on my soul and responsible for extreme melancholy, but never vouchsafe the reason for this mental anguish. I could well have done, in my miserable confusion. Poor Edleston was in a similar condition. He could not doubt my love. He could only wait for me to take him in my arms, and when the day for his departure to London drew near, and we had done no more than hold hands and sigh, he too could only look to the future. Then he was gone, and I was left to write poems to his memory. To confuse the crass multitude, I called him Thyrza. (xiii)

A GIRL CALLED CAROLINE

Parting with Edleston, even if on a temporary basis, left me all at sixes and sevens once more. And as if that were not enough to bear, I was immediately made aware of that curse of any gentleman who would be a gentleman: Debt.

My allowance on attending university had been set at five hundred pounds a year, payable in quarterly instalments. Even supposing dear Hanson had been punctual in forwarding the funds, this would still have been insufficient, as I soon found out, for the everyday business of living, at least like a lord and a Byron. Cambridge itself might not have been expensive, but I was a man in the grip of a most terrifying passion. I loved. I could conceive of no one better suited to be my eternal companion than Edleston. And yet I knew that to yield to such a love would be to damn myself forever. Therefore I determined upon the need for a surgical operation, on the mind and the desires. Come what may, I would steep myself in all the vices considered to be essential to manhood, and eradicate the memory of Madame Jeanette from my mind for ever.

But to descend upon London and plunge into the life of a Brummell requires one essential commodity: Funds. I had none, but this was surely no more than a temporary misfortune. For I owned Newstead, worth a hundred thousand if it was worth a penny, and I owned the mines at Rochdale, worth no doubt a hundred thousand more. It did not seem to me to be taking any sort of risk to borrow money to my requirements on a temporary basis, until I came of age. Of course I knew that I would require security, in the form of the signature of someone of repute who would undertake to repay the loan should I fail to do so, minors being held irresponsible in these matters in the eyes of the law. I also felt fairly sure that it would be unwise to approach Hanson, who might well report my intention to Mama, and cause me embarrassment. I therefore wrote Augusta, and asked her to stand surety for a small loan. To my utter amazement and disgust she not only refused, but returned a lecture upon the iniquities of debt. I was outraged. I could only feel that I had been deserted by the one person over all others I had supposed I could trust. Our correspondence ceased.

I was not to be thwarted. I had taken lodgings in London with the same lady who had been Mama's landlady in the past, Mrs Massingberd, and she, on hearing of my difficulties, arranged for me to meet certain representatives of the tribes of Israel, herself standing security. Thus equipped, I launched myself upon London society. I spent hours at my tailor. I spent equal hours at the rooms in Bond Street where Angelo and John Jackson shared their talents, and besides pursuing my gifts with the sword I also learned the manly art of self defence. Nor did I neglect my pistols, and soon made myself into one of the best shots in London, for now that I was approaching man's estate, who could say when I would be required to defend the honour of my name? I displayed my athletic prowess in other directions as well, my greatest feat being to swim in the Thames from London to Blackfriars, a distance of three miles.

But the main purpose of my descent upon London, to the total neglect of my Cambridge responsibilities, was finally to conquer Venus. To this end I visited Madame Dulcina, London's leading *entremetteuse*.

"My lord," she said, studying my card. "An honour." Which smacked too much of the fair Jeanette, but I was soon to understand that ladies of this variety have a certain language all their own.

"Mine, madame," I insisted. And perceived her closely studying my form. "Will I not do?"

"My lord," she cried. "You are a handsome man. Why, stoutness is all the rage."

A nasty barb. But truly I had permitted my weight to burst the bounds, so to speak, and actually tipped the scales at something over two hundred pounds, which as I am not a very tall fellow, made me very nearly as broad as I was long. I resolved then that I would remedy the situation, which had been partly encouraged by Jackson, as any would-be pugilist needs a lot of beef to stand up to punishment.

But I refused to be abashed. I had steeled myself for this ordeal with all the determination of a wounded soldier facing the amputation of his foot.

"I am glad to hear you say so," I remarked. "And what have you to offer me tonight?"

She pulled her lip. "Now let me see. . . ." And she seized my arm to escort me into an inner room where several young women sat around, dressed in bright if tawdry gowns, entertaining several gentlemen, although none of my acquaintance, as I had especially chosen an evening when I knew my friends were all at table. "What does my lord fancy? Harriet?"

The girl obligingly stood up. She was tall, and obviously strong, with black hair and handsome features. And clearly chosen to sustain the weight madame anticipated I would deposit upon her belly. But her gaze was too experienced. I had come here to learn, certainly, but no one was to know that save myself.

"Not Harriet," Dulcina said sadly. "Well, then, Joanna."

This was more my own height, and more my own size in every way, for she was distinctly fat, although young and attractive enough.

"You can have Joanna on the floor," Dulcina informed me, "and never know the difference."

Joanna giggled obligingly, and shuddered from stem to stern. Shades of Jeanette.

"My lord is difficult to please," Dulcina said, a trifle tartly. "Well, then. . . ."

"That one," I said, making one of those momentous decisions, entirely on the spur of the moment, which so often govern a man's entire life.

For at that moment a girl had entered the room, bearing drinks for the clientele. She looked hardly old enough to sustain the tray, was absolutely boylike in her slender thighs and her absence of bosom, but feminine enough in the mass of soft yellow hair which cascaded on to her shoulders, and *entirely* feminine in the demure sweep of her blue eyes.

Dulcina was taken aback. "Caroline?" she demanded. "But Caroline is only fourteen. She is. . . ."

"Reserved?" I demanded in turn, my heart pounding most painfully. For on a sudden I felt a flush of quite tremendous passion, and my breeches were threatening to burst. What more could a man ask, I wondered, than a woman who looked like a boy? And at fourteen, she was far too young to regard any faults of omission on my part with contempt.

74

"Indeed not, my lord. That is to say, she *is* reserved, for gentlemen of a special taste. . . ." Dulcina smiled, not a pretty sight. "But if your lordship is of such a taste, why she shall be yours."

The introduction was carried out somewhat publicly, setting the rest of the assembly to laughing and cheering at my taste for the unusual. Nor was the girl herself insensible to her position, for her pale cheeks immediately filled with blood, as she carefully set down her tray. "Will my lord take a glass?" she inquired, her voice little more than a whisper, while her eyes, turning up to meet mine for a moment, as rapidly lowered again. And in so doing sent a fresh rash of passion bounding through my system. But of a quite unexpected variety. On a sudden my sexual impulse disappeared and in its place there arose that *pure* passion which was the bane of my existence. In that moment I desired nothing more than to escort the girl from her iniquitous surrounds and keep her for ever as my own.

A lord, in love at first sight with a whore? The situation was preposterous, and so I answered perhaps more gruffly than I had intended. "No."

Caroline glanced at her employer, who shrugged, allowed herself a little sigh, and whispered: "Then if you will come this way, my lord."

We left the withdrawing-room to the accompaniment of more cheers and ribald comment, and I followed her up a brief flight of stairs and along a narrow corridor, dimly lit and redolent with the scent of men and women at play, as well as the occasional sounds of the players themselves, and arrived at an empty chamber, into which she ushered me, immediately closing and locking the door. I sat on the bed, turning round to do so, and discovered to my consternation that the young woman had already removed her gown, and that she wore nothing at all beneath. And if the suggestion of her had attracted me earlier, I was quite dumbfounded at this apparition. Her body was utterly slender, her breasts nothing more than slight mounds upon her chest, although her nipples were sufficiently pointed. Her belly lacked all pout, and her slit was attended by only the scantiest of pale brown wisps. Her legs were long, and well muscled, her feet delightfully formed. And above all that haunting pale face, those magnificent eyes, that splendid hair.

"My lord is displeased?"

Perhaps her voice was the most marvellous thing about her.

"Displeased? I am pleased, very pleased."

75

She crossed the room, every movement a dream, and sat beside me. "May I assist my lord?"

"In a moment," I begged, suddenly terrified of what I was about to do, supposing I could do it at all. For cocker had assumed a sort of half position, which I well knew could endure for hours, keeping me pleasantly titillated but in no condition to fulfil his proper function. "Can we not talk?"

"Whatever your lordship wishes," she said.

"I. . . ." I cursed the heat in my cheeks. "I would like to know how you come to be here," I said. "If I am not being too bold."

"Mama sold me to Madame," she explained, without a hint of knowledge that this might be an unnatural and hideous act.

By now I was deciphering her faint accent. "You are Scots."

"My name is Cameron, my lord," she said, licking her lips in an apprehension of her own.

"But I am also a Scot," I cried. And with a boldness which even now astonishes me, I seized her face between my hands and kissed her upon the lips.

There was joy. Her breath was sweet, her tongue tender and just bold enough to set me on fire. But I am cursed with imagination, and when I felt her fingers unfastening my breeches I could not help but wonder for how many other men she had accomplished such a task, identifying some of the middle-aged louts who still sat without.

"I . . . I am afflicted," I gasped. As she could see for herself.

"Not so, my lord," she protested, and slipped from the bed to kneel between my legs. For how many years had I dreamed of such a moment, and Caroline's beauty placed May's in the carthorse variety. Her touch was that of a goddess, the soft caress of her lips as she took me into her mouth the purest nectar. Yet still the image of her kneeling at the feet of some monsterish rake, surely her more usual occupation, had me in its grip, and harden I would not.

"My dear child," I muttered, seizing that golden head to draw her into my stomach. "I am afflicted. I will withdraw."

"No." She almost shouted, and in the same instant started to her feet. And bit her lip, while a tear stole down her cheek. "My lord, you cannot. Should you not be satisfied, madame will flog me."

"I will be satisfied, at least to *her* satisfaction," I promised.

"She will know, my lord. She will know. Please, my lord."

Her tone was filled with such abject terror I could not disbelieve her. But what to do? I was as desperate as she, for I knew that to leave unfulfilled now would ruin me for ever; Edleston lodged not a mile away. My gaze rolled around the room, seeking to rid myself of the ghastly images which were numbing my manhood, and alighted upon a stout cane, standing in a corner. And remembered May, and my childhood. If I dared. But somehow I knew that with this child I could dare.

"Then *you* shall beat *me*," I said.

"My lord?" Her head raised.

"Have you not done so before?"

She shook her head. "That is reserved for senior girls."

I could have shouted for joy. In this, at the least, she was mine. "Then tonight you become senior."

She hesitated but a moment, then completed the removal of my clothing. I knelt beside the bed, and a moment later she applied the cane with more vigour than I had supposed so young a child to possess. Six strokes had my senses whirling, and accomplished all that I could have hoped. I turned, still on my knees, threw both arms around her gentle buttocks, planted a kiss on those lips I intended to breach, lifted her up, laid her on her back on the bed, and was inside her in a gigantic bound.

Where now was the virgin who had never managed an orthodox erection? Gone for ever, I am happy to say. How shall I depict the feeling as her thighs closed on me, the moment of anxiety when I seemed to scrape through a desert, to be replaced a moment later by a rush of splendid lubricity which had me heaving back and forth, accompanied by a surge of positively demoniac carelessness, of consuming desire, so that I dug my hands beneath her to hold a buttock in each, and pulled her up while I pushed myself down, while my lips seized hers and my teeth clashed with hers and my tongue twined itself round hers, and I felt my cocker explode in a tumult of repressed passion, which might have been building for ten years for all I knew, and knew also, or at least, *supposed*, that my fears were ended for ever.

I have no very clear recollection of leaving Madam Dulcina's that night, but I do remember returning the next, and demanding the company of my Caroline, to be rebuffed. "Caroline is unwell," Madame informed me, and tapped me on the chest with her fan. "You were too ardent, my lord. The poor girl is a mass of bruises."

I sent her flowers, and withdrew to Cambridge. I desired no substitute. Indeed at that moment I desired nothing at all, not even Caroline herself. My elation knew no bounds. For the first time in my life I was master of my own soul, and of my own body. Over the next year I enjoyed myself as I had never suspected it was possible to do, whether at Cambridge, which I hardly spared the time to attend, as I realised I was accomplishing very little, and where indeed I hardly dared attend owing to a shortage of funds, or at Southwell. Here I cut a dashing figure. In my new confidence I could throw myself into the heart and soul of the community, flirted with Lizzie Pigot, who had remained my faithful correspondent, took part in local amateur theatricals, and wrote poetry; it was that autumn that I finally published, in a private edition, all those youthful stanzas at which I had worked so hard over the previous ten years. The edition was called *Fugitive Pieces*, and although I distributed it only to my friends or those I thought might be interested, I suddenly discovered myself the centre of all Southwell's interest. The good ladies of the village, and even more their daughters, pretended to be shocked by my eroticism, but truly they were more attracted by the suggestion that at the age of eighteen I had indulged in so much licentiousness.

Now of course I enjoyed this enormously, the more so as it was entirely a pack of lies. Upon one brief encounter with Caroline I built an entire lifetime of lubricity, allowing my ever fertile imagination to run riot, turning myself into a positive Defoe. And discovered that the gates of feminine hospitality were opened wide before me. Not, alas, that I took as much advantage of my situation as I should. I was simply too ignorant.

But life is never intended to be mere pleasure. However desperately I sought to enjoy myself, I remained a minor, with better than two years to go before I could attain my majority. Thus I remained also at the mercy of Mama, who hovered at my shoulder cursing me and begging me, screaming at me and weeping before me. Her theme was the wastage of my life when I should be at Cambridge. I could not explain to the dear old soul *why* I had not returned to Trinity – she would have had a seizure on the spot – but in the end I could stand her importuning no longer, and took myself back to the Happy Hebrews, once again under the kind auspices of Mrs Massingberd.

To be fair, these gentlemen were more than willing to help, and also to be fair, they were in business for profit and not charity. They ascertained the sum I calculated I required, added to it the sums I already owed, and came up with three thousand pounds, which would enable me to resume my preferred way of living until I was of age, at which time I should repay them *five* thousand, and be free of debt. Even I, unused to business matters, computed this to be a rather high rate of interest, amounting to thirty-three and a third per cent a year for each of the two years, but the simple answer was, take it or leave it, and when I considered that my actual worth on achieving my majority would be in the nature of two hundred thousand, to give away two and a half per cent of that vast sum in order to complete my varsity days in the manner to which I had been born did not seem too much of a sacrifice. Per cent, per cent, per cent. What drones, and fools, it makes of us all.

Thus I returned to Cambridge in the spring of 1807. And was not recognised. This was partly because there was no one there to recognise me. Most of my first year acquaintances had departed, even old Tommy Jones had died, and my new tutor, the Reverend George Tavell, had not such an easy manner. But it was also partly because I had lost a great deal of weight, having spent the previous summer and indeed this very spring working very hard at exercise, even playing at cricket in a heavy coat to reduce the fluids. From two hundred and more pounds I had come down to one hundred and forty, a remarkable achievement, and one I was determined I should never have to repeat. One meal a day, a few sips of wine, and a glass of soda water was my recipe for health, and although on occasion it left me giddy with hunger, it did wonders for the sharpness of my brain and of that other important part of my anatomy.

In truth I returned to my *alma mater* in no very settled frame of mind, for a variety of reasons, but even in the absence of people like Teddy Long, who had gone into the army, I suddenly found it a most entrancing place, the reason being an entirely new set of friends who suddenly appeared. Of these I will mention only two, Charlie Matthews and Cam Hobhouse. Matthews was the perfect companion, as full of spirits as a puppy, up to every scrape he could conceive, but withal a man of cutting intellect. He had, in fact, been the tenant of my rooms during my absence from Trinity, and had been warned to be careful of the furniture, for I was a damnably sharp fellow. Which was by way of being a compliment. Matthews of course turned the whole thing into a farce, and would warn visitors even to be careful how they turned the doorknob, less they incur the wrath of the absent lord. In him I think England lost a great and original mind, had he ever been able to turn it to any useful pursuit. (i) Cam was a vastly different proposition, as sober as a judge and looking like one, and yet the very best of fellows, as he has proved to me on so many occasions I cannot recall them all. Our friendship was the more odd as in my previous year he had not been a friend at all, leading that group who were opposed to me – and there was a considerable number – on grounds that I dressed outrageously, which is to say I was fond of wearing a white hat and a grey coat, and of riding a grey horse. (ii)

Once he discovered that beneath the hat there lurked a brain, however, he could not do too much for me, especially as he also had a literary bent, although his was towards prose, ever the nobler form of expression. Between us we worked very hard at our chosen avocations, whenever we could find the time, because I was now determined upon publishing, and for public consumption, and was revising all of my poems, adding lines here and deleting lines there, with a view of throwing myself open to the vulgar gaze at the earliest opportunity.

I say whenever we could find the time, for as usual there were far more important things to be accomplished at Cambridge than work. Serious things, to be sure; it was during this year that, together with Cam, Douglas Kinnard, (iii) and half a dozen others, amongst them Ellenborough (iv) and the Duke of Devonshire, (v) we founded the Cambridge Whig Club. But also all the pleasures that young men find. Swimming was ever a principal joy. We littered the bottom of the Cam with coin and crockery, all of which we dived for and retrieved at depths of twelve feet and more, while another of our aquatic pastimes was to cling to a heavy log beneath the surface and see who could hold his breath the longest.

That sport sufficed for our daylight hours. After dark we had recourse to more gentlemanly pursuits. In my new found Caroline-granted freedom I wished to be a leader in this field, and found myself at once disappointed and disturbed. That I might occasionally need the cane was no hardship to a hardened whore, and in fact my reliance upon this relict of my childhood decreased with every occasion. What I could not accustom myself to were the hardened whores themselves. They were never for me, and if I must necessarily play the man it was with no great enjoyment, which but reintroduced my innate melancholy, as I drearily recalled Mary Ann Musters' chilling comment upon my person; bought love was not for me, but save it was bought, where would I find the woman to regard me as a suitable or even a possible bedmate?

As a result I threw myself ever more heartily into the business of making mischief wherever I could, and I fancy surpassed even Matthews at his best in my ultimate ruse. A rule of the college in which I resided was that there should be no dogs in undergraduate rooms, even a small one like a bulldog I had lately acquired, named Smut. But the word was specific. I was thus able to perpetrate the most splendid wheeze by purchasing myself a large brown bear, which I installed in the turret room immediately above my own. Bruin was a splendid fellow, remarkably affectionate, which made him the more obnoxious to those Fellows of his acquaintance, as he was wont to give a literal interpretation to the word "bearhug". But when we went walking, he attached to the end of a stout chain, we were the centre of attraction.

In many ways, no doubt, this year of Tilsit, (vi) seen in retrospect, was a happy one. I sometimes think of it as the very last of my boyhood, and not merely in terms of physical age. It had a carefree quality I was never to know again, mainly because I supposed, at its beginning, that I had shrugged off the awful canker which had been inflicted upon my personality. I deluded myself. For not very long after I again took up residence, with Bruin *et al.*, I was visited by Edleston.

He had not changed in the slightest, save to grow yet more pale, as he had spent the year locked away in the vaults of his London office. But the eager friendship, the adoration with which he regarded me, was as before, just as my own pulse quickened at the very sound of his voice.

"I have heard you are become a man of parts, my lord," he said.

"A man acting the part, my dear Edleston," I assured him, holding his hand as we walked down a leafy lane. "Have you not done the same, this last year?"

"Never," he declared most vehemently. "When loneliness overtakes me, I lie in bed and dream of you."

So then, I was not yet saved from my affliction. Indeed, perhaps at that moment I realised that I would *never* be utterly free of it, for in those surroundings, of hallowed Cambridge, and at that time of life, not yet twenty, and in the presence of those laws, of England, I was forced to regard it *as* an affliction, perhaps more horrible than leprosy. Freedom of mind, as freedom of body, had not yet been enabled to come to my rescue.

And yet, resist him, at least in his presence, I could not. "It is less simple, at Cambridge," I told him. "But when I am done here, when I am of age, then, dear Edleston, my plans are unchanged. Then we shall seek our own destiny, in each other's company, and wherever it takes us, if we have to travel to China."

"Do you mean it?" the poor lad begged, looking me full in the face.

"I mean it," I assured him. "But the decision must be yours, as you are the younger, as you will have more to lose. But make it, in due course, and leave the rest to me."

Yet he was troubled, having more insight into me than I had supposed. "Then I shall," he said. "When the time comes. But for the present, why, I have a present for you." And he gave me a cornelian stone,(vii) beautifully shaped in the form of a heart, and almost seeming to throb with red blood. "Remember me," he said.

"I shall, for ever," I promised. "Nor will this stone ever leave my side."

Remember him I have, and if the stone and I have been from time to time separated, it is at my side now, broken in two pieces, alas, but none the less treasured for that. Because we *loved*. No human law has the right to dictate that emotion, nor to interfere in its display. And I gave him a bumper farewell supper, when fourteen of us sat down, and demolished twenty-three bottles of wine, beside sundry other beverages.

Yet the meeting plunged me into another of my melancholy fits, as I contrasted what I would be with what I was, and what I was with what I might become. Beneath the glitter of the laughing, carefree Byron there lurked a trapped soul, seeking freedom, seeking relief from his burdens, reduced to wishing that with a snap of his fingers he could rid himself of clubbed foot, crippling debt, and of callow England, all in a bound, and emerge a free, healthy and careless man. My confusion of spirit even led me this year to quarrel with Hanson, for being slow in forwarding my allowance, a stricture he certainly deserved, but I had not so many true friends that I could afford to antagonise any of them. I had even greater problems nearer to home with the discovery that my valet, Frank Boyce, had been guilty of fraud and indeed downright theft. I made what plea for mercy I could, but the poor fellow was still transported, and I was left to do nothing more than reflect upon the misery of the human soul.

But for writing, I doubt not I would have gone mad. With *Hours of Idleness* about to burst upon the public, I busied myself with reviewing, with writing satire, and even with the first half of a novel. Only the satire was, I think, of any value, but Crosby, the London agent of my printer, (viii) was reluctant to take it on as he considered it would give too much offence to too many important persons, and it did not then see the light of day. (ix) A pity, because Cam and I intended to publish in a joint volume.

In fact *Hours of Idleness* was very well received indeed, I having been unwise enough to use my own name. But sales were good, nor were the early reviews at all bad. I even received a letter from my cousin's uncle, Robert Dallas, praising my ability as a poet although somewhat critical – who was not, even amongst my Cambridge friends? – of the erotic or satirical content. He wished to call, and did so. I cannot pretend that I was not flattered by this praise from an already established man of letters, although it turned out that what he was really after was a loan. This seemed pointless, so I gave him two hundred pounds as a gift, although I could ill spare it myself. And discovered that I appeared to have accumulated him as permanent literary adviser.

But not all reviewers were kind. The *Monthly Mirror*, in the person of a Mr Twiddie, chose to suggest that I had not been flogged sufficiently at Harrow to have saved me from this venture into verse, a criticism that so angered me I promptly sent him a challenge. My very first, although I was not in the least afraid, as I practised with my pistols at Manton's every day. (x) In the event Twiddie apologised and the matter was allowed to drop.

But Edleston was much on my mind. I could not help but contrast the pleasure I had felt in his company, with the distaste I felt when in the company of women, again and again and again. I also could not help but consider, quite seriously, our likely social position were he to accept my offer to live with me once I had achieved my majority. Indeed, our *legal* position were it to become known. And formed on the instant that plan for travelling to the Levant which had already been roaming around my mind. I even mentioned the concept to one or two acquaintances, so that were it to come about it should not surprise them.

But actually, an exorcism was at hand. Deeply concerned with my uncertain condition, I determined one evening to revisit the one houri who had brought me unalloyed happiness. Madame Dulcina was overjoyed to have her noble client back again after close to two years, but to my request for Caroline she was forced to refuse. "Sweet Caroline has become very popular, my lord," she said. "She is booked for the night."

"Then I shall return tomorrow," I said.

"Tomorrow, as well," Dulcina said. "Oh, come, my lord, she will eventually be available. And for the time being, I have another fourteen year old, named Mary . . . besides, you must know that Caroline is no longer a child. Quite the contrary. She is a young woman. I doubt she will do your lordship much good."

But Mary turned out to have a sallow skin and lank black hair. "I will have Caroline," I insisted, my obstinacy being encouraged by the thought of that delightful creature lying there at the side of some great lout, or using those splendid lips to such advantage as she had revealed to me.

"And I have explained that you cannot, my lord," Dulcina said with great patience. "Any night this week. But I will put you down for next Monday."

Today being Tuesday. "I will have her now," I said.

"My lord, should you intend violence, I must inform you that I have friends, on the premises. . . ." And as if summoned, as no doubt they had been by some secret method, I saw two large young men standing just beyond the curtain.

"Violence, my dear madame?" I gave a careless laugh. "By God, should I choose to do you violence, I would settle those two louts for a start." For my pockets each contained a loaded pistol. "But I am a man of peace. The girl is a whore. She came to you upon a money payment, and no doubt earns you some income. I would buy her, outright."

She gaped at me. "My lord is demented," she said. "A whore?"

"How much, woman?"

"Well. . . ." She was clearly quite confused. "I could not possibly let her go for under a hundred pounds."

"The money is yours," I said, with all the grandeur at my command. "Just let me have the girl. Now."

DOMESTIC AFFAIRS

Caroline had indeed changed, but entirely for the better. Taller, her slenderness developed into titillating curves, her blonde hair curling on to her shoulders, only her face remained a mask of composure, no doubt a cultivated calm, for she was undoubtedly as confused as madame herself.

It was necessary for me to wait for some fifteen minutes, while she was extricated from the clutches of her client, and no doubt dunked in a hip bath, before being dressed and brought out. A reflection which somewhat cooled my immediate ardour, but I was committed to my course and had no intention of withdrawing.

"My lord?" she whispered, frowning, so that I wondered if she truly remembered me. "Madame says I am to go with you."

"For the rest of your life," I said. "Does that please you?"

Her tongue stole out and circled her lips, and she glanced at Dulcina, who stood beside her. "I am sure it pleases her very much, my lord," Dulcina said.

"Well, then," I said, beginning to feel embarrassed, "shall we leave?"

I escorted her from the brothel and down the stairs to the pavement, where we rapidly discovered a hansom. The door was closed upon us, upon me, for the very first time in my life alone in a cab with a woman, if one excepts Mama. "No doubt travelling in a hansom is strange to you," I remarked.

"By no means, my lord," she said. "I. . . ." She stopped, and I observed her biting her lip, and realised my mistake. Of course, she would have been hired out for private parties. Here was a fine beginning. I found myself becoming angry at her past. We travelled the rest of the way in silence, and arrived at Mrs Massingberd's establishment both feeling distinctly apprehensive.

85

"My lodgings," I explained, stepping down, and offering her my hand, which after a moment's hesitation she took.

"My lord. . . ." Once again the quick bite of the lip.

"Everyone will be asleep," I assured her, and escorted her into the silent house, and up the stairs to my rooms. By now I was becoming more aware of the girl rather than the whore. She smelt delightful, and clean with it. She looked delightful. And I had the evidence of my own memory that she was entirely at my disposal.

She turned to face me, only half visible in the gloom. "My lord. . . ." Once again the hesitation.

I raised my finger to my lips, stepped past her, lit the candles, and turned to face her once again. She was taking off her hat. I stepped towards her, and she stepped towards me. A moment later we were in each other's arms, and my tongue was exploring hers. Perhaps the thought crossed my mind that she did this every night of her life, had done this every night of her life for at least two years, and with a succession of low-born oafs not fit to kiss my feet. But she would do it no more, save with me.

I released her, and she undressed, allowing gown and then shift to slide to the floor, uncovering splendid white shoulders, delicious breasts, larger than I could have hoped, young enough to turn up, disappointing only in her slightly flattened nipples, slender belly, in which a gentle pulse throbbed, still narrow thighs which gave into the long, well-muscled legs I remembered. And between? Her hair had grown, not blonde but a gentle pale brown, and curled. It was dry, and I wished it to be wet. I knelt before her to kiss her, and felt her fingers stroking my hair.

"Will my lord use the cane?" she whispered.

I stood up, raising her from the floor as my fingers lodged on her buttocks. "Not this night, sweet Caroline," I promised her. "Perhaps not any night, ever again." There was confidence. But not misplaced. I *owned* this. I carried her, still holding her tight against me, my fingers exploring between her seething legs even as they held her from the ground, into my bedchamber, laid her on the bed, found that she had herself released my breeches, and was inside her in a moment and spent a moment later. I lay on my back while she completed undressing me and once again raised me with her fingers and her lips, so that I wanted to scream for joy, and entered her again, more aware of what I was now doing, able to watch those flickering eyes, to stroke that sweet wet hair, to caress those throbbing breasts and watch the tits come hard as my own. And knew, that I was as *good* a man as any, given the opportunity.

And awoke to a fine frenzy. I was in bed, but scantily concealed beneath the covers. Caroline was curled up on a settee situated against the wall, even less concealed, and Mrs Massingberd was standing in the centre of the room, suitably outraged. In my excitement of the night before I had forgotten to lock the door.

"A fine thing," she declared. "A fine thing. Turning my house into a brothel. I'll not have it." She pointed at Caroline. "Out."

The poor girl started to move instinctively, before recalling her unusual situation and glancing at me.

"She will do no such thing," I said. "The young lady is to be my. . . ." It was difficult to think of a suitable word. "My companion, from now on."

"Companion?" Mrs Massingberd's voice rose an octave. This is the problem of continuing to lodge with those, of either sex, who have known you in your youth; they persist in seeing themselves in *loco parentis* until they are disabused of the notion.

"I am even considering marriage," I said, warming to my task.

"Marriage?" Caroline whispered.

"Marriage?" shrieked the Massingberd. "To a whore?"

"Madam," I said, "you disgust me. If we are unwelcome under this roof, why then, we shall find another."

She glared at me for some seconds, then turned and stamped out, muttering, "Your mother shall hear of this."

An idle threat. For were she to run to Mama with any tale of my sexual misbehaviour, she could be sure I would inform Mama that *she* was standing surety for my alarming debt, and their friendship would have ended there and then for ever.

But Caroline was naturally at once alarmed and delighted. "My lord," she whispered. "There will be a great to-do."

She did not specify whether she was referring to her coming engagement to a peer of the realm or to the possibility of an avenging Mama descending upon our happy home.

"Tush," I said. "I will not be put upon by middle-aged women." And I held out my arms, to which she readily returned, for a morning tumble, the pleasantest of exercises, which I delayed only to inquire as to her reasons for leaving my bed during the night.

"My lord is a most restless sleeper," she confessed, and showed me a bruise on her ribs apparently caused by my elbow.

My ardour sated, and hers, I assumed, for I was still ignorant of what composed a female orgasm, or indeed caused it, I was able to consider my situation. "Certainly," I decided, "we shall remain not a moment longer where we are not wanted. I know a fine little family hotel in Bond Street where we may stay in certain comfort."

"But my lord," she protested. "The expense. . . ."

"Think nothing of it. I am worth thousands."

Her eyes widened. "Oh, my lord," she whispered, "you are so reassuring. But the scandal. They'll not permit it."

A problem which had already occurred to me. But one I could very easily solve, and entirely to my tastes. Caroline might have filled out a great deal, yet she was still slender rather than voluptuous, and her rather blunt features were quite asexual. "You shall be my brother," I decided.

"My lord?" It was the first occasion I had ever heard her raise her voice above a whisper.

"Did you not know I had a brother? We shall to my tailor immediately, and have you outfitted. Alas. . . ." I ran my fingers for the last time through those delightful locks. "These will have to be cropped, but nothing else need change save the necessity to encase those lovely limbs in trousers, and then, why, we may, no, no, we shall be *expected*, to share the same room for ever more."

She was amazed, so much so that she omitted to put forward an even more simple solution to our situation, that of eloping straightaway to Gretna. And indeed, had she done so, I would certainly have agreed, and who is to say it might not have been the most sensible act of my life? Caroline was undoubtedly a whore, but had I married her her faithfulness would have been assured, at least as much as any other wife's, saving only the one with whom I eventually became encumbered, and her marvellous beauty and equally marvellous willingness to accommodate my every requirement would have saved me a great deal of grief, while as to the scandal of a lord marrying a prostitute, while it would have been great it could hardly have been any greater than that to which my name is presently attached.

I speak now with hindsight. At the moment I did not wish Caroline to do anything more than lie on her back, unless it be to use her lips to advantage on my cocker. To have a willing woman entirely at my disposal, waiting there whenever I went abroad, anxious only to please, never uttering a cross word or a critical one, was heaven enough for a twenty year old. And my plan worked to perfection. My tailors fitted her out very rapidly with pantaloons and shirts and jackets and cravats and even drawers, for I did wish her to be genuine from skin to glove and besides it was such a pleasure slowly to strip a handsome young gentleman and watch him turn into a beautiful young woman, garment by garment. Thus we encountered no opposition from the Bond Street hotel, and settled down in perfect domestic bliss which quite drove all thoughts of returning to Cambridge or even indulging in any more poetry from my mind.

Until one morning, when I went forth for my stroll as usual, and purchased a copy of the *Edinburgh Review*.

I was of course in the habit of taking this paper regularly, as its literary criticisms were regarded as the most important in the kingdom, and I would be less than honest did I pretend I had not been waiting with some anxiety for it to notice *Hours of Idleness*. Imagine then my feelings when I turned to the requisite page, discovered with soaring heart that I was *there*, and settled down to read it on my walk back to my blue-eyed goddess. Imagine *then* my feelings as I slowly waded through the damning lines that followed. The fellow was a Whig – the paper was Whiggish in sentiment – but he had not spared me on any political grounds. Apart from taking me to task for attempting to hide behind the appellation of a Minor, for so I had honestly described myself, and indeed launching into a quite unnecessary personal attack, he proceeded to annihilate my compositions, concluding by relating them at best to *stagnant water*.

I declare my heart stopped beating for more than a second when I reached the end. The work had been published under my own name. There was not a soul of my acquaintance who did *not* read this infamous *Review*, therefore in one moment I conceived myself utterly damned, the laughing stock of the entire world, a man as ruined as if snubbed by the Prince.

I regained my rooms in a state of collapse, so that Caroline assumed I had had a seizure and was for calling a doctor. This I dissuaded her from doing, seized her and so filled her with my seed that she near exploded, then flung myself away from her and descended even deeper into the pit of despondency. I swear that more than once my hand stretched out to my pistols, and I was within an ace of blowing out my brains, while the poor child lay on the bed and stared at me in horror.

But I had known disaster before, and survived. Caroline came to my rescue with a bottle of claret, and having demolished that I requested another and then another, so that by nightfall I was literally roaring drunk, but instead of roaring, I seized my pen and a block of paper. They had seen fit to declare war upon me. Well, then, I would declare war upon them, the entire scurvy crew, every man who had ever written a word. I felt like the Angel of the Lord, come to blow the last trump upon all of their puerile meanderings, concerned to save only those few, Gifford, (i) Campbell, (ii) and one or two others, whose work was worthy of my approbation.

Thus *English Bards and Scotch Reviewers* was born. It was, and remains, one of my most *energetic* works. Which is not to say I have not, in recent years, regretted some of the statements I made, some of the reputations I blew asunder. Southey (iii) – I have no regrets for Southey. He was and is a lamentable laureate. Wordsworth (iv) – I have no regrets for Wordsworth. But Moore, (v) why, he had titillated my youth, made me part of what I am, and it was churlish for me to chide him with that very obscenity I had made my own. As for Scott, (vi) I believe I regretted those words the moment they were written. But Scott is a genius, and has the magnanimity of genius, as he has revealed to me often enough.

Meanwhile, I wrote, as I had never written before, as perhaps I shall never write again. (vii) And in between times, conceiving myself damned in any event, I *lived*. Here was stuff far more to Caroline's taste. From being buried in a bedchamber, she regained the laughing light which was her intended life, but with a great difference; she walked on the arm of a lord, and was known as his alone. Not that I was hers alone. If I would be an outcast, doomed no doubt to an early demise like dear Papa, I intended to go out in style. I dined with six and seven whores at my elbow, and used my sweetest to lure two and three and four back to my rooms; two of her friends, indeed, set up a permanent establishment with me, attending almost every night. I *wallowed* in dissipation, for with my free hand I gulped great quantities of claret wine.

No man can ever have fucked more furiously. I expended every last ounce of energy in my being, either into words or into the eager bodies of my splendid companions. I awoke in the mornings feeling even more exhausted than I had been the night before when going to bed, and was reduced to taking tonics to force myself once again into the mood for either composition or connection. I gambled and I drank. I associated with what is described as low company, and with old Tom Cribb even became an arranger of prize fights. (viii) For a space perhaps of two months I burned my candle at both ends and indeed in the middle as well, marvelling at the light it emanated, until upon returning one night, accompanied as usual by my lady friends, but without Caroline, she having remained in bed this day on account of feeling unwell, I found the hotel awake and alarmed.

My brother had had a miscarriage.

The sweet child had not even told me she was pregnant. Indeed, such was her terror of my discovering her in this burdensome female condition that she had deliberately induced the miscarriage, but being inexperienced in such matters had done herself an injury. The to-do can only be imagined, as the hotel staff, beginning their treatment on the assumption that the young gentleman had suffered some kind of internal haemorrhage such as we are told afflicted the unhappy Arius, (ix) began to realise their error. Of course we could not remain. The dragon who managed the house was very broadminded, and had no objection to my bringing the occasional lady, or two, home after supper. But she expected them gone again by dawn, and the realisation that I had been living a perfectly domestic existence under her very nose aroused her to fury.

With Jackson's aid I removed Caroline to Brompton, where we lived in perfect contentment, while to aid her recovery I took her down to Brighton, the weather now being almost summery. Here again she was passed off with great success as my brother, even amongst the members of the aristocracy who happened to be enjoying the sea breezes, which but serves to illustrate how irrelevant the name of Byron at that time was to these proud persons.

We were happy, or at least I should say that I was happy, and Caroline was sufficiently experienced even at sixteen to convince me that she was also. This despite letters alternately bullying and pleading from dear Mama, who had got word of the situation and was in a position better than anyone else to know I did *not* possess a brother, and also despite my quite lamentable financial affairs. For of the three thousand arranged for me by Mrs Massingberd at the beginning of the year more than a thousand had immediately been swallowed up in liquidation of my earlier debt, and the remainder seemed to dwindle as if eaten by mice, for even living in Brompton, or perhaps *because* we were living in Brompton, Caroline and I enjoyed our excursions up to town, to the gaming tables and the play and the opera and the theatre. Approaching midsummer all my available funds were gone and I owed large amounts in various directions, to my tailor, to my wine merchant, to heaven knows whom. The idea of departing England's shores suddenly once again became most attractive, for I conceived that there was no other way I could escape the importunities of my creditors, saving I could sell something. I actually approached Hanson with a view of reaching a settlement of the Rochdale affair out of court, being willing to accept nothing more than a sufficiency to pay my debts, at that time not yet ten thousand. The lazy fellow refused, as I now know because Mama made him, she being determined that my inheritance should eventually reach me in an intact form. Poor deluded dowager. She is dead, and I no doubt will soon be dead, the cause of our misfortunes is and ever was the burden of debt, and Rochdale is no nearer being mine.(x)

Creditors apart, however, that spring was one of the happiest of my life. I loved. I wrote, endlessly, not much of it very good, but my great work was completed and despatched to the printers. I engaged in disputations with the Fellows of Trinity, who were reluctant to grant me my MA degree, their law requiring attendance at the university for nine terms to justify the honour, and my total attendance did not really amount to three. But they could hardly refuse a peer of the realm, and the matter was amicably settled. There was also the odd feud, and the odd challenge. I particularly remember one with Hewson Clarke,(xi) who scribbled several offensive verses against me, and more especially against Bruin, who remained in residence, being tended by Boyce's replacement, Willie Fletcher from Newstead, and continued from time to time to disrupt the contemplation of those sacred cloisters. I was indeed requested to remove the dear fellow, as I would not attend myself, and seemed to give offence when I wrote back that it was my intention he should sit for a fellowship, pointing out that he worked at least as hard as anyone else, and was an amiable fellow to boot, who did not drink or whore or play at cards.

How long this idyllic existence might have continued I would not care to say. I was well suited, my mode of existence was entirely self-selected, I certainly had no wish to seek another until my twenty-first birthday, and the only change I contemplated was a removal of Caroline and myself to Newstead in July, for the disgusting Grey's tenancy came to an end in June. Consider then my feelings when I returned home one night from a debauch, having in the course of the evening become separated from Caroline, she stating that she would retire early because of a headache, to find, in the place of my charmer, a letter, pinned to a parcel, and inside the parcel twenty five-pound notes, neatly folded.

The letter was extremely well composed. In it she explained that while she valued my esteem and indeed my company, she was by nature a roving soul, and in addition, she had a penchant for *older* men more experienced in the art of love, and it was with one of that order she was leaving, he having put up the purchase money. It was quite one of the most damning and humbling epistles I have ever received, and for some moments it left me with recourse to nothing but tears, even as I formed the resolution to hate all women able to read or write from that moment forth.

Even worse than the clandestine way in which she had taken her departure was the suggestion that I had not done enough for her, either in bed or out of it. Of course at this distance of time I can see her point. As I have explained it did not then occur to me that if *I* was receiving pleasure *she* might not be, while she was well aware of my financial problems and lived in daily dread of the bailiffs or worse, she not being protected by her birth from the horrors of gaol.

But I was crushed. Sleep that night was out of the question, because the very pillows carried her scent. And every time I closed my eyes I saw that golden hair, that slender boy-muscled body, those marvellous little tits which just filled my hand; I heard her gentle whisper, could see the flash of her teeth as she smiled. Truly I can say, whatever I now am, woman has made me so.

And why, it may be asked, if I loved her so dearly, did I not gird on my sword, prime my pistols, and go in pursuit? She would have been easy enough to find, her lover easy enough to challenge. The fact is, once I discovered that I was not loved, I entirely *ceased* to love. The thought of her body, of her lips, of her hair, in the possession of another, still drove me to a frenzy, but it was a memory, as if she had died. I wept over the passing of *my* Caroline. Another's Caroline held no interest for me. So, Grey having packed his bags and departed, I went to Newstead, without my love.

But not alone. Hobhouse accompanied me, thus early setting his pattern of devoted friendship, for if he had never approved of the liaison, he knew how much it had meant to me. And I removed Bruin from Cambridge to take up his more proper abode, the Fellows having refused to honour his academic qualifications. While there was my dog Boatswain to greet me. I had forgotten the delight this great shaggy monster felt for my company. His welcome almost drove the melancholy from my mind.

But I was more than ever determined to leave England as soon as it could be managed, which meant the moment I reached the age of twenty-one. In the meantime, there was enough to do, in restoring Newstead from the ravages caused by a ten years' tenancy of Grey. I busied myself, spent far too much money, discovered that I possessed a willing harem of serving girls only too anxious to please their lord – and none of whom pleased me in the slightest, although one, a child called Lucy, managed to announce herself pregnant from my efforts – and was rendered desolate once again by the death of my dear dog. Truly I counted myself friendless in the world, having not yet come to estimate Cam at his true worth.

It will be seen therefore that I attended London for that most important of dates, 22 January 1809, in no very proper frame of mind. But I was about to become a peer of the realm, with all the privileges but also all the responsibilities of that exalted position, and I was never one to shirk my responsibilities.

My main reason for being in London at the beginning of the year, however, was provided by the imminent appearance of my *English Bards and Scotch Reviewers,* and also because I had at last persuaded Ridge to undertake the publication of my satire, suitably adjusted in accordance with the suggestions made by Dallas. He would have emasculated the entire thing, but while I went along with many of his criticisms, I allowed my anger at my guardian to overcome my common sense and indeed added even sharper lines in describing his "paralytic puling". Hard words, which I regretted, because I did not then know that he *was* subject to a physical ailment of an embarrassing nature, but which at the time I felt he entirely deserved.(xii)

For as a guardian he had ever proved the most disinterested fellow possible, while now that it came to a simple matter of introducing me into the Lords, which it surely was his responsibility to do, he once again declined to concern himself with my affairs. The whole business was in fact attended by an embarrassing amount of detail, the point at issue being whether dear Dad had ever married Mama at all, the ceremony having taken place in Scotland. Imagine, after eleven years of being a lord, suddenly to have my very legitimacy called into question. This disgraceful business dragged on for several months, put me into a very poor frame of mind, and quite spoiled what should have been one of the greatest days of my life.

In the event the date was 13 March, too close to an Ide for comfort, and I would have been entirely alone but for the sudden appearance of the faithful Dallas, come in fact to discuss my satire, which was then at the press, but determined to remain for my elevation.

The place was almost deserted. The good fellows might all have stayed away on purpose. I waited, Dallas at my side, both of us prey to very unhappy reflections, while my name went in to the Lord Chancellor. (xiii) There was some delay as Lord Eldon was actually talking some unnecessary business, and when the time came I was quite stiff with a mixture of chagrin and embarrassment. I looked to neither right nor left as I passed the Woolsack and reached the table where the oaths were administered. This done, the Chancellor approached me, quite courteously, and apologised for the delay, remarking that "these forms were a part of his duty".

I allowed him the very tips of my fingers in a handshake, bade him think nothing of it, and added, "Your Lordship was exactly like Tom Thumb; you did your duty and you did no more." (xiv) The fact of the matter was, I saw through his scheme, which was to entice me, either through the warmth of his greeting – as a young and inexperienced man he could have counted upon my embarrassment to respond to his approach – or by encouraging me to sit upon the right side, to appear as one of his party. I would have none of it, and turning away from him took my seat upon the left, listened to the inconsequential ramblings of my senile seniors for some moments, and then left.

Dallas took me to task for my coldness, but I explained my reasons, and also those for attending. "It was my duty," I said. "But now I have done it and with it. I shall go abroad."

In fact this now represented the only way in which I could avoid the most acute financial embarrassment, and even Hanson was brought to understand that it was the best course, provided he could somehow discover adequate funds to finance the journey. The point was that I could clearly live far more cheaply abroad, even while constantly travelling, than I could manage at home, with all my commitments. A peer of the realm has a great many of these, not least a duty to be available for the rescue of his fellow peers, or their descendants, should the occasion arise.

I can give an early example of this, for it was around this period that dear Falkland (xv) was killed in a duel. This was bad enough, but his family, to one of whom I was godfather, were left in the most dire straits, and to the four children sweet Christina (xvi) already possessed there had to be added the one present in her belly. I called to see her soon after this posthumous son was born, took tea with her, listened to her anguished pleas and watched the tears roll down those pretty cheeks, and could do nothing less than scribble a note for five hundred pounds, roll it into a tube, and leave it in my cup, that she might discover it when I was gone. Hanson was scandalised, but then he was hardly a gentleman.

Although in the event he was right in this particular judgement; my generosity to Chrissy was to cause some embarrassment later on.

Unfortunately, while I estimated that a similar sum would suffice for my annual requirements when in the Levant, perhaps a quarter of what I was currently expending in London, there was the business of outfitting a peer of the realm for such an undertaking. I do not speak of ordinary necessaries. There were also regimentals and weapons, as well as gifts to be disbursed to the eager and avaricious Turk, without which I was assured I would receive a very scurvy welcome. The cost of these trifles was frightening.

There was also the business of Hobhouse, for the good Cam had volunteered to accompany me. Alas, he had recently quarrelled with his father, and had been despatched into the wilderness without a penny to his name. His part of the proceedings would of course be a loan, as his expectations were on a par with my own, but it was a case of borrowing from Peter to pay Paul. In my desperation I even formed a plan of utilising Mama's remaining capital, a matter of three thousand pounds, but she was reluctant to relieve even her own son, without adequate security, and where was I to discover that? (xvii) Fortunately Hanson had a scheme, and a gentleman named Saw-bridge, with six thousand pounds to lend, and it was only the expectation of this kept my spirits high.

That, and the reception given to *English Bards and Scotch Reviewers*. It would be idle to pretend that it was well received by those mentioned in its pages, but it certainly made the public sit up and take notice, and a first edition of one thousand copies, which I had considered far too great, was gobbled up in no time at all. Then my satire was due along any day now, and I conceived I was becoming quite a well-known literary figure. It has sometimes been suggested to me, indeed, that by accepting payment for these scribblings I might greatly have alleviated my financial situation, but consider, would that not have lowered me to the level of a tradesman? I was the 6th Lord Byron, not some itinerant hack grubbing about for all the ready cash he could discover. I bestowed my share of the profits on poor Dallas, who was now ready to be considered my manager, and was a most conscientious and deserving fellow.

There remained one ambition I was determined to realise; before casting the dust of perfidious Albion behind me, I would be the lord of Newstead for one great occasion.

There was perhaps half a dozen of us, including Hobhouse and Matthews, of course, as well as Hodgson (xviii) and Wedderburn Webster, (xix) so it will be seen that we were a somewhat dissimilar collection. Yet our desire was to enjoy ourselves, and this we did, in our own various ways.

We dug for treasure. For while the work necessary to restoring the house had been in progress, someone had turned up a gigantic skull, so perfect in every way that it might have been buried only ten instead of near three hundred years previously. This grisly relic of Newstead's previous inhabitants so attracted me that I had it made into a drinking cup, which I used henceforth at meals.

More important, however, it set me to wondering what else might lie buried beneath those once sacred cloisters. Monks, always wealthy fellows, hearing the measured tread of the minions of Great Harry (xx) approaching to despoil them of everything they possessed, and already, no doubt, dreaming of a Romish reaction to return them to their glory, would they not have buried their silver and their plate, to escape the greedy talons of the marauders? So we dug, and we dug, and we dug, with myself supposing that the end of all my troubles was finally in sight. And found a great many other human remains – I seemed to be living on top of a cemetery – but not a single article of value. The monks of Newstead must have been asleep when invaded.

We also worked, at our own particular hobbies. I was revising my satire with a view to a new edition, the first having been praised by Gifford, no less. Hobhouse also wrote, and the others amused themselves in their own ways.

But principally we were there to enjoy ourselves. We never rose much before the middle of the day, took breakfast, walked or rode or strolled or read until evening, dined, and caroused until the small hours. I flatter myself that I was able to provide entertainment to any taste, even the most jaded. There was Bruin, chained to one side of the entry hall, as amorous as ever and as determined to join in the fun as ever. Opposite him there was Boatswain's replacement, of a similar great shaggy type but lacking his predecessor's natural affection; he was in fact half wolf, and acted the part. Then there was the human element.

Being surrounded with so much evidence of monkish behaviour, we could do nothing less than dub ourselves the merry monks of Newstead, clad ourselves in long forgotten robes and cowls, and behave like monks, within reason. We said no masses, but we drank a great deal of wine. We had no wives, but where was a monk to be found without some pleasures of the flesh? To entertain my friends I naturally had recourse to hiring some extra serving maids, my only requirement being that they be young and where possible attractive. These became fair game after midnight, whether in bed or without. We made the rafters ring as we chased through those hallowed cloisters, seeking our game, finding one, certainly, for they generally were more than willing to fall in with our wishes, and carrying her, stripped of her clothing, all flailing leg and waving arm, flying hair and giggling laughter, trembling breast and throbbing belly, into the great withdrawing-room, there to set about her to our heart's content. Those of us who were still up and doing, for it must be confessed that this aspect of life held no attraction for Hodgson, who preferred to retire to a study with a book.

And as men will, from time to time we quarrelled. Matthews, in the main, for he was a damnably quarrelsome fellow. He quarrelled with Webster, and determined to throw him from the window. Webster complained to his host, whom he had also irritated too often with his confoundedly petty habits and even pettier point of view.

"My dear Wedderburn," I pointed out. "If Matthews says he will throw you from that window, he most certainly will do so, for he is a man of his word. But you will come to no harm. The ground outside is uncommonly soft. Indeed, I may say that that window might especially have been created for defenestration."

He was not to be placated, and left, and the rest followed soon after. Hobhouse and Matthews left together, having formed the plan of *walking* the hundred odd miles to London. This they did, but naturally enough, managed to quarrel within a few hours of leaving Newstead, with the result that they refused to exchange a word for the rest of the way, this although they often passed and repassed one another before reaching the safety of Charing Cross.

And what of the noble lord, whose hospitality they had all been enjoying? Did I weep as I lay in bed supposing that this was the last occasion for a very long time that I would know Newstead as it should always be? Or indeed perhaps the *last* time. Did I enjoy my bouts with the serving girls? Oh, I did, while they were taking place. Did I brood over what might have been, and wonder about what might be? Of course. I was then, as ever at that part of my life, a sorely confused fellow. I wanted to leave England, for the sheer excitement of it, but I also wanted to stay, and be my own man. I wanted the Newstead party to go on for ever, at the same time as I dreamed of a buyer suddenly appearing who would pay cash on the barrel. I wanted to seize one of the girls, and discover Caroline, returned to my arms, eager only to please me, and I wanted . . . here was the most sinister of all turn of events, for like a man who has had leprosy, and been pronounced cured by a miracle, who spends the rest of his life inspecting arms and legs and body for some sign of the terrible taint re-emerging to haunt him, I discovered at Newstead that no woman, save she be as willing as Caroline and perhaps not even then, I feared, could provide so great a pleasure as a being like myself.

A week later, having bade Mama a tearful and recriminatory farewell, as she installed herself as chatelaine of Newstead, I was in London, seeking a passage on the Malta packet. But passages require funds, and there were none to be had. Hanson's friend of six thousand pounds turned out to be one of not quite two, and this would hardly satisfy even those creditors who knew of my intended departure, for of course we had not exactly bruited this abroad. It was necessary once more to have recourse to the happy Hebrews, and even they, not yet having seen a penny of their earlier money returned, or even the interest, were unwilling to cough up a great deal. I was in despair, conceiving myself to be utterly ruined, just a single step away from being dispossessed of everything I owned and still not able to take the blessed flight into the path of the sun that was all I dreamed of, when who should come to my rescue but dear Davies, suddenly flush from a successful run at the tables, with a loan of £4,800 which saved my bacon and left me for ever in his debt. Almost literally, for the poor chap has only recently been repaid. (xxi)

All of this delay meant that I missed the Malta sailing, and was forced to seek berths on the Lisbon packet, which was not due to depart until well into June. But the end was in sight. At the beginning of the month I was on my way down to Falmouth, accompanied by my servants, Fletcher, Old Murray, and a lad named Robert Rushton.(xxii) I had also accumulated a German fellow who had already travelled in Persia and therefore promised to be useful – while of course our party was completed by Hobhouse.

TWO GENTLEMEN

I can hardly express the feelings that animated my breast as at last I felt the sea beneath my feet, and watched England receding beneath the horizon; I did my best in some lines I sent to Hodgson, but they were necessarily written in anticipation rather than during the event. And the event itself was disrupted by a most disagreeable concomitant of sea travel: I was confoundedly seasick. However, we possessed an able captain, by name of Kidd, which is a seafaring title if I ever heard one, (i) and a fair wind, and actually made the Tagus in just over four days, which was by way of being a record.

And fell in love with Portugal at first sight, for all that it was a damnably dirty place populated by damnably dirty people, and ruffians to boot – on attending the theatre one night Hobhouse and I were beset by footpads and had to use swords and pistols to escape with our lives.

But the mountains were enchanting, the countryside more so, and the Tagus a challenge. I plunged in without ado, and swam across to Belem, with an ebbing tide driven by a fresh breeze. It was quite the bravest swim of my life, and I have in mind my later and more celebrated aquatic adventure. And we visited the splended palace which Beckford had built for himself, straight out of *Vathek*. An event which caused me some serious considerations, as in his life I could not help but see a forecast of my own. (ii)

But we were in a hurry to get on, and the ship for Cadiz being late in arriving, Hobhouse and I decided to continue across country. We hired horses, purchased saddles from an English expatriot named Ward, (iii) found ourselves a guide by name of Sanquinetti, and set out for the frontier and Badajoz, before pressing on to Seville. Here was experience, certainly, the brooding mountains, the sunless valleys, the craggy peaks with which we were surrounded left both Hobhouse and I amazed that modern armies could have campaigned across such inhospitable terrain. But then, the thought that they *had*, that the road along which we made our way had rung with the shrieks of dying men and horses, and run with their blood, made a deep impression upon us which was but heightened by our encountering a doleful procession, consisting of several Spanish soldiers escorting three men, two French prisoners and one of their own countrymen accused of spying, to be hanged. I knew no Spanish, and how I wished I had never learned French, for the pitiful pleas of the unhappy froggies was dismal to hear; they conceived themselves certain to be at least emasculated before being hanged, in itself a sufficiently unhappy prospect, and they also deemed that only an English officer could save them from their fate. But there was nothing we could do. They had seen fit to invade a country which had been their ally until very recently, and must perforce accept the concomitants of that decision.

And so we came to Seville, which at that time was the seat of the Junta and thus the capital city. And a very gay place it was too, where the English were as popular as in Portugal. But only certain types of Englishmen and only with the *hoi poloi*. We had been recommended two places where to stay, and visited them both, but as soon as the landlords, or in one instance the landlady, discovered we were English *lords*, and not merchants, she would have none of us. How Cromwell did overturn everything when he sent his Ironsides marauding. We eventually found lodgings, on the recommendation of the English Resident, Hookham Frere, (iv) with two maiden ladies, who liked our looks and cared nothing about our pocketbooks. Indeed they liked *my* looks so much that I could have accommodated myself a hundred times over during the three days we spent there, and I was upbraided by the elder of the sisters, just before leaving, with *not* having knocked on her door during the midnight hours; not content with snipping away a lock of my hair, she must give me one of hers, and this was no curl, but a three foot long plait, useful no doubt as a weapon to repel boarders, but scarce the sort of thing one could carry next to one's heart. I sent it home to Mama.

But neither of them was particularly attractive, nor did I have any wish to become embroiled in a local affair with a strange nationality which might involve me in Heaven knows what – I had already observed the speed with which a Spaniard whips out his knife when he conceives his women have been insulted, and who was to say there was not a brother lurking in the wings?

And so we contented ourselves with sightseeing, with watching the immortal Maid of Saragossa (v) parading the battlements, which she was required by the Junta to do every day, wearing all of her medals, to encourage the population, and in looking forward to making our descent upon Cadiz.

Ah, Cadiz. There can be no more beautiful spot on earth. I fell in love with it at first sight, and if I have never returned, it is certainly a place I shall revisit ere I die.

In Cadiz we were welcomed by the highest, entertained on the best possible scale. In Cadiz we saw our first bullfight, or at least, we crossed from Cadiz to a little neighbouring town, (vi) making the journey by water. It is impossible not to be thrilled by the martial music, the splendid costumes, the drama of a bullfight. It is also impossible not to be nauseated by the slaughter, and being Englishmen, we were less distracted by the murder of the bull than by the damage done by that fearsome beast to the horses. The sight of one of these splendid creatures staggering around the arena with his intestines trailing upon the sand was more than the average stomach could bear. Our first bullfight was also our last. (vii)

In Cadiz we saw the great Wellesley, (viii) elder brother of the Duke, land, and we heard the guns ring out for the victory of Cuesta. (ix)

Then it was on to Gibraltar, where we waited for the Malta packet. We walked a great deal, and climbed the massive rock to stare at distant Africa. And we listened to tales about the Levant, which resulted in a considerable upheaval in our domestic arrangements.

The German who knew Persia turned out to know nothing at all, and was dismissed. Sanquinetti turned out to be the greatest thief on earth, and was dismissed. Old Murray, who duly arrived at the Rock in the company of Fletcher and Robert, was not standing up at all well to the rigours of sea travel, and I deemed it best to send him home with a pension. Which left my two faithfuls.

But a conversation I had with a sea captain used to trading with the Levant caused me grave misgivings. He chanced to see Robert unloading some of my gear, and remarked on what a pretty boy he was.

"Why, yes, so he is," I agreed.

"And you plan to tour the Levant," said the good fellow, pulling his beard, and shaking his head.

"Why, sir, do you not recommend it?"

"For yourself, my lord, a grown man, even if a handsome one, it will be an experience to remember. But for that boy, why, he'll not survive it."

"Not survive it?"

"As he is now, my lord. Why, the Turks will jump for joy to see so splendid an object, and they will have him."

"Have him?" My mind reeled.

"Either to castrate, or to bugger. That is the fact of the matter, my lord."

"And will I not defend him, you think?"

"To the best of your ability, my lord. Yet will he be stolen away before you know he is gone. Believe me, sir, I have seen too much of it. I would wager you five pounds, my lord, that that boy does not remain at your side a week."

I began to understand for the first time that travelling to strange lands is not merely an exercise for the ears and the nose and the mouth and the eyes, but also for the senses and the emotions, and the brain. But my mind was made up on the instant. Perhaps it had been half made up already. I sent Robert home with Murray, with a letter instructing his father to deduct twenty-five pounds a year from his rent to pay for the boy's education, and privately thanked God for his and my lucky escape.

Then it was hey ho for Greece.

We visited two of the Mediterranean islands before reaching our goal. At Sardinia we were made most welcome by the Resident; at Malta the Governor, Ball, one of Nelson's bold seadogs, hardly deigned to notice us at all, and it cannot have been every day he was visited by an English milord.(x) However, Malta had its compensations, as it was here I began work on this very Memoir, and although *that* edition had a short existence, I doubt I have made many changes in rewriting it. While also in Malta I indulged a flirtation with a Mrs Constance Spencer Smith, an Austrian lady who enjoyed some notoriety for having taken part, while in Paris some years before, in a plot against Napoleon, which had all but cost her her life. She had escaped in romantic circumstances, and was now seeking ways of passing her time as her husband was away in Constantinople, where he was with the British legation. I was undoubtedly one of those ways, and while I enjoyed the sensation of being pursued by a sophisticated and attractive woman, and even went so far as to swear my undying love for her, accompanying my troth with a promise of marriage when I returned from the Levant, I suspect we both knew we were but play acting. For one thing she was several years my elder, and for another, a flirtation is a perfectly accurate description of our liaison.

I was permitted to caress her quite delicious breasts and entered, for the first time in my life, at least the portals of paradise. For consider the female breasts I had known, or at least possessed. Caroline and her friends had all been sixteen or less, small and almost hard; Lucy had been like fondling a cabbage, and an overcooked one at that. And there had been no other. But here was a woman, full grown and in the very prime of her beauty. These were too large for my hand, and delightfully firm, and possessed of the very faintest of sags, so that I could lift them away from her chest, allowing them to lie in my palm. Her lips were also mine, but beyond that she would permit nothing, and I, poor ignorant youth, was unable either to persuade her or take her by force. In my defence I must say that she was the first *lady* with whom I had ever been closeted, as opposed to serving girls and whores, and I was distinctly apprehensive about the whole thing. But in fact it was with a sense of some relief that at last I found myself on board the good ship *Spider*, and sailing for Greece.

No doubt I had waited all my life for that moment. The sight of those mountains rising out of that wine dark sea, the very breath of them, brought back all my childhood pleasures in the Highlands of Scotland, but with an emphasis, a delight, an *awareness* I had never previously known, which quite drove thoughts, pleasant or unpleasant, about dear Constance from my mind.

It was on the morning of 23 September that I first caught sight of the peaks of the Peloponnesus, our convoy at that moment being in the channel between Cephalonia and Zante, and knew that I had at last found my spiritual home. Hobhouse felt the same, although perhaps in a different genre. To him Greece was living history, and he was never without his compass and his guidebook and his historical tome, referring to this deed and that, planting his foot here and then there to insist that the event in question had happened *there*, and nowhere else. But to me, Greece was merely *living*, although asleep beneath the heel of the proud Turk.

I can do nothing more than recall, most briefly, our adventures. How we came into the harbour of Patras, and dashed ashore to feel the hallowed soil beneath our feet. How we seized a prize, a Turkish merchantman out of a French Ionian port, with great firing of guns and excitement amongst our crew; and our passengers. How we anchored off Prevesa and saw the moon rise above the Bay of Actium. How we went ashore in our best regimentals and were soaked to the skin by a seasonal but most unwelcome downpour. How we were shown Ali Pasha's palace, as it was called, an empty barracks, but populated by a pack of fierce Turkish soldiers, all mustachios and pistols and knives. How in the company of some local dignitaries and Lieutenant Oliver we visited the ruins of Nicopolis, and found only desolation.

It was now that we bade farewell to our naval escorts, and plunged northwards for Jannina, the seat of Ali Pasha's government. The journey took the better part of four days, the first by boat to Salora, and thence on horseback across the mountains. It rained, the food was unusual, and our bedding even more so, for it was invariably on the ground and shared with an army of companions, of whom bedbugs were only the skirmishers. Hobhouse complained, and Fletcher grumbled, and your lordship laughed and enjoyed it all hugely. Here was living, at last. What a nonsense it made of your polite drawing-rooms, your aimless conversations, your sanctified manners. Within twenty-four hours we were learning to belch like the very best of our escorts.

And then, Jannina. There were houses, and domes, and minarets, clustering amidst the orange groves on the edge of the lake, dominated by the mountains which rose sheer behind them. It was a most awe-inspiring sight, until we approached closer and found the arm of a man, with part of the shoulder still attached, hanging by a string from a tree. Perhaps I had dined too well, for I vomited in a bush.

In Jannina we were welcomed as royalty. Ali Pasha himself was away, "concluding a little war", but his people could not do too much for us, gave us the best of quarters, and refused payment for anything, while the English Resident, Captain Leake, although ill with a fever, also took great care to see to our needs. For never before had any English travellers visited this remote and barbarous country, much less a milord on his tour. The hospitality we received quite overcame our initial revulsion, and the people themselves, and especially their magnificent accoutrements, could not help but arouse our admiration. I bought several Albanian dresses, at some fifty guineas each, but the price was worth it; with so much gold decoration they would have cost two hundred apiece in England.

In the absence of the Pasha we were received by his grandson, Mahmout, a boy of ten, rouged and in general painted like a woman, who most gravely entertained us to coffee and sweetmeats, ordered the women withdrawn to their bedchambers that he might take us on a tour of the palace, and wondered at so great a man as myself being

allowed to travel so far from home while still so young, and with so
limited an entourage. Next day was the first of the Mohammedan
feast of Ramadan, which continues for a month, and during which no
one may take food or drink while it is light enough to distinguish a
grey thread from a black. But once darkness did fall the entire city
became alive with entertainments, puppet shows, jugglers, dancing
girls, storytellers, with eating and with drinking and doing everything
else as well, so far as I could tell, for here I must say that the Albanian
women were quite the most beautiful in feature I had ever seen. I
longed to be able to sample some of this splendid animal passion, but
they were none of them available. Hobhouse and I were taken to the
public baths, and given to understand that if we wished dalliance there
were *boys* within. We stared at each other in amazement, and Cam
began to laugh.

And I? Had I not, in my most secret heart, come all this way for just
such an opportunity? I did not know, for sure. Besides, with
Hobhouse at my side it was possible only to consider the strictest
orthodoxy. I also laughed, and together we fled.

Soon we were allowed to depart for the Vizier's headquarters at
Tepelene, accompanied by his secretary and servants, a priest, and an
Albanian soldier named Vassily to act as guide. We were also accompanied by Fletcher and our Greek dragoman, George. It was a hilari-
ous journey, on reflection, for while Hobhouse and the main party
hurried ahead, fearful of the weather, I lingered, with Fletcher and
George and some of the servants, and was caught by the mother and
father of all thunderstorms, which had our guides taking off for their
lives, George firing his pistols in desperation, Fletcher consigning his
soul to the Almighty, and myself laughing, the whole accompanied
by an orchestra of peeling thunder and dazzling flashes of lightning,
shrouded in impenetrable rain. For some hours were were quite lost,
although only a short distance from our destination of Zitza.

The first day was a representation of our week's journey to the
Pasha's headquarters, for it rained every day, the roads went from bad
to worse, and our quarters, when we could find them, descended
further the scale of human comfort, although ideal for goats and fleas.
Hobhouse was scandalised, and claimed he never slept a wink, while
poor Fletcher had by now clearly resigned himself that he was on his
way to hell.

But Tepelene compensated. Here was a military city, raised from the beautiful to the sublime by the aura of arms and men. And what man can resist the glow of martial fervour? Here were Albanians, in all the glory of their long white kilts, their gold worked cloaks, their crimson velvet gold-laced jackets and waistcoats, their silver mounted pistols and daggers; here were Tartars with high caps and equally well armed; here were Turks, with long pelisses and turbans; here were black slaves holding horses, kettledrums beating, couriers arriving and leaving, boys calling the hours from the minaret of the mosque. I swear that even now, at a distance of several years, I can remember that day as yesterday.

Once again we were treated as royalty, which I endeavoured to match by donning my best red regimentals, and equipping myself in addition with a sabre to show that I too could be a man of war. For was I not going to meet one of the greatest warriors of his time, who had raised himself from a simple robber chieftain to be the despot of a great empire, which only paid token loyalty to the Porte, but went its own way in splendour? And was he not one of the most fearsome of masters, who had slain countless men, women and children with his own hands?(xi)

In fact he was small, very plump, and gentle, with a fine face, light blue eyes, and a white beard. His manner was at once dignified and charming. He rose to receive me – a rare honour – in a large marble paved room, which had a fountain playing in the centre and scarlet ottomans all around the walls. He paid me gracious compliments, said he could have told I was a great man even had he not been informed of it because of my small ears, curly hair, and little white hands, and claimed he looked upon me as a son and would have me regard him as a father during my sojourn in his country.

And no son could have been better treated, as when the time came for us to move on we were accorded a royal escort to protect us from bandits, with which the country abounded, and in addition discovered that our supplies had been arranged and we were allowed to pay not a penny for them. This from the man who had once had fifteen beautiful women drowned in sacks in a single night because of a *rumour* that his son was being unfaithful to his wife.

He also invited me to visit him, whenever I wished, but preferably at *night*. An invitation I never made use of, certainly suspecting what lay behind it. *And* now sometimes regret. Would it not have been a fine thing, to be loved by Ali Pasha? But at twenty-one, and with staunch Cam at my elbow, I was a perfect coward.

The rains having abated, our return to Jannina and thence the coast
was made in half the time it had taken us to make our way inland, but
on arrival there was a delay, for our information was that the country
south of us was even more bandit-infested than the Vizier had supposed, and we decided to take his advice and proceed by sea, but of
course it was first of all necessary to procure a vessel.

Still, the few days that we spent kicking our heels were useful, at
least to me. Hobhouse continued with his inspection of everything he
could discover. I wished to think, to recall the events of our journey,
from the leaving of Falmouth to the present moment. For certainly I
had enjoyed a great many strange experiences, and the Muse, never
long willing to leave me in peace, was again stirring in my bosom. It
was now that I allowed Cam to read my Memoir. He was scandalised,
and convinced me that I also should be. Together we burned the
scurrilous pages, a stupid act I have often regretted. And yet, write I
must. If my prose was obscene, I determined to proceed with my
autobiography in verse. On the very last day of October, in that year
of 1809, I began to write a poem, after Spenser – whose *Faerie Queen*
was one of the books accompanying me – which I called *Childe Buron's
Pilgrimage*.

In suggesting that we return to the Morea by ship, Ali Pasha had of
course been concerned to preserve our lives. In the event, the voyage
was very nearly our last, for immediately after leaving Salora – and
running aground into the bargain – we encountered a fierce autumnal
storm, which quite drove our Turkish captain – the Turks are notori-
ously bad seamen – to distraction. He and his men called upon Allah to
save them, the Greeks in the crew prayed to their Saints, George called
the name of his wife, Fletcher supposed his last moment had come. The
waves threw our little craft about like a cork, the mainmast split, and
even I abandoned all attempt at levity, wrapped myself in my cloak,
and lay down to await whatever might come.

After an entirely dismal night we came safe into a little bay quite
close to Prevesa. But the voyage decided us that robbers were the
lesser of two evils, and we continued our travels on foot.

Our spirits soon recovered. The climate, now the rains were done
with, was delightful; we could bathe in the sea every day. And we
were now approaching classic Greece itself. And I was writing something, for I laboured at every opportunity, which I *knew* to be worthwhile. I was happy, and could see no reason ever to return to England.

Indeed, I wrote Hanson to say as much, but this was by way of being a threat, for as usual there were no letters and even less remittances awaiting me at my various stops, and I was endeavouring to spur him to action.

Thus we made our way to Missolonghi, a dismal, fever-infested place on the edge of a swamp which the locals honour with the name of lagoon, from whence we crossed the gulf of Patras, where we replaced George, who was less an interpreter than a robber himself, with another named Andreas, and journeyed to Vostitza, where we lodged with the Cogia Basha, who was a Greek, a wealthy young man by name Andreas Londos. He was only twenty, but an utterly delightful fellow, a little reserved at first, but as we were forced to spend some days with him, the winds being too contrary to permit us to cross the Corinthian Gulf, he became much more friendly.

We passed our time in shooting, and it was while we were out after woodcock one day in early December that I fired at, and hit, an eagle. It was only wounded, but unable to fly, and was quite the most tragic sight I had ever seen. I endeavoured to save it, but it pined, and died in a few days. To this day I have never fired at another bird.

It was also while we were at Vostitza that we gained a valuable insight into the Greek character, which I had been concluding was entirely debased from the greatness of the Homeric heroes, in that they seemed content to lie supine beneath the heel of the vicious Turk. But one evening Londos was playing at draughts with a local doctor, who happened to mention the magic name of Rhiga, the man who, twenty years before, had attempted to organise a revolt against the conquerors, and had been barbarously executed. The transformation in Londos was remarkable. He threw over the board, jumped upon the sofa, and with tears streaming down his cheeks gave vent to a thousand patriotic exclamations, ending by singing the Greek version of the *Marseillaise*, the *Deute Paides*, or *Greeks Arise*. This sudden effervescence of patriotism was coming from one who had been trusted by the conquerors with a position of responsibility. We were amazed, and I at the least would not be surprised should the Turks be faced with another revolt, and in my own lifetime.

But finally on 14 December we managed to cross the gulf, visit deserted Delphi and gaze at Parnassus, and thence make our way to the greatest city of the ancient world, Athens itself.

★　　　★　　　★

110

We entered Athens on the evening of Christmas Day, having spent the most miserable Christmas Eve of our entire lives in a deserted village called Scourta. Not that the date was of importance in these climes; the Turks of course do not recognise the festival, and the Greeks adhered to the old style calendar, and to them Christmas was still some ten days away.

But Athens had an effect upon our senses akin to that of Cadiz. Not in beauty, to be sure, for it was a narrow streeted and somewhat decrepit village, nothing more. But it clustered at the foot of the Acropolis.

Our destined lodging indeed was beneath the very shadow of the immortal hill. It was a double house, owned by Mrs Tarsia Macri, the widow of a former British vice-consul. Our half of it, the smaller, and connected to the main dwelling by a corridor, consisted of two bedrooms and a sitting-room, which opened into a courtyard. Small, but sufficient for our wants, while our daily needs were cared for by the widow and her three daughters, by name Mariana, Katinka and Theresa, not one over fifteen, and each a rare beauty. Theresa, indeed, had just celebrated her twelfth birthday, and was the loveliest of the lot, to her splendid dark hair and eyes being added a clear complexion and a straight nose only just tending to hook at the end.

We were naturally delighted at the prospect of being looked after by three such houris, but for the time being our ambitions went no further; we were in the capital of the ancient world, and wished to do nothing more than look. This occupied our first few days, our escort being the current British Vice-Consul, Spiridion Logotheti. But far more important a companion was Giovanni Battista Lusieri, who called the moment he learned we were in town. He was a Neapolitan painter, married to a Franco-Greek, who had been commissioned by Elgin to make drawings and then to superintend the dismantling of the sculptures which the noble vulture was bringing home to delight the British public. (xii)

Now of course I knew all about these marbles, and indeed had seen some of the first when they were shown in London shortly before my departure. I had thought little of them, and less of the act of larceny by which they had been obtained. I thought little of them now. But Lusieri proved a very valuable fellow, in his knowledge of ancient Greece and especially ancient Athens. He was to prove valuable in more than that, had I but known it.

Athens, then, for all its apparent decay, was a heavenly place, at least to weary travellers. Undoubtedly this was in part due to the fact that we *were* travellers, and from Albania. An idea of the way in which we had grown accustomed to roughing it may be gained when I say that my room at the widow Macri's was actually occupied when I arrived, by an Englishman named Galton, who had delayed his departure for some trifling reason. And I did not even complain, but waited patiently if uncomfortably for him to leave two days later. While Fletcher turned to and slept on the floor without a comment apart from his usual.

There were the ruins, which were everywhere to be discovered, usually upon the payment of a small bribe to the local official. Then there were the people themselves. If it has been gathered that I felt no very great admiration for a nation which could lie docile beneath the heel of a conqueror for so long, I will say it was impossible not to warm to the charm, the gaiety, the ability to find enjoyment in the most menial of tasks, which is the characteristic of the average Greek. We had seen little of this in the mountains of Albania, or in one-night lodgings with total strangers. But Mrs Macri made us part of the family, cut a door in the wall to connect the two houses, and showed us a delightful community life, shared with our neighbours, which made us feel utterly at home within hours.

And then there were the three graces, all smiles and gentle curves and sinuous movements. We had no better means of communication *than* smiles and looks and beckonings, for they spoke no English and we spoke no Greek. But communication between the sexes is never confined to mere formalities. A look may be far more instructive than a speech, a touch far more inspiring than a stanza of the greatest poetry ever written. And indeed my surroundings inspired me to write as I had never dared before.

I doubt I had ever been so introspective before. And undoubtedly it was to do with being in Athens. For here was introspection on a vast scale. The temples were crumbling, but enough remained, for anyone with the slightest imagination, to *remember* them as they were. When we rode out to visit Marathon, while John Cam poked around for exact sites and stations, I could stand and stare, and *hear*, and *see*, Miltiades rallying his men, the vast Persian host splashing through the gentle waves, the onward march of the armoured hoplites, the enveloping movement of the two Greek wings. I could hear the clash of spear upon shield, the whirr of the arrows in the air, the shrieks of dying men. This had happened, where I stood, a mere twenty-two centuries earlier. And what are twenty-two centuries in the awful span of Time?

But then, where were the Greeks who had so boldly assailed the greatest power in the world? I suddenly realised that they were not gone, but merely submerged by events. Who, having heard Andreas Londos singing his song, could doubt otherwise? And the events were not merely those of physical conquest by the Turks. It was the world's attitude to anguished Athens. I suddenly saw, in Elgin's foul plan, the greatest despoliation since Alaric sat on the steps of the Capitol. My breast overflowed with shame for my countrymen, and the words of castigation flowed from my pen.

Our visit to Marathon was part of a lengthy excursion which Hobhouse at last persuaded me to take, tearing myself away from the quiet pleasures of composition in the Macri household. We toured the entire surround of Athens, managed to get ourselves lost in some caves, and returned home again on 25 January 1810. Hobhouse was immediately for setting off on another and even lengthier expedition. I cried off. The Muse was stronger than ever. But my creative urge, which I had assumed would be quite uninterrupted while John Cam was away, was about to be ended in the strangest way. Only two days after my conscience departed, my morning's study was disturbed by a young man named Nicolo Giraud.

NIKKY

He introduced himself as Lusieri's brother-in-law, and said that the painter was this very day removing one of the Caryatids from its proper setting to the hold of a ship, and wondered if I would care to see the operation. I decided I would. Monsieur Giraud seemed an extraordinarily pleasant fellow, very young, only fifteen as it transpired, and blessed by belonging to two of the most interesting nations on earth; to the liquid good looks, the dark hair and long lashes, the aquiline nose of the Greek he added the sparkling fervour and interest of the Frenchman. And he was disposed to be pleasant, for he had heard a great deal about me from his brother-in-law, and was most anxious to make the acquaintance of a milord.

We climbed the sacred hill and thus considered the act of sacrilege. It seemed to me the very stones cried out as the wondrous marble girl was removed from her ageless perch, and in her place a slab of concrete slapped over the broken base. The whole thing was so suggestive of a Hunnish rape that I felt quite out of sorts, and rode out of the city only half aware that I was accompanied by the boy.

"Will my lord bathe?" he inquired, catching me up as I gazed upon the gentle surf rolling in from the Aegean.

"Aye." A moment later we were stripped to our drawers and disporting ourselves amidst the fishes. What memories came back to me that day, of the Cam and Matthews, and of Edleston. How happy had I been then, compared with the discontented misanthrope I had become.

And yet, I reflected, *had* I been happy? Had I not even then sought more than I could have, or at least, more than I dared take, in England? But here I was in Greece, where to take a girl, for pleasure, was considered the unnatural act. I left the water, my cocker making patterns on my small clothes as a result of my considerations, and found Nicolo standing beside me, in a similar state. And how beautiful he looked at that moment, with water smoothing his dark hair and dripping on to his shoulders, with his thin garment sodden and clinging to his flesh to outline every aspect of his body.

"My lord is like a god," he remarked, and lay down, on his back on the sand.

I sat beside him. "As you are, Nicolo. Or any man, caught in the right mood, the right garb."

"Some more so than others," he remarked with a wisdom beyond his age, and then moved, in such a way that his garment became somewhat disarranged, and his cocker peered through the fold, and harder than I had suspected.

I gazed at it with pumping heart. Never had I received so open an invitation. But he was not disposed to leave it there. "I would be my lord's friend," he remarked. "If I am considered worthy."

I turned away from him in self horror, rolling on to my face and my stomach, the better to protect myself and to hide my desire, while of course the touch of the sand but increased the urgency of it.

"My lord does not like me," he said, sadly, and dusted the sand from my bottom, very gently, sending shivers running up and down my spine.

"I like you too well," I groaned.

"My lord," he cried. "My lord, I am yours."

I turned my head, and found him kneeling beside me, and his drawers had been discarded. Here was beauty. I can say it now, unashamedly. Since returning from my travels, and indeed since setting out on them again, I have been fortunate enough to discover that the reciprocated love of woman, the *shared* love of woman – an aspect of life of which I then knew nothing – is an emotion unequalled by anything else life may have to offer. But it is an emotion, a pleasure, a love, composed of so many things as to defy analysis. It is complicated, confused, a knowledge but never a certainty, liable to be turned into despair by the slightest mishap, the slightest alteration in mood by either of the participants. The love of a man for a man is the *purest* of all emotions. At least I have found it so. No doubt I speak without proper experience. If Nikky was the first man I ever truly loved, physically as well as mentally, he was also the last, and who can blame me if now, sometimes, in my despair at the collapse of my life and my reputation, I look back on those sublime months and wonder if I had not done better to retain that perfect liaison for the rest of my life.

But my complete happiness with Nikky lay in the future. On that

115

January day even as I admired those hard muscled thighs, that flat belly, that hairless chest, the still wet thrust of his marvellous cocker, the tightness of his eager balls, even as I reached for it without the ability to stop myself, I conceived myself to be utterly and inexorably damned.

We did no more than embrace, caress our mutual cockers, bring ourselves to mutual ejaculation, and return to the sea for another, more primeval bathe. Yet was my life once again cast into a sea of doubt and misery I had not known since Edleston. Nikky called every day, and we went swimming every day. My fondness for this sport was well known, and there was no comment. In Athens there would have been no adverse comment in any event. And we dallied with the ultimate, without seriously attempting it through a mixture of ignorance and uncertainty.

Things were in this pretty situation when Hobhouse returned. And recognised the state of affairs immediately, for John Cam knew a great deal more about me and my hidden fires than we ever discussed or I even suspected. Thus he suddenly became a livewire of activity and enthusiasm, throwing himself into the business of entertaining me as he had never done before, the while regarding Nikky with utter distaste and not fearing to show it.

But John Cam knew that the only sure cure for my deepening affliction was to remove me from the source of the disease. As I knew myself. After all, I had never intended to linger in Athens even this long. My problem was at least partly genuine, however. In all the near twelvemonth that I had been absent from England, I had received not a letter from Hanson, and certainly not a remittance. From Mama I had had some communication, mostly a recapitulation of current news events, as if I was not able to obtain and read newspapers for myself. But from my faithful friend and lawyer there was a deathly silence, and my funds were running low. I despatched several bitter epistles in his direction, but the uncertainty as to whether I *would* be able to continue my journeys or not, even supposing I really wished to, merely added to my overall dejection.

The break, when it came, was sudden. On 4 March the sloop of war *Pylades* moored in the Piraeus, and Captain Ferguson called and offered a passage to the Turkish port of Smyrna, departing the next morning. It was all too much for me in my then mood. I left the matter to Hobhouse and went swimming with Nikky, well knowing it was for the last time. John Cam certainly would have no doubts, however desperately he had to scurry around to get us packed and ready. The next day we were embarked, and waving farewell to the fabled city. I amused myself with writing verses – to Theresa.

So once again I sought to escape myself, by travelling. And once again, I suspect, proved myself of little value as a companion. Even John Cam was moved to criticise my endless moods, and as a result, after all but a year in each other's company, we had our first rift. But of course it was in the main caused by Nikky, and by Hobhouse's fears for my future.

A three-day voyage brought us to Smyrna, where we were entertained by the British Consul-General and his wife, Mr and Mrs Francis Werry, and from whence we visited the ruins of Ephesus. I was by now at once accustomed to and somewhat bored with these endless accumulations of dwindled stone; one ruined temple is much like another. And yet the *feel* of these places, the knowledge that here feet had trod, and eyes had looked, and voices had spoken, two and three thousand years into the past, still had me in its grip, and a most melancholy grip it was as the jackals howled through the deserted streets, all that were left of the teeming multitude.

We spent almost the entire rest of the month of March in Smyrna, waiting for a passage to Constantinople. The time was not ill used. Hobhouse continued his journal, and I completed the second canto of my *Pilgrimage*. I took Buron into Greece, and left him there. I myself could not foresee the future, except in the most gloomy terms.

At last we left, in the frigate *Salsette* with Captain Bathurst, which was proceeding to the Turkish capital to carry our ambassador, Robert Adair, home to a well-deserved retirement. The Werrys were desolate to see us go, Mrs Werry, a woman of past fifty, putting down a flood of tears and even insisting on snipping a lock of my hair – so I cannot have been *so* disagreeable, whatever Hobhouse's comments. Our journey northwards was very slow, due to contrary winds, and indeed we remained fast for a fortnight at the entrance to the Dardanelles. But this gave us the opportunity to explore the Plain of Troy, for I at the least have no doubts not only that the city once stood but that the mighty siege did indeed take place, whatever the imputations of the blackguard Bryant.(i)

But it was during this enforced if enjoyable halt that I accomplished one of my greatest aquatic feats, that of swimming the fabled strait, as

Leander had done to get to grips with his beloved Hero. We crossed by ship's boat to the European shore, and in the company of a Mr Ekenhead, a lieutenant of marines, I plunged into the icy waters. Because the sea was distinctly and unpleasantly cold, far more so than I had been led to expect, and this, added to the force of the current, proved greater even than my strength. After we had been carried a mile and a quarter below the castle from which we had entered, we were forced to ask to be taken out, to the amusement of the sailors and other travellers. But I was not so easily to be defeated. As our journey continued to be delayed, I went swimming every day to accustom myself to the temperature of the water, and extended my strength by diving for tortoises flung overboard. And so on the morning of 3 May we tried again, the frigate having been forced by the strength of the current to anchor close in to the Asiatic shore. Once again we crossed to Europa castle by boat, and dived in. One hour and ten minutes later I emerged a mile and a half farther south, on the Asiatic side, Ekenhead having made the land five minutes earlier. My triumph was tempered by the reflection that Leander had not only immediately plunged into the arms of his beloved – supposing his frozen cocker had been able to do its manly duty, which mine would certainly have not – but had then swum back again, and all before dawn. Truly they were giants in those far off days.

A week later we came to Constantinople.

From a distance there could be no question that we were approaching one of the great cities of the world; the skyline as a gentle breeze took the *Salsette* up the strait was a mass of minarets and domes and tall cypresses. But it was dusk before we dropped our anchor off Seraglio Point, and then it was gloomy in the extreme, for not a sound could be heard and not a living thing discerned. Nor was this first impression of the heavy hand of the Turk dispelled when next day we went ashore, as the first thing we saw was a dead body being gnawed by dogs; they were stripping the skin from the skull as you or I might peel a fig.

At least we reflected that our impressions could hardly get worse, and indeed they improved considerably after we had paid our respects to the Ambassador. Adair himself was ill, but his secretary, Canning,(ii) turned out to have played in the Eton and Harrow match of 1805, and he remembered me even if I didn't remember him. He could not do enough for us, and Adair offered us rooms in his own home.

These we declined, but we were clearly welcome and dined with him whenever possible.

Happiest of all events, in Constantinople there arrived a letter from Hanson, and a remittance for five hundred pounds, which was like a cup of water to a desert traveller.

Yet the two months we spent in this great and ancient city are amongst the least pleasant of all my memories. For a variety of reasons. First there was the disagreeable realisation that in Constantinople the British, that valiant nation which at this time was almost alone in resisting the mighty French empire, were considered as very small beer. All Europeans were so regarded, but the French for their present power, and the Austrians, for their *ancient* power, were held far superior to us even by those who had seen a British battle fleet sailing majestically up the Dardanelles. (iii) My personal chagrin was intensified by the failure of the Porte to pay any heed to my rank. I was forced to decline my first invitation to visit His Sublime Majesty when I discovered that not only would I not have a private audience, but I would not even have a privileged place in the procession, being slotted in behind Canning. Poor Adair was quite upset, and even produced the Austrian Ambassador, the recognised arbiter of Constantinople etiquette, to convince me that there was no alternative. I refused to be humoured and withdrew my company for three days. (iv) But such is that most cursed of all human weaknesses, curiosity, that I eventually succumbed, and when Adair went to pay his farewell respects I took my place in his entourage like any commoner, and for what? This Grand Signor, this Mahmoud II, never even deigned me a glance. Indeed, he deigned no one a glance, but merely rolled his eyes from side to side. He was a most splendidly dressed fellow, in a robe of yellow satin bordered with sable, and a diamond encrusted dagger besides other jewels, and he sat on a most gorgeous divan – Hobhouse remarked that it suggested a four-poster bed – encrusted with pearls and precious stones, but to me he looked perfectly puerile. I preferred Ali Pasha.

A second cause for discontent was the changing attitude of Hobhouse. Having seen me slipping into Turkish ways in Athens, he had taken on a most profound dislike of all things Mohammedan, and was inclined to say so on every possible occasion, thus increasing my realisation that if a man really wishes to sample the life of other countries he had better do so without taking one of his own countrymen along as a companion. I wished to see, and feel, and even do. He wished to condemn, and retired in haste from a wine cellar we visited in Galata where a bevy of handsome young boys did a dance for us, all posturing backsides and waving cockers, which he described as absolutely beastly. Perhaps it was, but only to us, and we were in *their* land.

But the most disturbing reflections to which I was exposed had nothing to do with either Turk or Constantinople. They arose as a result of the letters I received from home. Hanson's, while as I have said it included that most welcome event, a remittance, was in the main nothing but a catalogue of financial problems and departures. Rochdale had not been sold or even bid for. Some minor lands I held in Suffolk *had* been sold, but no money had been received, owing to a fault in title – how I seemed plagued by these mishaps! Newstead was still not producing its proper rental, and the good fellow even suggested I would do best to sell *this*, my ancestral home. He supported his argument by pointing out that such a step would not only liquidate all my debts at a stroke, but the residue, set at the most modest rate of interest, would provide me with a far greater income than I could ever hope to obtain from my rents. But, sell Newstead, where my poor ailing mother was living? I could not contemplate such a step.

Mama's letters, with their hints that she was ill, were no more cheerful.

Then there was a letter from Hodgson, giving me the good news that *English Bards* was into its fourth edition, and that I was thus quite a well-known fellow, *in absentia*. But he also informed me that he had received a communication, sealed, but which he suspected to be a challenge arising out of some remark I had made in my satire. This he was keeping until my return, as clearly I could not respond at a distance of several thousand miles. But it seemed just one more straw to load on the camel's back in convincing me what a sea of troubles awaited my return to my homeland, supposing I ever did. And why should I, I wondered?

And Hodgson's letter contained worse news even than this. For in a casual sentence he also informed me that Edleston had been accused of indecency.

The news came as a profound shock. For if I appear not to have thought about my dearest friend since leaving England, or perhaps since adventuring with Caroline, yet had I done so a great deal.

My affairs with women had none of them been overwhelming successes. The taunt with which Caroline had left my bed was burned too deeply into my heart ever to be forgot. My dear Austrian promised much, but had never permitted me fully to display my talents, and who could tell what would happen then? And besides, there was the personality of woman herself, which at that tender age, I was still only twenty-two, appeared as a frightening imponderable.

Contrast this with the utter pleasure I had known whenever in Edleston's company. The only cause of uncertainty there had been a suggestion of aridity, in an emotional as well as a procreative sense, attendant upon devoting all my love to him, and the very definite fact of the criminality of our liaison. But deep in my heart, had not my journey to this remote part of Europe been entirely to discover whether such a love *would* be arid? To this moment, to be sure, I had only tasted, never swallowed. But I was determined to go the whole distance, in my most clear headed moods. Otherwise my journey was an entire waste. The problem was, to do so when encumbered by English companions all breathing English morals down my neck, and far worse, all eager to bear witness to my every act.

But I had at least tasted, in complete safety, and considerable enjoyment. Edleston had done nothing more than that. And now stood accused and no doubt condemned – for in *this* business the two are synonymous – when far from my side, alone and friendless. What were my feelings? Disgust? Jealousy that he should have sought another? That was unfair. Sadness? Fear? I really cannot identify any of them. I only know that I was angry, but whether with John himself, with myself for being absent from his side, with the laws of England, with the eagerness of gossiping tongues, or with the very laws of heaven which make us what we are, I cannot say for certain.

But the anger was there, and easily observable to my friends. The *Salsette* being now ready to return with Adair from Constantinople, we took passage aboard, but as usual I fear I was a poor companion. Indeed, being confined upon the ship with naught but male companions, all looking askance at my black mood, but increased the virulence of my temper. I felt almost murderous, although I could not have named a victim, and may even have threatened some such crime. All in all one of the most miserable periods of my life, and sufficient to make John Cam realise that our friendship if not ended, would hardly grow by continued intimacy. Besides, he was anxious to regain England and set about publishing his journal. We bid a farewell in Piraeus, but I will not pretend I was sorry to see him go. I felt like a prisoner being released after a long incarceration.

But yet I was reluctant immediately to plunge into the ultimate life of vice I so eagerly sought. I returned to the widow Macri. The girls were overjoyed to have me back, sorry only to learn of Hobhouse's departure. Their mother was equally pleased. Neighbours came in to dine, and I regaled them with my adventures in the Turkish capital. We caroused until late in the evening, and then I retired to my bed. I had barely got beneath the covers when my door opened. I sat up, and was amazed to discover Mrs Macri.

"Madame?" I demanded.

"You expected my daughter."

"Well . . ." I began in some confusion.

"I have seen the love in your eye, my lord, just as I have seen the love in Theresa's eye."

"I do assure you. . . ."

"And I, my entire family, are flattered that a great gentleman should be so pleased with one of our humble station. My lord, I am here to give my assent to your wedding."

I could only goggle at her in total horror.

"It will be a fine match," madame continued. "She is young, and strong, and able, and loving, and you my lord, above all men, will know that she is a virgin."

"Madame . . ." I gasped.

"There remains only the question of a settlement," the dragon continued, still speaking quietly, hands clasped in her lap. "I have considered the matter deeply, my lord, and considering your lordship's wealth and title, I think a sum of twenty thousand piastres will be entirely suitable."(v)

I could only continue to goggle at the monster. Which encouraged her to come closer.

"You are surprised," she remarked. "So the girl is young. But she will grow. And she will make you a good wife."

I began to laugh. I could not help it.

The widow Macri stopped, a few feet from my bed. "The price is too low?" she inquired.

I sat up, and took hold of myself. I had no wish to offend the old beldam, and after all, had not Caroline's mother made a similar transaction, and with a much less moral objective in mind? "My dear madame," I explained, "I am a lord, a peer of the realm, a ruler of my country. . . ." Well, that was stretching imagination a little, but I still fully intended to make my way in the Lords on my return to England, and perhaps attain the highest offices in the land. "I cannot marry a Greek . . .", another occasion for choosing words with great care, ". . . girl. I must marry a lady, a duchess, a countess." And preferably one with a large rent roll.

She sighed, and nodded, but did not seem entirely put out. "I had feared as much." She sat on the end of my bed. "But you can still have the girl. I will not insist upon marriage. She is fond of you, and will care for you, and be good to you."

Another occasion for goggling, as such utter immorality I had not suspected to exist. After all, the woman had some pretensions to position in this community.

This time she took my silence a different way. "The price is too high?" she inquired. "Well, then, let us settle for ten thousand. I will accept nothing less."

"My dear madame," I resumed. "Theresa deserves a better fate than to be forced into the bed of a rake like myself. In any event," I hastened on, as the widow would have protested, "I do not have ten thousand piastres. I have barely enough to live on as it is."

She frowned at me. "You are a milord."

"Oh, indeed I am. But a penniless one."

"Penniless?" Her voice rose an octave.

"Farthinglcss."

She peered at me for some moments, and then got up. "Then I must ask you to leave my house, sir. And instantly."

I had already resolved upon such a course of action, but this was somewhat precipitate. I was not even allowed to bid farewell to Theresa before I was evicted.

But my plans had already been laid. I intended visiting the Morea, where the son of Ali, Veli Pasha, held sway, and to which I had been invited, and where, I hoped, I might begin that investigation into my true nature which had haunted me for so long. Alas for the schemes of men. Even as I prepared for my journey, who should appear in Athens but Sligo,(vi) also determined to visit the Morea, and equally determined to have me as his companion. This was intolerable. Apart from the interference with my plans which such an instant replacement for John Cam would provide, Sligo, while personally the pleasantest of fellows, travelled like an oriental potentate, with more than twenty in his party, including even a resident artist to record the scenery. In point of fact, and much to my relief, we only kept company as far as Corinth, and there parted.

In the event my entire visit to the Morea was a disappointment. I duly reached Tripolitzka, the capital of Veli Pasha, and was indeed made welcome. And discovered myself once more to be a coward. Veli had no doubt heard of me from his father, and sought to succeed where the lion had failed. He was certainly younger and a deal more prepossessing. He was also far more public in his affection, constantly throwing his arm around my shoulders and hugging me against him, and making the most lewd of suggestions. All of which I resisted, without knowing why. Except sheer fright, which I was reluctant to admit. The fact is I trembled upon the brink, much as I had done with Mesdames Jeanette and Dulcina a few years before. My pride would not allow me to become the acolyte of some semen-stained old whore, be it male or female. To discover myself I needed a male equivalent of sweet Caroline, someone who, perhaps more knowledgeable than myself, would yet submit to being the lower partner – in every possible sense – and allow me to pursue my goal in my own way.

But this was not apparent to me at the time. I was aware only of confusion, and very rapidly fled to Athens, arriving in the middle of August, to discover, as is so often the case, that a man may spend a lifetime searching while omitting to notice that the object of his quest lies beneath his very nose.

Because obviously I could not return to my lodgings at the widow Macri's. I therefore sought the assistance of Lusieri, who recommended that I seek bed and board at the Capuchin convent situated at the foot of the Acropolis. (vii) Here a few students were taught by the monks, and there were several vacant cells, more than sufficient for Fletcher and myself, for to the pair of us was my expedition now reduced. This seemed an entirely sensible project to me, and thereto I removed myself – it was scarce more than a stone's throw from the Macri household. To find myself plunged into a perfectly masculine paradise, where upon my first attendance at dinner I was fondly kissed upon the cheek by one of the novices, who wore a loose robe and nothing else. Undoubtedly I had, all unwittingly, found the sanctuary I sought, but there was more. With me, the mere act is never sufficient. I am a man of emotion, of passion, of feeling. Where I cannot feel, with my head and my heart as well as my cocker, I am lost. I know this now. Perhaps I was less aware of it then. But it was in any event irrelevant, for seated at the far end of the table, who should I descern but my old friend Nicolo.

I should have known, of course. For why else should Lusieri recommend this place had he not an intimate acquaintance with it through his brother-in-law? And in the months I had been away, Nikky had not changed, save perhaps for the better, his hair soft and black, his olive features hauntingly beautiful, his complexion still as clear as day, with never a trace of unseemly hair to mark his chin.

On the first evening he was the most aloof of the lads. But I understood the reason. He was piqued at my departure from Athens, leaving him behind when he had offered me his all. I smiled at him, and called him by name, and having dined well and drunk well, my senses inflamed by the precocious manhood with which I was surrounded, I invited him to show me to my chamber.

"Georgio will do it," he said.

"*You* will do it," I commanded, rising to my feet. My dining companions looked surprised at this evidence of decision on my part — they had earlier discovered in me only a pleasant companion. Nikky hesitated, looked sulky, shrugged, and rose, to walk before me to the door, from whence I bade the company farewell. He secured a candle, and led the way along the hallowed passageways, with me at his heels, a prey to the most remarkable reflections. For on the one hand I was irresistibly reminded of that gay frolic at Newstead, and set to wondering about my friends, about Matthews and Hobhouse and Hodgson and even dear foolish old Webster, set me to recalling Edleston and Clare, set me to thinking the strangest of thoughts, while my cocker remained in a state of half arousal which had me thinking of that first encounter with blue-eyed Caroline.

While I was yet a prey to these confusing and disturbing thoughts, we arrived at the door of my cell. "No doubt your lordship wishes to retire," Nikky remarked.

"Indeed," I agreed, "but not alone." I sauntered into the room, amazed at my nonchalance, wondering why the mad pounding in my heart, the guilty lurches of my belly were not revealed in my face. "Will you not keep my company a while?"

He hesitated, then closed the door, remaining on the inside. "I had thought I had no place in your life," he said.

I turned to face him. "You, Nikky? Of all men, none ranks with me so high as you." A somewhat exaggerated speech, at least in retrospect, and one which would certainly have angered Hobhouse. But this was different. Hobhouse and I were *friends*. There is no nobler expression of human relationship, and it is an oft debased word. This lad and I were about to become *lovers*; I did not doubt the outcome for a moment, as he had stayed. Lovers are seldom friends. Indeed, there is something about love that is inimicable to friendship. The one is a river, broad and deep and slow running and reliable. The other is a millstream, bouncing and effervescent, changing in an instant from depths in which one may drown, to shallows in which one comes hard aground and is left stranded, to sluice gates in which all hell lets loose and one emerges amazed at having retained life, much less sanity.

And Nikky was clearly already in love. "My lord," he whispered, and sank to his knees before me, an act both of obeisance and serving to bring him closer to that object he longed to possess. "I love you. I loved you from the moment of our first meeting, and I will love you until the hour of your death."

Which seemed to me to be looking unnecessarily far into the future. The present was what mattered here. For I also had donned a loose robe in which to dine, and if I had prudently retained my drawers beneath such a lascivious garment, this was a small obstacle to eager hands. A moment later they were about my knees and slipping to my ankles, and Nikky's lips were exploring where only Caroline's had ever gone before. And obtaining a similar result, as he took me entirely into his mouth and used his tongue to devastating effect.

But this was a game at which two could play, and indeed it was this aspect of the situation which had brought me hither. I raised him from the floor, spread him upon my narrow cot, and gave myself over to the pleasures of exploring another man's body, in our culture *almost* the most forbidden of sexual acts. But its very outlawry made it the more attractive, while it was something I had longed to do ever since I had found myself swimming beside Clare.

And Nikky's beauty extended far below his face, as I remembered from our first set-to on the beach. Here were slender thighs, silky down, tightened balls and the most beautifully shaped cocker. He was not of course circumcised, and this was my only disappointment, as I had thought nothing quite so compelling as the beauty of the Turkish boys Hobhouse and I had seen dance in Constantinople. But truly it would have mattered very little had he been ugly. A cocker is a cocker, and can never fail to delight. And here was one at my complete behest, slowly filling with blood, slowly swelling, twitching of its own

126

whenever he tightened his muscles, beginning finally to trickle before at last giving vent to a tremendous explosion.

While mine remained inflamed and eager for the main business of the evening. But first we must lie together and kiss and suck, with never a word spoken, for what need was there of words? Until he himself turned over and presented me with his rump, suitably arranged at a proper angle from the bed. He had to do more, as entry in these circumstances was not only strange to me but is somewhat difficult at the best of times. The necessary lubrication was soon forthcoming however, and such was my anxiety that the deed itself was completed and consummated only seconds later, leaving me gasping and in a sad state of confusion, certain of only one thing, that if the 5th Lord Byron had gloried in the name of the Wicked Lord, what would posterity say of the 6th, only supposing they could ever discover the truth about him?

HOME THE WANDERER

I awoke in a state of some confusion, which was increased by the continued presence of Nikky, who had spent the night in my arms. And as we were both fully rested and restored in vigour, another set-to was necessary before we departed for our respective studies, for I was not wasting my time, but endeavouring to learn Italian, as well as revising the second canto of *Childe Buron*, in which I was covering my earlier Greek travels and experiences.

This day, however, I would have none of them, for I was the victim of some most disturbing considerations. On the one hand, my sexual instincts were delighted with what I had experienced. But this in itself was a cause for confusion, for while I had much enjoyed fingering Nikky's cocker and raising it to erection, and looked forward to doing this again, it really had not been so very much more pleasurable than fingering my own, which could be done at will and without fear of discovery and condemnation. The real pleasure of our set-to had been the possession of his splendid, small, tight buttocks, and when I allowed myself to think about this in earnest, I recalled that perhaps my principal delight in Caroline had been her rear end as well, which, as she had been a young girl, had also been small and tight and almost masculine in its delight. It had never crossed my mind to ask Caroline to permit sodomy, I would have been far too terrified of her reaction, but supposing such a woman could be found, was it not possible that she would grant me an equal or perhaps an even greater delight than Nikky?

Wishful thinking, for I could conceive of no female of my acquaintance who would be willing so to turn nature inside out.

My next consideration concerned my guilt. Because however normal such behaviour was in Athens, I was an English milord. Who eventually would have to return to his own country. Last night's tumble was for the moment privy to Nikky and myself. But for how long? Even supposing he did not boast of his conquest to his fellows, and far worse, his family, there was Fletcher. That good hearted and licentious but, alas, utterly orthodox fellow had the cell next to mine. He was a heavy sleeper and we had made little noise, but could he fail to observe Nikky's nightly pilgrimage to my bed? There was a grim prospect, to be at the mercy of one's own servant.

And lastly, there was Nikky himself. At that moment I think I was genuinely in love with him. He was certainly all that one could wish in a lover, at once beautiful and utterly devoted. I had turned my back upon too much love in the past to wish to do so now. For where would I, with my crippled leg, ever find a woman to adore me so extravagantly? I could command servants to my bed, but Caroline and Mary Ann had sufficiently illustrated the true feelings of their sex towards a cripple. Even Constance had no doubt been prepared to love me merely because she had never seen me without my boots on. Constance. My God, I had entirely forgotten that temptress, still waiting for me to return to Malta as I had promised. How long ago she seemed, and how uninspiring. Still, no doubt she had forgotten me as well, and fastened her grip upon some other hapless youth.

But the memory of her added yet another straw to the burden that was momentarily growing more heavy upon my back. "*Crede Byron.*" It seemed to me that circumstances were conspiring to make a mockery of that proud motto.

Thus confused, uncertain, I wandered the streets of Athens, going far from my usual haunts and more into the Turkish quarter of the city, as far as the port, my head spinning, my heart and my body calling out for me to return to the cloistered peace of the convent, to the adoring looks of my Nikky. And it was while in this mood, and a long way from arriving at a decision, that I strolled down a leafy lane between the high walls of two houses, and heard a woman sing.

The quality of the sound was quite delightful; it broke through even the depths of my reverie and had me raising my head to discover from whence it came, for all that I could understand only a few of the words, as she was singing in Turkish. But that she was near at hand was undeniable. And that the possessor of such a voice would also be the possessor of a beautiful face seemed equally undeniable. Without further thought I said, in a mixture of Turkish and Greek, having by now picked up a smattering of each language, "Are there then nightingales in this place?"

The singing ceased, and for a moment I feared I had lost her. Then she said, and even closer at hand than I had hoped, "Night-ing-ale? What is this, night-ing-ale?"

She was clearly on the far side of the right-hand wall, a mere few inches of bricks and mortar distant.

"A bird," I explained. "Which in northern climes is renowned for the sweetness of its voice, but which would have to bow its head in shame were it to hear you sing."

Another brief silence. Then: "You are a *gaiour*."(i)

"Am I accused or congratulated?"

She laughed, and the sound equalled her singing. "I would be as you, were it possible. Alas. . . ."

"At least let me see your face."

"Impossible. This is the garden of the harem of Hussein bin Hassan."

Of whom I had never heard, although from the size of the place I concluded he must be a wealthy gentleman. In any event, I was not to be put off by that difficulty.

"In which you are alone," I pointed out. "Or you could not even speak with me. May I not look over the wall?"

Once more the hesitation. "It is very dangerous."

"A state of affairs upon which I thrive," I boasted, not entirely untruthfully, and assuming that she referred only to myself. The deed itself was trivial. The wall stood only six feet high, and the muscles in my arms were as strong as ever. A simple heave, and I had my elbows and even one leg upon the top, and could look down into the garden. My first harem. And a place of rare beauty it was too, with carefully watered grass, not the most common of sights in this arid land, above which shady palm trees slithered in the gentle breeze, and in the centre of which a marble fountain gave forth a cooling dampness. Best of all, the garden was entirely walled, with a single door on the far side no doubt giving access to the interior of the house. But this door was presently closed, allowing the most perfect privacy to prevail within.

And if the garden was a place of shaded beauty, what was I to make of the girl, for she could be no more, who stood by the fountain, to which no doubt she had retreated, gazing at me with wide brown eyes? Her form was slender as a boy's, and well delineated by the afternoon sunlight playing upon the silk of her pantaloons, illustrating that she wore nothing beneath and that her legs were perfectly shaped, while above . . . but she had observed my interest and interposed the fountain between her crotch and my gaze. Which allowed me to concentrate upon her upper half, which was encased in a heavily embroidered pink bolero jacket, not fastened in any way, and thus allowing the soft brown chest to dominate the afternoon, while as she moved I even caught a glimpse of pink nipple. Above and behind this was a cascade of midnight hair, issuing from beneath a small jewelled cap, also in pink, and descending nearly to her thighs. And then the eyes, for the rest of her was concealed by a white gauze mask which was far more opaque than her trousers. And which, I estimated from the fact that it was slightly askew, had been hastily donned as she heard me scrabbling up the wall.

"You are too bold," she said.

"And thus deserve a reward, would you not say?"

She hesitated, and then walked round the fountain. The darkness at her groin pressed against the silk for an instant as she moved, and then a gust of the breeze caught the material from behind and flattened it around her bottom, two curving delights of the uttermost magnificence. I truly suspect I have never since beheld such utter loveliness, and its effect upon me, suspended in an exhausting and undignified position as I was, served to reassure me upon at least one of my earlier considerations.

She apparently found me no less interesting. She came closer yet, and while staring at me with knitted brows. "You are the English milord," she said suddenly. "I have heard of you, of your beauty. . . . " She checked herself and the flush rose above her *yashmak*.

"George Gordon Byron, at your service," I agreed, and swung up my other leg to sit astride the wall. "And that I have not yet heard of you, sweet lady, is entirely a crime. May I ask your name?"

"Haidee."

"And may I not see your face?"

She glanced right and left. "It is forbidden."

"Ah, but is it not forbidden for me to be here at all, much less talking with you? What is one forbidden act, more or less?"

Again the quick glance, and then she reached behind her and released the mask. And capped the entire episode. For the face was worthy of the body and the hair. Straight nose, wide red lips, little pointed chin, the whole adorned by a delicious shy smile.

"You are the most lovely thing these eyes have ever beheld," I said. "Had I died without seeing you, Haidee, my life had been that of a pauper."

"My lord is too kind," she said, and restored her mask. "And now you must go. To be found here. . . ."

"Go?" I demanded. "Without at the least touching you? Oh, my exquisite child, that I could never do, if I must spend the rest of my days upon this unhappy perch."

For I was quite inflamed. If there was one thing I wished to do more than any other it was to plunge my weapon into a female slit, if only to reassure myself that I was still capable of such an act. But such a slit, so much perfect beauty. . . .

"You must promise to remain upon the wall," she said, coming closer.

My turn to hesitate. But surely she would herself release me from my promise, and soon. "You have my word."

She stood beneath me, and stretched up her hands. I held her fingers, they were warm and just a trifle damp.

"Haidee," I whispered, "my Haidee." I ran my fingers down her arm to her elbow, and reached down for her breast, for the act of reaching up to me had quite displaced the bolero, and two splendid mounds, small, but brown and capped by a delicious dart of pink, were exposed to my desire. She misunderstood my intention, and had tilted her head back for a kiss. But I could kiss and fondle at the same moment. I bent lower, my fingers touched her flesh moments before my lips . . . and the garden door opened.

I wasted no time, having no desire to compromise either Haidee or myself. "Until tomorrow," I whispered, then swung my legs over the parapet, and dropped back into the street. From behind me there came a flurry of noise, amongst which I discerned my sweetheart screaming, which she did as prettily as she did every other thing. Almost immediately a door opened farther along the lane, and a couple of very ugly fellows emerged, all waving scimitars and ready to do me the most serious of damage. But this sort of adventure I had craved for it seemed all of my life. How often had I proved my skill, either at quick firing into a barn door or at the more stately accuracy demanded to shatter a bottle trailing over the stern of a fast moving ship? The only thing I had ever doubted was my ability when faced with the heart stopping danger of an armed man. I need not have worried. Even as I turned to look at them my hand was emerging from my pocket, holding my first pistol. I fired too hastily, but then, I had no great intention of killing anyone as a result of my escapade. And the mere fact of the shot was sufficient. The noise and the whanging of the bullet from wall to wall discouraged them, and they ducked back into the doorway, while I, laughing maniacally, hobbled along the lane and round the corner and into a broader and more populous thorough-fare. No doubt several of those who passed me by had heard the shouts and the sound of my shot, but they chose discretion rather than valour, and within half an hour I was safe back within the walls of my cloisters.

And safe in more ways than just one. Never can I recall having been in a better humour. I had slept with the boy of my choice, gone abroad, and discovered the woman of my choice. We had been inter-rupted, but the future lay before us. No girl could have allowed herself so much intimacy with a total stranger and not been prepared to grant me the furthest extent of her love. I had proved myself a perfect Zeluco, a man who took his pleasures as he found them, lived life to the hilt, and was prepared to accept the odds that came against him.

That night I indulged myself to the utmost, and enjoyed comparing the eager love of Nikky in my arms with the prospects of an equally eager response from Haidee, whenever we could manage to find each other some privacy. For I never doubted that she would be waiting again for me, behind the wall, and in my silly innocence I equally had no doubt at all that it would be possible for her to escape the harem from time to time, to the safety of a tryst.

Nonetheless, for my own safety, I had Fletcher accompany me when I returned to that pleasant suburb by the sea. For this was an escapade he not only could understand, but one with which he was in the fullest sympathy, having found in the women of Athens the most perfect companions, at least amongst the lower orders. It was two hours after noon when we made our way down that leafy lane, to be alerted by a great noise, coming, it seemed to me, from the very door of the house in which my charmer lived. Nor was the lane as deserted as yesterday, but there was a goodly crowd of people, Greeks as well as Turks, gathered to oversee the proceedings.

I prudently halted on the very edge of the crowd, and engaged an onlooker in conversation. "Whatever is happening yonder?"

"Hussein bin Hassan is about to drown one of his wives."

I stared at the fellow.

"Drown a wife? How may a man drown his wife?"

"It is the Turkish law, did you not know? A wife who has been found unfaithful shall be tied in a sack and thrown into the sea." The lout grinned at me. "Sometimes the sack takes a full minute to sink. It is all screaming and wriggling arms and legs."

Once again I stared at him for some seconds, while my stomach turned over and my brain seemed to be seized in an icy grip. In my careless callous concern only for the satisfaction of my own lust I had condemned the sweet child to the most horrible of deaths.

Fletcher caught my arm. "We'd best be off, my lord," he muttered. "If they drown the guilty wife, what do they do to the man?"

"Flee?" I muttered. "And leave that child to her fate?" Suddenly the cold horror and fear dissipated, and was replaced by a burning heat. "Follow me," I commanded, and pushed my way into the throng. My heart pounded, and my mind seemed to be singing. Was not this what I had always dreamed of doing, standing foursquare to the world, my pistols in my hand, defying my enemies to do their worst? What did it matter that I was the guilty party, and defending a crime? At least a crime in *prospect*, even if it had not been one in fact, as yet.

The crowd parted before my advance, and a glance over my shoulder revealed Willie hurrying behind, face pale but determined. By now the entire crowd was moving, forming a sort of procession, while I could hear a high pitched wailing, which was no doubt my Haidee screaming her last, although any sound as far removed from that magnificent voice with which I had fallen in love could scarcely be imagined.

Haste was imperative, for already I could see the water, and the crowd was beginning to *growl* its anticipation. But I was nearly there. A last push between two lads, and I emerged on the shore, to see the head of the procession, a small, pockmarked fellow with a grey beard, but most splendidly dressed, who could be none other than Hussein bin Hassan himself, followed by two other small fellows who presumably were his brothers or his eldest sons, and then four men carrying between them a sack, which wriggled most desperately and from which the spine-chilling wailing was proceeding, and then by four other men, either other members of his household or perhaps witnesses.

I counted these eleven my only opponents, for the crowd was mainly Greek and I could not see them interfering to assist the crime of their hated overlords, but even so the odds were long enough. Yet I did not hesitate for a moment.

"Hold there," I commanded, leaving the safety of the mob to stand alone in the afternoon sunlight.

134

They paused and looked at me. I advanced, my hands in my coat pockets, resting on my pistols, while Fletcher, immediately behind me, actually drew one of his weapons, appearing to inspect the priming.

"Will you commit murder?" I demanded.

"Murder, my friend?" inquired one of the witnesses. "This woman is guilty of adultery, and is suffering the prescribed penalty."

"Adultery?" I cried. "Tush. She did not even allow me a kiss."

That threw them into confusion. Their heads went together and their muttering rose into the morning air. No doubt such an admission on the part of the male was unknown in their society.

Then Hussein himself stepped forward, and I followed Fletcher's example and drew my weapon.

But his tone was mild enough. "You are the English milord," he remarked. "I have heard of you. This is no business of yours. Withdraw, and nothing more shall be said."

"I shall withdraw, with that poor girl on my arm," I declared.

"You would attempt to come between a man and his wife, between a criminal and the law?"

"There has been no crime. If you insist upon it, there *shall* be no crime," I said. "You have the word of an English milord. But I will not stand by and see a woman drowned."

Hussein gazed at me for a moment, then gave a contemptuous snort and turned away. "Continue," he snapped. "And have done."

"By God, sir," I shouted, stepped forward, seized him round the neck with my left hand, while with my right I levelled my first pistol and fired, with great deliberateness, my shot striking the stone upon which the four assassins were standing, causing them to drop their quivering burden in great alarm. Meanwhile I had restored my spent pistol to my pocket and seized its fellow, which I pressed against Hussein's temple. "When she dies, so do you," I said.

He was so surprised he did not even wriggle. Indeed I believe he had quite lost the power of speech. Not so his friends and relations, who had not expected their morning's entertainment to be so dangerous. As one man they took to their heels, leaving their victim and their master exposed upon the shore.

"Open the bag," I commanded Fletcher, and the faithful fellow stepped forward, knife in hand.

"Haidee," I said. "My dear, sweet Haidee, I can only beg you to believe that I shall be your protector from this moment forth, that I shall love you and cherish you for the rest of my days."

The woman emerging from the sack stared at me as if she had never seen me before in her life, as indeed she had never seen me before in her life. Here was no Haidee, sweet and seductive, but a middle-aged harridan with a nose like the beak of a trireme.

In my dismay I released Hussein, at the same time being forced to consider what sort of a household he maintained, for assuming this lady *had* been guilty of adultery – supposing she could possibly have found someone to accommodate her – there could be no question that Haidee would soon have committed the same crime, which suggested that all of his wives were equally anxious to put horns on their lord. Which was not entirely surprising when one considered the fellow.

However, there I was with a quite unwanted damsel on my hands. I could not consign her back to her sack, for the crowd was now entirely upon my side, and cheering me to even greater deeds. But I was a sorely confused and concerned knight errant as I assisted her to her feet. For it seemed more than likely that this afternoon's work would have considerable repercussions, which I had been prepared to withstand with a view to attaining the soft beauty of Haidee at the end. But for this creature. . . . "Let's be off," I said to Fletcher, and he was eager to agree.

We hurried the female up the street and through the crowd, who continued to cheer us, past the house of my beloved, all barred and grim, with a couple of armed Turks standing outside, although they made no move to interfere with us, and gained a secluded alleyway.

"Now then," I said. "What's to be done?"

"We'll take her to the convent," Willie decided. "You'll want a cell for her, my lord." He winked. "Close to your own."

"For God's sake, Willie," I cried. "This is not the one of whom I spoke."

The woman was meanwhile watching us both anxiously, as it did not appear that she understood English.

Fletcher scratched his head. "My lord, I do not understand."

"We have rescued the wrong woman," I explained with great patience. "Indeed, it seems that mine does not require rescuing at all. Now, to bed this one would turn me into the most continent monk who ever lived, and that I'll not risk. Willie, you must find a place for her."

He scratched his head some more, clearly still not entirely understanding. But finally he nodded, seized the bewildered beldam by the arm, and disappeared. I discovered later that he removed her to a house of ill repute of which he had become a regular customer, and there installed her, after a suitable payment from my coffers. A rum business, where one has to pay for a girl to be taken into a brothel. (ii)

As I had supposed would be the case, my adventure was the talk of Athens, and possibly of the entire Middle East, for a while. And yet the authorities made no attempt to molest me. It may be that they had no wish to incarcerate an English nobleman, or it may be that Hussein did not press charges, for it did occur to me, so remarkably ugly was his intended victim, that the very accusation of adultery might have been trumped up as an excuse for getting rid of her. Certainly it was difficult to account for Haidee's survival, unless she had managed to convince her husband that she had been assaulted rather than compliant.

But in the circumstances I did not dare add fuel to the fire by attempting to renew my abortive liaison, and so was reluctantly compelled to relegate her to a memory and to a place in literature. My friends indeed presumed it best for me to absent myself from Athens for a while. This fitted in well with my various plans. I had already determined to get rid of the faithful Willie before he discovered my relationship with Nikky. I therefore secured him passage on a boat for England in November, a very necessary step in any event, as apart from wishing to send letters home, my affairs, from the odd letter I received from Hanson, were going from bad to worse, and he was once again suggesting that the only solution to my impossible financial situation was to sell Newstead, a step I was equally determined to resist. Instructions in this direction were carried by Fletcher, and in addition, as he had undoubtedly been seen at my side in the fracas, I was removing him from the vicinity of Turkish vengeance.

I followed him soon enough, departing with Nikky for another tour of the Morea. But in fact my own thoughts were turning to home. Such a journey was clearly necessary, in view of the continuing depressing news I received from Hanson. In addition, letters from dear Mama continued to suggest that she was not in the best of health, a condition no doubt partly induced by the embarrassment of being constantly dunned for my various debts. I could do little less than go to the rescue of the poor old soul. And it was a challenge I was suddenly eager to face; for the events of the past few weeks had given me great confidence in myself – I felt I had at last truly attained the stature to which I had always aspired. Yet another reason encouraging me to leave, at least for a while, my beloved Greece, was a tertian fever which I had contracted, and which returned with unfailing regularity to reduce me to a shivering wreck. A sea voyage and a year in England would undoubtedly drive the ague from my bones.

But however loathe I am to admit it, the prime reason why my decision finally settled on a return to England was the cursed gift of the Muse which a capricious fate had seen fit to bestow upon me. *Childe Buron's Pilgrimage* seemed to be burning a hole in my portmanteau, and I had written an additional work, which I called *The Curse of Minerva*, in which I lambasted the thieving proclivities of the infamous Eldon. I was also at work upon another, satirical work, *Hints from Horace*, in which I was encouraged by the news that my *English Bards* was now in a fourth edition. A writer's anxiety to inflict himself upon the public is like a drug, which can only be resisted for short periods, and it was now two years since I had enjoyed that pleasure.

Thus the decision was finally taken, and in the spring of 1811, after giving a farewell dinner to all of my Athenian friends, I boarded the good ship *Hydra*, *en route* for Malta, travelling, remarkably enough, together with a cargo of the infamous marbles themselves.

I took Nikky with me. I really could not contemplate leaving him behind both because of his utter devotion to me and because of the way he had nursed me through my illness. Nor were his family the least concerned to see him go, foreseeing for him a much happier future in my company than in Athens. Of course I had no intention of taking him back to England; that would have been far too great a risk. But I intended to place him at School in Malta, where his education could be completed, and where he would be waiting for me when I chose to return, for I was determined that my visit to England would be for the purpose of settling my affairs, and nothing more. If, as seemed entirely probable, I was going to be forced into selling Newstead, then I could conceive of no reason whatsoever for my remaining in that cold and limited country. I would make proper arrangements for Mama, and then hasten back to the blue skies, the warm seas, and the even warmer inhabitants of the Mediterranean. How little one suspects the future.

This suggestion that our separation was going to be little more than a few months did a great deal to reassure the poor lad, although he was desolate at the thought of even this brief parting. For my part, however, I underwent the strangest change of heart when the mountains of

Greece finally sank below the eastern horizon. Put me down as fickle; I would not deny the charge. Yet so long as circumstances are unchanging, I am the most faithful of men, and however *much* my circumstances have changed over the years, it has never been of my doing. Indeed, in seeking marriage, I wished only to discover a pleasantly unchanging existence, content to lie in the arms of the same woman night after night. Fate, and my wife, decreed that this Nirvana was to remain a dream. But so it was with Nikky. In Athens, living at the convent, seeking him whenever I desired more than just a tumble, living my own life – and despite my ill health it was one of the very pleasantest periods of my entire life – I would have been happy to find my love nowhere else. Yet as I say, once we were uprooted from the scenario in which our relationship had seen its first act, my feelings altered. Perhaps it was through sailing on an English ship, surrounded by Englishmen and the constant reminders of the life to which I was returning, but I was happy to see the brown hills of Malta rising in the west, and installed Nikky in his new surroundings with all possible despatch.

This was necessary in any event, as it was now time to face my beloved Constance, give her the reasons for my delayed return, and convince her that I should be in England only a brief while before again seeking her arms. But of course she knew better, nor, I suspect, was she altogether displeased to see the approaching end of the affair.

The month I spent in Malta, therefore, waiting for a passage to England, was a massive exercise in mutual hypocrisy, in which we sat together and walked together and held hands together and kissed together, and made plans together for when I returned, each certain that he or she was entirely satisfying the other's doubts, each knowing that it would be a relief when the parting finally came. This at least is how I reason the matter. For when the time *did* come for me to board the frigate *Volage*, however hard she tried, she could muster very little physical evidence of grief, and I had the entire long voyage home to arrive at the conclusions I have just related.

I may say that throughout this month I continued to be debilitated by a constant recurrence of the tertian I had first contracted in Greece, which left me for the most part devilishly depressed, and I was overjoyed to have nothing but the sea air to breathe, and which in fact very soon restored me to health. But it was an entirely *intellectual* health. No doubt my excesses in Athens, crowned as they were by the

139

superficial Constance Spencer-Smith, had left my emotions quite flaccid, while more than ever my fertile imagination was stirring with a desire to write, and publish, and speak, and take my place in the forefront of affairs. Thus I dreamed of founding a literary periodical, in which I could satirise and romanticise and criticise to the limits of my ability. And why not? Sufficient of my friends, and Hobhouse for sure, were similarly inclined, and I do believe that had my entire life not been caught up in a hurricane breeze so soon after my return to England, from which I have only just escaped, battered and breathless and entirely unsure as to whether I am standing on my head or on my heels, I might have settled down with John Cam into a politico-literary existence, which would no doubt have made me much happier although it almost certainly would from time to time have landed me in gaol.

But what a dismal prospect met my eyes when I finally alighted at Sheerness. The month was July 1811, and it was raining. Hobhouse, I discovered, was on his way into the army or at best the militia, in an attempt to placate his father. Davies was on his way to gaol, part of the cause being the five thousand pounds I still owed him and was unable to pay. My own affairs were descending rapidly from bad to worse. My mother was ill. And Bruin was dead. He had, it appeared, just pined away in the absence of his master. It seemed to me that the entire two years and twelve days that had elapsed since I had set sail from Falmouth might have been a single night, in which I had rolled over in my bed and awakened to find the world just a little bit greyer than on the previous evening.

Even the literary plans with which my brain and my portmanteau were bulging seemed likely to come to naught. I took my wares to Dallas, showing first of all my satire. He expressed grave disappointment. I then produced *Childe Buron's Pilgrimage*. This he read with great interest, but at the end revealed positive alarm.

"Mind you," he was at pains to explain, "some of the poetry, and all of the descriptions, are first rate. Absolutely first rate. But I very much doubt, well. . . that the public are ready for anything quite so explicit. And about you. It could be an autobiography."

"Well, it is not an autobiography," I lied angrily. "It is a work of art."

"That may be," he agreed, "but anyone reading this will find it very difficult not to identify Buron with Byron. Why, even the names are too closely linked. We shall have to consider."

At which I took offence and myself off, leaving the manuscript in his hands, however.

As if this were not annoyance enough, I was suddenly appraised that my mother was far more seriously ill than I had supposed. In fact I felt some considerable guilt, after having been away for so long, at having dallied in London for a fortnight before setting out for Newstead. But apart from the problems I have already mentioned, there was the main one of lack of funds. I had dreamed of eventually returning to my ancestral home with my affairs entirely in order, with an income more commensurate with my position, with nothing but good news to restore the dear old soul to a happiness she had never known. And found myself as usual baulked by the tardiness of Hanson, by innumerable legal problems the most of which I did not even understand, by delays which seemed to stretch endlessly into the future. And most of all by a crippling lack of ready cash. Some idea of my straits may be gained when I say that on the news that Mama might be really ill, I determined of course to set out without delay, but even so had to discover Hanson and raise a loan of forty pounds for the journey.

This took time. I had not yet left my London hotel when a servant arrived with a further bulletin. My mother was dead.

THE MOST FAMOUS MAN IN ENGLAND

Anyone reading these pages will not need to be convinced that Mama and I had never got on. Disappointed in my appearance at birth, regarding me – no doubt correctly – as a prime cause of her husband's desertion, her joy at my becoming Lord Byron rapidly dissipated into gloom as she realised the inheritance was going to bring more problems than pleasure, she could hardly be blamed – at least, I can hardly blame her in retrospect – for occasionally venting her anger or her bitter humour at my expense. And yet she loved me. There can be no doubt of that. Her letters alone had always been waiting for me on my travels, her good wishes alone had sped me on my way.

And I had loved her. Better from a distance, to be sure, but none the less sincerely for that. My grief was for a few days almost unbearable, accentuated by guilt, for I had paid scant attention to her oft repeated suggestions of gathering illness, and indeed it was some relief to me to learn that she died suddenly of a seizure in consequence of yet another large account being brought to her attention. But the account itself had been of my creation.(i)

I reached Newstead as rapidly as I could, and was overwhelmed again. She lay in state in the withdrawing-room, and the servants were in mourning. The business of the funeral, the arrangements and the outfittings of the mourners, left me mentally exhausted, and yet filled with a wild, almost a demonic energy. I could no more have walked slowly and solemnly behind the coffin than I could have jumped over the moon. I could not go. I could not watch. I commanded Robert Rushton to the hall and had him don the gloves with me. We sparred as dear Mama was laid to rest.

An action which was undoubtedly misunderstood by all who learned of it. And such was my notoriety in a year's time that *everyone* in England eventually heard of it. No doubt here began those rumours that I was a *strange fellow*. For feeling a grief too strong to be admitted. (ii)

But fate, having seen fit to welcome me back to England with utter disaster, was not disposed to leave me there. It was almost as if the malign goddess had been waiting for me, for two years, to open the floodgates of her wrath. While still prostrate under the burden of Mama's departure, unable to attend to business, of which there was a great deal, unable to think, I learned of the death of Charles Skinner Matthews. This would have been terrible at any time, but the actual circumstances were horrifying. For diving into the Cam, as we had spent so many pleasant hours doing together, he had had his foot trapped beneath a great log lying at the bottom of the river, and so had drowned, unable to communicate with his friends above, who assumed he was but playing, with success, our old game of who could longest hold his breath.

Remarkably, this second shattering blow restored some presence of mind. There was a deal to be done, and I found solace in action. With death all around me it was time to consider the possibility of my own. I drew up a will, attempting to make sure that all who had been faithful friends of mine, from dear Willie upwards, should be looked after when I left them, bequeathing £7,000 to Nikky, and leaving the bulk of my estate to Augusta.

I would have done this anyway, as she was my only remaining close relative. But as it happened the death of Mama accomplished one favourable result, in that it ended our estrangement. She wrote her condolences, I replied with mine on the growing resemblance of her family to a rabbit hutch, for her third had just been born, and within weeks we were once again on our old footing of literary intimacy.

Then there were my estates to be inspected and improved and my affairs to be put in order. A great deal of money would have to be spent on renovating the farms at Newstead, but Hanson estimated that once this was done my income would be several thousand pounds a year, more than sufficient. The problem was that great and growing burden of debt which hung over me like a cloud, which was in no way alleviated by Mama's scanty portion or by Hobhouse's repayment of the loan he had borrowed to make his tour with me. I was in the unhappy position of being unable to improve my estate until my debts were liquidated, and being unable to liquidate my debts until my estate was improved. In this perplexity the news from Dallas that John Murray was willing to publish *Childe Buron's Pilgrimage* seemed hardly relevant, especially as he wished certain changes to be made. I have never been one for changing my poems at the whim of publishers. Murray, like Dallas, was disturbed at once by some of my more outspoken criticisms of our government and its servants, especially my remarks on the pusillanimous Convention of Cintra,(iii) and by some of my more earthy passages. I had no doubts on either score, and insisted the offending lines should stand. When he joined Dallas in suggesting that the work was flagrantly autobiographical, however, I agreed to change the name, and *Childe Buron* became *Childe Harold*, with just an acknowledgement that it was written by myself.

This done I forgot about it, having more important things on hand. At this distance of time I am amazed by my attitude. Murray was actually offering six hundred pounds for the copyright, a sum which not only would have been acceptable enough at any time, but which that early pointed to my poetry as a possible source of income equal to my rents. And I would have none of it, pointing out that I was the 6th Lord Byron, not some grub street hack seeking to be paid for his labour. (iv) I bestowed the copyright on the always hard-up Dallas, and allowed him to make what profit he could. Then it was off to Rochdale to see what could be done about my other property, the sale of which, I was fast coming to realise, was my only hope of becoming solvent. And was greatly relieved. That the mines there were extremely valuable was undoubted. That they would eventually be mine to dispose of seemed certain. And that I would be able to sell them at a good price seemed equally certain. I returned to Newstead in my best humour since leaving Greece, to be greeted by yet another shock. Fate had twisted my tail, as usual, and added a fourth death to the year's already melancholy tally: John Edleston.

I had not seen Edleston since returning. I had had no wish to do so. In part this was due to the news I had received while in Constantinople; he had sought his pleasures elsewhere and apparently more publicly than was permissible in England – which of the two had piqued me more I would not care to say. But in part it was also due to my own feelings, my own sentiments. I had abandoned Nikky in Malta, but as I have already indicated, my feelings even for him underwent a profound change the moment we left Greece. Perhaps I had played myself out. Perhaps I had realised that however enjoyable a pretty boy might be, he could never be the most important thing in life. Perhaps, indeed, looking for new fields to conquer, I had remembered that

Robert Rushton remained at Newstead awaiting my return. And in the event found that I felt nothing more than friendship for him.

Yet Edleston's death, coming so hard upon the heels of so many others, upset me profoundly. I am a confoundedly sentimental fellow, too much given to looking over my shoulder in a blaze of rose coloured images. Now I could think only of that unforgettable month at Cambridge, of how we had walked and talked and planned. Of what might have been. And as usual I found my solace in verse, and wrote some of my best poetry to his memory, addressing them to the name I had bestowed upon him, Thyrza.

And yet, in the most curious fashion, John's death came as a relief to me. For where is the point in writing a Memoir if one does not explore one's deepest thoughts? Edleston was a delightful memory, but also a sword hanging over my head. Alone of those in England he knew of my secret desires, my secret ambitions. I discounted Hobhouse, not only because he was a friend rather than a lover, but because however much he suspected, he did not *know*. And now that I had sated myself in that direction, and turned my back upon all things carnal, as I supposed, I desired no lurking memory suddenly to appear and confound me.

Business affairs soon called me to London, as well as a letter which arrived from the Irish poet, Tom Moore, issuing me with what amounted to a challenge. It seems this was his second, the first having been despatched while I had been on my travels, and kept in England by my friends who suspected its contents and could see no way of my dealing with the matter while at a distance of several thousand miles. This was galling, as it imputed some reservations as to my courage. Even more annoying was the reason for the quarrel at all. I had no enmity for Moore. Indeed he had long been one of my favourite poets, and it will be remembered that I had used his erotic verses to good effect, as I had supposed, when courting Mary Ann Chaworth. But in *English Bards* I had poked fun at a duel he had once fought, abortively, with Jeffrey of the *Edinburgh Review*. The quarrel had in fact been mended before shots had been exchanged, and the two protagonists had shaken hands. Whereupon the pistols were taken out to be unloaded, and it was discovered that only one had been loaded at all. Now, my reference to the affair had been intended to disparage Jeffrey, the lout who I am still sure was responsible for that damning review of my *Hours of Idleness*. (v) I was ignorant of the fact that the pistols had been Moore's, and that he had indeed been twitted with having insured his own survival by using only a single ball. Hence his anger.

I could not of course apologise. At the same time, I was reluctant to kill a man I admired – I could foresee no other outcome were he opposed to so accurate an eye as my own – and especially to kill him over a mistake. I therefore wrote him in reply, informing him of the error, and then of course announcing that my second would call upon him whenever he wished. As I had hoped, this mollified him, and indeed he suggested we meet, which we eventually did at the house of Sam Rogers, (vi) an occasion at which Tom Campbell was also present. The whole event was one of the great days in my life, for here I was, admitted on terms of equality with three of the leading literary men of the time. I found them charming, Moore best of all, and for the next week or two indulged myself in a perfect round of intellectual gatherings. My mind was so stimulated by these events that I allowed myself to be trapped into a metaphysical controversy with dear Hodgson, he being increasingly alarmed at the evidence of Atheism, or at least of a lack of belief in Christianity, as revealed in my writings, I having been incautious enough to permit him a glimpse of *Childe Harold*. I'm afraid we reached no agreement, save that he concluded I was destined irretrievably for the fiery furnace.

More important, my confidence restored on every front, I began once again to interest myself in politics, and determined to speak as soon as I could discover a suitably radical subject.

For a brief while, then, I was happy. I conceived myself settled into a way of life which would continue into the foreseeable future, playing my part in the literary pursuits of London, enjoying my rights, in every sense, as lord of Newstead, eventually selling Rochdale to liquidate all of my debts, and best of all, as time went by, slowly and steadily establishing myself as a man of parts in the Lords, with a future perhaps of ministerial rank and a place in the history books. Ah, what fools dreams make of us all, when stark reality lies just around the corner. There was I, meandering through life, and all unaware that I was standing on top of a volcano, which exploding, would catapult me into an orbit too fast for mortal man. Immediately after Christmas a letter arrived from Dallas informing me that Murray intended publishing *Childe Harold's Pilgrimage* on 1 March, the coming year being 1812.

In fact the announcement of this date dismayed rather than encouraged me. For I was now intent upon fulfilling what at that time was the ambition of my life, to make a major speech in the House. And I was a little bit disturbed, in view of the comments of Dallas and Murray and others – although it was gratifying to know that Gifford had entirely recommended the work (vii) – at the consideration that the levity as well as the critical content of the *Pilgrimage* might reflect adversely on my parliamentary career.

The subject was at hand. The miracles – supposing they are miracles – of the industrial revolution, coinciding as they did with in effect the twentieth year of the longest and hardest war in which this country has ever been engaged, (viii) had caused, as will be remembered, a severe dislocation of industry and an ever increasing burden of hardship was being thrust upon the labouring class. Nowhere was this more readily apparent than in my own county of Nottinghamshire, where the genius of Arkwright and others, enabling one man to do the work of several in the mills, had thrown hundreds out of work and daily threatened the livelihood of hundreds more. Not unnaturally the Luddites, (ix) being *Englishmen*, had resented thus arbitrarily being reduced, with their families, to starvation, and mere protest being useless against the most hidebound government this country has ever had, they resorted to action. Frame burning became the sport of the masses, and the outrage of the propertied classes.

The Tories reacted with typical vigour. Dragoons patrolled the fields, ready to crush the slightest spark of revolution, and a Bill was brought before the Commons, and duly passed by them, inflicting the death penalty on anyone convicted of this most dreadful crime. Here was my signal. The Whigs as a party were opposed, but in the main, I suspected and soon in fact learned, merely because they conceived it their duty to oppose the government in everything, and besides, so Draconian was this new law that they had high hopes it would rebound upon its perpetrators. For me, however, it was a simple act of humanity to combat with all the means at my command so hideous a measure.

I worked at my speech during longer hours than I had ever bestowed upon my poetry. Nor did I intend to be at the mercy of several sheets of paper, but committed the entire declamation to memory, so that when at last I rose to speak I was bubbling with words and with ideas and with energy. And with defiance. Memory took me back to Willie Fletcher and myself standing before the eleven terrible Turks. But here I was alone, and facing a far more numerous band of terrible Tories. Yet I blasted them to silence with the fury of my eloquence. I

147

began quietly enough, reminding the great men assembled before me that I was "a stranger not only to this House in general, but to almost every individual whose attention I presume to solicit". Then I pressed on to enumerate the horrors the passage of such a Bill would inflict, the obloquy it would bring upon any nation infamous enough to allow such a measure to become law. I spoke of my travels in Greece and Turkey, countries which we are in the habit of regarding as amongst the most oppressed and degraded in the world, and could not help but compare the happy contentment of the average Greek to the misery of the Nottingham workers. And I concluded quite brilliantly, anticipating the Bill become law. "Suppose one of these men," I said, "as I have seen them, meagre with famine, sullen with despair, careless of a life which your Lordships are perhaps about to value at something less than the price of a stocking frame, suppose this man surrounded by the children for whom he is unable to procure bread, is dragged into court to be tried for this new offence, by this new law. Still, there are two things wanting to convict and condemn him; and these are, in my opinion, twelve butchers for a jury, and a Jeffreys for a judge."

I believe they were scandalised. Certainly they unshipped their heaviest guns, Eldon and Harrowby,(x) to answer me. But amongst the Whigs, although there was a certain feeling that my delivery had been over theatrical and lacking the dignity of true parliamentary procedure, my stock rose to a tremendous height.(xi) This was on 27 February. Publication of *Childe Harold* had been put back for some days, but it yet came within a fortnight. And so it was that the young lord who had announced himself as an unknown on the floor of the House awoke one morning to find himself famous.

Murray had printed a first edition of five hundred copies, which I considered sufficiently ambitious. Publication was finally 10 March, and by the thirteenth the entire stock was sold out. And from the very start the discerning public elected to discover myself in its hero, and even better, or worse, elected to suppose that every episode described had actually happened, with myself as the central character. It was Southwell over again, on a vastly expanded scale, with every dream of violence or lust or passion or anger which I had ever experienced, and set down, as authors will, suddenly translated in the eyes of the multitude into pure fact, and a young man of twenty-four revealed as a perfect satyr.

The effect upon myself was the more difficult to bear, as I knew I was as guilty as they considered me, but in a different way, for of course the poem contained no mention of Edleston or Nikky. Bearing this burden, which caused me to reflect carefully upon how much I talked, lest I be careless, even upon how much I smiled, I was the more easily identified as the rake of the century by those twittering females who had inebriated themselves upon Harold's adventures, and when I further withdrew into my normal reserve, assisted by a weakness they none of them even suspected to exist, a monumental shyness, had them all wondering why, in view of my accepted past, I was not smiling and paying court to each of *them*. There is no woman in the world can resist such a challenge. The result was that overnight I became the most sought after man in London. A mishap which left me as confused as delighted, and which for some three years, as I have said, had me whirling along in the midst of a hurricane breeze of emotion and recrimination and ambition and disappointment and love and hate as to leave me as you see me now, a man ruined in health and reputation, but one determined to fight his way back into at least his *own* self respect.

My first indication of the sudden fame to which I had acceded arrived in the form of invitations. On a sudden, it seemed, every hostess in London wished to have me in her drawing-room, and there were days – I do not exaggerate – when the street outside my lodgings – I had taken rooms at 8 St James's Street, above a draper by name of Dollman – was crowded with carriages from end to end, every one bearing a delightfully scented envelope with a command to attend this soirée or that ball, this dinner or that reception. Now for all my earlier nonentity, I was not a complete tyro in society. My oratorical prowess had already made me a frequent visitor at Holland House, (xii) where that Whig leader and his wife held sway. Nor were we a purely political gathering, for Elizabeth Fox was something of a bluestocking, and I was as welcome to introduce Rogers and Moore and Campbell to her table as I was to bring myself. But what this Holland House Society largely lacked was feminine company, for the very good reason that like dear Papa's first wife, Elizabeth Webster had cuckolded her husband with the greatest publicity, and with Lord Holland, and after being divorced, had immediately married her lover.

I would not like you to suppose she was behaving in a unique fashion. I suspect that the only husband I have ever encountered without a pair of horns is myself, and that my wife was not the sort of woman to dally is my misfortune, nobody else's. But Lizzie Fox had performed her amours, as I say like Lady Carmarthen, in too public a fashion, and however much she might be regarded as a friend by the wives of the Whig nobility, her house was barred to them by propriety.

Thus, however familiar I might be with male society, I was distinctly nervous at the prospect of finding myself the centre of a group of gabbling females, and this was the first cross my fame had to bear. Holland House had to compete with all the other great hostesses of the day, and I was soon making a nightly entry into such formidable portals as Lady Jersey's,(xiii) Lady Westmoreland's,(xiv) and many others. There I was surrounded, by men and by women, all eager to inspect me, as if I were some strange animal but newly incarcerated in their menagerie, all eager to glance surreptitiously at my foot, all eager to hear me speak, expecting pure poetry and blasphemous experience to hang on every word, and all eager to obtain my opinion on any matter that interested them, most of which were totally unfamiliar to me. What could a poor poet do but preserve the haughty cast of his features, permit himself few words and fewer smiles, while maintaining the dignified good manners demanded of his class? All of which, apparently, convinced everyone that, as was natural in view of my devastating past as revealed in the *Pilgrimage*, their company bored me silly.

Which, such is the perverseness of human nature, but made them the more anxious to return, like moths around a flame. Within a week I was indeed becoming bored by the whole thing, by the succession of faces, young and old, pretty and ugly, and shoulders, and arms, by the succession of inviting eyes and lips and smiles, none of which made the slightest impression upon me for the very simple reason that, in my innocence, I had no idea what they were inviting me to do. I had no suspicion that every one was a whore at heart. These were women of my own class, or even superior to it, for there was the odd duchess amongst them. In any event, I kept reminding myself, I am but a nine days wonder, at once for my rank and my orphanage and my speech and my limp as much as for my poetry, and by the end of this season will be quite forgotten.

Until the evening at Lady Westmoreland's, when my hostess herself appeared before me, leading by the hand a small, slight young woman, with upswept pale gold hair and a remarkably youthful face, not at all pretty but intensely animated.

150

"My dear Lord Byron," Lady Westmoreland began. "I would have you meet. . . ."

At which point the introduction came to an end, for the young woman suddenly freed her hand, permitted me a long and somewhat hostile stare, and then turned and walked away.

CARO – THE FIRST PART

I was intrigued, but nothing more at that moment. She had at the least acted differently to any other woman I had recently met. But I must again emphasise that I did not then appreciate that almost all the giddy females with whom I was surrounded wished to find themselves in bed with me. Indeed, I now realise that during those first weeks of my fame I must have turned down at least a dozen invitations of this nature, merely because I did not recognise them to *be* invitations. My time was more taken up with sifting through the enormous volume of mail I had suddenly started receiving, for a goodly part of it consisted of letters from young women all over the country, stating their love for me in quite unequivocal terms.

In addition, Caro was not the sort of woman to send any man, and least of all this man, home with his head full of lustful dreams. True, her curveless body made me think a trifle wistfully of Caroline or Theresa Macri, but I deemed myself to have outgrown *them*. And also true that Moore and Rogers were willing to gossip about her, and describe her as quite an eccentric, but I had no idea what they meant. What was undeniable was that although she was a Ponsonby, and therefore a descendant of one of the oldest families in the kingdom, she had married William Lamb, eldest surviving son and therefore heir of Lord Melbourne, even if the gossips would have it that he was not that gentleman's son at all, such being the habits of feminine nobility.(i) Now the Lambs were *not ancien régime*. Their blood had only very recently turned blue, and had gained this distinguished colour through the medium of lending money at exorbitant rates of interest, a profession frowned upon by their peers – mainly because *they* had no cash available to lend – and certainly not calculated to make the family any more attractive to a victim of the practice, like myself. In addition to all this, Caro was not only older than I, but she was a mother into the bargain.(ii) And yet this was to be the

152

woman who more than any other changed the entire course of my life.

After our first encounter, several days passed until, on visiting Holland House, I discovered her sitting with my host and hostess.

"Lord Byron," said milady. "I understand you have not yet met Lady Caroline Lamb."

I bowed over her hand, but could not resist a question. "The offer of an introduction was made to you before, Lady Caroline. May I ask why you then rejected it?"

She raised her head. Her face was pale, but there was a peculiar sparkle in her hazel eyes. "I changed my mind."

"Caroline is the most unpredictable of women," Lord Holland remarked, no doubt to prevent my taking offence.

"All women are unpredictable, my lord," I rejoined. "It is their most delicious quality." And discovered that my newest acquaintance was staring at me, nor did she either blush or look away when discovered.

"And what is *your* most delicious quality, Lord Byron?" she inquired, while I was discovering that her voice, a delightful drawl encumbered with an even more delightful lisp, was the most fascinating thing about her. Fool that I was, I should have understood from past experience that once a voice attracted me I was done.

"Insincerity," I told her. "It is an essential accompaniment of writing poetry."

She smiled. "As is wit, no doubt." She rose. "I am to ride."

I bent over her hand once again, inhaled her perfume, and quite without knowing why, murmured, "I should feel the poorer were our conversation not to continue, at your pleasure."

"I shall be at home tomorrow morning at eleven, Lord Byron," she said, and was gone.

Next day I duly took my carriage to Melbourne House, an erstwhile residence of the Duke of York.(iii) Here the entire family was ensconced, the senior Melbournes on the ground floor, William Lamb and his wife and son on the first. A somewhat unusual and to my mind unnatural arrangement, but as I was so soon to learn this was an unusual and somewhat unnatural family. Indeed it was on this very day that I made the acquaintance of the most unusual and unnatural member of it, for as I limped up the stairs to the first landing, I passed an open door, and encountered a maid, all blushes and curtsies. And heard a voice from within.

"Who is the gentleman, Louise?"

I handed her my card without saying a word. She giggled, and curtsied some more.

"Lord Byron, my lady."

"Ah," said the voice. I could not see into the room, and I would not deliberately look, but I knew I was being inspected, and from top to toe. Yet as nothing further was said, and the maid was withdrawing, I continued my climb, and was announced into the junior *ménage*.

Here, to my chagrin, I found not Lady Caroline, as I had antici-pated, but both Rogers and Moore.

"Poet's corner," said Irish Tom.

"I do assure you that I have no intention of intruding," I said, somewhat coldly, for I really was put out, having hoped for a *tête-à-tête* with the lady.

"Nor are you, my lord," Rogers agreed. "It is we who are appar-ently the intruders. Why, her ladyship was here with us but a moment ago, having just come in from riding, and being somewhat dishevel-led and hot. We she would talk to, but the moment *your* name was announced she scuttled from the room to change."

Which quite mollified me, the more so as within minutes Caro herself returned, in a clean gown and with her face glowing from the application of soap and water. Yet was the morning entirely unsatis-factory. The conversation was brilliant enough, but there was too much of it, and in my heart I knew I had come not for conversation. After a brief while I took my leave. She accompanied me to the door.

"I fear you are bored," she remarked softly.

"Not with your company, my lady," I said. "My friends I see every day. I had hoped. . . ." I paused to smile at her.

She did a most extraordinary thing, raising her finger to brush it across my lips. "When you smile, you are beautiful," she said, and hesitated herself, looking slightly shocked at what she had said. Then she seemed to collect her thoughts, and flushed.

"Perhaps I could call again," I said. "I am free this evening. Eight o'clock?"

"My dinner hour."

"Ah. Well then. . . ."

"But you shall be welcome, my lord," she assured me.

"Dinner, my lady?"

"You need not eat." She had apparently heard of my abstemious habits. "*I* dine alone. Your conversation would no doubt save the

154

meal from being tedious." Once again the quick flush. "I shall be alone, Lord Byron. I do promise you."

Thus I paid my second and more fateful visit to Melbourne House. It was yet March, and dark by seven. The stairwell was dim, even with its flickering candles; I succeeded in passing that first landing without interruption and to my gratification was clearly expected, for the door swung open before I could knock, and a page, a young and pretty boy, resplendent in scarlet and sepia, was taking my hat and coat and stick, and then showing me into the dining-room. Where a large mahogany table was empty save for Lady Caroline, seated at the very end, although there was another cover set. She wore a pale blue tunic over a white linen gown and looked hardly older than twelve.

"My lord," she said. "You are the most punctual of men. And I had not expected you to be." She was in fact half-way through a light supper.

I bowed over her hand. How my heart thumped. I knew I was the veriest tyro at the sport which was rushing upon us; she supposed I was the blackest rake walking the streets of London. And I did not even know what I proposed, what I wanted, what I dared.

"Will you take something?" she invited.

"Thank you, I have already eaten." I glanced around me. "Your husband is not at home?"

"Dear William is never at home," she said. "A glass of wine?"

"Thank you."

"You may serve the wine in the drawing-room, Charles," she instructed the hovering pageboy, and I held her chair for her as she rose. "I live a solitary life, my lord, save for those friends who come to call, and for my son, of course. But he is not very well." (iv)

I walked at her side. "I am sorry to hear that."

She glanced at me. "As *you* were not very well as a lad, I am told."

"On the contrary," I said. "I was as strong as an ox."

Once again the quick glance. "Oh. I. . . ."

"Was judging me by my misfortune, perhaps," I said, beginning to regret that I had come.

"A limp is hardly a sign of ill health, my lord," she said, seating herself upon a settee, and motioning me beside her. "It was a tale I had heard, and like all tales, is now proved false. I had hoped it was true, because then I could suppose that my George would eventually grow to be as full of health and vigour as you undoubtedly are." She allowed me a quick smile. "Perhaps even as full of genius."

Which threw me into confusion and dissipated my pique. I could only flush and attempt to murmur some platitude.

"But you are," she insisted. "I have read *Childe Harold*. There was genius in every word." She raised her glass, Charles having been in attendance. "I would like to toast its success."

"That is already assured," I said, somewhat brashly. But I drank the toast, and discovered that Charles had withdrawn, although the double doors into this large room remained open. And indeed for the first time I noticed the room itself, which was a trifle over-furnished so as to suggest a vulgarity of taste, but was certainly large, and lush, and comfortable. And seated in the centre of it as we were, our conversation at the least was sure to remain private.

Caro leaned back with a sigh, considering her half empty glass. "I should like to write," she said, and gave one of her quick smiles. "Or do you suppose such accomplishment beyond woman?"

"On the contrary," I protested, never having considered the matter.

"I should like to do so many things," she said, sitting up again. "You have travelled. Clearly, from your writings. I should like to travel." She rested her elbow on the arm of the settee, her chin on her hand. "I should like to have visited Constantinople."

"Women in the east do not enjoy the freedom that they do here," I pointed out.

She smiled, dreamily. "Oh, if I travelled, *when* I travel, I shall do so as a *man*."

My turn to sit up straight.

"I could easily pass for a boy," she said, quite unaware that she might have surprised me. "And think what an adventure that would be, my lord. They have a way with boys, have they not, in the east? They would find me already prepared."

This time her cheeks did faintly flush, as she glanced at me. While I was speechless.

She waved her hand and set down her glass. "I say what I think, and people are shocked by it. Are you shocked by it, Byron?"

It was the first time she had used my name.

"I. . . ." I chewed my lip. "I am delighted."

"You are a poor liar." She got up, took a few steps away from me, then turned to come back. "You *are* a poor liar. Why do you stay? I will certainly shock you some more."

Impossible, I thought. "I do assure you, Lady Caroline. . . ."

"My friends call me Caro," she interrupted. "Caro William, if identification is necessary to separate me from my sister-in-law, Caro George."(v)

"I should be honoured."

She stood above me, considering me, one finger on her chin. "When you smile," she said once again, "you are beautiful. When you do not smile, you are no less beautiful, but it is a dark, sinister beauty. As your poetry suggests that you are a dark, sinister man. *Are* you a dark, sinister man, Byron?"

Her conversation was really the most alarmingly direct I had ever encountered. It was at the same time the most invigorating I had ever encountered. And I was becoming more confident, more master of myself. "A man cannot help what he is, Caro. He is usually made so, not born to it. In my case, perhaps, I suffer from both."

Once again the long consideration. Then without warning she sank to her knees, leaning against mine. "If I loved," she said, very softly, "it should be such a man."

Here was an invitation far too clearly stated to be overlooked even by a simpleton like myself. I leaned forward to kiss her lips, and a moment later was irretrievably lost.

(How simple to say. And no doubt the eager multitude, should they ever read these words, passionate as they are for *romance* no matter how great the improbability, will accept it as such. A kiss, and immediately two minds, two bodies, two souls, are as one.

But I had been kissed before. And since. And, God willing, I shall be kissed again. There are women, there are men, who with a kiss can indicate a multitude of emotions. But the gamut is limited. A kiss can accomplish so much, a kiss can accomplish so little. Below and above, there are realms into which the mere touch of lips, the mere intimacy of tongues, cannot attempt. That I became lost with Caro in a matter of moments had nothing to do with our lips.

The touch was delightful. Her breath was delightful. Her tongue was entirely knowledgeable without being overbold. And while our mouths yet held one another, she raised herself from her lowly situation, placing her hands into mine and inviting my assistance, which was readily granted. A moment later she was in my lap, legs drawn

157

up, and our kiss was gaining in intensity, while my hands, as man's hands are wont to do, slipped across the bodice of her tunic, seeking a path to breast and nipple. The journey was undoubtedly difficult, as there was no obvious way through the realms of material, and I was hoping to be shown, as she was obviously most passionately endowed, when to my utter surprise her hand closed on mine, to lift it from its goal, and replace it *on her ankle*, this having been exposed in the course of our set-to.

Consider the implications. A touch on the wrist, a squeeze of the hand, invites a man's hand onward and upwards. He knows then that swelling breast and quivering nipple is within his reach, provided only he proceeds with caution and with love and with gentleness. He does *not* know whether such intimacy will lead to what he seeks most of all, at least when in the company of a lady; my experience *with* ladies, such as Constance Spencer-Smith, had led me to understand that such an ultimate lay a long way in the future.

But the invitation, from exposed ankle, can lead only one direction.

And then consider, that this was a *Lady*, and one of the best born in the land. Who thus encouraged my hand to seek its glory in its own way. For a moment I was quite paralysed, but she continued to hold my lips with hers, to vent her passion upon my tongue, to move her body against mine. Once again the invitation was implicit.

I encountered silk clad calf, and silk clad knee; the folds of her gown and her petticoat closed over my wrist and my forearm. I found silk clad thigh, and then a garter, and then, dare I believe it, naked flesh. Here was experience enough. In my many tumbles, I had certainly touched feminine thighs and feminine buttocks. But this was in the act of completing my own gratification. Here my cocker was trapped within my breeches, crushed by her weight, to be sure, but completely separated from her glory. This voyage must be undertaken by hand alone. And from her anxiety as she kissed me there could be no doubt that she wished me safe to harbour. I slipped between, found wisps of the purest silken hair clinging to her groin, and a wet dampness beneath. There I paused, totally at sea, totally unable to continue, from sheer ignorance, and she took her lips from mine, for an instant.

"Move, please move," she whispered. "But don't stop."

I slipped my hand to and fro, now so far as to grasp buttock, now forward to caress hair, and was rewarded with a series of sighs, such as I knew I had heard before, but all too seldom, and never so convincingly, and then she gasped, and her lips left mine, and I felt her breath filling my ear. And stared in horror at the page, standing in the doorway.

But however great her ecstasy, Caro had seen him too, and in one instant had scooped a commonplace book from the table behind the settee, placing it on my lap, while sliding from that perch herself to sit beside me and turn the pages most earnestly, while my hand remained trapped in that most magnificent of valleys.

She raised her head. "Yes, Charles?" she asked, with quiet seductiveness.

"My lady rang?" inquired the scurvy fellow.

"I did not ring," she said. "But as you are here, Charles, you may as well fill our glasses."

This he did, while my fingers remained caught in that perfumed and unforgettable trap, and then withdrew.

"*Did* you ring?" I asked.

She smiled, and kissed my chin. "No. But I instructed him to enter at a certain hour. After all, you might not have been all I dreamed of."

"And was I, all you dreamed of?"

"All," she assured me. "Providing you do not stop now."

"And what of me?" I asked. "Am I a creature of stone?"

"Your turn will come," she promised me. "But not here. Not tonight. I will come to you, where we may be alone. This I promise, whenever I am able. We shall *love*, Byron, because you can love. Believe me that."

And so was I initiated into the pleasures of woman, than which there can be nothing finer.) (vi)

I returned home in a fine frenzy, having promised to visit her again on the morrow.

(And this despite the fact that my cocker was totally unsatisfied, and like to explode into my breeches or into my hand. Yet I touched him not at all, nor sought solace elsewhere. I had learned, on the instant, that there is more to love than the mere satisfaction of self. To have that trembling, noble creature literally melt into my hand was a joy I had never suspected to exist. To accomplish such an ecstasy in mutual happiness was clearly a heaven to which I could now aspire. I retired to my bed, and considered all the females I had known. Now I understood what had driven Caroline Cameron from my side. Now I felt like Adam, when Eve had pressed upon him the fruit of the Tree of

Knowledge. Now, on a sudden, childhood fancies, and callow selfishness, were behind me, and I had become in an instant a man.)

What else could I but love, adore, worship the creature who had made me thus? So she was married, my elder, not particularly beautiful. She was mine, or she clearly intended to become mine, in a fashion no other woman had even considered.

I could hardly wait for the morrow, and was only abashed to discover Rogers upon my doorstep. "I took the liberty, my lord," the wretched fellow informed me, "as I am attending Lady Caroline's, and I assumed you would be also."

I nearly pitched him straight through the door, and then refrained. For after all, it was necessary for us both, Caro and I, I mean, to maintain appearances. No doubt she had already arranged it that we should eventually find ourselves alone. "It shall be my pleasure, Sam," I assured him. "We shall travel in my carriage."

The day, I remember it well, and for a multitude of reasons, because in point of fact it was one of the half dozen most important days of my life, fully worthy of standing beside those other unforgettable occasions, the date of a man's birth, his attaining the age of maturity, his wedding day – to which it led directly – or indeed his day of death, was 25 March, the year 1812, with Bonaparte already trudging hopelessly towards Moscow.(vii) As I trudged towards my Waterloo.

Not entirely unwittingly. For as we entered Melbourne House, and essayed to climb the stairs, me listening for the sound of that imperial voice once again issuing from behind the door, and in my new found understanding of femininity, wondering if *it* had ever gasped its love in such frenzied tones – what *knowledge* I had suddenly gained – I tripped, and fell to my knee, which is universally recognised as the worst of omens.

"Are you injured, my lord?" Rogers inquired, helping me to my feet.

"Not physically," I said. "I know not what it holds for the future."

"William stumbled," the good fellow pointed out, "and yet gained the kingdom against all the odds."(viii)

I preferred not to conjecture, and a moment later we were shown into the same withdrawing-room where I had known such joy the previous night. But what a transformation had taken place. All the furniture was pushed back against the wall, a small orchestra scraped away at their fiddles, and the centre of the room was filled with posturing couples, some twenty of them, grasping each other in the most lascivious fashion as they indulged in the waltz, that new craze which had just penetrated our shores from iniquitous Germany.

Rogers of course was immediately for finding a partner and indulging. I was scandalised, both on behalf of the general indecency of the whole affair and because my charmer, far from making a special journey to the door to greet me, but waved an airy hand and continued to lavish her body upon the hands and arms of an utter lout. Had I then dreamed yesterday? Was this the woman who had whispered her love to me, while sitting on my lap? In my confusion I sank to a sofa, perhaps the very sofa on which we had reached such ecstasy, and found myself next to a young woman.

"Lord Byron," she announced, looking very surprised, cheeks pink and breath threatening to flee.

"I have that misfortune," I groaned.

"I am Anna Isabella Milbanke," she said, and when it became obvious that such information meant nothing to me, she added, "I am Lady Melbourne's niece." And when this also failed to elicit any great comment on my behalf, my swinging brain being a little uncertain as to who exactly Lady Melbourne was, she continued yet again. "I have just finished *Childe Harold*, my lord, and found it most interesting. Shall I tell you why?"

In a space of seconds I had met my doom, all unwittingly, and even more unwittingly, been unable to discern, from that so exact delineation of herself, from that so confident determination to give me her impression of my genius, that this girl was the most unusual I was ever to meet – far more so than Caro herself – sent by a malign Fate to procure my destruction, if such a thing could possibly be accomplished. (ix)

161

CARO – THE SECOND PART

"I'm sure I would be flattered to hear your opinion," I lied.

"Well," she said, "I found the poetry very fine. Very fine indeed. But it was not the most interesting part. That was the character of Childe Harold himself."

"Indeed?" I inquired, expecting a diatribe.

"There was a tortured soul," she remarked, a dreamy expression coming over her face, and to tell the truth, she was not at all bad looking, her features handsome rather than pretty, her dark brown hair very luxurious, her figure, so far as I could gather, plump and possibly even voluptuous. "I see him as a man trying to escape from the curse of his background, his upbringing, perhaps the weaknesses in his own character."

This from a girl younger than myself.(i) I was quite amazed, and while remaining in stunned silence, received a sidelong glance and a quick smile.

"Am I very wide of the mark?"

"Why," I began, considering the matter, when we were interrupted by my charmer, flushed and exhilarated and panting from the dance, which made her decidedly attractive.

"Byron," she said. "Will you not waltz?"

My anger returned on the instant, and I heaved myself to my feet. "No, my lady," I said. "I will not waltz, because I do not waltz, because I *cannot* waltz, as a glance at my person would convince you. What is more, I abhor the idea of the dance, and so will bid you farewell."

She stared at me in total surprise, and I turned to Miss Milbanke. "Your servant," I said, and limped for the door.

Where I was joined by Rogers, who had overseen although he had not overheard, as I had spoken as quietly as possible.

"Whatever is the matter?"

"That is no company for me," I said, as I went down the stairs.

"Indeed, I would have said so from the start. Nor for Miss Milbanke. You would do better to cultivate her."

"She is too intelligent for me."

"Perhaps." He opened the door of my carriage for me. "Yet is she a great heiress. She'd set your affairs in order for you." He winked. "All of them."

Impertinent fellow, I thought as I drove off. At that moment, marriage, to any female, was the furthest thing from my thoughts. I would have liked to ape Hussein bin Hassan, but with the entire sex in my bag, ready to be dropped into the briny. And to think that only the previous night she had reached ecstasy at my touch.

I reached my rooms in a frenzy of anger and despair, commanded Fletcher to bring me a bottle of claret, and sat down with my pen. But for once even the Muse was absent. And for what, I kept asking myself? The woman was not even attractive, except when in the grip of her emotions. While she was undoubtedly far too forward for me.

I finished my bottle, staring morosely at the wall, and was alerted by a knock on the door.

"I will not be disturbed," I said.

"Begging your pardon, my lord," Willie said. "But there is a young gentleman to see you."

I turned my head. "Young gentleman? What young gentleman?"

"Well, as to that, my lord, I doubt he *is* a gentleman. He is a page, my lord."

"A page? Ha." She wished to make amends. "He will have a message for me," I said. "Bring it in and give the fellow a shilling."

"Begging your pardon, my lord, but he says the message is by word of mouth, and must be delivered to you alone."

"He does, does he?" I pushed back my chair and got up, stumped to the doorway. "Out with it, boy." For he was undoubtedly Caro's; he wore the scarlet and sepia uniform I had observed the previous night, and might have been the same fellow Charles.

Except that he was not. For when he raised his head, I found myself looking into those startling hazel eyes that belonged to my beloved.

I was so surprised, and dismayed I could not speak. For however wonderful it was to see her, to have her here in my own rooms, my imagination could not cope with the risk to both our reputations.

"My mistress instructed me to deliver her message to you personally, my lord," she said. "If you wish to hear it."

I pulled myself together. "Of course I do, young fellow. Charles, is it? You'll come into my room. Thank you, Willie, that will be all."

Fletcher nodded to himself, and withdrew. I could not help but wonder if after all he suspected my relationship with Nikky. But I was not prepared to consider that at this moment. My heart was pounding. She had come to me. My anger with her dissipated on the instant.

She stepped into my bedchamber, and I closed the door, and turned the key in the lock. She faced me.

"You do not look very pleased to see me."

"I am appalled at the risk you run."

"And do you not consider love a risky business, Byron?"

"Oh, my sweet," I groaned, taking her in my arms. I kissed her hair, each ear, each eye, her nose, her chin, and her lips. I lifted her frail form from the floor to hold her in my arms.

"Oh, Byron," she whispered in my ear. "How I love you, Byron. How I adore you. How can I ever apologise to you for this morning?"

"I was foolish."

"You were right," she insisted. "I was the foolish one. How can I ever atone to you? I shall never waltz again. I swear it. Byron, my sweet. . . ."

(I set her down; her fingers were already tearing at her buttons. I attended to my own clothing, watched her nakedness loom before my eyes. Slender as a boy, to be sure, with hardly any breasts at all, her flesh the palest of white beneath which blue veins hurried on their way. Pale gold hair, a match to her head, thatched her groin, so fair was her colouring. Her legs were splendid, too long for her body and beautifully shaped. They were the most beautiful thing about her. But not quite. Her beauty lay in *herself*, her enthusiasm, her abandon, her utter femininity.

I had her in my arms again, naked, moving slowly towards my bed while she squirmed on my chest and arranged for cocker to find its way between her legs. But when she hit the mattress and fell backwards, she was reaching down to arrange him on her belly.

"No haste, Byron," she begged. "No haste." She kissed me. "Use your hands."

As I had done the previous night. But I was still a novice at this game, and to be guided, to grasp her buttock while my wrist lay between her thighs, so that she could saw herself to her heart's content, and this time watch, where last night I had been afraid to look, the colour flare in her cheeks, her eyes dilate with pleasure, and show their whites, her tongue seem to swell and fill her mouth, which in turn flopped open. And know the utter delight of conquest myself, as cocker swelled with blood and jammed himself against her fluttering belly. How many opportunities for similar glory had I wasted, I thought. How many women could have lain in my arms, unable to contemplate any other existence. Had I only known.

She smiled, and kissed me for a while. "Come inside," she said. "But gently, Byron. Gently."

Once again she guided me. "I cannot bear your weight," she said. "Use your elbows."

I kept my body just touching her, while I slipped in and in and in, sadly disobeying her instructions for I could not hold myself in check. And indeed I was spent long before I had intended it, and then my weight did descend upon her, so that she gasped, and pushed against me, and I rolled away to lie on my back.)

For a moment there was no sound, save for our breathing. Then she rose on her elbow. "What do you think of Annabella?"

I had no idea of whom she was speaking. "Do I know the lady?"

"My cousin-in-law, Miss Milbanke."

"Is her name Annabella? I thought. . . ."

"She was christened Anna Isabella. But we have shortened it. Did you like her?"

"She seemed a shade too intelligent."

Caro bit me on the chin. "Did you *like* her?"

"I have not considered the matter. I *love* you."

"If you liked her I would jam a knife in her ass," Caro said, with sudden vehemence. "Anyway, she would bore you. She wishes to talk only of things she has read, problems she had solved. She does not wish to *do*. Stay away from her, Byron."

"Willingly. But oh, my sweet, to have you here . . . suppose we are discovered?"

"Would you be ashamed to be discovered with me, Byron?"

What a terrible question. "By no means. I. . . ."

"I would like the world to see me here, Byron, naked on your chest. I would like most of all my foul mother-in-law to see me here. I would like her to walk in that door this instant. I would like to run down the street and up the steps of her house, naked as I am."

165

She gave some indication of getting up, to my alarm. I hastily hugged her closer.

"Were we discovered," I said, "I might have to kill your husband in a duel. I should not like to do that."

She rested her head on my shoulder. "You are right. William is a dear man. He neglects me. But all men neglect their wives. Will you neglect your wife, Byron?"

"I have not considered the matter."

"But you must. You will. You will marry, and I will lose you."

"I will not marry. Not while I can hold you in my arms."

"Oh, Byron," she whispered, settling herself once again.

"But we must be cautious, my sweet," I said. "I have already been closeted in here, with a page, so far as Fletcher knows, for upwards of an hour. I will be arrested for sodomy."

She raised her head to stare at me.

"So you must go, my dearest," I said. "Until we can meet again."

"Will we *share*, Byron?" she asked. "I must share. Everything. I must have your soul. And I will give you mine."

"We will share, Caro."

"Promise."

"My word."

"Then I will go. Next time, my page will be a page. And he will tell you when we may meet again."

"I will come to the ends of the earth," I promised, in a fine fettle of romantic fervour.

"Then make me happy, once again, before we part."

"I wish I could. But I very much fear. . . ." A short lifetime of dissipation had left cocker unable to do his duty at periods shorter than three hours, if then.

She smiled, and kissed me on the mouth. "You have hands, Byron. I will settle for hands."

I should repeat, I was never in love with Caro. I know that now. I knew that very shortly. But for a brief, mad midsummer's spell I mistook my fascination, my utter delight in her wild, irrational yielding, for love. And there could be no doubt – possibly there *can* be no doubt – that she loved me with a fervour like to bend the already weakened fibres of her brain.

For some three months, then, she filled my every thought. I lived from Caro to Caro, terrified when, as happened often enough, and at all hours of the day and night, she visited my rooms in the guise of a page, gloriously happy when I was able to call upon her at her home, and discover the place empty save for the lads who so willingly made themselves scarce. I saw none of my male friends, except at soirées where Caro was on my arm, I abandoned correspondence, even with Augusta, while as for poetry, I could not understand how I had ever wasted the time in such a puerile pursuit.

We loved. We fondled each other's bodies, we searched each other's minds. She told me of her childhood in Italy, of her dreams, even of her brief and stormy affair with Godfrey Webster.(ii) She told me of her nights with Willie Lamb, and rendered me half wild with jealousy. She told me everything that she did, from sitting on the pot to talking with her child. Her desire to share was the most extravagant thing about her.

And she expected such confidence in return. Alas, weak vessel that I am, and far too delighted at being able to share myself, I reciprocated with abandon. I spoke of secrets – Edleston, Clare, Nikky – which I had supposed ever locked in my heart. Lovers do not contemplate the future, except as a continuation of the present. Lovers do not *fear*. Not while they are both sure of the other.

And we *outraged* society. A fact of which I at least was blissfully unaware. For this great game in which we indulged, even if it was played with varying degrees of fervour by everyone of our acquaintance, was ruled by a rigid set of laws. A wife's eldest child must be her husband's. Well, Caro had fulfilled that requirement. (Nor, such was her addiction to masturbation rather than intercourse, was she likely to perpetrate a bastard, at least at my hands.) But an affair, however widely it may become known, must be conducted with discretion. A husband should never be forced to the point where he will call his cuckolder out. Else were all London society decimated at a stroke.

And indeed, at the end of it all I might well have found myself looking down the barrel of Willie Lamb's pistol had I not finally been brought up short. It happened one evening when I was climbing the stairs of the Melbourne residence, knowing that Caro waited above, alone and anxious, and passed that never-to-be-forgotten door on the landing, and encountered the same maid as before.

"My lord," she said, curtseying low. "My mistress invites you to visit her."

"I have a prior engagement."

"But I insist," said Lady Melbourne, she having been standing in the shadows of the doorway. "After all, Lord Byron, should we not know each other, as I at the least know so much about *you*."

I was in a difficult position, as this was my mistress's mother-in-law, and in addition chatelaine of the entire establishment. But my stomach filled with lead. Clearly I was in for a very unhappy time.

"The fault is mine, Lady Melbourne," I protested.

"You have been preoccupied," she agreed. "That will be all, Lucille." And she herself walked before me into a small parlour, where she seated herself in an armchair. There were several candles burning in this room, and so for the first time I had the opportunity of actually inspecting her, although to be sure I had seen her from a distance from time to time. But such distant views had been coloured by my knowledge of her, that she was Yorkshire country stock, a Milbanke, who had married the moneyed Lambs and by the power of her own personality risen to the top of the social tree, whatever the numerous obstacles placed in her way. But those glorious days were well in the past, and she was scarce less than sixty. (iii) So then, what did I expect?

I have no idea, save that she was totally unlike *any* expectation. No doubt her face was lined, but the ravages of age were skilfully concealed beneath her powder; her arms, which were bare, for she wore a ball gown, were plump and well rounded, her bust still full, and her thighs no larger than a middle-aged matron's should be. In addition her features remained very fine, a trifle bold, and completely dominated by her eyes, which were large, and dark, and imperious.

While I was thus engaged, *she* was inspecting *me*, and then motioning me to a seat. "You *are* a handsome fellow," she said.

"You delight in flattery, my lady."

"And you?"

"I prefer the truth. You are a beautiful woman."

Her expression, which was a trifle severe in repose, broke into a most charming smile. "Almost I can understand what Caro sees in you." The smile died. "Are you determined to ruin her?"

"My dear Lady Melbourne. . . ."

"Or if not her, at least yourself," she continued as if I had not spoken. "What do I hear of you? A promising young man. An able speaker. A man with prospects. Even able to write poetry, if that is an accomplishment for which a nobleman should wish to be remembered. And you are handsome with it, and surround yourself with an air of mystery which is becoming. All of London is at your feet, Lord

Byron. Who knows, all of England is at your feet. And your greatest ambition seems to be to throw all of it away."

"My dear Lady Melbourne. . . ."

"It is not enough," she continued, "that you conduct this affair with the most flagrant openness. Do you not suppose all of London knows Caro comes to your rooms? Oh, that fault is hers. The fault is yours for humouring her. She is not strong in the head. If you are not already aware of that, I am telling you now. She is excitable to the point of lunacy. You have not observed this yet. But you should have. All is plain sailing at the moment. But should the slightest obstacle be placed in the way of her ambitions, you will see a different Caro. Believe me, that one will terrify you."

This barb in fact struck home more shrewdly than she knew, for I was not so unobservant that I was unaware that Caro was not a woman to be thwarted in any desire. Even the slightest interruption of her pursuit of sexual pleasure could have her quite vehement.

No doubt it showed in my face, for Lady Melbourne's tone softened. "I have spoken at length, and most disagreeably. Believe me, Byron, I seek your salvation no less than my own, and that of my family. Tell me who you would bed. I could procure her for you. No matter who she is," continued this quite astonishingly bold woman. "If you would but exchange her for Caro. Why," she said, and once again vouchsafed me that unforgettable smile, "I would replace her myself, my lord, were you so minded."

Another quite astounding proposal, and one I should have fled without hesitation. But it came in the midst of a quite astounding conversation, which was taking place in the midst of a quite astounding summer, the sort of halcyon days one dreams about but seldom manages to experience. Fortunately for poor mankind; we are not intended to fly quite so close to the sun without melting.

"My dear Lady Melbourne," I temporised, which she took to be acquiescence.

"Then kiss me, you foolish boy," she said, and leaned forward.

(As I stepped back into history. This woman had cut her swathe through London society, through all the bloods of England, through, if rumour were to be believed, the Prince Regent's own bedchamber, before I had been born. And remained as anxious, indeed, as *hasty* a lover as in those far off days. She required hands, certainly, but in no Caro-desperate fashion. Hands for her were means to an end. My fingers were guided first of all to her gown, to be unfastened, while her tongue explored my mouth, and her hands slid inside my jacket to caress my ribs and my back.

"Show me," she whispered. "Show me how Childe Harold makes love."

Once again I was at the mercy of that accursed book. Or was it that inspired book? I released yards of material, but when I would have stripped her she gently restrained me, and had me raise her skirts to her waist. For her legs remained very fine, to be sure, but well shaped, and *active*. As her bottom was firm. And what am I to say of those gates of paradise which she exposed to me as she sank back on to her settee, holding my hand so that I was compelled to follow? Her hair was tinged with grey, a totally foreign phenomenon to me, but none the less attractive; her scent was sweet, so sweet indeed that I understood she must have deliberately perfumed herself for the occasion, and thus our encounter was no casual accident.

And when I would have sent my fingers in advance, as I was by now experienced in doing, she allowed me but a second's exploration, and then whispered, "Is Childe Harold shy?"

A moment later I was in, and she was rocking her body in a series of great sighs. It was all a little hasty for me, used as I was by now to a lengthy process in which my own satisfaction came at the end of a long masturbatory bout, and so I sawed to and fro, the while enjoying the pleasure of watching so magnificent a matriarch becoming my slave, of uncovering still splendid breast and tumescent nipple, of kissing eye and mouth and nose before exploding with a violence I had never previously attained.)

Then for a while we lay together, cheek to cheek. "Promise me," said my charmer.

"It cannot be done suddenly."

"I do not expect it to be done suddenly." She raised herself on her elbow, discovered, it seemed for the first time, that I had disarranged her bodice, and pulled my head into that delightful valley to half smother me. "So long as it is done, Byron." Then she released me and sat up. "And do not forget my other promise."

A dizzying experience, and one from which I was not to escape unscathed, although I did not realise it at the time. Indeed for the next three and a half years I was virtually this woman's slave, mentally, if not physically. And suffered for it. I do not mean that she was a *bad* woman, in the real sense. But she was confoundedly meddling, and confoundedly determined to have her own way, and in a position of wealth and power to accomplish this ambition.

Our clothing restored, she herself showed me to the door. "Write to me, Byron," she commanded as she kissed me goodnight.

Away from her side, I at last had the opportunity to think. And realised I had been seduced, purely to interfere in my relationship with Caro. I was so angry I nearly returned to Melbourne House on the instant, for she would undoubtedly still be waiting, and there would have to be explanations. But I was exhausted, and chose bed instead, and there did not sleep, but reflected at depth and with some uneasiness.

Because much of what Lady Melbourne had suggested rang true. Even I, besotted with my golden haired boy-girl, could see that she was not the most stable of characters. In our brief liaison we had not so far had a cross word, but it was possible to discern the molten rivers running beneath the translucent surface of her radiant personality. And our affair could not continue in its present form for ever. We must either come to a violent parting between ourselves, or between Caro and her husband. And suddenly, that the latter was the more likely was no longer an exciting prospect. Quite apart from a sudden uncertainty as to whether I would wish to undertake a prolonged exile – in the midst of my new-found fame and social fortune – with such an unstable character, there was the dazzling prospect opening up before my eyes of every noble lady in the land beckoning me to her bed-chamber. For if I had so attracted Lady Melbourne, what fields might not lie open to my conquering host? And more, where such a prospect might, a few scant months before, have induced even a feeling of boredom, on the basis that all cats are grey in the dark, I was now understanding this to be a complete misapprehension, clearly only indulged in by those men too dull to understand, or too inhibited to indulge, the preferences of their various partners. I had further to consider that Caro was no beauty, while Lady Melbourne, if undoubtedly one once, was but a relic of her former self. But when I considered all the ladies I had recently met who were beautiful, and wondered what *their* particular preferences might be, and allowed my always overwrought imagination to wander over the prospects at hand, I felt quite dizzy with ambition and expectation. I could even console myself, and my conscience, with the reflection that Lady Melbourne was undoubtedly right, and it would be for Caro's own good to have our affair terminated.

But how, there was the question? In my innocence I assumed that a mere matter of a hint, combined with neglect, would work with her as it had worked with Constance. I wrote her next morning, excusing my non appearance on the grounds of political requirements, as I intended to make another major speech in the Lords. This earned me a fiery epistle, combining her regrets with her understanding with her damnation for my neglect with her encouragement for my future as a minister. And in fact I had not been lying, for I was preparing a speech on the Catholic Claims Bill, once again aligning myself with those unfortunates whom society seemed prepared to consign forever to the netherworld. This was less well received by my Whig friends. The suggestion was that I was becoming too much a radical, whereas in my heart I wondered if the rumours about Caro and myself were not indeed acting to my disadvantage.

It was at this time also, that to add to my distractions, Chrissy Falkland emerged from my past, and from her home in the wilds of Derbyshire wrote me the most passionate letters, the poor deluded girl having assumed from my gift of five hundred pounds a few years previously that I had acted out of love for her, a love she was now determined to convert into marriage. Off-putting replies did not work with her either – she had come to the absurd conclusion that my lines to Thyrza were directed to herself – and I was driven half wild with her endless letters bidding me come to her.

But at least she was too far removed to come to me. Caro lived just round the corner, so to speak, a point I had overlooked. After a fortnight had elapsed since our last meeting, a time I had filled with frenzied activities and with equally frenzied letters of explanation, the one thing I had omitted to take into my calculations came to pass; one evening a scarlet and sepia clad page presented herself at my door.

Willie Fletcher broke the news, because I was with friends, Hobhouse and Moore, the former having just returned from Ireland. He stood in the doorway, rolling his eyes and shrugging his shoulders, muttering about a messenger. It was some seconds before I understood what he meant.

"Tell the lad I'm busy, Willie."

"My lord. . . ." The poor chap was looking positively terrified, clearly afraid that she might force an entry. As I suddenly realised she might very well do.

"If the message is urgent, ask him to wait," I decided. And rolled my eyes myself; clearly she could not wait in the antechamber. "Well, Hobby," I said, "it seems that there is some matter for me to attend to."

"We'll leave of course," said the good fellow, getting to his feet. "I'll have some more tales to tell you when next we meet."

With a pounding heart I ushered them into the antechamber, and found it deserted. A moment later my door was bolted behind them, and she appeared on the garret staircase which led to Fletcher's room, having removed her hat and fluffed out her hair.

"Caro," I said. "We agreed that coming here was far too risky for you."

"And what of your coming to Melbourne House?" she asked, in a deceptively calm tone.

"Well, I . . . I have been most terribly busy," I explained, escorting her into my parlour.

"With other women." It was not a question.

"Oh, dear me, no," I protested. "With parliamentary business. Did you not read my speech?"

"I never read parliamentary speeches."

"Ah, well . . . do pray be seated."

"I did not come here to sit down," she pointed out. "I came here to kill myself."

"Eh? Oh, really, Caro. . . ."

"But before I do that," she said, continuing to speak in a perfectly calm voice, "I am going to kill you."

"Sweetheart," I said. "Why don't we sit down and. . . ."

"And before I do *that*," she went on, "I am going to tear this place apart."

All this while she had not raised her voice, so that I was quite unprepared for the storm which followed. For without the slightest further warning she leapt at my table, where I had been scribbling a few lines and where the draft of another parliamentary speech was lying, and cleared it with a single sweep of her hand, before overturning the table itself and kicking my inkwell across the room, leaving a spatter of blue on my carpet.

I was too bemused to move. And, dare I confess it, the man who had faced eleven terrible Turks without the slightest hesitation was aware of a remarkable feeling of alarm. I did not know exactly how she was to be stopped.

"Books," she said, hardly raising her voice above a whisper, and reaching for my shelves to start a perfect avalanche.

"Glasses," she remarked, upending a tray.

The door opened and Fletcher stood there. "My lord. . . ."

"Get him out of here," Caro commanded, and now she was weeping.

"You'd better withdraw, Willie," I suggested, and he seemed quite pleased to close the door behind him.

"Caro," I begged. "Let us sit down. . . ." Supposing there would be anything left for us to use, for she was at that moment overturning a chair.

"Wine," she said, selecting a bottle of best claret from my sideboard, and from which I had taken but a single glass. "You like wine, do you not, my Byron?" Saying which she stood against me and poured it over my head.

Here at least she was close enough to be resisted, and I seized her wrists. Whereupon the tears became a perfect flood and she collapsed at my feet.

I scooped her up, she was as light as a feather, and both covered in wine as we were, found the remaining chair and sat myself in it. "Caro," I said.

"Byron," she wept. "Oh, say you love me, Byron."

"I love you, Caro."

"Say you will never leave me. Say it."

What could a man, any man, in my position do? "I shall never leave you, Caro."

"Oh, Byron, Byron. Make love to me, Byron. Make love to me. I adore you,.Byron."

(She was fumbling at my breeches while she spoke, but alas, our recent exertions had not been such as to leave me in a terribly amatory state. As she very rapidly discovered.

"You don't love me," she moaned. "You don't love me."

"I adore you, Caro," I vowed. "But sometimes. . . ."

"I will attend to you," she promised, entirely removing my drawers. And indeed she did, realising a dream I had known since childhood, it may be recalled, when I had first watched May at work upon her "Man, Man". Since then only Nikky's lips had ever accomplished my dearest wish. But now Caro got to work, and sent me into a seventh heaven of utter delight. Nor did she desist even when I was fully equipped for battle, but pushed me back into the chair while she continued to kneel before me, and within a few further seconds rendered me incapable of further combat that night, at the end imbibing herself, something I would never have expected.

And then subsiding, her head on my thigh, her body quivering for I believe she had induced her own climax while attending to me.)

"Now you are mine, Byron," she whispered. "Now you are mine. For ever."

I very much feared that she was right.

MY LADY

Sanity returned with the dawn, and with Caro's departure. But it was a very sombre sanity. Because undoubtedly I was lost, whenever in her sublime company. Therefore was I lost unless we could be separated. I said as much to Lady Melbourne, as soon as I could obtain another *tête-à-tête* with her.

"Is she *that* fascinating?" my lady remarked. "I would never have suspected it. But I agree that matters have reached crisis stage. Even Lady Bessborough is asking questions, and she has nothing between her ears save wool."

Lady Bessborough being Caro's mother.

"What's to be done?" I begged. "I fear I am the weakest of men. I desire only to be *governed* by a good woman. You offered me the pick of London's beauties for my bed. You would do better to offer me the pick of England's heiresses for my bride."

"It is a matter I have been considering," she agreed. "But it must be someone close to me. I'd not lose the pleasure of your company, my Byron. Yet finding you a wife will be quite meaningless while you are Caro's slave." She frowned at me, still holding my hand. "Are you *sure* you wish the affair ended?"

"If it can be, without hurting Caro."

"Perhaps," she said brightly, "you are nothing more than an infatuation. In which case the remedy is simple. Separation, as you say. I am sure you have been neglecting your property, your affairs. Why do you not pay a visit to Newstead?"

"Willingly. But she will follow."

"I do not think so. I will arrange for William to take her out to Brocket for a while."(i)

"Well, then . . ." I began, reluctant to abandon the fleshpots.

She shook her head. "Brocket is too close to London. She must know that you are beyond her reach."

I sighed, but accepted the inevitable. And indeed, my affairs certainly needed attending. I had, in fact, and very reluctantly, allowed Hanson to place Newstead on the market, and he was confident of finding me a buyer, and soon, and one prepared to meet our price. Therefore my time at the old place might be limited. Hobhouse accompanied me, but we did not remain immured in the country for very long. As soon as we were informed that Caro had left London we returned. This was mainly on account of politics, for during my brief absence I was elected to the Hampden Club, this being a perfect hive of reformers. Upon my return to town I duly attended this august gathering, into which I had been introduced by a nobleman I knew only slightly, the Earl of Oxford. I could not imagine why he had taken the trouble, although he claimed to have noticed my speeches in the House and to have determined that I was just the man for his revolution, whenever it came. Of course this was a damned lie, and he had been bidden to it by my magnificent Lizzie, but as I had nothing more than a nodding acquaintance with either her or her husband at that moment I was quite flattered. (ii) Until I sat down with them. The reformers I mean. I then realised that while I was, and am, and ever shall be, totally dedicated to reform, of just about everything from the Poor Law to our abominable system of government, I will never be able to feel any affinity for the *reformers*, they appearing without exception as a scurvily petty-minded lot.

The upshot of all this, as I have suggested above, was an invitation to one of Lady Oxford's parties. Here was flattery, at least to someone in my position. With only two exceptions – and sometimes I doubt even that – Liz Harley was the most exceptional woman I ever met. Or even heard of. I knew all about her, of course. How her marital misdemeanours, commencing far sooner than propriety allowed, had surrounded her with a family of the most beautiful children which unkind society referred to as the Harleian Miscellany; how she was at once the most lovely, the most intelligent, and the most witty woman of her age – not that this was designed to impress me greatly or so I thought, as she was past forty by the time I encountered her; (iii) and most important, at this early stage of our acquaintance, how she was the centre of a circle of all the radical minds of England. Indeed, although I came to know her very well very shortly, I have a suspicion that politics were always closer to her heart than sex, and that is saying a great deal.

I attended the soirée, of course. And not to put too fine a point upon it, fell in love.

I am aware that this misfortune would appear to have overtaken me several times in the past. But consider, what is love? It is adoration, based perhaps upon a mental as well as a physical consideration, but dictated entirely by what our feeble minds can at the moment grasp. It is possible I loved May Gray. My brain was undeveloped, I existed by feel, and she was prepared to assist me to do that. I loved Mary Ann Chaworth, because I was just becoming old enough to appreciate female charm. I loved Eldeston, because he supplied that charm and that companionship without any of the disagreeable rivalry which seems inescapable where two members of opposite sexes get together; I loved Caroline Cameron, because in my then state she supplied my every want; and how pale and insignificant the whole crew of them seemed when compared with the possible delights of Haidee.

And so I had become famous, and sought after, and had found myself in love with Caro. I have explained this already. Here was no beauty, but here was nobility, breeding, and above all *knowledge*, on a scale I had not suspected to exist, save in my wildest dreams. But she was as wild and irrational as any dream, and like to be more trouble than she was worth. Yet when I entered Liz's drawing-room I still loved her, this I swear.

Until I had bowed over my hostess's hand. Until I had looked at that raven hair, that flawless complexion, those marvellously chiselled features, that swelling bosom . . . here was Haidee come to life, a Haidee doubled or more likely tripled in age, but perhaps the more beautiful for that. And when I compared what I had heard to what I could see! This woman, from all accounts, would make Caro seem like a virgin in bed, just as she made Caro seem like a village maiden in looks. I could do nothing more than stammer, while she smiled, most graciously, and remarked, in that so quiet, so calm voice of hers, "Lord Byron. I had supposed, for one fearful moment, that you should never tread these boards, so *busy* you have been. But now you are here, why, my season is complete. And you are as pretty a fellow as they claim. Those must be the fullest breeches in all London."

I remember little more of the evening, not on account of the utter abandon of her language – I had been warned of this – nor at the spectacle of such words emanating from such marvellous lips, but mainly because I was confounded to observe that she had already a cavalier in attendance, and he was that absurdly deaf lout, Hamilton. (iv) I staggered home in a state of inebriation, without having taken more than a single glass of wine. To discover that life was not quite so simple as I had fondly hoped and imagined. Caro had also returned to town.

This became apparent to me even as I left her ladyship's house, for as I walked to my waiting carriage there was a hiss from a dark alleyway – so great was the crush of her ball that our equipages were parked all along the street – and as I turned, reaching into the pockets of my greatcoat for a pistol, who should I see but a pageboy, issuing from the shadows, her face wearing that unnaturally *quiet* expression which promised utter disaster.

"Caro?" I gasped.

"Byron," she echoed.

"But. . . ." I looked from left to right at the empty street. Empty, that is, save for the coachmen and cabbies, several of whom were glancing in our direction. "You must be mad."

"I am, mad with love for you," she informed me, by now having reached me to seize my hands. "Oh, Byron, Byron, how could you?"

For a moment I did not understand her meaning, and so landed myself in an even deeper trough. "Well, my sweet," I temporised, "as to that, the lady's husband and I are partners in our ambition to improve the lot of this unhappy country before we descend into actual revolution."

She frowned at me. "Liz Harley?" she demanded. "She is old enough to be your mother. I'll not be jealous of that harridan."

Would she had kept her promise. But for the moment I was greatly relieved. "And am now on my way home, early as you'll see. Caro, this is the most outrageous behaviour. Should it be discovered. . . ."

"I should shriek for joy," she announced, far too loudly. "I care not who finds out, Byron. Oh, Byron, Byron, how could you let us be separated?"

"My dear Caro," I said, speaking as reasonably as I could, while wondering how the devil I was going to cope with the situation, "I had absolutely no say in the matter." For surely a man is allowed a little lie in such circumstances. "I cannot gainsay your own husband."

"You can, and you will," she announced. "I will have no more of it. I see it now, Byron. They mean to drive us apart. They mean to leave no stone unturned to separate us. Well, they shall not succeed. Prepare yourself, my own dear love. I have but a few necessary preparations to make, and I shall be with you, for ever. We shall fly to those eastern parts where you found true happiness, and where I will bring you truer happiness yet. Just be patient for a little while, Byron, and all our troubles will be over."

She stood on tiptoe, kissed me on the mouth, and ran back into the alleyway. After a moment's hesitation I ran behind her, for I really could not permit her to roam the streets of London in the middle of the night, unaccompanied. But when I reached the far end I heard only the clip clop of horses' hooves. No doubt her Charles had been waiting with the mounts.

I returned home in a sad state. Just be patient, she had promised me. And then, an elopement. The ultimate scandal which would prevent my face ever being seen in polite society again. Well, it can be said, this is exactly what has happened to me, and without the excitement or the pleasure of an elopement in the first place. But I am no hand at foretelling the future. And besides, Caro and I were played out. I knew that then. Had *Lady Oxford* suggested an elopement I would have been at her window with a ladder before the sun rose. But Caro . . . dear, sweet, fascinating, unstable Caro? It would have been an act of madness on either side.

But what to do? She was a determined woman, and I could not consider what would happen were I merely to refuse her. I spent a sleepless night, and then was relieved next day when a note arrived by the faithful Charles, somewhat incoherently written, to be sure, but promising me that her wild act had been a result of nerves, and that I need have no cause for alarm. I sank back in sheer relief, and allowed myself to be lulled into a sense of quite false security.

So the summer appeared to pass, peaceably enough. I attended Lady Oxford regularly, but she, although always apparently overjoyed to receive me, gave no further hint that she might be willing to exchange Hamilton for Byron, which was frustrating in itself. That she had use for my talents as a leader of the reform party, however, was obvious, and it was at her house that I had the great pleasure of meeting Princess Caroline, whom I liked enormously, probably because of her miserable married circumstances; certain it is that she was not the most attractive of females.

Remarkably, this meeting was very rapidly followed by one with her husband. At a ball given by Miss Johnson he was there, and I was informed that he wished to meet the author of *Childe Harold*. It may be believed that *I* had no wish to meet *him*, but in the circumstances this was a royal command which could scarce be avoided. I therefore accepted the inevitable, allowed myself to be escorted forward, and was, although I hate to admit it, charmed. He had actually read the poem, and more, revealed himself well acquainted with other poets as well, and went out of his way to flatter me. I even made plans to attend his next levee in order to come to know him better, but I was prevented, to my disappointment. I had no idea then that I was soon to be required to take sides in that most unhappy of all marriages – excepting only my own – and that he and I were in fact never to speak again.

Of course during this period, I also saw Caro quite regularly. We met at balls and receptions, and we had our moments alone together in her house. But she was more carefully watched than before, and these occasions were infrequent. I explained to Lady Melbourne that I was doing my best to end the affair, but that clearly it would take time. I preferred such apologies to be by letter, because when in her presence I felt overwhelmed by her personality and quite prepared to kick Caro down the stairs if she asked me.

But it was a frustrating period. There was I saddled with a mistress I no longer loved, and one who was as like as not to ruin me, desperately in love with the most beautiful woman in London, who smiled at me and persisted in her quite outrageous conversation, but would do nothing more. I could not take her on to the dance floor, as could others, and murmur sweet nothings into her ear as we waltzed. I was at the mercy of *her* willingness to flirt with me, and I had no idea how to proceed, boldness being ruled out of the question by my fear of being laughed at. Liz preferred to laugh, or I should say, to smile, quietly and confidently and sometimes contemptuously, than do anything else. It was this last that I feared. She sailed through life like the proudest of swans, and I was too aware that in many ways I was an ugly duckling.

Yet as I say I was lulled into a sense of security, feeling that Caro's passion had to be on the wane, and that my own fortunes might even be looking up. If I could not get close to Liz, well then there was her daughter Jane, a creature almost as lovely and quite as outspoken as her mother, while she had some claims to be even more intelligent, or at least educated, as she once told me she had learned all of Shakespeare off by heart, and recited quite enough of it for proof. *She* appeared more than willing to reciprocate any advances on my part, and as July drew to a close I seriously considered abandoning the mother for ever in favour of the daughter.

But *as* July drew to a close my world came tumbling down yet again. On the twenty-eighth of that month Charles arrived with a note, very brief and to the point.

"I shall be with you tomorrow. For ever. Caro."

I was horrified. Just when I was seeing my way through the wood, so to speak, utter catastrophe. I sat and stared at the fateful epistle for some time before rousing myself, to send Willie round to Hobhouse's rooms. If ever I needed a friend it was now. "I shall go down to Harrow," I said in my letter. "If you will accompany me."

Back came the reply that of course he would, and indeed that he would attend my rooms at noon. Which seemed to me to be time enough; Caro rose no earlier than did I, normally. And in fact good Cam was at St James's Street before the appointed hour. I was already packed, Fletcher was ready, we had a coach standing by, and were prepared to make the most precipitate of flights, when we were arrested by a thunderous banging on my door.

We gazed at each other like two conspirators about to be arrested, and Hobby ran to the window. The situation was worse than I could possibly have imagined, for outside there was gathered a considerable crowd, all staring at my lodgings. There was nothing for it. "You'd best open the door," I said, and slumped into a chair.

He obeyed, and came face to face with Caro, but no pageboy today. She had decked herself out in the most fantastic of disguises, far more likely to attract attention than to permit her to pass unnoticed. For she hid beneath a very old and well-worn cloak, which was sensible enough, but it only reached her knees, and below it were to be seen scarlet stockings encasing those delightful calves, while if her straw hat was undistinguished enough, she had omitted to remove an emerald pin from the ribbon, so as to cause confusion as to whether she was a lady, whore, or dandy in disguise. In addition her face was flushed and bore every mark of agitation. But this was at least partly at seeing Hobhouse. Without hesitation she continued on her way, up the garret stairs to Fletcher's rooms. He for his part, revealing a streak of cowardice I had not suspected in him, went the other way, *down* the stairs to Dollman's, muttering over his shoulder something about having to buy a new hat. This with a perfectly good beaver sitting on my table.

Thus deserted I went outside myself. "You'd best come in," I said. She came down the stairs, glanced right and left, and entered the apartment, not hesitating in the outer room, but going straight into the bedroom.

"Byron," she declared, discarding her cloak to reveal herself dressed as a page, as usual, and throwing both arms around my neck. "Oh, Byron, my love. I have done it. We are free."

"Free," I groaned, kissing her. "We are most damnably trapped."

Another knock on the door. "Byron?" It was Hobhouse, regaining a fraction of his manhood. "Are you there, Byron?"

"What does *he* want?" Caro whispered. "What is he *doing* here?"

"He is my friend," I explained.

"You need a friend, to elope?"

"Ah." But I was in no condition to explain that. "Perhaps if you were to come outside and talk with him."

"Like this?"

"If it embarrasses you, I will obtain some female clothes. Give me one moment."

"If you do not return, I shall kill myself."

I nodded, somewhat wearily, and closed the door behind me, sending Fletcher downstairs to procure some clothing from Mrs Dollman. Hobhouse poured us each a glass of brandy.

"It cannot be, old fellow," he said. "You will be ruined. Worse, you will not even be happy."

"You must convince *her* of that," I said.

"I shall," he declared, and Fletcher having returned with the feminine garb, a moment later Caro was in our midst, refusing a glass herself, and taking on that seductively quiet expression which I knew to be the prelude to a storm.

"Lady Caroline," Hobby said, speaking most earnestly. "I must beg you to reconsider. Lord Byron is the most honourable of men, and will of course acquiesce in whatever you demand, but my dear lady, please think. You will bring ruin upon both of you. Exile from England, for a start. You will never again see your son. My lord here will never again speak in the House, and a most promising career will be nipped in the bud. I do not speak of the anguish you will bring to your relatives, to those who hold you dear . . . my dear Lady Caroline, can you not see it would be best for us all were you to return home?"

All this while she had been gazing at him, scarce blinking, which aroused some alarm in my mind. But she replied quietly enough.

"I shall not go home," she said. "I *cannot* go home."

I realised the worst, that she had spoken of the affair to her husband, or her mother, or perhaps both. "Well then," I sighed. "My thanks, Hobby, but there can be no alternative. We must go off together."

"You shall not," Hobhouse cried. "Over my dead body."

"The dead body will be mine," Caro shouted, suddenly coming to life, and leaping across the room to seize a court sword which I had carelessly left on a table.

"Stop her," Hobby bawled.

I ran after her, seized her round the waist, imprisoning her arms, which forced the sword to her side.

"Do not be afraid, Bryon," she promised, kicking me on the ankle. "I shall kill us both."

"Caro," I begged. "For God's sake, Caro."

But by now our legs were inextricably bound up together, and we fell over with a most frightful crash. While we lay on the floor, gasping for breath, and Hobhouse wiped sweat from his brow, there came a new pounding on the door.

"Lord Byron?" It was the faithful Dollman. "Lord Byron? I shall send for the watch."

"My God, no," I groaned. "Hobby dissuade him."

Hobhouse hastened outside.

"But do not leave me alone," I shouted, for Caro was still wriggling in my arms, having got her breath back, and was also attempting to bite me.

Fletcher hastened in. "My lord."

She had released the sword. I kicked it towards him and regained my feet, carrying her with me.

"You hate me," she announced.

"I love you, Caro." Well, what else could a gentleman say? "But I cannot love you if you persist in this madness. I may well come to hate you then. But stay, and enjoy my love, and your responsibility."

"You love me?" she whispered, and fell to kissing me, much to Willie's embarrassment. And to Hobhouse's, for he now returned, having persuaded Dollman not to take any action.

"What's to be done?" he moaned. "What's to be done?"

"I shall go home," Caro announced, which left us all dumb. "They will wish to spirit me away. They intend sending me to Ireland. It was that dread possibility which forced me to it. But I will go, Byron, if you command me."

"I . . . I . . . it would be best," I said a trifle weakly.

184

"Then I shall. I shall sacrifice myself for your future, my dearest, dearest lord. But you must promise to call, at least once more. Friday. Promise me that."

"I promise," I swore, while Hobhouse raised his eyes to heaven. But it was the only way to make our peace.

In fact our problems were a long way from being over. Before we had even got her into my carriage she had changed her mind again, and was refusing to return home. We eventually persuaded her to go to the house of a mutual acquaintance, and from there she was reclaimed by Lady Bessborough. But of course the scandal was the talk of London, nor was it to be alleviated during the rest of the summer, for she managed to postpone her eventual departure to Ireland by pretending that she was pregnant, and that the journey might induce a miscarriage.

But finally the date of her departure was confirmed, it was 6 September, and she wrote me to ask for a last meeting. I could not help but accept, and was at least secure in the knowledge, when I called at Melbourne House, that we were being watched to prevent any catastrophe. As if such a consideration mattered to Caro! We were scarce seated together, on that fateful settee, when she was whipping up her skirts with one hand and producing a pair of scissors with the other, beseeching me to snip a lock of that most private hair to remember her by. I could do nothing less than agree, but the event affected me profoundly, and our farewell grew tender, on my part perhaps a shade too tender, and I do recall that in a letter I wrote her, which I fondly imagined would be my last, I declared how much her love had meant to me, how much indeed I had loved her, did love her, and would always love her.

Yet I would be lying were I not to confess that once I knew she was on the ship for the Emerald Isle I did not immediately feel an overwhelming sense of relief. It seemed to me that like a drowning man who has suddenly found his hand fastening upon a saving lifeboat, I was coming up for air after being submerged beneath the briny for a long six months. And as if to suggest that the entire universe was suddenly moving in my favour, Hanson announced that he had a buyer for Newstead. A Mr Claughton, clearly an agent for some more respectable party, for he was a lawyer himself, was prepared to offer £120,000. Here were all my misfortunes banished at a stroke, my future secured, with a wealth which would make me utterly independent of anyone in the world.

"I am the happiest of men," I confessed to Lady Melbourne. "I feel that after having been lurking in purgatory since birth I have suddenly been granted access to heaven."

"On account of a little money," she said scornfully, she never having known the lack of that essential commodity. "Really you do amuse me, Byron. But I congratulate you, as I congratulate you upon escaping Caro's clutches, at least for the moment." Sinister words which I did not immediately heed. "And what will you do with your new-found freedom?"

"Make you my mistress."

She smiled, and kissed my cheek. "You are too wearing for me, Byron. I sometimes think you are too wearing for yourself. Would you like my opinion?"

"I doubt I shall survive without it."

"It is that you should marry, and at the earliest opportunity."

"At twenty-four?"

"Most men leave it too late. You are free, you are wealthy, you are healthy. . . ." She frowned at me. "You *are* healthy?"

"In the direction you mean, certainly. I suffer from a recurring tertian fever which I contracted in Greece."

"Which is hardly contagious, and indeed, will make you more acceptable. Believe me, there is no woman can resist nursing a handsome invalid. But what woman would resist you in any event, Byron? You have but to name her."

"Then I shall. Meg Elphinstone."

Lady Melbourne frowned once again, and this time far more deeply. "Whatever for?"

"Well," I said, feeling my cheeks begin to burn. "She is reputed to be the wealthiest heiress in England." (v)

"And that is an important consideration, in a man worth better than a hundred thousand? She is not exactly a raving beauty."

"She has red hair. I adore red hair."

"I can think of a dozen eligible young women with red hair," Lady Melbourne said with great patience. "Nor can you be sure it will last. I had red hair once."

"She is fond of me. I can see it in her gaze."

"Every woman in London is fond of you, Byron. Or would be, given the chance."

Oh, if I had married dear Meg. All my troubles would have been ended at a stroke.

"Well, then," I said. "I shall marry Lady Jane Harley."

"*What?*"

"Well, you cannot deny that *she* is beautiful. And well connected. And even due for a little inheritance." Although the Miscellany was so numerous whatever Oxford left would have to be somewhat divided.

"I never heard such nonsense in my life," Lady Melbourne declared. "Such obscene nonsense, too."

"Obscene?"

"Will you deny you seek the mother through the child?"

"Why, I. . . ." But of course it was true enough. Although passing through Jane on the way would have been enjoyable enough.

"There," she said. "You are a perfectly horrible man, Byron." But she smiled as she said it, for of course had I not passed through her own daughter-in-law on my way to her? "No, no, we shall find you someone who fulfils all of those requirements, beauty, wealth, a fondness for you, but one who, in addition, is free of the taint of London scandal, and who, in addition, *admires* you."

"Dear Lady M," I said. "Now you are creating fantasies. However much the lovely creatures may wish to have an adventure with me, I doubt there is one who actually admires me."

"I can think of one," the devastating old lady said. "My niece, Annabella."

My total surprise must have shown on my face. Of all the young women of my acquaintance, Annabella Milbanke had been least in my thoughts as a possible wife.

"But consider," Lady Melbourne suggested. "Annabella is at least younger than you, which cannot be a bad thing. She is perhaps not beautiful, but she is certainly handsome. You tell me that you wish to be managed, well, she is strong willed and knows her own mind. And she is an heiress."

"And do you think she cares for me at all?"

"I repeat, she admires you," Lady Melbourne said. "I think of all the qualities a husband may wish in a wife, that is the most important. Far more so than love. Think about it, my dear Byron."

Which I did, whenever I had the time. For I was not merely pining over Caro, nor merely feeling relief at her departure. Owing to her calls upon my time and my emotions I had done very little writing that summer, save for a diatribe against that iniquitous dance the waltz on which I worked in a desultory fashion whenever the spirit took me.

Now I was determined to steep myself in composition. But not in London. I found it impossible to work in my rooms, expecting as I did every moment to hear that thunderous rap yet again. I took myself to Cheltenham, where I considered myself safely removed from the hurly burly.

The fact was, I was confoundedly miserable. Caro might have been too exciting to live with; her memory was far too exciting to live without. And memory is such a damnable selective sense that it is inclined to concentrate only on the good times. To make matters worse, however much we might be separated by the breadth of the Irish Sea, she continued to write, epistles of undying love to which I was hard put to reply without reawakening such an ardour as would have her taking the next packet.

Thus weakened, and confused, and unhappy, I drifted inexorably into the dangerous orbit of the Milbankes. For of course I now know that Lady Melbourne's contemptuous dismissal of such as Margaret Mercer Elphinstone and Jane Harley was merely inspired by selfishness. Were I to marry either of those desirables I would be out of her reach, for ever. And of all managing women she was the most. Whereas Annabella, now, her very own niece . . . it is scant comfort to me, from the depths of perpetual exile, to consider that she misjudged that young woman's character as badly as did I.

In any event, I in due course submitted my proposal, in writing, from the depths of Cheltenham and through the medium of my elderly confidante. The reply was a complete surprise to me, and, I fancy, to Lady Melbourne as well: Annabella refused me. She was most complimentary about my talents, but then proceeded to dissect my character in a way I would not have supposed possible for a twenty-one-year-old girl. I doubt her assessment was meant to be read by me, but Lady Melbourne duly forwarded the offensive document, in which the young virago pointed out that she felt my character was overlaid by the passions aroused in my youth – how little she knew the truth of her careless statement, as she based her judgement only on a reading of *Childe Harold* – and felt that she could not really consider herself capable of ruling such a wayward spouse. In a sense this was flattery, but once again my emotions were sorely confused, on the one hand anger at being rejected, on the other intrigue at the woman who could take so formidable a step. And over all, of course, relief that the fatal day when I should have to tie myself to any woman for life had once again been postponed.

But all other matters, even the absence of Caro, were put from my mind only a few days later. For there arrived a letter from Lady Oxford, inviting me to spend some time with them at their country estate of Eyewood. "It will be a small party, I fear," she wrote. "And I trust you will not be bored, but all our friends seem to have deserted us for this season." A patently uninteresting list of absentees then followed, transparently a prelude to her final sentence: *"Lord Hamilton is shooting grouse in Scotland."*

LIZ

I discovered that we were an even smaller party than I had suspected, for I was the only guest. We sat five at supper, as in addition to the Earl and Countess, there were Lady Jane and Lady Charlotte, she being just twelve and an absolute beauty, even prettier than her sister. His lordship was very easy, and our conversation roamed over a variety of subjects of mutual interest, Lady Oxford playing her full part. And never can she have looked more bewitchingly beautiful, in a crimson gown which allowed her magnificent shoulders and breasts full exposure, her black hair descending in gentle folds past that splendid white flesh. I felt quite giddy, for surely I could have been invited to such a family gathering with only one objective in mind, and I could hardly wait for the meal to end.

It eventually did, the two girls kissed Mama and Papa, and to the amusement of all, me as well, and then retired. Soon to be followed by Harley himself. He drank a second glass of port, rose to his feet, and said, "I retire early. And rise early. Good for the health. Do you rise early, Byron?"

I was still debating which line to take when he answered himself.

"No, I suppose you don't," he said. "Lie abed, eh, composing poetry." He gave a brief laugh, and left the room.

The butler was still present, refilling our glasses, so we sat in silence for a while. Then the worthy fellow also withdrew, closing the double doors to the winter parlour – the days were already drawing in and there was a great fire blazing in the grate.

And contrary to her usual flow of provocative conversation, Liz continued to sit quietly in her chair, gazing at me to be sure, and from time to time sipping her port.

"A delightful dinner," I remarked. "Eyewood is a delightful place. And you have two delightful daughters."

"I have several delightful daughters," she pointed out. Her voice was one of the quietest I have ever known. Her whole demeanour was the calmest I have ever known. "Does that disturb you, Byron?"

"Why should it?"

She finished her wine. "My husband is a quiet man," she said. "A very good man. An *enthusiastic* man. About horses and dogs, and politics. I am also very enthusiastic about politics. We make a perfect pair. Are you enthusiastic about politics, Byron?"

"Oh, indeed I am. The right sort."

"Of course," she agreed. "Unfortunately, Edward is not very interested in sex. At least, I suppose he *is*, in his own way. But he finds it embarrassing. He wishes to be done with it as quickly as possible. Do you find sex embarrassing, Byron?"

All this still spoken in that so quiet, so confident voice.

"I don't think so."

"I thought not, as I have read *Childe Harold*. I am a woman who must be made to feel, Byron. Can you make a woman feel?"

"Well, I. . . ."

"Did you make Caro Lamb feel? Or perhaps I should still use the present tense?"

Ah, so that was what she was brooding on.

"Caro and I are friends, my lady. But nothing more."

"I am glad to hear it." She got up, the taffeta of her gown giving a gentle rustle. "I do not suppose she would be good for you, over any period of time." She crossed the room, stood beside my chair. "I think you and I may do very well together, Byron."

I seized her hand, and she allowed me the gentlest of smiles.

"When the time comes," she said, and freed herself to pull the bell rope. The butler was there immediately. "I shall retire now, Masters," she said. "You will show Lord Byron his room."

The fellow bowed in my direction. "If you will accompany me, my lord."

I got up, a sorely puzzled and somewhat disturbed man. I kissed Lady Oxford's hand, and received a gentle squeeze.

"Sleep well, my lord," she said. "Eyewood is a peaceful place."

"Then I'm sure I shall," I agreed, determined to keep up my end no matter how hard my heart was pounding. And so followed the butler along an interminable corridor, and up interminable staircases, my room being apparently situated in one of the wings of this place, and so eventually came into the care of Fletcher, who assisted me to undress before blowing out the candle and leaving me to my slumbers. As if such a prospect was possible. For never before had I been quite so cold bloodedly interviewed, at least on such a subject, and never had I been left quite so high in the air.

Foolish Byron. Had I not known, from the moment of the invitation, what Lady Oxford wanted? And what Lady Oxford wanted she would most surely have. I had not been beneath the covers fifteen minutes when a door I had not previously observed, situated in the inner part of my room, opened, and there she was.

(She carried a candle above her head, the flickering light seeming to bathe her face and hair, only faintly illuminating the soft blue of her undressing robe.

"In bed, my lord?" she asked.

I was already out of it, and reaching for her. She smiled, and placed the candle on the table.

"I am a very wicked woman, would you not say? I am quite wanton. I am old enough to be your mother, Byron. Have you thought of that?"

"I have thought of you, my lady, and of no one else, for too long." Once again I sought to hold her, and once again she side-stepped.

"Nevertheless," she said softly, "I am sure I should be punished."

She shrugged her shoulders, and her undressing robe slipped from her shoulders, rested for a moment at breast and at hip, and then clouded around her ankles. She wore no nightgown. And how I wished for several more candles, or an entire chandelier crammed with them. I had known she was beautiful, but never had I expected to see so much beauty before me in the flesh, except perhaps from Haidee. Certainly not, dare I say it, in a middle-aged woman, and a mother several times over. But even without the support of her stays her breasts sagged no more than delightfully, and they were as large and as round and as pink nippled as I had dreamed in my happiest midnight slumber. Her belly possessed the slightest of pouts, and even the stretch marks which lurked to either side of her navel did no more than increase the attraction. Her groin was a luxuriant black forest, her legs long and slender. Her perfume filled the room, and her smile added to that quiet voice no less than to what she was actually saying swirled around my head like incense.

"A woman like me," she said, "should be *whipped*."

I stared at her, uncertain I had heard correctly.

"And then forced," she commanded. "For how else may I know that I have sinned?"

I drew a long breath, and removed my nightshirt.

"I see you agree with me, my lord," she said. "But be sure I will not lightly submit. I will resist you."

This was the game she wished played, and I could understand that Harley, no longer in his first youth, might well find it too tiresome. For me it was a sudden call to inebriation of the senses, to accomplishing all I had ever wanted, it seemed. Well, almost all. And perhaps, I thought, even *that* was possible in the coming tumult.

And now I understood also why my chamber had been chosen in a remote wing of the house, far removed from servants as well as children as well as lord. For as I reached for her she ducked my arms and fled to the other side of the room, pushing a chair out of the way as she did so, and causing it to fall over with a crash. Yet her movements were carefully calculated to avoid me but not to escape me. My hands slid across her shoulders, discovering that they were lightly coated in a sweet smelling oil which made her the harder to grasp at the same time as it increased the sense of the touching fingers.

She reached the wall and turned, hair flying, breasts inflating and subsiding as she breathed. I slowed, covering her from the front, and she laughed, deep in her throat, then lowered her head and once again attempted to pass under my arm. I caught her round the waist, but my grip slipped on the oil, and my hands slithered down over thigh and bush, while I lost my balance and fell to my knees. Whether she also tripped or whether she felt she had led me sufficient of a chase, she also collapsed to the floor, and I was enabled to turn and grasp her ankle.

She rolled on her back and kicked at me with her free leg, but I dragged her across the room to the bed, seized her wrist, and plucked her to her feet.

"Only your hand, Byron," she said. "Only your hand." Thus signifying that we were about to enter the second phase of our remarkable set-to.

I swung her round, panting myself, and thrust her face down across the bed. I had not had the time to inspect her back before, but this was as splendid as the rest of her, and her buttocks, if larger than I usually preferred, were none the less magnificent. They cried out to be struck, in my present frame of mind. They cried out for a great deal more than that, but I decided to continue in her vein for the moment. My palm

193

crashed into that splendid white flesh, and she gave a jerk and a little moan of mingled pain and pleasure. I hit her several more times, while she quivered and *cooed*, and then abandoned all pretence and sank to my knees beside the bed to kiss and part the glorious mounds.

Alas for my hopes, she also was roused to the necessary pitch, and rolled beneath my lips, presenting sweet scented forest where I had desired heaving dunes. Yet was I neither abashed nor hesitant, and boldly sent lips and tongue where she wished, so that she sat up in her delight and hugged my head into her body, leaving me breathless. "Now, Byron. Now."

I released her to climb on to the bed, and she thrust at me with her nails. I fell on her belly, and was surrounded by flailing hand and flailing leg and flailing hair. Our faces banged one into the other and she bit my chin. I thrust myself downwards, crushing her beneath my weight, and slowly separated her legs. I found myself between and got hold of her wrists and spread her arms. Our bodies rubbed against each other and I felt myself slipping into the treasured goal, as she herself confirmed with a tremendous jerk of passion, working herself against me and over me, closing her legs on mine, throwing my arms aside to seize my shoulders and draw her nails through my flesh, so that I came in an unimaginable surge of pain, and remained rocking to and fro for some seconds afterwards, the while gazing down on that tear-stained face, for she had wept during her orgasm, on that dishevelled hair, on that flaccid mouth and those small white teeth, felt her gasping breath playing on my face even as I felt her gasping belly flutter against mine, and knew that at last I had been to bed with a *woman*.)

She left me at dawn, and I slept. By then I needed it, for never had I spent such an unforgettably tumultuous night. Never had I been so exhausted. Never had I felt so sated. We had kissed and coupled and wrestled and fought and laughed and groaned and moaned and wept and thrashed our bodies against each other's for some six hours. There was no part of her beauty my fingers or my lips had not explored, no part of mine had not felt the imprint of that lovely face, the soft caress of that flowing hair, the gentle scouring of those brilliant white teeth.

And yet, when we encountered each other a few hours later, she was as perfectly groomed, as wickedly, wittily self contained as I had ever known her. The night seemed to be a dream, and I must make conversation with her husband, listen to her play the piano, walk and gambol with the girls and the dogs, and wait for the night, to discover what indeed was reality.

And to be reassured, if at the same time slightly alarmed. For it is a characteristic of woman, or at least *most* women, that when they discover what they like, they are by no means inclined to vary in the slightest. This is indeed their greatest weakness, and leads me to the answer to a riddle which no doubt puzzles a great many of them. Oxford was himself a prime example but there are sufficient cases to be discovered, where a lucky fellow is married to a most magnificent woman, beautiful, indulgent, passionate, perhaps even wealthy, and yet, after a few years of marriage, the fellow is dallying with all and sundry, sluts who are capable only of passing on the clap, chambermaids who should not attract a second glance. And why? With all that splendour his to command? Because of course, it is not his to *command*. It is his to indulge, but in a chosen direction. Here is the true secret of a relationship, supposing it can be discovered. Variety. And I do not mean of the body, the shape, the curve, the scent, even the voice. The woman capable of understanding that it lies within *herself* to satisfy her husband, time and again, will never find him astray.

Liz Harley, for all her intelligence and her marvellous femininity, had never chosen to learn this simple lesson. Thus the next night, and the next, and the night after that, we consumed some six hours in a wild contest which sent chairs flying and had candles flickering, had us sweating and exhausted, and bruised and battered, and utterly sated by dawn. It seemed, and in her case was. I was less happy; I could not help but wonder if instead of tiring of her lovers Liz merely wore them out. Yet however perverse my longings, here was the most contented society in which I ever lived. Caro had been tumultuous enough, but the tumult had extended beyond our bed, had sought to poison my very life. With Liz the tumult ended when she *left* my bed. Our days together, and we spent all day together, were pastoral idylls, in which we walked and talked and played the piano and discussed events, her calmness going a long way even to diminishing my moods and depressions, and these were considerable.

I had cause. I had not been very long at Eyewood before all the world knew of it, and knowing Liz, knew too why I was there. The vital information progressed to Ireland, and brought a letter by return, addressed not to me, but to Liz herself. She was upset, at least as upset as she ever allowed herself to be. And this, I was to learn, was a great deal more than even I suspected. For the time being, she replied to Caro's accusations and inquiries with her usual calm assurance.

But there was more than just letters to annoy me. The infamous Claughton now decided to renege upon our contract. He was obliged to pay the first £25,000 of the purchase price of Newstead by the end of the year. He actually paid £5,000, and then announced that he had reconsidered and wished to be excused from his obligations. *That* sent me up to London in great haste, as may be imagined. Secure in the knowledge that I was about to become a wealthy man, I had relaxed my monetary discipline, and considerably increased my debts. Now here I was back again where I had begun, only considerably worse off. In the circumstances I did not feel inclined to let the wily lawyer, or his nameless client, so easily off the hook, and was for taking the matter to court. Hanson persuaded me otherwise. How this despicable breed clings together. But his arguments were convincing enough, that if we agreed to settle, say on a total payment of another £20,000, we should at least be £25,000 the richer and able to place the Abbey once again on the market, whereas merely to go to court would abandon the whole business in Chancery for the foreseeable future. Of course I agreed, but gained no credit by it, and the detestable Milbanke, who had now decided to write to me on a regular basis, having refused my hand in marriage, went so far as to accuse me of a flintlike hardheartedness in squeezing another few pounds out of the defaulting contractors.

Her comments I could withstand. Even if I was reduced to such a state that I was forced to sell the majority of my horses and let my grooms go, and could scarce raise the hundred guineas necessary for a picture of Liz, which I was determined to have. Caro's importunities were less easy to bear, as she now demanded the return of all her gifts. These trinkets she had showered on me during our brief affair, and to tell the absolute truth, I had by now forgotten for the most part what they had been, or where they now were, as I was forced to confess to her, whereupon she accused me of giving them to other women – what other woman would have accepted them? – and in a fine fettle of rage, having by now returned to England although confined at Brocket, she assembled a group of lads and maidens, lit a huge bonfire, on which she burned all of my letters – but alas only *copies*, as I later discovered – and an effigy of myself, while these acolytes danced round and round the flames. It may be imagined what a scandal that caused. I'm afraid that between her and Claughton I was reduced to a very ill state of mind, so much so that I once again considered leaving England.

Caro was not the only reason for my decision; I was just becoming aware that I was a man marked by my political opponents, and this at the moment when I was beginning to lose all of my political fervour. For to say truth I found Parliament a confoundedly dilatory and boring place. Reform I wished, and more deeply than I believe a great many people suspected. I had not spoken up for the Nottingham frame breakers, for the disenfranchised Catholics of Ireland, merely to forward my political career. I had felt a deep compassion for these unhappy people, a deep longing to see their wrongs righted. There were innumerable other causes I wished to espouse. But what did I see when I looked around me? Despite my efforts the Luddites were still being hanged. The Irish question remained as implacably unsolved as ever. Injustice to all who did not wholeheartedly support the Tory majority remained the rule of the land. It seemed to me, as it seemed to the majority of our circle, that only by direct action, by a revolution – properly conducted, of course – could the vicious inequalities of our land be set right. No doubt, as I attended the Lords less and less, I became more and more outspoken over the dinner table, and no doubt there was ever a spy present to remember my words and repeat them to eager ears.

In fact we were all of us becoming increasingly aware that we were watched, and reported, and recorded. How deep and how long and how vicious were governmental memories I was to discover only three years later, but even at the time, with a sale for either Newstead or Rochdale as apparently distant as ever, with debts piling up around me, with my reputation already in tatters from Caro's wild carryings on, I began to feel that I had tarried too long in England, and that it was time to escape once again to those sunny climes where I had become a man.

My considerations in this direction were assisted by the fact that Oxford was himself feeling the draught of official disapproval. That his house was the centre of disaffection had become too widely known, and no doubt it had been intimated to him that it might do his health good to spend a year or two abroad. Here was a pleasant prospect.

From which it will be gathered that soon enough Liz and I were back in the seclusion of Eyewood together. She was herself, as I have already said often enough, the sunniest of women, and withal always ready for a display of her utterly wicked humour. As when Caro, ever importuning, wrote me and reminded me of her parting gift, which I still possessed in a little box in my bedchamber, and begging a similar return that she might embed it beneath her pillow.

"She is the most persistent of females," I groaned.

"And she will continue to be so," Liz agreed. "You had best humour her."

"You would have me send her some hair? From *there*?" I was aghast. "Will that not merely reawaken her ardour?"

Liz gazed at me for some seconds, and then gave that unforgettable smile of hers. "A time for witchcraft, dearest Byron. Do you not agree? There is a pair of scissors on that table." And she hoisted her own skirts above her waist, as we were alone at the time.

Certainly she had enough to spare, and if it was of a darker colour than my own, I doubted Caroline would be able to tell the difference. I had the good sense – I was at last becoming able to understand women – to snip out *two* locks, one for the purposes of our subterfuge and the other for myself, which pleased her enormously, as there can be no doubt she had that in mind in making her suggestion.

It will be seen therefore that despite my financial and political problems, and despite the constant menace of Caro, we managed to be happy from time to time. More than that, I had even managed, during the preceding months, to write again. In addition to preparing *The Waltz* for the press, I had composed an Arabian adventure, mainly based upon what I had seen and heard during my travels, but also drawing upon what I had myself experienced, for I was determined to immortalise Haidee in print. This I called *The Gaiour*, and these two were now about to be published, despite the continued strictures of Dallas as to my indecency. But I am afraid I was becoming weary of a literary conscience ever sitting at my shoulder, and gave him short shift. *The Gaiour* indeed attracted quite as much attention as had *Childe Harold*, and my literary fame once again bounced to the top of the tree, even as a fresh set of whispers began to accumulate around my reputation. At least some of them were based on fact, for it was now that we became aware that an addition to the Miscellany was apparently imminent.

This was a considerable shock to my dear love, she having supposed she was beyond the reach of such mishaps. And it was the more inconvenient because plans were by now far advanced for the Oxfords to depart these shores for sunnier climes. And I of course had every intention of accompanying them, supposing I could raise the necessary funds; Oxford was willing to accept my presence as his wife's cavalier, but not if he had to keep me into the bargain, nor could I possibly have placed myself in so invidious a position.

But there we were; Liz had definitely missed two periods. Looking back on the event there can be no doubt it was all caused by sheer aggravation. For although my darling maintained that superbly nonchalant air to all the world, and even managed to fool me over long phases, she actually was much less calm under the surface than she pretended, and perhaps suffered more than an outgoing person by reason of bottling up her emotions. For in addition to my irritations caused by the default of the despicable Claughton and my various other financial woes, Caro now began to press for a meeting with me. This Liz quite firmly refused to permit for some time, and I imagine it was worry over it brought her low. When she finally did give me permission to see the wretched girl, this seeming the only way out of the constant bombardment of messages and letters, she promptly relaxed sufficiently to discover it had all been a false alarm and place our minds at rest.

The fact was, Caro had now descended to those menaces she was to use with devastating effect in the future; i.e. she threatened to repeat to the world at large everything she could remember of our intimate conversations. It was now for the first time that I realised what a fool I had been to permit myself to trust such a creature, but it was too late. Thus if I approached our meeting with every desire to strangle the worthless bitch I kept myself under the most rigid control, put forth all my charm, and endeavoured to gain the victory by sweet reason rather than anger. And appeared to succeed, because she was herself in a reasonable mood that day. She still wanted the return of her gifts, but her principal fancy was to see me, to touch my hand. She really was quite pitiful. And her sole demand was that we should meet from time to time. I deemed the crisis ended.

But my desire to leave England was accentuated. Hobhouse was already on his way, he having secured a mission which would carry him through the courts of Northern Europe. He had begged me to accompany him, but I lacked the wherewithal, and in any event, the idea of tramping through the snows of Russia did not appeal to me in the least. I am a warm-blooded creature, and I desired the sun.

And of course when I could finance a trip abroad I wished to accompany the Oxfords, for now that Liz's alarms had been proved false, their plans for departure were again in full swing. But raising money proved next to impossible. I could not even advertise Newstead once again, as the Claughton business was still hanging fire. In my despair I begged Hanson to sell everything in the place not included in the original contract, all my silver, my books, everything movable in fact, just so he could raise me a few thousand pounds. But as usual he procrastinated and I was left in the lurch. I became seized with a sense of desperate isolation. Liz was the only friend I possessed in the world – save for the omnipresent Lady Melbourne – and at her behest and with her encouragement I had become far more of a radical than I had ever intended. It was she who pushed me into presenting Cartwright's petition to the Lords calling for a reform of Parliament.(i) We had close on two hundred thousand signatures, and I made a moving speech. Imagine my horror when only one lord rose in my support, and that was the madman Stanhope.(ii) Even my Whig admirers of a few months before feared to be seen speaking to me. Parliamentary reform was anathema in the midst of the struggle with the French horror, and all who supported it were regarded virtually as traitors to their country.

It was also Liz who encouraged me to accept an invitation to visit Leigh Hunt(iii) in Surrey gaol, this itinerant scribbler having been imprisoned for libelling the Regent. Moore accompanied me, but Moore had nothing to lose, being an Irishman as it was. In the event, I enjoyed the evening very much, and found Hunt a pleasant fellow. But of course this escapade as well as all my other radical adventures were carefully noted down. Thus isolated from all but a few friends, feeling the pinch of poverty, blackmailed by a heartless wench, not knowing where to turn save into the arms of my beloved, the final blow fell.

With the coming of summer Harley decided he would wait no longer, informed me that I could join them in Cagliari, which was their chosen destination, as soon as I was able, and took his lady and himself to Portsmouth. Liz and I bade each other a tearful farewell, our grief assuaged by the thought that our separation would be of only a few months. But we both knew each other too well, in our hearts. I was never to see her again.

And with her went my freedom, although I did not then realise it. But with Liz beyond the sea, Caro acting as maniacally as ever, my own affairs drooping from bad to worse, I found myself more and more inclining towards taking Lady Melbourne's advice, and finding myself a wife. It was a decision I postponed as long as possible, to be sure, considering several eligible ladies only to drop the idea, or to have it dropped for me. On the one hand my instincts told me a successful marriage would lead to the solving of all my problems, on the other the man in me rebelled at the concept of associating a feminine will with my wayward and masculine mode of existence.

Yet when a man embarks upon a course of action, he is likely to continue, perhaps without intending to, long after the reason loses its pertinency. So it was with me. I dallied for almost a year following the departure of the Oxfords, while all the world understood I was looking for a wife, and at the end could do nothing better than pen another proposal to that unfailing critic of mine, that Princess of Parallelograms who lurked in her north country lair. This was a formality, part of the game with which I was deluding myself. I supposed. After all, the girl had refused me once. It was unlikely that she would accept me after so long a break in our acquaintance.

But the remarkable girl did. (iv)

BOOK THE SECOND

GUSS (i)

My grief at the departure of Liz Harley from my life was in fact assuaged far sooner than I had supposed possible, because of course it was only a week or two later that you came to visit me.

I remember you, standing in the doorway, as if it were yesterday. I remember even my slight feeling of annoyance, when Willie Fletcher announced you. I was sitting quietly, with a bottle, brooding. Liz had just departed these shores, and I was desolate. The last thing I desired was a relative, especially a relative whom I knew only through letters, descending upon me.

And yet, when I saw you, I felt a sudden sense of gladness. You wore a dark blue velvet coat. See how I remember? And you looked hot, as well you might on a June evening. Your hat was also velvet, I think, and trimmed with ostrich plumes, and your gown was a beige lawn. You looked utterly beautiful.

At the same time, I even knew why you had come. The only reason why you *would* come, unannounced and unexpected.

I took your hands to kiss them, and you embraced me, and kissed me on the cheek. You smelt delicious, and you trembled just a little, with nervousness, which made you the more delightful.

"My Lord Byron," you said, in mock humility? "Pray forgive this intrusion."

"Intrusion?" I cried. "How may a sister ever intrude upon her brother?" I took your arm, and escorted you to a chair. "Willie, some tea." I sat you down, and sat beside you. "What brings you to London?"

You flushed, and lied most prettily. "A visit. Nothing more."

Then I knew for certain. But we talked for some time, about your daughters, then you had but three, about gormless George, about Six Mile Bottom, about everything under the sun except what was uppermost in both of our minds, me wondering how much it would

205

involve, you no doubt remembering how you had failed to support me in my hour of need, and whether or not you would be rebuffed.

But the conversation was easy enough. I made jokes, and you laughed. A woman with humour, I thought; a rare creature. And then I reflected that it had to be so, as you were my sister, and a great gush of warmth came out of me. I could wait no longer. I took your hands again, and pressed them between mine, and said, "Now, Augusta, tell me how much you need."

You gazed at me for a moment, eyes wide, mouth slightly open, pink spots in your cheeks. I swear you have never looked more beautiful. Well, I lie at that. You *have* looked more beautiful. But I had not at that time observed it.

"I'm your brother," I reminded you, as you appeared to be struck dumb. "I am here to help you."

"Oh, Byron," you whispered. "I am destitute. George spends his life but a single step ahead of the bailiffs, and I am left to survive as best I can."

"How much?"

"Anything you can spare. Just to tide me over, until. . . ." You did not finish the sentence. You had no expectations, save through me, and I knew that as well as you.

"How much?"

You gave a pretty little sigh, and raised your shoulders. "Two hundred?"

"Surely more?"

You licked your lips. Another charming gesture. "No. It will do, for the time. But if it is too much. . . ."

"I think three hundred would be safer," I said. "I will make out the cheque in the morning."

"Oh. But. . . ."

"You were not thinking of returning to Cambridge tonight?"

"Well, I. . . ." Again the quick lick of the lips.

"You shall stay here," I decided. "In any event, you will not be able to obtain the funds until tomorrow."

"Here?" You looked around you.

"There is a bedroom through the back."

"Ah." Once again the quick look.

I smiled at your modesty. We were brother and sister. But I was still a gentleman. "You shall sleep in my bed, my dearest Sis, and I shall

206

sleep on this sofa. Fletcher will make me up a bed. There, it is all arranged."

"But I have not even a maid, or a change of clothes."

"I shall obtain you a maid, and a wardrobe. If only you will stay."

"Byron," you whispered, and leaned forward to kiss me on the cheek. "For the first time in my life, I feel I have come home."

The next morning, as we sat together drinking our chocolate, arrived an invitation to Lady Davy's to meet the famous de Staël. (ii) I invited you to stay over and come with me, and you agreed. I think you were looking upon these few stolen days as your first holiday in years, certainly since tying yourself to George Leigh, and you were spending them in the company of your famous brother. We explored London together, and you were thrilled every time I was recognised. And we enjoyed ourselves. We discovered we had identical senses of humour, identical interests, even identical moods.

Then came the night, and we attended the dinner, that fantastic affair in which de Staël took on the best brains in England, and sent us home reeling from close exposure to so much mental majesty.

"Remarkable," I said, as Fletcher admitted us. No doubt I had had a glass too many of wine, for I had some difficulty with the word.

"Do you like women like that, Byron?" you asked, also revealing a slight tendency to slur.

"No," I decided. "Willie, fetch a bottle of port, and then you may retire."

The good fellow obeyed, and climbed his garret steps. It was approaching three in the morning, and almost daylight all over again.

"Neither do I," you decided, half falling on to the sofa. "She is too like a man. A woman should be a woman."

"Well said." I poured two glasses of port, held one out.

You blinked at it. "I wonder if I should," you said. "I really must be away tomorrow."

I sat beside you, and we touched glasses. "Why?"

"Well . . . there is my home to be seen to. My children. . . ."

"Cannot Nanny look after them for a few days?"

"I have already been absent a few days. Besides. . . ." Your tongue stole out and circled your lips in that so fascinating gesture of nervousness. "I am sure you are tired of sleeping on this sofa." Your eyes came up as you said those words, and those well-remembered pink spots appeared in your cheeks.

Had that most terrible of thoughts already crossed your mind? I know you say it had, but I have always wondered how much of your confession was not inspired by a determination to take upon yourself the sins of your baby brother. The truth is that up to that moment I had never considered the matter at all. I considered it *then*, with a terrible suddenness, for I sat beside one of the most lovely women I had ever known, sipping port, my senses just sufficiently distorted to make a nonsense of right and wrong, of rule and convention.

And attempted to smile. "You would find me uncomfortable were I to crawl in beside you," I said. "I am told I am all elbows and knees, when sleeping."

You continued to gaze at me for a moment, then sighed, and finished your port. "I have never enjoyed anything so much as these past few days," you said.

"Then we'll not end them," I declared. "I insist. You can spare another week. I too have been happy, dear Sis, and I had not expected to be, not at this moment, certainly."

Once again the gentle sigh. "How wonderful it would be, were we not brother and sister," you said, half to yourself. And then you glanced at me, and smiled. "But not wonderful at all, as I would not be able to sit here with you on your sofa."

Your hand rested on mine, and I lifted it and kissed it. "Not wonderful at all, my love," I said. "I would have no other sister."

I waited for you to pull away, but you did not. Instead you remained gazing at me, and your flush was slowly fading. "Are you a *bad* man, Byron?" you asked at last.

"They say I am."

"I know what they say. Are you?"

I forced a smile. My heart was pounding so hard I was sure you could hear it. Because I now knew what was going to happen. What nothing on earth save a fire or an earthquake could then prevent happening. Oh, where was that fire and the earthquake? And how splendid that they were absent.

"Indeed I am, Guss." This being the first time I had ever used that name. "I am a Byron. Would you have me different?"

"Guss," you whispered, and swayed towards me. "No one has ever called me Guss before."

You were very close, and your eyes were half shut. I seemed to be enveloped in your perfume. "Then that shall be my name for you, for ever more," I promised, and brushed your lips with my own.

For a moment we remained almost motionless, our breaths clouding, then your mouth opened, just a fraction, and your tongue touched mine. My hands came up to close on your waist, slide over the bone of the corset, and reach your breasts, and you gave another little shiver, and moved, but not away; you slid round my cheek to whisper in my ear.

"I cannot resist you, Byron," you whispered. "Do with me as you will. Please."

Was ever a man faced with a more burning decision? And one which I knew could be made in only one direction. You *were* the loveliest thing I had ever seen, for now you had fallen against the back of the sofa, and your eyes were definitely shut, while your bosom rose and fell slowly and rhythmically. And here was no slender girl, but a voluptuous woman, every bit as well endowed as dearest Liz, but a dozen years the younger. But you were my sister.

And you were presenting yourself to me in a way no woman had ever done before. Caroline Cameron had been purchased. My servants had been commanded. Caro Lamb and Liz herself had *commanded*, bidding me follow their whims and their pleasures, and I had been happy to do so. Lady Melbourne had been the most commanding of all. I had in fact for some time been longing to display my new-found abilities in the arts of Venus to some less experienced creature. It had never crossed my mind that I could be so presented with a mature mother of three. *And* you were my sister.

For here was the most insidious attraction of all. The man in me longed to strip your clothes away, to gaze upon what I was certain would be a most marvellous body, to take possession of it. But I had taken possession of other delightful bodies before. It was the Byron in me, the Zeluco, which cried out for me to make love to my own sister, to commit the ultimate sin against convention and gossiping society. And I knew, deep in my heart, that this same compulsion was driving you towards destruction as well.

Yet I still temporised, fool that I am. I still supposed that we could steal something of what we wished, and leave the rest, the ultimate sin, untouched. I could look, I could touch, you could do the same, should you wish, but an incestuous connection need not happen. There goes the boy, unaware of the forces which will always command a man.

I put down my glass, and lifted you from the sofa. You were heavier than I supposed, and it required a considerable effort, which you assisted by putting your arms around my neck. I held you beneath the knees and beneath the shoulders, swayed slightly, and your hair pressed against my cheek. Once again I was surrounded and over-whelmed by the scent of your perfume.

The bedroom door was ajar. I pushed it with my toe, and it swung inwards, and I laid you on the bed. Then I discovered that your eyes were again open, and that you were gazing at me as you had earlier. And then too I discovered that I was less a man of the world than I had supposed; I knew too little about the intricacies of feminine garb.

As you recognised. You sat up, as I sat beside you, and we kissed. And this was a real kiss; our mouths moved on each other's, our tongues explored each other's; I felt your hand sliding down the front of my shirt, and hovering at my waistband, and I seized it to place it where it wished to go. And felt once again that marvellous tremble seeping through your body.

You moved your mouth, and inclined your head for me to reach the buttons at the back of your gown. I fumbled them loose, receiving another rush of scent as your marvellous flesh became uncovered. And you still held my cocker, releasing him only to stand so that I could ease your gown down from your shoulders and around your hips.

You smiled at my clumsiness, and turned away, to attend to your own petticoats. I tore at my jacket and breeches, threw them on the floor, dragged off my boots, and gazed in wonderment at your drawers. I had never before seen a woman in so modest a garment. You saw the expression on my face, and flushed, and hesitated, and I knelt before you to slip them down about your ankles, to gaze at so close a range at those marvellous white legs, so long and strong and perfectly shaped, to press my lips into the soft contour of your thighs, to allow my hand to wander where my lips still dared not go, and trace a pattern through the deep red brown of your crotch.

I heard you pant, and saw you strain at the ties of your corset. I got up again. There was no haste. There was no need for haste. There would never be need for haste again. You held the bedpost, and I released you from your prison, allowing it too to slip to the floor while my hands massaged the tortured flesh, slowly slipping round, under your arms, to hold your breasts. Your crowning glory, my own dear Sis. Never can there have been breasts like yours, so large, and yet firm, and you had fed three children. They sagged, but so had Liz's, and hers had been equally magnificent. No, not equally. Hers had been inferior. She had not possessed such nipples, so huge, so hard, scraping into my palm.

You turned away from me, and lay down. You lay on your back, cushioned on your hair, your arms above your head. Your right side was closest to me, and you raised your left leg. You were making sure, consciously or unconsciously, that you were at your most beautiful, and I watched you suck your belly flat and hold your breath. You needed none of that, my darling. I loved you then, I love you now, with a passion I had not suspected to exist within the human mind.

And yet, I still supposed I could stop, before too long. I could still bend over you, and kiss your mouth once again, and then straighten. I could bend lower, and suck each nipple in turn, and hold the breasts in my hand, and yet straighten. I could kiss your toes and your calves and your thighs, approaching always the goal I ultimately sought, and turn away. I could bury my face in that sweet-scented forest, and drive my tongue before . . . and I could feel you tremble as you came. The first I had ever induced with other than my cocker or my fingers, and the best of all.

And then I knew that stopping was not for me. That we were damned, or blessed, above all others. At the moment it seemed blessed. I remember cocker was a huge molten mass of inflamation, so that I was terrified I would burst all over your belly. Would that I had. Sanity might have returned, and to us both, for long enough to save us from ourselves. But we would neither of us accept that possibility. I crawled above you, and your left knee went down even as you spread your legs. Your eyes were again open – had they been open all the time? – and were wide, and anxious, and desiring. I slipped towards you, and was inside you in a moment. Never can a woman have been so welcomingly wet and yet so filled with sensation. I felt your legs closing about mine even as your hands tightened on my shoulders. I found your mouth and sucked your tongue, and felt your lips go slack as you came again. But only seconds before I.

We did not sleep until well into the morning. We preferred to play, and smile, and kiss, and couple, and explore. We refused to allow ourselves to think. Thought was an enormity.

And when eventually we did sleep, it was in each other's arms. I had never slept in a woman's arms before. I have always been far too restless, and besides, once the deed was done, once my passion was abated, I had always wished only to be alone. I had no wish ever to be alone from you, my dearest Guss. Nor was I even restless.

211

What dear Willie thought, for undoubtedly he knew, as when he would have entered the parlour he would have seen the sofa empty, does not bear consideration. But Willie was, and is, a faithful fellow, and gave no sign, nor did he even disturb us by tapping on the door.

Yet arouse we eventually had to, to sit up in bed and stare at each other. Sleep had interrupted our idyll, and we were aghast. And yet, you were more beautiful than ever, with tousled hair and sleepy eyes, and no doubt you found me the same. We looked at each other, and you opened your mouth, and I stopped the words with my own. And then for another glorious half an hour time stood still and the world without had no meaning.

At last you could speak. "I must go home," you said.

"Why should you not stay here for ever? Become my housekeeper. Many sisters keep house for their brothers. No one could criticise, my darling. Stay here, for ever."

"I have three children."

"Well, then, I shall take a larger apartment. You may have your children here."

"You hate children."

"I shall love yours."

"I also have a husband."

"That lout? Is he ever there?"

"Yet am I married to him. I must go back, Byron. I must."

"Next week," I decided, and so it was settled. I find it difficult to recapture the delight of those ten days. We walked together and we rode together. We attended soirées and dinners together, for by now it was well known that Augusta was in London, and visiting with her brother, and you were invited wherever I was. You gloried in my fame and my popularity and my *sangfroid*, and I gloried in your quiet beauty, your superb demeanour, and above all, in our *secret*. How pale all other women appeared, how insignificant all other men. We loved and we shared, on a scale none of them would dare approximate. We were giants, they were pigmies.

But we also talked, as we lay in each other's arms, your sweat mingling with mine, your legs wrapped around mine. "George would never miss you," I would say. "I doubt he would observe you had gone."

You bit my ear. "Am I that insignificant?"

"*He* is, in our world. I shall love your children, Guss. I shall adore them as I adore yourself."

212

And you would shake your head. "I must go home. This is madness, Byron. Magnificent, midsummer madness, to be sure. But none the less, madness. Why, were it to become known. . . ."

"How can it become known?"

"It can. It will. It must. These things always do."

"Well, then, we shall laugh at them."

"We shall have to leave England."

"What could be better? I intend to do so as soon as my affairs are in order, in any event."

"You cannot, Byron. I could not live without you."

"You shall not live without me. You shall come with me. And all the rabbits as well."

You sighed. "I cannot. I cannot, I cannot, I cannot. I cannot stay here with you, another hour. It is too dangerous. You would be ruined. I would be ruined. George would be ruined. . . ."

"George is already ruined."

"Oh, Byron, life is not the amusing game you pretend it is."

"I know that, Guss, and better than anyone else. What would you have me do?"

You hesitated, then kissed me again. "It would be best if you were to marry."

"*Marry?*"

"That would allay any doubts, any suspicions. We could still see each other."

"Very seldom."

"Would our meetings not be the more glorious for that?"

"Marry," I muttered. But of course you were right. "She must have money. There is no other reason for it."

"Of course she shall have money."

"Well . . . whom? I had planned Charlotte Harley. In due course."

"You cannot wait. Nor is it certain she will inherit a penny. What about . . .", you frowned, delightfully and thoughtfully, "Adelaide Forbes?"(iii)

"I could never love her."

"Silly boy," you smiled, and kissed me on the mouth. "I do not wish you to love her. I wish you to love me. But Adelaide, because she is so plain, will be perfectly undemanding, and you may live your own life. She is certainly an heiress."

"Hm," I said disconsolately, yet resignedly. Had you asked me at that moment to throw myself from the window, I should have done so without question. "Adelaide it shall be."

Alas for the dreams of man. On Monday 5 July, I attended a small party given by Lady Heathcote, and there encountered Caro.

I had thought, and I had hoped, that I was through with crises in this direction. I had seen her once or twice during the spring, but always at large gatherings, and in a moment of misguided generosity I had allowed Murray to send her a copy of *The Gaiour*. I had assumed that we were on terms of friendship, nothing more. Now, when she entered, I greeted her as warmly as I had greeted every other woman in the room – there were perhaps twenty of us altogether – and to my amazement she did not reply, but merely turned and walked away. I recognised at once that she was in the grip of one of her more extreme moods, but did not relate its cause to myself. My dearest wish, indeed, was to learn that she had taken up some new liaison.

It was a waltzing party, and therefore an occasion at which I was very much in the background. I sat myself on a settee in the corner, where I was from time to time joined by my hostess or various other guests. To my concern, however, I discovered that Caro was also not dancing, and the waltz was her favourite occupation. She preferred to seat herself on the opposite side of the room, to stare at me. I began to feel vaguely alarmed.

Eventually it became time for supper, and I was to take in Lady Rancliffe. We proceeded together towards the dining-room, when I suddenly discovered Caro standing in the doorway. It was necessary for me almost to brush her as I passed, and she seized my hand and pressed what felt like the blade of a knife against it, murmuring, "I mean to use this."

"Against me, I presume?" I remarked, being unable to think of anything else, and being distinctly alarmed that Lady Rancliffe might overhear. I declare I was all of a twitter, and could hardly eat, attempting to reassure myself that it was just another of her bravados, but of course I could not leave the table and my partner to sit beside her and endeavour to soothe her. I did, however, manage to discover her when we rose. "Caro," I said, trying to be as cheerfully nonchalant as I could. "Why are you not dancing?"

"*You* ask me that?" Her voice was low, and absolutely seething with passion.

"Well, I do wish you would," I said, preserving my calm. "If you do not, it will be imputed to me, and I really would not like that."

Here we were interrupted by Lady Heathcote, all smiles. "We are to dance again," she said brightly. "Come, Lady Caroline, you must begin. We have seen too little of you on the floor."

"Oh, yes," she said, and turned to me. "May I waltz now?"

"I have just asked you to," I said. "You should waltz with every gentleman in turn, that is able. You are the best dancer in London, are you not?"

She stared at me for a moment, and then turned and ran out of the room.

"*Well*," said Lady Heathcote.

"I'm afraid I have offended her," I said. "If you will permit me, dear Lady H, I shall withdraw."

"Oh, Byron," she said. "I do not think that is necessary."

"Nevertheless, I would like to. Perhaps you should go to her."

She hesitated, sighed, and nodded. "I shall. You'll come again, my lord. Please."

"Of course." I bade my farewells and withdrew, but not to bed. I sat up, with a bottle, and congratulated myself on having escaped without a scene, and spent most of the night thus. Indeed, it was getting light when there was a banging on my door. I had by now moved from my St James's Street residence – well, I had to after Caro's exploit there – to rooms in the Albany. I got up, my heart pounding, and watched Fletcher proceed down the hall, and sighed with relief when I discovered it was Lord and Lady Ossulstone.

"Why, Ossulstone," I cried, quite bewildered. "How good of you to call. Lady Ossulstone. Fletcher, you'll prepare a punch."

"I have not come here to amuse you, my lord," Lady Ossulstone remarked, looking extremely angry, and at the same time extremely ugly, as she was not the most beautiful of women in any event. "I have come to tell you that you should be ashamed of yourself."

"I?" I was more dumbfounded than ever.

"You mean you don't care?" mumbled Ossulstone.

"I'm sure I shall," I agreed. "And deeply. Could I only discover what this is all about."

"Ha," remarked Lady Ossulstone.

"I say, well, perhaps he really doesn't know," Ossulstone said. "I mean, what, give the chap the benefit."

"Ha," said Lady Ossulstone once more. "You mean you do not know that Lady Caroline has attempted suicide?"

In the aftermath of that disaster I more than ever inclined towards a precipitate departure from those unwelcoming shores. But alone? I could not face that. Nor could I, after the lapse of little more than a month, merely chase behind Liz, even supposing I could raise the necessary funds. For she was gone for ever, replaced in my heart and my mind by my own sweet Sis.

I could not live without you. Certainly I could not remain in London after you tore yourself away and went home to Six Mile Bottom. A week later I was there as well. To renew our idyll. I had always loved the east country. I remembered how happy I had been at Cambridge, and here we were only a few miles distant.

Perhaps, I told myself, perhaps you told yourself, that once within the confines of your own home, surrounded by your children and all the evidence of your responsibility as a wife and a mother, your mad passion would die, and dying, consume mine with it. What fools we were. What glorious fools. To descend from my carriage, and see you standing there, with your three little girls around, with your own nanny waiting to remove them after they had greeted their Uncle George, made me wonder where I had spent the first part of my life, that I had neglected this domestic bliss. To watch you going about the ordering of your household, conferring about the daily menu, commanding here, requiring there, was to transport myself into a seventh heaven. And then, with the coming of the evening, and the lighting of the candles, with the children departed for bed, we could sit down to supper like the oldest of married couples, and smile at each other through our glasses of port, and know that a few scant minutes separated us from each other's arms. For the house was small, and my bedchamber necessarily adjoined yours. It required no more than a tap on the wall to summon me through the deserted hallway.

"This is madness," you said yet again, as I closed the door behind me. But you wore nothing at all, the days were still warm, and you were the most beautiful object I had ever seen, could ever see, will ever see.

"Did she really try to kill herself?" you asked, your head on my shoulder, while we rested in the midnight hours.

"I have no idea. I have no idea how much of what she says or does is intended, and how much just the result of her own uncertainty."

You gave that little tremble, which I now know denotes fear equally with pleasure. "I hate her, for involving you in such a scandal."

"And I almost love her for it, as it ends for ever the hopes of my marrying Adelaide Forbes. The family were aghast."

"They wrote to me." You propped yourself on your elbow, your nipple touching my shoulder. "But you must marry, Byron. You must, you must, you must."

Never had I heard you quite so vehement. "Why the haste?"

"You must," you said, and lay down again.

Now it was my turn to raise myself on my elbow, and kiss those lips, those eyes, that chin. "We are brother and sister. We can go where we like, do what we like, say what we like. No one can gainsay us. No one can criticise us. No one can say a word against us, saving only they manage to find themselves in this very room together with us."

"Suppose you so?" You threw your arms around my neck, and hugged me close. "Oh, my dearest, dearest, Byron. Mortals were not meant to sin as we, and escape the wrath of heaven. There is the surest way in all the world for us to be found guilty, and it is already done. I have missed a period."

"One period?" I queried. "Liz Harley missed two, earlier this very year, and discovered it was no more than a false alarm."

"Liz Harley is past forty," you pointed out. "And I have never needed to miss more than one in the past to be sure. I really am as fertile as a rabbit."

I kissed you on the nose. "So perhaps you are pregnant. Who can possibly say it is not George's? He *does* sleep with you?" Horrid thought.

"Whenever he happens to be here."

"Well, then, surely he has been here at some time during the past two months?"

"I suppose he has."

"Then we have nothing to worry about. Even supposing the child is the spitting image of me, *you* are very nearly the spitting image of me, so he will merely be supposed to have taken the Byron looks."

"And suppose he looks like an ape, with hair on his arms at birth?"

"Eh?"

"Is that not the mark of an incestuous child?"

Here was a potent point, and one I had forgotten. But this was certainly supposed to be the case.

217

"At least," I pointed out, "as the damage is done, there is no need for us to hold back further."

To which you agreed, albeit a trifle reluctantly. You were obviously very frightened.

As was I. I was so agitated I even made a clean breast of things to Lady Melbourne, or at least, allowed her sufficient hints to establish a certainty in the matter. She was appalled, the more so as London was already beginning to stir to rumours that wherever one saw Lord Byron one was equally sure to see his sister. This was acceptable enough. What was not was our own weakness, the weakness of any couple in love. The light of sheer delight shone in our every gaze, whenever we looked at one another, a tell-tale sign of which we, of course, were quite unaware. Lady M now joined the general consensus that I should marry, and as speedily as possible, and she added her opinion to yours, that the child, should it really be on its way, would certainly be a monster. And at last I understood the enormity of what I practised and what I risked, and like a trapped animal turned this way and that, seeking some spell to break the awful hold.

I tried the bottle, after so many years of careful sobriety. I indulged with Sheridan, and we made a fabulous pair. But he was so far steeped in an alcoholic haze that he was good for only a few hours. A better drinking companion was George Colman, (iv) who I now met for the first time, and could consume more wine than any man I have ever known, all without turning a hair. His conversation was not on a par with dear Sherry's, but at least he would still be talking when the prince of speakers was snoring in his chair.

I continued to be besieged with letters from Seaham, the Milbanke country seat located in darkest Northumberland, and from whence Annabella, having elevated herself to the position of my conscience entirely by having *refused* my hand, dissected my character with great regularity and much apparent sorrow. No doubt she meant well, but she was somewhat tiresome, the most when she took me sharply to task for taking "poor" Claughton to law, entirely in an attempt to get some of my money out of him. She considered that he had offered far too much for Newstead in any event. The absolute effrontery of it.

And I tried, always without success, to raise the funds to escape back to sunny climes. But Claughton, indeed, remained in front of my prospects like a dark shadow. He would and he wouldn't. He offered sums to be rid of his contract, then did not pay and left me with nothing.

It can therefore be understood, by you if by no one else, my love, that when in September I visited Aston and the Websters my heart was not really in any condition to indulge in the childish flirtation which was all Fanny at that time wanted. (v) I was not even prepared to seduce the child utterly, as I was given the opportunity to do. Fanny could encourage the most delicious of carnal thoughts when I was actually in her company. But once we parted, my mind turned immediately in your direction, and although the poem I wrote that night, which I consider the best thing I ever did, is assumed by all the world and certainly by Fanny as being directed at her, it was of you I thought as I penned these lines. I can repeat it now, entirely from memory:

> She walks in beauty, like the night
> Of cloudless climes and starry skies;
> And all that's best of dark and bright
> Meets in her aspect and her eyes;
> Thus mellowed to that tender light
> Which heaven to gaudy day denies.
>
> One shade the more, one ray the less,
> Had half impaired the nameless grace,
> Which waves in every raven tress,
> Or softly lightens o'er her face;
> Where thoughts serenely sweet express,
> How pure, how dear their dwelling-place.
>
> And on that cheek, and o'er that brow,
> So soft, so calm, yet eloquent,
> The smile that wins, the tints that glow,
> But tell of days in goodness spent,
> A mind at peace with all below,
> A heart whose love is innocent!

The event of course brought a distinct cooling between Lady Melbourne and myself, and she chose to suppose that the fault had to be entirely yours, merely on the grounds that you were the elder. Nor could I dissuade her. As a result our correspondence began to slacken.

And I attempted to turn myself from the dreadful path by work. But even my work was no more than an apology for my love. *The*

Bride of Abydos, as you may recall, defended the theme of incest. And earned me considerable criticism. *The Corsair* was more in the nature of an escape, into those sunny climes and warm seas that I so loved, that I so wanted to regain, if only you would have come with me, my sweet. But you would not, and I must pour out my heart into verse. (vi)

The next few months were utter misery to me, as within *another* month there could be no doubt about the event. I visited Six Mile Bottom over Christmas, and indeed finished *The Corsair* while I was there, but by then your belly was well swollen and we could do no more than talk, and remember, and perhaps plan, just a little. And put up with George, who strutted the place in fine style at expecting a fourth child, and with so little effort on his own part.

"In and out," he boasted to me one night after supper, when you had retired. "In and out, and I would say not more than once. Well, what do you expect, in the summer, with the ponies to follow? And yet there it is. I tell you, Byron, I must be the most potent fellow in the kingdom."

It was all I could do not to stuff the decanter down his throat.

So I worked, and I boxed with Jackson, and I brought myself a macaw and a parrot as their company was infinitely preferable to that of any human in my circumstances. I moped over Bonaparte's abdication, and wrote a contemptuous poem to his memory, and I even formed a scheme to visit Paris with Hobby. But of course I could not go, with your time so near. And so it was that April rolled around, and you gave birth.

To a perfectly normal child, our own Elizabeth Medora. You were overjoyed, and I could not allow you to see how disappointed I was. For my selfish desires had grown and grown, and our conversations at Christmas had led me to believe that, had the child turned out to be the monster you feared, you might have taken the step I desired above all others, and eloped with me. Am I not a monster myself?

But you were at once relieved and happy, and I could not help but feel the same. I gave you £3,000 to pay George's debts, and insisted it was a gift and not a loan, despite your protests. I still insist that it be so treated.

But what was I to do then? You were feeding the blessed infant, and could not make yourself available. And we were into another summer. What a summer. Do you remember how the sun shone, how all the world seemed to come to London, making it the capital of Europe for that splendid season? You know my feelings on monarchy, upon the whole aristocratic conspiracy which tramples the lives of ordinary folk, and yet even I could not help but thrill to the spectacle when each day as I walked abroad I was as like as not to see the King of Prussia, or the Emperor of Russia, or Prinny himself, or lesser lights like Blücher or Wellington, parading our streets. Never can there have been so many parties, so many dinners, so many gatherings. And I attended them all. I swung along from drunken ball to drunken ball, varying my time only by spending the remainder of each night drinking with Sherry and Colman. I even indulged a flirtation, with some child called Henrietta (vii) something or other, I quite forget her last name, who claimed to be a Swiss exile, or that her father was, and wrote me the most touching letters, requesting only that she be allowed to see me. Of course I granted the wish, found her quite pretty, and invited her to bed. Would you believe that the silly girl was overcome with revulsion? What had she expected, from Lord Byron? She fled, and I laughed. I doubt I would really have gone to bed with her, even had she stripped there and then. I was in love, and I have never been able to love more than a single woman at a time. But *they* had given me a reputation, and in my mad mood I would live up to it.

So I wrote. *Lara* was an immediate sequel to *The Corsair*, and in it I could forget. (viii) And I experienced Caro's tantrums and madnesses. And forgave her. Even her. In fact, my sweet, I committed an unpardonable sin. To choke her off, I told her that I was in love, and more in love than I had ever been, or that I would ever be again. And when she accused me of lying, I allowed her a glimpse of one of your letters. There was no signature on the page, and I assumed that she was too excited to notice more than the sentiment. But I am afraid she did.

And I finally concluded that terrible affair with Claughton, out of which I eventually made £25,000, and regained Newstead once again. And was able to take you there, for a first and as it has turned out, a last visit.

You came with all your children, even my own. And why not? Newstead was their home as much as ours. And at Newstead there was enough for them to do, enough staff to see to their wants, and leave us in peace. We explored. Hand in hand we walked those hallowed parks. We stood together and gazed into the lake, and I stripped and plunged in, while you smiled at my youthful energy.

221

Indeed I regained all the fervour of my youth, and indulged in such half-forgotten pleasures as shooting open soda water bottles with my pistols, while you marvelled at my accuracy.

And we loved. I found your bedchamber every night, and we lay together, and loved together, and were happy, together. Do you remember when we carved our names on that tree? Perhaps they are there yet. Perhaps they will remain for ever, twin souls seeking a way through life, together.

And while we loved, we planned. We selected a wife. Your choice was Charlotte Leveson Gower, and you undertook to make the necessary proposal. My choice, to which I was reduced, I must confess, with some uneasiness, was Annabella Milbanke. But you were allowed first go. I really supposed that Charlotte was a more pliable prospect than that Princess of Parallelograms.

But Charlotte refused. Her letter, a mass of contradictions and confusions, arrived while we were sitting together at breakfast, if you remember.

"Oh, dear," you said. "I had really hoped." And you gazed at me with those great eyes. "What's to be done?"

"I have written Miss Milbanke," I said.

"You promised to wait."

"Indeed I did, and indeed I have. I have the letter here. Would you like to read it?"

You scrutinised it.

"That is very fine," you said at last. "Not that I suppose it will accomplish a great deal. I doubt that young lady ever intends to marry. You know how many she has refused already."

George Eden, certainly; (ix) Billy Bankes, probably. And there may have been more.

"I do. Then shall I tear it up?"

"Send it. She can do no more than refuse you."

"Again."

"And what will you do then, Byron?"

"I shall leave this country. I am quite determined on it. I promise you, the moment her refusal arrives, I shall make my preparations and trouble you no more."

"Do not say that, Byron."

"Well, then, come with me."

"I cannot. Oh, Byron. . . ." You reached across the table to take my hand.

"Then allow me to carry you off."

"Oh, Byron. . . ." Your eyes filled with tears, and I was gentle enough to change the subject.

"We shall wait on the refusal."

But I would have done. Oh, how I would have done. Oh, how I wish I had.

BELLE – THE FIRST PART

No man can ever have been so utterly dumbfounded as I when that cursed letter arrived. I happened to be at Newstead, entertaining my sister and her family, and it was placed on my table, with the rest of my post, as I sat at breakfast, with Guss opposite. I opened it without a care in the world, expecting another character dissection and found instead this wayward young woman declaring that the sole object of her life was to make me happy. Ye Gods. Suppose she had set about making me *unhappy*?

I remember my heart seemed to miss a beat as I perused the damning document, and then I passed it to Guss without a word. She, meanwhile, observing the way my cheeks had paled, had become quite agitated. But she was greatly relieved when she had read the letter.

"There," she said. "Your problems are over."

I attempted to lift a cup. My hand shook so the tea was spilled in the saucer. "What's to be done?"

"A great deal," Guss decided. "You must write her again, and immediately. And you must leave for Seaham right away."

"Seaham?"

"Well, you wish to see her, don't you?"

I could only stare at her in anguish. Because I did not wish to see Annabella, at that moment. I was overwhelmed by the enormity of what I had done, of what had happened to me. I had accumulated a wife. In my position. When my heart was set upon leaving England. When my affairs, if temporarily relieved by the money we had extracted from Claughton, were as tangled as ever. When my heart was irretrievably engaged elsewhere.

And what a wife. I knew nothing of her, save what I had gleaned from her letters, and these were as inconsistent as it was possible to imagine. But she was a Milbanke. Lady Melbourne would be my aunt. That at least was an encouraging thought. But Caro would be

224

my cousin-in-law. What would *her* reaction be? I could not envisage it. I wished above all else that I could snap my fingers and wake up and discover the whole business done with, and Annabella sitting opposite me instead of Guss.

As if I would really ever replace Guss with anyone. It was her strength saw me through the next tumultuous days. Going to Seaham was at the moment out of the question, as it was very necessary for me to see Hanson and arrive at some true picture of my financial prospects. But I dared not even go to London. I contented myself with writing letters, to Annabella, of course, conveying my delight at the happy prospect in front of me, to Lady Melbourne, informing her that she had gained a nephew – and giving her full credit for the ultimate success of our courtship, as she had begun it in the first place. And Guss and I spent our last happy days together. It was now that we carved our names in that old oak, a memory of a brother and a sister, stealing those few precious moments they had never known as children.

But we could not linger for ever. Too soon it was necessary for Guss to return to Six Mile Bottom, and for me to go to town, and face Caro.

In fact there was no explosion at all. Caro had decided to play the romantic and wish me nothing but joy. I was greatly relieved.

Because I had more than enough on my plate as it was. I was very anxious to make a proper settlement upon my wife, and considered the sum of £60,000, or the equivalent of £3,000 a year for twenty years, to be adequate. Hanson of course pointed out that this was being unnecessarily generous, especially as the young lady had expectations of her own, not from her father, to be sure, he being confoundedly pinched, but from her uncle, Lord Wentworth, her mother's brother, who was an elderly fellow and reputed to be ailing. He also was interested to discover where the £60,000 was coming from, but we were on the way to regaining full title to Newstead, and he was confident of selling it once again for £120,000, so it seemed to me quite reasonable to see that half of the money went to my wife.

For I was quite determined to have a *successful* marriage, now that the die was cast. I even paid up my bets, quite cheerfully. These arose from youthful enthusiasm for bachelorhood, several years before, when I had given odds of a hundred to one in guineas that I would never face the altar. Naturally all my *friends* hastened forward to collect their dues the moment the news became known.

And in fact this was the first discordant note I discovered. The

Milbankes were quite absurdly anxious to shout the coming event from the highest mountain. It was in all the newspapers far sooner than I had deemed possible, or than I considered seemly. And was as quickly contradicted by the *Morning Post*. Here was a fine to-do. Naturally I suspected the hand of Caro in such an embarrassing situation, but when I called on the editor, Parry, and he showed me the offensive letter, I realised it was not in her hand. I could only deny the denial.

Meanwhile, Annabella and I carried on our distant romance. Her letters were naturally somewhat querulous, wondering when if ever I intended to visit her home, nor did she seem to appreciate that my honour demanded I make all the necessary arrangements for her future security, before taking up my prize. And of course it was quite impossible for her to understand the habits of old Hanson; I still hardly understood them myself. He was at his very worst at this period, and when I supposed all was arranged for a meeting between himself and the Milbanke lawyers, he suddenly took himself off to Ilfracombe in Devon, about as far away from London as he could manage while remaining in the kingdom, leaving me as usual thoroughly in the lurch.

I could only endeavour to placate my beloved by the tenor of my letters, reminding her that I desired only to be reformed, or if possible made again, by the love of a good woman. She had but to command, and I would obey. It is quite incredible, even four years later, that I should have so wished to place myself in the power of so wretched a woman, but the sentiments were at the moment genuine. I felt the hand of God in our so strange arrival at a betrothal, when it would have seemed that every possible factor was opposed to it, and I truly supposed that the wicked creations of Childe Harold and Conrad were laid to rest, that Zeluco had taken himself from off my back, and that a new Lord Byron would emerge from those dreadful ashes, the model of a married man. In short, I did my very best to convince myself that I was in love.

But by the end of the month I could delay no longer, and on 29 October I left for Seaham.

It was a Saturday, as I recall, and I actually left London in a far more settled frame of mind. True, Hanson had not yet returned, but I left a message for him to the effect that he should join me in Durham as soon as possible. More important, I had persuaded Hobby to act as groomsman, and this had done a great deal to reassure me. Not that he needed very much persuading. In common with all of my friends he assumed I was taking the most sensible step of my life.

But perhaps more important yet, I was working again, and at something quite different from anything I had attempted in the past. Douglas Kinnaird had approached me with an invitation to write the words for a musical composer who was going to publish the real old undisputed Hebrew melodies. Can you imagine an infidel like myself being intrusted with such a task? I was delighted and enthusiastic.

Yet I travelled with a heavy heart. Make no mistake, I was determined, then, to make the very best of my marriage, to be an ideal husband, to cherish and honour my wife, and in time, I hoped, love her as well. But I was giving up my freedom, and what man does not mourn the loss of that irreplaceable blessing? And I was giving up my dearest love, although being the optimist that I am I hoped this might not be on a total basis. But more than any of these, I could not discover within myself any *sexual* passion for the woman I was about to marry. I reminded myself of course that we had only met on one or two occasions; it is difficult to fall in love with the most passionate of letters – they are of use only to *remind* one of love, and to rekindle the embers – and in fact her letters had never been passionate. I told myself that so far as I remembered she was an attractive girl, and certainly well endowed with womanly curves, but how I wished the very thought of her would bring cocker up hard and excited, as for example the very scent of Liz Harley had done.

I broke my journey north at Six Mile Bottom. I conceived it the very last day of my freedom. George was away, and Guss and I were able to walk and talk, and consider. She was distressed at the fact that I was paying my first ever visit to my future wife, empty handed. To tell the truth, I had not even considered the matter.

"You should certainly have a present."

"Of what? Jewellery?"

"That would be acceptable."

"Would you believe I lack the funds? To buy anything of real value, anyway."

"Oh, Byron. Let me. . . ."

I smiled at her. "I had forgot the matter, truly."

"Well, then, a poem. Write her a poem. That is free as air, and is your peculiar talent. She will be overjoyed."

"A poem? To Annabella?" I considered the matter. But my brain

227

seemed entirely dead. A poem, to Annabella? I could imagine no words, no rhymes, to fit the subject. "I am presenting her with myself. Surely that is sufficient."

Guss frowned at me. "Are you sure you love the girl? Sufficiently for marriage?"

"I shall love her, I promise. I am ever tardy at new attachments. I shall love her."

I shall love her, I told myself as I travelled north.

The journey took longer than I had anticipated, and it was Wednesday evening before my carriage rumbled down the drive of the Milbanke home. The house glowed with candles, but apparently I was not expected, which was somewhat offputting, for there was only a butler to greet me. He took my hat and coat, and showed me into the parlour. "I will inform Miss Belle, my lord," he said, and left me alone.

Here was a fine welcome, I thought. In fact I was not in any event in the best of humours. I was still put out by Guss's strictures, and I was tired by the lengthy and uncomfortable journey. And now to be left alone like some journeyman come to force himself upon the family . . . the door opened, and there she was.

She was very simply dressed in a pale green dinner gown; ballooning shoulders and sleeves, but leaving her neck exposed, yet with a very modest *décolletage*. Her complexion was better than I remembered it, and her hair every bit as lovely, dark and rich and long. But, possibly through nervousness at meeting me after so long, her face was *tighter* than I recalled, mouth and chin seeming immovable, even as she forced a smile and came across the room.

Her hand was extended, although she did not speak. I raised her fingers to my lips. "It is a long time since we met," I ventured.

She licked her lips, not at all the way Guss did, but anxiously and quickly. "We . . . I must apologise," she stammered. "We had expected you earlier. I will fetch my parents."

She hurried from the room and returned a few moments later with the august couple, who no doubt had been hovering. Milbanke I liked. He gabbled a bit, and what-ho'd a great deal too much, but he seemed a genuinely good-hearted fellow. Lady Milbanke, fair Judith, was entirely different. She seemed to shroud me with her gaze, her smile was cold, and she was the possessor of an alarming and crushing sniff.

"We expected you on the weekend, my lord," she remarked.

"The roads are bad," I explained.

"Indeed?"

"Some mulled wine," Milbanke decided. "Mulled wine." He pulled the bell rope. "You like mulled wine, my lord?"

"I like any wine, Sir Ralph," I said, and received a sniff from the distaff side.

"Won't you sit down?" Annabella begged, moving towards the sofa.

"I'd prefer not, if you'll excuse me. I have been sitting down for three days."

"Point taken, what? What?" Milbanke glanced at his wife, and flushed. "But it is good to see you, my lord. Good to see you, what? So much to be done. So much to discuss. So much to be planned. Weddings, what? Nothing but work and expense, what? You'll have to go through the guest list, what? Three hundred and fifty at the last count."

I stared at the doddering old fool in consternation. "Three hundred and fifty?"

"Oh, we shall fill the church," Judith said. "It will be a great occasion. Seaham will have known nothing like it."

I drank some wine, and discovered Annabella gazing at me.

"You think that is too many?" she asked.

I drank some more wine. "Far too many, if I may say so."

They stared at me.

"Weddings," I explained, "are private affairs. They concern the bride and the groom, and their respective families. As I have no family, save my sister, I shall inflict only my groomsman on you. You no doubt know of him, John Hobhouse."

This brought forth a most devastating sniff. "We have heard of the gentleman," Judith said, as she might have heard of Attila.

"He is your best friend," Annabella said. "We would have expected no one else. But what of your other friends? Mr Kinnaird?"

"A groomsman, and no one else," I said. "That is my philosophy."

"Oh." She looked at her mother.

I knew I had to settle this matter immediately, once and for all. Three hundred and fifty guests? The entire village *en fête*? Why, I should die of embarrassment.

"And a church," I said. "No, no, I doubt that is a good idea, if I may say so."

"Of course you may say so, what?" Milbanke ventured.

His wife silenced him with a glance. "Where would you be wed, Lord Byron, if not in a church?"

"What is wrong with this very house, Lady Milbanke? It is a most charming house. And we shall obtain privacy."

She continued to regard me as if I were a snake for some seconds longer. Then she said, "Of course we shall bow to your wishes in the matter, Lord Byron. And now, Sir Ralph, I think we should dine."

Clearly I was never going to be close to my future mother-in-law. But in fact, no sooner had I gained this initial, and most important victory, than I felt myself warming towards the entire family. No doubt the mulled wine had a deal to do with it, reviving at once my spirits and my limbs, still frozen and cramped after my long journey. So as we sat down to what was a most excellent dinner I determined to reveal the other side of my character.

I spoke of my travels, I spoke of London, I told them of Kean, (i) who was by way of becoming a friend of mine. I put out all of my charm, and certainly old Milbanke seemed delighted. So did Annabella. I could see her anxiety melting away as she must have reasoned, and correctly, that much of my earlier disagreeableness had been the result of fatigue. Even the dragon was smiling at my jokes by the end of the meal, and I reckoned I had scored not only a victory, but a minor triumph as well.

"Draughts," Milbanke said as the port was brought. "We play at draughts after dinner. Do you play at draughts, my lord?"

I could only goggle at him.

"Or Belle could play us a tune on the piano," Judith suggested.

Belle was more adept at discerning danger signals. "I'm sure Lord Byron is extremely tired," she said, quietly.

I could have kissed her there and then. "I am," I said. "Oh, utterly exhausted. Tomorrow, I shall be a new man. But if I could possibly be allowed to retire. . . . Sir Ralph? Lady Milbanke?"

"Of course, my dear fellow," Milbanke said. "Of course. Thoughtless of us, what? Three days on the road. . . ."

"My lord left London on Saturday," Judith pointed out, like drips of icy water falling on a windowpane. "That is *five* days, Sir Ralph. I am *sure* he is exhausted."

"A good night's sleep will do wonders, I assure you," I said, cursing my mathematical inaccuracy, and rose. Belle also got up, and came with me to the door.

"I am so happy," she said, "that we are together at last."

230

I kissed her hand. "And I am the happiest man in all the world," I lied. "Tell me, what time do you rise in the morning?"

"About ten." She squeezed my fingers. "There is so much I want to show you."

"There is so much I want to see," I agreed, although I doubt we were discussing the same thing. "Good night, Belle." It was the first time I had used the diminutive myself, and she seemed pleased.

I gained my bedchamber, and sat down for Fletcher to draw off my boots.

"Well, my lord," he said. "They seem an amiable family."

"Fletcher," I said. "You are a fool and a blackguard. Go to bed."

Which he did, being used to my moods. Was it a mood? I assumed so at the time. I reasoned at great length. I was still tired, I was still brooding on Guss, I was apprehensive about the whole thing, I was in strange surroundings, I had been invited to spend an evening pushing little bits of wood about a board, the port had been of inferior quality, why, any man would have been put out. But not sufficiently to have an icy hand seeming to close on his stomach. I had kissed her fingers, I had squeezed her hand. I had inhaled her perfume, I had endeavoured, without success, to look down her bosom. I had heard the rustle of her gown, always a pleasure to me, and I had listened to her voice. And cocker remained as limp as if I had tumbled the whole day long. I knew then that I was on the road to disaster. And yet I could not stop myself. The wheels of a marriage had been set in motion, and short of proving myself the most abominable cad, I could do nothing to stop them now.

I slept badly and awoke early. But I was entirely reluctant to rise. I felt that it was necessary for me to prepare myself very thoroughly before once again risking exposure to the sniff or the what ho, or indeed to Belle's somewhat muted admiration. I chose to think of it as admiration because that was the word selected by Lady M. I personally was uncertain *how* I would describe my future wife's attitude, save that the word thoughtful would come into it. There it was. She was *thinking* about me, a good deal of the time. Far too much of the time. I have never cared for women who *think*. They are creatures of mood, creatures of instinct. A woman who begins to think, about any man but especially her fiancé, is a woman about to become a menace.

The fault was mine, of course. For two years, indeed, she had done little *else* but think about me, and had revealed as much in her letters.

231

Possibly the damage was done, but if I *was* going to marry her, I had best set about correcting the earlier mistake. She could think about me all she wanted, when we were separated. When we were together, she must do nothing more than *feel*.

My course thus charted, I rose and dressed, and descended for breakfast. It was just noon, but I discovered that I was alone, the family having already eaten. Too late I remembered that Belle had told me she rose at ten. Then where was she?

"Miss Belle has gone for a walk," the butler said.

To do some more thinking, no doubt. I could not but regard this as a sinister development. Yet she returned a few minutes later, windblown and pink-cheeked, but looking the more attractive for that.

I kissed her hand. "I'm afraid I overslept."

"You were tired," she said. "But I so wanted to show you my favourite walk. Along the cliffs."

"I have finished breakfast," I said. "And am at your disposal."

She hesitated, no doubt having just made that particular walk, then smiled and said, "Well, then, if your lordship is ready."

We walked side by side, down a path, and through a wicket gate which gave access on to the cliff. "Isn't it marvellous?" she asked.

Well, I suppose it was. The wind was fresh off the North Sea and more than a hundred feet below us was whipping the waves into whitecaps, and sending them pounding against the rocks. But it was also uncommonly cold, and the sun had quite forgotten to make any effort to find its way through the curtain of grey which obliterated the sky. The last time I had consciously stood on a cliff to look at the sea had been at Sunium, just outside Athens. I remembered that it had been so warm I had taken off my coat, and the heat and the gentle surge of the sea below me had so entranced me that I had carved my name on a great pillar there, the remains, so it is said, of Neptune's temple.

Perhaps a shadow crossed my face, for she sighed, and turned away. "I grew up here," she said. "No doubt my spirit has absorbed a great deal of this bleak climate."

I held her hand. "I am sure there is nothing a warming fire will not cure."

She raised her head, her eyes asking a question.

"And I am a perfect cauldron," I assured her.

"It is easier to be consumed by heat than frozen by cold."

I refused to be put off. "It is also a deal more enjoyable, if one is going to be consumed by anything," I said, and kissed her on the mouth. Her lips remained closed, so closed indeed, that I was forced to suppose she had never been kissed before, especially as she blushed alarmingly.

"We should go in," she said, giving a tug on her hands.

I would not let go. "Belle," I said. "Belle. We are going to marry. After all these years. Belle. . . ."

"Believe me, my lord," she said. "I am overjoyed. I am the happiest woman in the world. But we must go in. Did you not know, the lawyers have arrived. Yours as well as mine."

I was not pleased at having to forego our *tête-à-tête*, but on the other hand I *was* pleased that Hanson had finally turned up, and indeed the rest of the day was taken up with perfectly amicable horse-trading. The Milbankes were delighted with my proposals, and gave no thought, or at least asked no questions, concerning where the £60,000 was to be found, supposing Newstead was not sold. On their part, they offered a settlement of £20,000, which was far more than I had expected. This was just as well, for Sir Ralph, rather like myself, had absolutely no ready cash and there was going to have to be a great deal of mortgaging, and in fact only just over £6,000 was ever actually raised. The rest was put out to interest, from which sum Belle's pin money of some £300 a year was to be found. But in addition to these sordid details she also had great expectations from her uncle, Wentworth, and all in all it seemed that in the course of time we were going to be a very wealthy couple. Could we survive that long.

The lawyers had to be entertained, of course, and it was midnight before we adjourned to bed, whilst next day there was more discussing and planning, everyone in fine good humour, except the main protagonists. I was becoming desperate. I simply had to discover, and very soon, whether I could love this girl, physically.

But at last it was all decided, our signatures were duly appended to the documents, and the legal luminaries departed for their journey south. "What a relief," declared Sir Ralph after dinner. "To have it all settled. Rather good, what? Settled a settlement. And now, draughts." He was a most confoundedly single-minded fellow.

But I could hold myself back no longer. "If you will forgive me, Sir Ralph," I said. "As it is now all settled, may I beg to be allowed an hour alone with Belle?"

"Whatever for?" demanded the dragon.

"*We* have things to settle, as much as anyone else, dear lady," I said, over-indulgence in wine causing me to be somewhat flippant.

She glared at her daughter, and Belle hastily rose. "I'm sure Lord Byron and I *do* have much to talk about, Mama," she said, and preceded me into the small parlour. "I do wish and beg, my lord," she said, "that you would not tease Mama quite so much."

"You have my word. But Belle. . . ."

"Whatever are you doing?" she cried.

"Shutting the door," I explained. "And locking it."

"My *lord*."

"Belle," I said, crossing the room and taking her hands. "I shall never tease your mother again. I swear it. But you must swear to forgive my moods. Belle, Belle. I am a man. I am Childe Harold. Have you forgotten? And you are the most beautiful thing on earth. . . ." Well, that was stretching a point, but in fact as she had commenced to breathe somewhat heavily and her face was filled with colour she was becoming more attractive every moment. "And we are betrothed," I reminded her, "beyond hope of recall . . ." An unfortunate turn of phrase . . . "and I can wait no longer to hold you in my arms."

This I was accomplishing as I spoke, sliding my hands round her shoulders to bring her against me. Nor did she resist, but allowed herself to be pressed against my bosom.

"Oh, Byron," she whispered. "You know so much, and I so little."

"Then it shall be my pleasure to be your mentor," I said, and kissed her hair, it smelt delightful, and her forehead, and each eye, and each ear, and her nose, and was rewarded with a certain flicker from the direction of my breeches, before I arrived at her mouth. "Your tongue, my sweet. Grant me your tongue," I whispered.

Her head jerked back. Her eyes were enormous.

And her mouth was open. I thrust forward, and gained the touch I sought, but no more than a touch, and she was away again.

"My lord," she protested, now pushing against me. "Is that not unhealthy?"

Here was a point of view which had never occurred to me before.

"My dearest Belle," I said, once again holding her close. "We are to be married. We shall sleep in the same bed every night for the rest of our lives. . . ." Poetic licence, to be sure, especially as I still preferred to sleep alone, but rendered necessary by the circumstances. ". . . we shall be sharing every inch of our bodies. I am going to *lie* with you, Belle. Besides that, a kiss is nothing."

"Oh, my God," she whispered, and I released her again.

"You do understand what is entailed by marriage?"

She flushed. "Of course I do, my lord. I. . . ." She bit her lip. "I had assumed I still had a few months in which to prepare."

"To prepare?" I cried. "To anticipate, you mean. To enjoy. To wish passed in a second that we may get down to the true business of love. And why should we wait a moment, as we are now betrothed?"

Saying which I again folded her in my arms, nor would I accept her mumbled protests or even her vain attempts to push me off. We wrestled for a few moments in the centre of the floor, my weight insensibly carrying her back, until her knees touched an armchair, and we fell into it, I winding up sitting on her lap, from which position I could do nothing better than assault her breasts as well as her lips, discovering that these were as promising as I had estimated, being large and firm. Her struggles subsided, however, her tongue even achieved a measure of enthusiasm, and I conceived the crisis past, as well it might have been, had we not immediately been interrupted by a knock on the door. Perhaps we had made a noise, or more likely the dragon was merely cursed with curiosity.

Instantly I was on my feet, and Belle was sitting up, straightening her gown and a perfect furnace glowing in her cheeks. The moment, which might I believe have prevented a lot of future unhappiness, one way or another, had it been permitted to continue, was gone, and she bade me a chaste and nervous good night.

Next morning I observed that she was at great pains to avoid being alone with me, even foregoing her customary suggestion that we take a walk, and when I invited her to do so, pleading an attack of the vapours which soon had her retiring to bed. So I was left with nothing to do but play draughts with Sir Ralph, and consider my situation, which seemed to me to be alarming in the extreme. I realised I would have to take the bull by the horns, so to speak, and when my betrothed once again opted to leave her bedroom, I was forced to assume my most masterful demeanour and once again insist on being left alone with her.

But this time she avoided the parlour and opted for the study, which left less room for wrestling, and in which she could seat herself behind her father's desk, which she assumed would prove a formidable barricade against frontal assault. "I must sit down," she lied prettily, "as I really am still feeling a little weak."

"I am sorry to hear it," I said. "Can it be something we ate?"

She decided not to take *that* bait, as I was still standing before her in perfect health. "No, no," she said. "I have been subject to this ailment from birth. Although . . ." she hastily continued, having observed my expression, "it is not at all serious or contagious."

I sat on the desk. "It shall be my business to see that it in no way interferes with our happiness," I promised. For if it was seduction she required, then seduction she would have, and I would permit not a trace of my very natural resentment to be visible. I took her hands. "Oh, Belle," I said. "There is so much I want to say to you, so much I want to do to you. . . ."

"My lord," she said uneasily, beginning the tug of war.

I would not let her go. Instead I bent my head, and after a moment she allowed me her lips.

"I am not a monster, Belle. I am a man. A man in love." Well, that was true enough, even if *she* was not the object of my adoration. "A man with red blood in his veins. As you are a woman. Belle, I must love you. I must love you now. I must. . . ." I drew her up from the chair, and she came willingly enough.

"Do you really love me, Byron?" she whispered. "I had been so afraid. You act so strangely. So coldly. Oh, Byron, if I thought you really loved me. . . ."

"I do," I promised her most fervently, kissing her hair and her eyes and her nose while my hands once again roamed those splendid mountains, all without discovering a way inside, and so abandoned that sport to slide down her shoulders and caress her bottom, which also seemed to possess all the right qualities. She positively melted into my arms, even tried some kissing of her own, and I counted my victory won, and was trying to decide whether she would accept it on the desk against which we were leaning, there being no other suitable surface save the floor, when she suddenly seemed to recollect herself, wriggled free as I was taken entirely by surprise, and gained the door, flushed and panting, and looking, if truth be told, quite delightful.

"I promised Mama I would assist her in the kitchen," she said.

But the day was mine. And I counted a final victory but a brief period off. I was as pleased as punch, because for a moment there she had really aroused me, and I could foresee no real difficulties when we properly came to grips, which was a great relief.

But next day she remained in bed, her vapours having returned.

This annoyed me. Yet would I have overcome my anger with determination had I not been disagreeably disturbed by the arrival of a post, which had followed me all the way from London, containing a most piteous appeal from Miss Massingberd. Her mother had died, it seemed, and the daughter had inherited all the debts. Amongst which were still mine, unpaid, and for which she was being dunned most desperately, with the threat of gaol hanging immediately above her head unless relief was forthcoming, and most shortly.

This threw me into a deep depression. "*Crede* Byron." I had, in point of fact, if not forgotten those earliest of my commitments, decided to ignore them as my creditors had not actually been pressing. It had not occurred to me that they would apply immediately to my surety. And the worst thing of all was that there was nothing I could do about it. There was nothing I could do about anything. I walked the cliffs by myself in a fine frenzy of desperation, the enormity of what I had done seeming suddenly to strike me squarely between the eyes. I was in debt up to those very eyes; my properties were as far as ever from being sold; I had contracted marriage to a woman I did not love and could not see myself loving while she continued in this vein, and upon whom I had settled a fortune I did not possess.

I could see no way through the morass which lay before me, and truly looked down on those cold and windswept waters beneath me and wondered how they would feel when entered from a height of over a hundred feet. It might have been best for all had I jumped.

But I did not, returned to the house, and retired to bed myself, so that when Belle decided to appear I was absent, and it was two days before we again made each other's acquaintance.

"My lord," she said, at breakfast. "I am so glad you are recovered." But she spoke tartly, and I realised that *she* was angry with *me*, for having absented myself for a day, while she made a habit of it twice a week. And I had not yet regained my sunny disposition. I rose immediately, bowed to Lady Milbanke, and said, "Belle, I would have a word with you, if I may. In private. If I may."

She glanced at her mother, got up and walked out of the breakfast room without a word. This time she returned into the parlour, and allowed me to close the door. She did not look at all like the shrinking young woman of a few days previously. But I was not disposed to take note of *her* moods.

"Belle," I said. "This constant manoeuvring, as if we were two prize-fighters, is no basis for a marriage."

"Indeed it is not," she replied, much to my surprise. "But I wonder if you truly ever had any intention of marrying me?"

I stared at her in total surprise. "We have signed a settlement."

"Bah," she said. "What is a settlement? What love have you ever shown for me? What presents have you ever given me? You have come here without even a ring to seal our engagement."

"Belle. . . ."

"When we are together, what do you talk about? Your adventures and your sister. Your *sister*." Her voice rose an octave.

Had I really mentioned Guss so often? I supposed I had, but I could not remember doing so to distraction. Yet Belle was certainly distracted. There were tears in her eyes, and suddenly she seized a vase and threw it on the floor. Shades of Caro.

"Belle," I said again, and caught her arm as she was about to attend to some more china. "Belle. Love you? I would think I had shown my love for you in every possible way. Oh, dear, dear, Belle, it is you who seem reluctant to reveal your love for me. . . ." My hands were seeking once more to caress her into acquiescence when she suddenly pulled free again and jumped away from me.

"Love," she shouted. "You call that love? That is carnal lust. You would feel that for a whore." And she bit her lip to suggest she had never used such a word before, which I can well believe to be true.

"Belle," I said, once more advancing.

"Keep away from me," she shouted. "I have agreed to marry you. I thought . . . I thought you were a sensitive creature, a poet. Not a rake and a lecher." And this after reading *Childe Harold*, and no doubt *The Corsair* as well. "I know my duty," she continued. "I am sworn to be your wife. When that time comes, *if* that time ever comes, I shall submit to your lust. Submit, submit, submit. But until then I demand to be treated with respect and with true love. I demand it," she cried, now completely bursting into tears. "I demand it. Or we had best annul the entire engagement now."

BELLE – THE SECOND PART

Was ever a sinner granted a more directly aimed shaft of saving light from a benign Providence? I had to do nothing more than launch another amorous assault, and her pride would have demanded she implement her threat. And I, poor deluded fool, could think only of how to avoid such a catastrophe, for her look was so stern, her whole demeanour so agitated, that I counted myself already lost. Unless I could appeal to her basic femininity. But I had not studied Kean's technique in vain. I gave a gasp, staggered back, and fainted into the sofa like your most accomplished maiden.

Belle was defeated. She gave a shriek of fear, and dropped to her knees beside me. "Byron," she wailed. "Oh, my dearest Byron. Forgive me. I did not mean to hurt you so."

I allowed myself a sigh, and an open eye, at the same time running my fingers across her shoulders and down her back, for a fainting man is really not responsible for his actions. "Indeed you have hurt me, sweet Belle," I groaned. "And yet I would beg your forgiveness. And have you understand that whatever I do, it is because of love for you." A pretty speech, and a pretty damning speech as well, for it melted her entirely, and left her as she supposed in command of the situation.

"I do understand, dear Byron," she said, and kissed me tenderly. And then rose, encouraging me to sit up. "We are a strange pair," she said, truthfully enough. "You, so overbubbling with genius, and with *passion*, and I, perhaps similarly endowed . . ." what effrontery ". . . but not yet permitted to reveal myself to the world. Nor can I, even to you, until after we are wed. I cannot, Byron, much as I would wish. I beg you to believe this."

"Oh, I do, I do."

"Well, then, my solution to our problem is this. That you should return to London. Do not look so shocked, my sweet. Our separation will be brief. The preparations for our marriage will go ahead. And then, then I may come to you with all the innocent eagerness of a wife. Say that you agree this is our best course, my lord."

Of course I agreed. I do believe that had I spent another day in that house I would have suffocated.

It may well be asked what prompted me to adopt this suicidal course? Well, of course, partly I was motivated by that greatest of human curses, pride. I had proposed to this girl, and been refused. I had proposed again, and been accepted. I could not contemplate the gossip and scandal that would surround a broken engagement. Had I been able to foresee the scandal and the gossip with which I was to be surrounded just over a year later I would have laughed at my innocence.

And, again partly, I was driven by a sense of necessity. I was *aware* that I was surrounded by enmity, by jealousy, at my alarming literary success, by concern, at my more and more radical leanings, by loathing, on the part of those who listened to tales of my amatory adventures and conquests. And my support was dwindling. Even Holland was growing wary of showing himself too much to be my friend, and dearest Liz, that surest pillar of strength, was reposing in Sardinia. I counted myself a friendless waif in the vicious jungle that was London society, and knew that the only way I could regain my former esteem was by making a safe and honourable marriage.

But most of all, and I admit it freely, I was now becoming decidedly interested in this young prude who was to be my wife. I could not help but consider that the sole cause of our bickering was her *in*experience in the art of love, and my *ex*perience. But this was a state of affairs which had to alter, and in my favour, as she knew and acknowledged.

I had sufficient other problems on my mind. Claughton, having paid up his contracted deposit, had assumed that this restored his right to Newstead, at least for the coming year, while he endeavoured to raise the next portion of the purchase price, and Hanson had convinced me that the man was obviously sincere, if temporarily pinched, and that therefore we could do nothing better than go along with him. Hence my generosity in the matter of Belle's settlement, as I really had assumed my days of poverty were behind me. But the rascal now chose this worst of all possible moments to inform us that he definitely could not complete the purchase, nor could he pay another penny.

Here was catastrophe. I could not possibly contemplate setting up a married establishment when my creditors were already inclined to trail me around the country, hands outstretched. I wrote in this vein to Belle, stating the exact facts of the situation, informing her that Hanson as usual was confident of finding another buyer, and suggesting it would be by far the best thing for us to wait a year, or perhaps two, before setting up house together. After all, we were both young, and we had already waited two years since my first proposal.

To my amazement her reaction was that I was seeking only to toy with her affections, and had no intention of honouring my engagement at all. Compared with me, in fact, Claughton was a knight in shining armour. It was to be a wedding this year or nothing.

Thank God for the bottle. And for friends like Kean, and Moore, and my faithful birds, even if one night when I was in my cups the beastly parrot nearly removed one of my fingers. And thank God for Guss, who endeavoured to calm my tangled nerves, but the dear thing really went about it the wrong way by reminding me of how much Mignonne (our pet name for Medora) resembled her handsome uncle. (i)

Yet, as I have said before, the wheels of a marriage, once set into motion, are not easy to stop. As if in a trance I applied for a special licence from the Archbishop of Canterbury, to enable us to wed as and when we chose, and without the inconvenience of banns, and on Christmas Eve, with snow thick on the ground and settling around my heart, Hobby and I set out for Seaham.

We started together, but did not long continue, for as we arrived in the east country he went on to Cambridge, while I lingered at Six Mile Bottom. I would of course have visited Guss for Christmas in any event, in view of our late departure – the Milbankes had hoped for a Christmas wedding, with all the attendant festivities, but I was not to be so trapped – but actually a break in our journey was an absolute necessity, for never can there have been a colder winter, at least that early. Our people could scarce keep their seats, and even inside the coach the pair of us nearly froze.

But Six Mile Bottom was the most agreeable shelter a man could find. Here was tranquillity. Here was the one woman with whom I could be utterly at peace. And here I wrote a letter begging to be released from my engagement. Perhaps it was sheer nervousness, such as I am told afflicts many men on their way to the altar, perhaps it was some more deep-seated sense of onrushing disaster, but I knew then that my marriage was doomed. Alas, how to separate our deep felt *senses* from the gift of clairvoyance? Guss persuaded me not to send the fateful document, and instead we continued our journey.

Slowly. The cold increased, the roads were bad. We read a new edition of Gibbon sent me by Murray as a sort of wedding present, and enjoyed it thoroughly. Oh, to write such *epic* stuff. And to *know* so much. Shall I ever attain such stature, such certain immortality? There's a glimpse of the future I'd appreciate.

On we trundled, slowly but alas surely, Ferrybridge, then Sheffield, then Thirsk, just north of York. I'm afraid I welcomed the endless delays, the miniscule progress. Hobby pretended to be shocked, but I wonder how he would have felt on the way to his own wedding? "An execution," I said. "That is how I feel, dear old friend. Why should I not walk slow?"

But no thunderbolt came from heaven to decide the matter for ever in my favour, and why should it, as the Deity had offered me an escape, and I had refused to take advantage of it. From that day to this, I do believe the Fellow has washed His hands of me. So it was that at eight o'clock on the evening of Friday – ever an unlucky day – 30 December 1814, after a week's travelling, we arrived.

To the usual welcome. We had been expected on Christmas Eve. This time there was not even Belle to greet us in the parlour, but we were shown straight to our rooms and told to dress for dinner. I reflected that every husband shackles his own ball and chain, and did as I was bid, patted Fletcher on the shoulder as Charles I no doubt bade farewell to his own faithful servant, and took myself downstairs, to find Hobby already there, with mouldy Milbanke, and Belle, who on hearing my step leapt up and positively ran to meet me, throwing both arms around my neck in a fashion she had never previously indulged, so that I was forced to believe she was impressing Hobby.

But her tears were real enough – of joy, I presume – and there were no remonstrances at all while I was clutching her to my bosom and we were both mumbling our undying love.

From which pleasurable occupation we were interrupted by the dragon.

"My lord," she remarked. "How very nice to see you, after all."

"Well . . ." I began, and peered at Hobby.

"The fault is mine, Lady Milbanke," said the noble fellow. "Bad roads, snow, why, I felt my first duty was to present the groom safe and sound, and not disrupted by a toss into a ditch."

The sniff he received rocked him back into a chair. "Winter is ever thus, Mr Hobhouse. And now. . . ." She made an airy gesture. "I doubt not my husband has forgot his epithalamium. I *know* the cake is stale. As for our guests. . . ."

It turned out that despite my insistence there were several of these. A man called Hoar from Durham, a confidential agent of Sir Ralph's, and his wife, and the Reverend Thomas Noel, Rector of Kirkby Mallory, an illegitimate son of Lord Wentworth's – what right had they to criticise me? – who would perform the ceremony. But he was an open, good-hearted fellow, who I was able to charm, as indeed I charmed the entire assembly at supper, partly as usual owing to the effects of Sir Ralph's excellent mulled wine, and partly at my gratification at being so warmly greeted by dearest Belle. I began to feel positively optimistic.

Still I deemed it best to sleep in next day, and give Hobby an opportunity to nose around. Which he did to great effect, but in a direction calculated to restore my gloom, for after a chat with the Milbankes – and Belle, I imagine – he informed me that they were convinced all of my financial problems were due to Hanson. They even went so far as to doubt the dear old fellow's probity. This was extremely disagreeable, not only because the thought that my future in-laws should spend so much time dissecting my affairs was disagreeable, but because in my isolated condition Hanson was one of the few rocks upon which I could build any confidence, and to have that reduced to dribbling sand was more than I could bear.

But I put a brave front on the matter as that evening was the *rehearsal*. Hobby acted the part of Belle, and Hoar gave him away. Everyone was in the best of spirits, thanks as usual to the mulled wine, and the event went off very well, ending at midnight when we shook hands for the New Year. This was Saturday. New Year's Day was Sunday, and the horrid event had been fixed for eleven o'clock on the morning of Monday 2 January.

On the day, worst of omens, I was up early, and unable to stay in bed, so that I commanded Fletcher to dress me in my full garb, white gloves and all, whereupon I descended into a deserted house, save for the servants, took a hasty breakfast, and went for a stroll in the grounds, despite the fact that it was still quite dark, so overheated mentally that I could ignore the cold. For a while. It soon drove me inside again, and I took refuge in that study where I had nearly conquered Belle. I sat at the desk and discovered, to my amazement, a copy of Sandys' translation of Ovid. Now, who had been perusing

243

that manual of love? I turned the pages, soon found myself reading, and was interrupted by Noel, dressed in full canonicals.

Hobby arrived soon after, and then Sir Ralph and Judith.

"Well," said the dragon. "A fine day for a wedding." She seemed determined to be cheerful. "Who's for tea?"

We all dutifully accepted the offer, and the tray was brought in, but her hand rattled so much that more liquid went on to the floor than into any cup, and we were quite relieved when the other parson, the Reverend Wallace, finally arrived. It was now half past ten, so Hobby and I retired up to my room until summoned.

"Well, old boy," Hobby said. "Now is the hour."

I could not speak a word, but sat on my bed.

"You'd best fortify," he recommended, and poured me a glass of port.

A knock on the door summoned us, and we went down to the drawing-room, where the two parsons, Sir Ralph, and Lady Milbanke were waiting. Cushions were already placed on the floor, but I was not required to kneel until the very moment. At five to the hour exactly Belle appeared. She wore a very simple muslin gown trimmed with lace, and a white muslin curricle jacket over. Her head was bare, which was a surprise to me, but her hair had never looked more lovely.

She was accompanied by her nurse, the infamous Clermont, whom I had not really noticed before, nor did I notice now. After all, however one holds on to a nurse as long as possible, the bonds of childhood intimacy are surely severed with marriage. How little I knew of either my wife or the evil genius who hung around her neck like a millstone. (ii)

But Belle herself, on this morning, looked utterly composed. She gave me half a smile, and remained gazing at me while Noel placed us on the cushions, and the others took their places, Sir Ralph next to his daughter, with Hobby next to him. Lady Milbanke and Mrs Clermont waited to one side.

Wallace conducted the service. I remember that when he came to the part "with all my worldly goods I thee endow" I could not help glancing at Hobby with a half smile. But Belle's responses were absolutely clear, and she never once took her gaze from my face.

The only discordant note came with the fitting of the ring. This I had regarded as the one good omen in the entire history of my engagement, for shortly after Belle's letter of acceptance had arrived, one of my gardeners at Newstead, in turning over the soil, had discovered a long lost wedding ring of my mother's, and I had determined there and then that we should use it at my own wedding. But now it was discovered that the band, a plain gold one, was too large for Belle's finger – and no real wonder, as she was slim where Mama had been stout. She herself took the disappointment with a smile, but the sniff behind me rattled the window-panes. Indeed the dragon had cause, for she was weeping, but I am informed that this is not uncommon amongst mothers of the bride. Alas Belle, determined that the ring should remain on her finger, secured it there with a length of black ribbon, produced by the infamous nurse. In a trice my mood was changed. Black cannot possibly be regarded as other than an unlucky colour.

But a moment later, ring or no, there could be no gainsaying the fact that Belle and I were well and truly married.

The ceremony over, we signed the register, and I kissed the bride. It was a chaste kiss, and yet her lips moved on mine, and gave some promise of better things to come. But she was weeping as hard as her mother, now, and was soon removed by Mrs Clermont to change for the journey to our honeymoon house at Halnaby.

Meanwhile I had to endure a kiss from Judith, as well as from Hobby, and much hand shaking from Sir Ralph and the two parsons. At least we were spared the epithalamium, but not some other indulgences, for despite my insistence the bells from the neighbouring church of Seaham suddenly began to ring, while several of the village worthies discharged their muskets outside the house. Yet I felt no anger. In fact, I felt nothing at all, neither emotion nor dejection nor elation. It had happened, and now I could only abide by the circumstances.

Belle was gratifyingly quick about her toilette, and returned within forty minutes. She looked quite lovely in a slate-coloured satin pelisse trimmed with white fur. Our goodbyes were speedily made, but I was hardly aware of anything until I was seated in the carriage, shaking Hobby's hand. He seemed to me the only concrete factor in the entire business. Together we had braved the perils of the east, and returned unscathed. When I thought of the Albanian bandits, the tremendous storms, our near wreck at sea, how much had we endured. And how much had we looked forward to enduring in the future. All come to naught. My God, I thought as I stared at his smiling face, I shall never again return to Greece.

The carriage was moving, and he was tugging, and I must let him go. I leaned back in my seat, and looked at a strange face, some child I had noticed around the house. I could only stare, in total consternation.

"You remember Meg?" Belle asked from beside me. And when I continued to stare, she added, somewhat sharply. "My maid."

"Here?" I demanded. "With us?"

"It is too cold for her to travel on the box, my lord," Belle explained, gently, but with just a hint of asperity.

I was suddenly angry. Indeed I suppose anger was the emotion which had been most lapping at my consciousness throughout the morning. "Oh, come now, sweetheart," I said. "Tell the truth. You were afraid I might rape you on the journey."

Pink spots appeared in her cheeks, but she did not reply.

"Well," I said, "as she is your maid, I am sure she knows all about you. Willie knows all about *me*." I opened the hatch, allowing a blast of icy air to enter which had both the women shuddering. "Willie, are you there?"

"I am here, my lord," answered the good fellow.

"Tell her ladyship that you know all about me."

"Indeed my lord. Whatever you wish."

"Please close the hatch," Belle said, still speaking softly. "It is very cold."

I closed the hatch. "Will I not get a kiss for it?" I was being hateful, I knew it even at the time. But now anger was being joined by fear. I wished warmth, and passion, and laughter. I could have ridden for ever through the snow with Guss seated at my side. And here was only patient resignation.

She was frowning, and moving her eyes, to indicate she was embarrassed by the presence of the maid. But it *was* her maid, and I was fast slipping into one of my devilish moods. I seized her face between my hands and kissed her mouth, forced it open with the fury of my assault, got hold of her tongue and sucked it into mine by sheer strength, released her to watch her fall against the cushions, gasping and pink cheeked while Meg attempted to pretend she was looking out of the window.

I expected Belle to say something, but she pushed herself up and sat in silence. Had she spoken I would have apologised there and then, but as she preferred not to, I kept quiet myself. And so we rode into the snow. It had been noon when we left Seaham, and it was forty miles to Halnaby, so clearly we were on the road for some time, as it was impossible to travel very fast. We rumbled along, with an occasional slither to bring the women anxiously upright. I grew bored and longed for conversation, but every time I turned towards my wife, she turned to look out of the window. Clearly she was angry with me. Well, bugger her, I thought, and had the strangest of thoughts. She was my wife. She was bound to perform my will in a way not even Caroline had, perhaps. And I was a different man to the innocent boy who had worshipped at that Paphian altar.

I shook my head to rid it of the clogging filth, found I could not succeed, and attempted to cure myself by singing one of the Albanian songs I had learned on my travels. I hoped I might thereby induce a thaw, as surely she would ask what the wild, martial music was. But she gave me a single scandalised glance, and continued to stare out of the window.

We passed through Durham, and the bells began to ring. "Ringing for our happiness, I presume," I said, and was once again ignored. I sat there for some time longer, then I took her hand. "My dear Belle, I apologise for my ardour. Believe me, it is better to possess a husband who desires than one who does not."

Still no reply, and she endeavoured to free the hand.

"Just as I imagine many a man would enjoy a wife who is dumb," I said, attempting to introduce some humour into our situation. "But I prefer conversation."

Still she merely gazed at me, although she ceased her attempts to free herself.

"Belle," I said, as gently as possible. "We cannot go on like this. It will come to an annulment. It must."

My threat had its effect. She licked her lips. "Not on my account, my lord," she said.

"Then we have nothing to fear," I promised her. "But oh, if you had married me two years ago. How much happier we should have been."

She closed her eyes, as if I had caused her pain. But her hand remained in mine. And so, eventually, we came to Halnaby.

Halnaby was Milbanke territory once again, and Belle's spirits rose accordingly. She was quite gay as she descended from the carriage to greet the assembled servants, dominating whom was another old nurse of hers, a Mrs Minns. I followed more slowly. Quite apart from the fact that I was frozen half stiff, I never liked displaying my limp to strangers, and strange servants least of all. But the warmth beckoned, and I followed my bride inside, through a gauntlet of greetings and salutes.

"You'll wish to see your rooms, my lord, my lady," Mrs Minns decided, and led us up the stairs, while below us Fletcher and the butler unloaded our boxes. Our bedrooms, the smallest in the house, and facing north, would you believe it, in the dead of winter, had connecting doors, and in each room a fire blazed to give some semblance of warmth. It was by now quite dark, and neither of us had eaten more than a morsel, during a halt at the inn of Rusheyford. Yet I felt very little hunger, at least for food.

The fact was, the sensation of being married, of *owning*, had been growing on me throughout the final hours of our drive, as Belle's hand had lain in mine, and now that we had come into the light and the warmth, and I could again see how becoming she looked in her fur-trimmed pelisse, I began for the first time to feel a real passion for her.

Which she, apparently, was a long way from reciprocating. She turned to me with a smile. "Well, my lord, safe arrived. You'll wish to lie down for a while before dinner, I have no doubt. Minns, you'll send Meg to me."

"Of course, Lady Byron," Minns said, obviously savouring the elevation of her erstwhile charge.

I had remained by the door, and now I checked her. "You'll do no such thing, Mrs Minns."

"My lord?"

"I wish to lie down," I said. "Most certainly. But not alone. And without the aid of a maid." They glanced at each other in consternation, and I contributed a smile of my own. "We *are* honeymooning, Minns."

She burst into a ridiculous giggle, and fled the room. I carefully closed and locked the door behind me.

"My lord," Belle said. "Byron. You know how the servants gossip."

"My lady," I said. "Belle. You know, and they know, the reason we are here." I advanced towards her.

"My lord," she gasped, and backed away from me.

"Belle," I said, reaching for her. "We are married. You can have no more scruples."

She evaded my hand and turned away for the next room. "You must give me time, my lord. Byron," she cried, for I had caught her round the waist.

"No time, my dear delightful duck," I whispered in her ear. "I have none to spare." She smelt delightful, and she felt delightful as she wriggled in my grasp, quite unavailingly.

"You'll tear my gown," she said, once again almost pulling free, so that I overbalanced as I reached after her again, and we fell together, fortunately not on the floor but across a sofa. She was on her face, and I knelt above her, looking down at a row of buttons. "I shall indeed tear your gown," I said, being filled with a sudden maniacal lust. Cocker was hard, and I was going to *love* this girl. I knew I could do it, now. "It is meant for tearing."

I ripped away the buttons, and uncovered white shoulders and then a corset. Never have I felt quite such a rush of passion. I stood up and released my breeches, sending my drawers after them. Belle seized her opportunity to roll over and sit up, gazed in horror at the enormous battering ram which was to be her fate – and I do believe mine was the first such thing she had ever seen in her life, for she was an only child – and fell back again with a sigh, pretending to faint. At least I assume it was pretence; if it were real it was short lived.

I whipped her skirts up to her chest, was pleasantly relieved to discover that her legs, if sturdy and not as long as I liked, were none the less well shaped and muscular, and gloated over a fine pubic patch, all dark and *glowing*.

"Byron," she said, having recovered, and endeavouring once again to sit up. "I beg of you, Byron."

I pushed her back, and she no doubt felt cocker on her thigh, for she gave a moan. "Byron," she cried. "Byron," she shouted. "Byron," she shrieked, for a moment later he was in, encountering some opposition, to be sure, from virginity as well as tightened muscles as well as a complete absence of lubrication. But he would not be stopped this night, and it required no more than a few seconds of tumultuous movement to relieve my passion and turn her cries into despairing sighs.

Slowly I pushed myself from her quivering form. "Now we are married," I said.

"Oh, God," she whispered. "Oh, God."

"Marriage is His invention," I pointed out.

"I am on fire." She suddenly realised how she appeared, and pulled down her skirts.

"Losing one's virginity is a painful business. So I have always been told." I sat beside her. "It will be easier from now on."

Her eyes opened, and she stared at me for a moment. "Never," she said, and rolled on her side, to face the wall.

"Oh, really Belle," I protested. "So I was hasty. My God, I have waited better than two years for that moment. Had I *not* been hasty you would have considered me a very tardy fellow. Tonight I will teach you the real business of love. I promise you."

"Never," she whispered again, still facing the wall.

I decided to let her recover in her own time, and went into my room, closing the door and summoning Fletcher. Even the tumble had failed properly to warm me, and I now discovered that my throat was sore. I was well on the way to catching a cold. I stood at my window and watched the snow flakes drifting by, shrouding the house in silence, so that I could hear the murmur of female voices from next door. Belle had summoned Meg. I wondered what they were saying to each other.

Dressed, I went downstairs to explore this gloomy, empty place, and was agreeably pleased to discover a well-stocked library, while the butler was on hand with a glass of sherry. But I was left very much to myself, and the house grew even gloomier, and I was just beginning to get angry again when she appeared, dressed in a very high necked and long sleeved gown – but this may well have been to afford some protection against the chill, which was not abated even by the fires – and with her hair carefully dressed. She looked as composed as ever, but was faintly breathless as she caught sight of me.

"You'll take a glass of sherry," I said.

She hesitated, then did so, and indeed tossed it off. And seemed to feel better. "I am uncommonly hungry," she said.

"Well, then," I said, taking her arm. "Let's to it. The sooner we eat the sooner we can get to bed."

She started to look at me, and then turned away again. I held her chair for her, and we sat at the head of a long and empty dining table. My throat was now very raw, and I preferred to drink than to eat. But to my distress Belle turned out indeed to be hungry, and withal a very *hearty* eater. I watched chops and beans and bread and tarts and pastries and cheese disappearing down that delightful throat and wondered where she put it all.

"You *do* intend to sleep with me?" I asked.

She swallowed, and drank some wine. "If you wish me to."

"The decision must be yours," I said. "I usually sleep alone, as a matter of fact. It is a habit I have formed."

Her head came up, and she gazed at me. "You are married now, my lord," she said. "We each have a duty. To the other."

"Duty," I said. "Is that how you look upon it?"

"I would hope to look upon it in a different light, with the passage of time, my lord," she said. And let her hand creep across the table. "I wish to make you happy, Byron. I wish to be your wife, in every way. In return I ask only your patience. I know little of the real world. My knowledge is gained from books. Be patient, I beg of you, my lord. And you will find me all you wish."

A pretty speech, and my moods are ever short lived. I raised her hand to my lips, and kissed it. "Patience is not one of my more obvious virtues, sweet Belle. But for you I shall study it. I promise." I gave her a squeeze. "Shall we retire? It will at the least be warm."

I undressed slowly and comfortably, before my fire, even managing to ignore Fletcher's prattle. I had dined well – if not so well as her ladyship, to be sure – and drunk well, and I felt pleasantly amorous. She was far better looking than I could have hoped, and I had no doubts at all that once her initial reserve was overcome she would be a delightful bedmate. It seemed to me that my fears and troubles and tantrums were over, and I was full of determination to make our marriage a success, to love her and to honour her, above all others.

And so I knocked on the door separating us, and was welcomed by Meg, who curtsied, and backed away from me, but far too sombrely, allowing me none of the girlish giggles I had anticipated upon such an occasion. Belle was nowhere in evidence, and was clearly already in bed, around which the crimson drapes had been drawn.

"Off you go," I told the girl, and she hurried through the door, which I then closed and locked. I crossed the room, and slowly drew the curtains.

She was sitting up, in a high necked nightgown, and with a cap on her head, although her hair was loose and allowed to tumble on her shoulders. Now, I had considered this approach at some length. I was truly sorry for any roughness I had revealed during our earlier tumble, but at the same time that had been invaluable in creaming off the worst of my passion. I was prepared for a long, slow, and delightful

251

introduction to matters sexual, such as I had known with Caro, but at the same time I was determined that this was going to *be* a sexual occasion, and no other. For how else may a man spend his wedding night?

And so, as I crawled in beside her and drew the curtains behind me, I smiles at her, and said, "Do uncover, sweet Belle. I have never seen your breasts."

She stared at me as if stung, and her arms folded themselves across those orbs.

I refused to be put out, and gently moved the protective barrier, releasing the bow at her neck. Her nightgown fell loose, although not loose enough. I put my hand inside to caress the soft, still cool flesh beneath, the flaccid nipple; she had beautiful breasts, nearly as large as Guss's, and splendidly firm. My lips wished to follow my hand, while I felt her gasping breath upon my neck, and a moment later she was twisting away from me again. I caught her shoulders, but she had already rolled on her belly.

"You promised patience," she mumbled.

"And I am being patient."

"Please," she whispered into her pillow. "I cannot. I cannot, I cannot, I cannot. Not tonight, my lord. I am aching. I . . . I have a headache. I am . . . I am ill, my lord."

"Ill?" I knelt above her, looking down on that slender body, scantily concealed by the clinging muslin.

"With fear. With. . . ." I swear she was about to say disgust, but she choked away the word. "With innocence, my lord. I beg of you to spare me this night. Tomorrow. . . ."

"How can tomorrow be any different, my dearest?" I asked, moving her hair to kiss the nape of her neck. "The difference can only come with experience. I shall be gentle, I promise you."

"No," she said. "No, no, no." And she seemed to force herself farther into the bed, spreading her legs to give herself purchase.

Fatal mistake. For cocker was ready for battle, as was my mind similarly inflamed. And she was my wife, bound to obey me in everything I desired. I looked down on that white shrouded form, and could make out her backside and the slit between. I panted with a sudden wild impulse. How often had I dreamed of such a conquest, and how often had I turned away in fear, or been turned away by events. But this night there was naught to say me nay.

I raised the nightgown, slowly, lifting each leg in turn to free the material, and gazed upon quite the most splendid bottom I had ever seen. I spread her legs wider yet, while she clung to her pillow and whispered, I know not what. But she, poor innocent, supposed that while her belly was glued to the sheet she was in no danger. I could proceed at will, and this I did, with some difficulty, to be sure, but at last with a *stab* which brought her head up and forced a scream from her lips. Yet was she helpless, pinned at once by my posture and my weight, and within seconds she was again mine, but more fully than ever had woman been before.

BELLE – THE THIRD PART

She made no demur, beyond her earlier struggles. Indeed my climax was followed by a complete relaxation on both of our parts, and within seconds we were both asleep, equally exhausted.

But for me sleep lasted for too brief a while. By midnight I was awake again, with a sudden start, for I had been dreaming, and supposed myself in hell, and with my arms around a woman. No doubt Proserpine.

I could remain there no longer, arose and wrapped myself in a dressing gown – the fires were burning low and it was distinctly cold – and sat at a desk in the corner of the room, to write to Augusta. I have never felt so low, in fact, so *damned*. It was a return of the dreadful guilt a young boy feels after masturbation, a consuming emotion I had not known for too long. And like all such reflections, quite without point – at least at the time. For Belle awoke in a much better humour than after our first tumble. I do believe her innocence was such that she assumed I had had my way with her without causing her any more pain, and she was greatly relieved. Better yet, a letter arrived *from* Guss, full of congratulations. Reading her delightful, undisciplined scrawl quite restored me to an equal temper.

Belle having raised herself to the necessary pitch by imbibing several sherries before lunch, we retired to bed that afternoon – there was really nothing else worth doing, so cold was the weather. I put forth my very best efforts, displaying every inch of knowledge I had accumulated over the years, and accomplishing nothing towards satisfying her. When I would stroke between her legs she adopted an attitude of patient resignation; when I would use my lips and tongue in that hallowed region, she positively tightened her muscles so much that I was all but crushed and had to withdraw in order to breathe. Having failed in that direction, I decided to attend to my own necessities, and made an entry, slowly and carefully. And despite her reluctance I do believe she was aroused, because certainly I had a much easier passage than on the previous day, and so did she.

To be sure it was intensely irritating to be informed, as she managed to accomplish without actually saying the words, that she considered she had done her duty as a wife and a martyr. I was content for the time being, that she would yield to me whenever I wished – and she was a voluptuous and thus most attractive young woman – and that, in the course of Nature's good time, she would feel some spark of passion arising from those most passionate of regions. I was almost happy, worked on my *Hebrew Melodies*, wrote Lady M a glowing account of my marital prospects, and even commenced to enjoy life, removed as I was from creditors and comparisons.

Yet my nights continued to be interrupted by the most fearsome of nightmares. I heard creaks and groans, and awoke shivering and anxious, convinced that assailants were breaking into the house, assassination in mind. Sent by whom? I did not know. I only knew they had to be combated, and so arose, and stole from my chamber, dagger and pistol in hand, to find – nothing. And staggered back to bed, where my wife would also be awake and trembling, she knowing nothing of my mental anguish, only the physical evidence of my fear.

And one such night, as I rested my head on her breast and she stroked my hair, she made a singular remark:

"I wonder whose heart will break first, yours or mine?"

Yet I could not resist teasing her, and not entirely in the best of spirits; her extraordinary *goodness* often irritating me to extremes. And so when, in her mathematical way, she sat down to reason out my midnight miseries, I was wont to point out that clearly there was a streak of derangement in my family, on both sides, a Byron having once committed suicide and a Gordon having attempted to destroy his own home by fire. Had I known how seriously she took these humours of mine I might well have paused to think.

But she smiled patiently at my sallies, and indeed I began to accept patience as her prime virtue, which satisfied me well enough until I could replace it with a better. I even wished she could transfer some of it to me, for my business post continued to reveal the most alarming state of affairs, *my* affairs, my total indebtedness now amounting to no less than £30,000, with a total income scarce a tenth of that sum. Hobhouse, indeed, to whom I had confided the worst of my situation, now re-erected the spectre which had been haunting my innermost thoughts for some time, as to whether or not old Hanson was truly a man of probity.

In this disturbed frame of mind, nothing of which of course I dared communicate to Pippin, as I had commenced calling my dear wife – I had ever in memory her overstrong reaction to my earlier attempt to unburden my finances on to our joint shoulders – our honeymoon came to an end and we returned to Seaham. For a brief while this was a relief. I was still resolved to make my marriage a success, and to be as much a model husband as was within me to accomplish. But I had early recognised that Belle and I had little in common. In the first place she was very much a stranger to me, as well as being a pretty and attractive woman, and I have never been able to find myself alone with a pretty and attractive woman without wishing immediately to make love to her. Had I had my way, we should have done nothing else throughout the honeymoon. And *had* I had my way events might have turned out very differently, and far better for both of us. But Belle as I have indicated regarded sexual matters as an unpleasantly necessary concomitant of marriage, and would far sooner walk, ever a burden to me, and talk, about matters which interested me not in the least, or read, rationing my endeavours to a nightly tumble before slumber, for which she invariably fortified herself with wine and great mental resolution.

In the second place, she appeared to regard poetry, or at least, my poetry, with contempt, and this, after all, was what I could best do when required to occupy my time in intellectual matters. While as for composing verses to celebrate a *Hebrew* litany, she was appalled. But then, she was appalled by my every attitude in regard to religion, which closed another promising avenue of conversation.

And yet, neither of these unfortunate aspects of our relationship which in a mistress would have verged on the catastrophic, appeared to me at the time to be so misplaced in a marriage. Judging by most of the marriages I had observed such a state of affairs was entirely ordinary, and once we had produced an heir Belle and I would no doubt go our own way in contented adultery or good works, as did so many of my acquaintances. I was therefore perfectly happy to regain the seclusion of Seaham, where at the least I was spending no money that I did not have, and where even a nightly session of draughts with old Milbanke served to pass the time.

But I knew I was borrowing the time. I could not spend the rest of my life with my in-laws; indeed, a scant fortnight of that sniff was close to driving me from my mind. I also knew that my destitution was not going to cure itself, and my presence was obviously necessary in London, where indeed Hobby was searching for a suitable residence for me. Now it seemed to me that the obvious course was for me to make the journey by myself, as it was now the end of February and the very dead of winter, attend to my business and hopefully be successful in that direction, appropriate our leasehold and see that everything was in order there, with Belle to follow as soon as the balmy breezes of spring thawed the snow. To my mind this was rendered doubly urgent by the fact that she had already missed one period, and it seemed at least likely that the hoped for event was already on its way, and would hardly be improved by a long and jolting journey.

But to my utter surprise, when I acquainted her with my intention, she absolutely refused to permit me to travel alone.

At this I lost my temper. Because of course my desire to escape from Seaham was equally a desire to escape from Belle herself, at least for a brief season. I had planned to stop at Six Mile Bottom, and I had planned a reunion with my old friends in London. I had not planned to do either of these things with a wife in tow.

But however I raged, she remained adamant, bringing forth all her virtues, if they be virtues, of stubborn patience. Well, I had been warned of these characteristics, often enough. Which but made me the more angry, especially when my planned departure had to be put back for nearly a fortnight while my lady made ready. I sank into one of my blackest moods of depression, which lasted until we were settled into my carriage. I remember that Judith leaned through the window to bid us farewell, and to say, tearfully, "Take care of her, Byron."

"Take care of you?" I demanded of Belle as we rumbled down the drive. "I had supposed you quite capable of taking care of yourself. I didn't want you in the first place."

She merely looked out of the window with a frozen smile on her face. But she was learning a little of how to cope with a husband, and by resolute good humour had somewhat improved my mood by the time we reached Six Mile Bottom. Yet my smiles covered a considerable agitation. Belle and Guss had never met. How would they react, one to the other? How would I react, to the presence of both of them? I had dreamed of Guss too often during the preceding two months. I longed for her touch. I longed for a great deal more than that. But with Belle at my side. . . .

257

The carriage came to a halt, and there was only the yardboy to greet us. "Wait here," I told Belle, and went inside. The house was equally deserted, save for a maid.

"The mistress is resting, my lord," she said. "She had not expected you . . ." she licked her lips, "now."

Because of that damnable delay. "Well, tell her I am here," I said. "And with Lady Byron."

Who was at that moment entering the hall, having grown tired of standing in the cold.

"Mail," I explained, thumbing through the letters which were addressed to me, and seizing upon one from Hanson. Alas for my hopes of a miracle. Another would-be purchaser had faded into the dusk. "I fear," the dear old dishonest soul had written, "that our best, indeed our only course is to place the property at auction, with a suitable reserve of course."

Never before had he been so pessimistic. Such a step would indicate to the world – at least that half which did not already know my precarious position – that I must sell at any cost, and that I was unable to discover a reasonable purchaser. I crumpled the letter in my fist, black bile once again welling out of my belly to overwhelm my spirit, and turned, and watched Guss descending the stairs.

How beautiful she looked, her hair loose on her shoulders, seeming to glide as she came towards me. I scarce heard the introductions, and indeed the two ladies had to make their own. I waited only to seize her hands, and kiss them. But she drew away almost immediately, with a gentle smile. "I am sure you are exhausted," she said. "My dear Lady Byron, you are quite pale."

"Belle, please," Belle said. "We are sisters."

"Belle," Guss said. "Supper will soon be ready."

They chattered, about everything under the sun, while I waited, and chafed. I took refuge in George Leigh's port, and had half consumed it by the time the meal was served. In my carelessness I ate too much, and then drank the remainder of the decanter, while they continued to prattle away, as if they had indeed been sisters, separated for at least a week.

But eventually the meal came to an end, and Belle looked at me inquiringly. "You *are* looking tired, my sweet Pippin," I said. "Off you go to bed."

"Are you not coming?"

"In a little while. Guss and I have things to discuss."

"Then I shall wait for you."

"Go to bed," I snapped. "Off you go. We have things to discuss. Private things. We don't want you around."

She gazed at me for a moment, pink spots gathering in her cheeks, then rose without a word, kissed Guss on the cheek, and left the room.

"That was hateful of you," Guss said, also rising, and preceding me into the parlour. "Only to be excused on the grounds of drunkenness." For she knew me well enough to discern the truth of the matter.

"Guss," I said, limping behind her. "If you knew how I have missed you, how. . . ." I caught her hand, and she turned. "Oh, Guss," I whispered, and endeavoured to take her in my arms.

To my consternation she resisted me. "Byron, please. Why don't you go to bed. With your wife."

"With my wife?" I shouted.

"Sssh."

"With my wife?" I lowered my tone. "I am here to see you, my darling. To hold you in my arms." Once again I endeavoured to draw her close.

And once again she pushed me away. "It cannot be, Byron. You are married, and she is a sweet girl. It cannot be."(i)

I was dumbfounded. I had set such store by this meeting, had dreamed of it for so long, and here she was refusing me as if we were strangers. I retired to bed in a very sorry frame of mind, which was increased almost immediately by an attack of the most virulent indigestion. I cried out in pain, so much so that Belle, whom I believed had decided not to honour me with her presence this night, came in to discover what was the matter.

"Go away," I shouted. "Get from my sight. I hate you. I hate the whole lot of you. For God's sake leave me alone."

Bitter words, and when my own torment had somewhat quietened, I heard her sobbing in the next room.

Here the fault was mine. I admit it freely. But the fact was that I was not myself. Quite apart from having had far too much to drink, and having been in pain, and feeling entirely frustrated, my brain was a torment of despair, for amongst my other letters had been one from Hobby informing me that he had secured the lease of 13 Piccadilly Terrace from the Duchess of Devonshire, this being a most suitable residence for newlyweds who were also clearly going to be the delight of London society. But I could imagine no more expensive property in all London. It seemed to me as if every misfortune I had ever known was coming together in one huge mass to overwhelm me and make a mockery of my plans for happiness.

A more experienced woman than Belle would have understood there was some deep-seated cause for my misery, for my apparent anger with her. A less selfish, a less self-contented woman would have endeavoured to understand what a curse it was to be poor. And a more intelligent – as opposed to merely learned – woman would have read *Childe Harold* and indeed everything that I had written with more than merely superficial interest, as she was married to the creator of those fantasies, and thus she would have endeavoured to understand something of the anguishes which roamed my brain. Belle was incapable of understanding anything beyond her own point of view. When she wished to air her feelings on a subject she could appear most learned and even sympathetic; but these were mere words. Deep in her heart she regarded any opinions, any emotions, any desires not felt by herself with the utmost suspicion and revulsion, and so certain was she of her own impeccable virtue it never crossed her mind that narrow-mindedness is the greatest of all vices, because it excludes the possibility of *charity*. Therefore the tragedy of our marriage was equally her responsibility.

I write these thoughts with hindsight, and after deep reflection. At the time I was not capable of such analysis. Dejection, despair, when coupled with indigestion, and I was now commencing a chronic case of this debilitating disease, are not dispelled in a moment, or even a day. I was aware only of misery, which I sought to assuage by consuming all of George's port I could discover, which further fuddled my senses and made my own approach as narrow as Belle's. Throughout our stay at Six Mile Bottom I hated her. But then, I even hated Guss, for refusing me the one thing I supposed would cure me. I railed at them both, taunted them both, and am afraid I was more than a little indiscreet from time to time, although I am hard put to recall exactly what I said. Certainly their faces grew longer and longer, and they were even given to whispering together against *me*, the ultimate disillusionment.

It was while I was in this utter pit of despondency that Belle announced she had missed her second period, and therefore there could be no doubt that I was to become a father.

*　　*　　*

Thus we left Six Mile Bottom for town. I was even in a sufficiently good humour to bid a warm farewell to Guss, which I now know was carefully noted by Belle. But I did not notice *that*, and indeed our arrival in London and the establishment of our residence at 13 Piccadilly was accompanied by every evidence of domestic bliss.

On the one hand, whatever the rent – which was in fact the alarming figure of £700 a year, exactly what I was receiving from Belle's dowry – the house was delightful, and if it was so large that we necessarily had to employ a retinue of servants, there was at least also a place for my old charwoman, Mrs Mule, who had faithfully followed me from abode to abode as I had fled around London, and who was now granted a permanent establishment.

On the second hand, my health was suddenly better than it had been for some time; I am always happier as the warm weather approaches, and summer was now close. Also, as Belle was now officially pregnant, our sexual encounters, which had remained the main cause of disaffection between us, were of course ended for the time being, and she became much less afraid of me.

There was a fourth reason for my contentment, although when I heard of it I was amazed and dismayed: Belle actually invited Guss to stay with us, and in fact she joined us within the week. I could not help but ask my wife if she possessed a wish for self destruction, without considering what construction she might put upon the question. And indeed Guss was a continual torment for me, as deprived as I was of conjugal relations, and once again in full health, I was quite desperate. She remained adamant, however, that we could not resume our old camaraderie for the time being, leaving me indeed unsure as to whether she *ever* intended to grace my bed again. The fact was, she had also been guilty of that most unfeminine of occupations, thought, during the two months that we had been separated, or even, I suspect, since the news of my engagement. And thus had decided that we had sinned most grievously. Nor, with so many other people in the house, and especially my wife, was I able to change her mind by *action*.

And yet the mere fact of her presence, her ability to laugh with me, and by doing so even to bring a smile to Belle's face, added to my brief contentment.

But of course the principal reason for my uplift in spirits was being back in London again, being able to see my friends, being able to work, if not at poetry, at other artistic pursuits, for it was now that I allowed myself to be nominated to the sub-committee of management for the Drury Lane Theatre, with almost *carte blanche* in deciding what plays should be performed, of being able to encourage promising poets, in particular Coleridge, as I remember.

It was during this time that my *Hebrew Melodies* was published, to the usual fanfare of criticism and objections, and to the usual rapturous applause from my public. We sold all ten thousand copies very rapidly, and Murray made a profit of £5,000. He at least was equally happy.

But best of all was being able to extend my friendships, for it was now that I had the pleasure of meeting Scott. We had corresponded, of course, as I corresponded from time to time with every literary figure in the kingdom. But his visits south were rare enough for us never actually to have seen each other. Now Murray managed to arrange a meeting, and we took to each other immediately. We had of course differences of opinion which in lesser men might have been serious. He was appalled at my licentiousness and my atheism, and was convinced, indeed he prophesied, that both would change as I grew older, that I would become the most reactionary of men and that religion would be my solace. "Me a Methodist?" I laughed. "There is no chance of that."

"None at all," he agreed. "But I would wager that you become something far more sublime. I see you as a Roman Catholic."

Which was – and is – a sufficiently unlikely prospect. For my part I found his High Church Toryism irritating, the more so as I was convinced it arose from choice rather than deep-felt belief.

But we could recognise the genius in each other, and we could recognise too that neither of us would ever be hidebound, or narrow, or unable to listen to another point of view. And we were both lame, which created a bond.

And we liked each other.

I'm afraid Belle saw little of me during those early months of our marriage, as I spent most evenings at the theatre, for which she had little affinity, even had she been able to go, because it was about this time that her uncle finally died, and she was forced to flee north for a few days, while when she returned, apart from swelling belly she was in mourning. But as she liked it better this way, we were settling into a perfect married routine, with my spirits higher than they had been for a very long time, when the blow I had always dreaded fell on my shoulders like the blade of an axe.

An utter scoundrel named Randall, to whom I owed a trifling sum, less than three hundred pounds, without the slightest warning or ultimatum, sought and obtained a judgement against me for debt.

The fact was that my numerous legion of creditors, having observed that I was happily married to an heiress and had taken up residence in a most palatial town house, had sat up and begun to take notice. And when in addition Wentworth's death was made public, releasing all those millions which were to accrue to my wife, they decided it was time to act, and I do believe that the infamous Randall had been appointed as the forlorn hope, so to speak.

Which is an accurate enough description of his and my situation. For I obtained nothing at all from the Wentworth estate. There was something *coming*, but the whole business, as usual, was so tied up in legal fog, that it had to be relegated to the realms of Rochdale.

Yet the judgement had been given, and I was displayed before all the world as an insolvent debtor. I surrendered to fate, and placed Newstead at auction. Our reserve was that modest figure of £120,000 which had been offered and accepted only two years previously. To my utter horror the bidding stopped at £79,000 despite the efforts of my friends, who took it up to £95,000. But no genuine buyer could be found to meet them, and the property had to be brought in. In my despair I even considered accepting the actual figure offered, but sober consideration, when I could spare the time to *be* sober, convinced me that was tantamount to committing suicide. For once the £60,000 I had so carelessly settled upon my wife was allowed for, the remaining £19,000 would not even have paid half of my outstanding debts.

To add insult to injury, the Milbankes, learning at last of my impending ruin, invited me to betake myself to Seaham and make it my home. Suicide was certainly preferable to incarcerating myself in darkest Northumberland with only the sniff for company.

I did my best, when I was able, which is to say, when I was sober, a state of affairs I permitted as seldom as possible, to be gay. But I do believe these attempts made matters worse. For Belle seemed unable to sense my mood, so concerned was she entirely with her own affairs, and would commence with a bright smile when I was obviously feeling at my lowest, or greet my own smiling countenance with a gloomy sigh. She was of course entirely aware of our financial difficulties, but she regarded them as *my* financial difficulties, never having experienced anything of this nature before, nor could she consider them as at all serious, in light of the property I owned, and our joint expectations. There can be nothing more galling to a man with an insoluble problem on his mind than for his wife to say, "Oh, do stop worrying. Everything will surely be all right."

By the end of August my nerves were so frayed, my spirits so depressed, that I could sit still no longer. I abandoned wife and home and friends and fled to Six Mile Bottom.

This proved once again to have been a mistake. George was absent, but Guss was dismayed to see me, especially with Belle in such a condition, now only some three months from her delivery. (ii) She steadfastly refused to allow me any liberties, despite my near piteous condition, and what was I supposed to do, rape my own sister? Worse, she took the side of the Milbankes, recommended that far and away my best course *was* to go to Seaham, bury myself there for a year or two, far from debtors and indeed from the possibility of accumulating debts. An idea I was forced to ridicule. For my creditors had got wind of the proposed removal, and would have none of it. Orders and executions were being secured on all sides, and I do believe had I left London on even the suggestion of permanency, they would have moved in the following day and sold me out.

I returned to town in no happy frame of mind, to find that this most dreadful of ever remembered summers was continuing on its merry course. Consider: That the news of my insolvency had even reached Murray, and he, stout fellow, had sent me a cheque for £1,500, representing this to be fair profits from the sales of the *Hebrew Melodies*. What, was I to be reduced to receiving charity from a publisher? I sent it back.

Consider: That the one work on which I had been able to labour since my marriage, *The Siege of Corinth*, now completed and out to be read, was found to contain a plagiarism of *Cristabel*. I was horrified, for the crime was quite unconscious. Yet I had heard *Cristabel* performed, and in the company of Scott, no less. I could only apologise and scrub the offensive lines. (iii)

Consider: That I poured all my energy into securing for Drury Lane the best of talents, either on the boards or in their scripts, and failed most miserably. For stars I even approached the irresistible Siddons, but she was well suited in Edinburgh and would not travel south. (iv) For plays I tried Sotheby, (v) and Maturin, (vi) and even Coleridge, as he owed me something, and came up with nothing worthwhile. I seemed to be pursued by an evil genius which turned my every scheme into ashes.

And consider: That my despair, my misery, my failure with Guss, had left me the most sourly continent of men. Which no doubt played its part in my blackest moods. Until there came the night I could stand the utter loneliness of my crowded existence no longer, and approached my wife in her bedchamber.

She sat before her dressing mirror, Clermont brushing her hair. For this familiar of the dragon had been deputed to attend her mistress during the pregnancy. Her back was to me, but she smiled at me in the mirror. A kindly smile, immediately ruined by her words, for she said, "Why, Byron. Are you not at the play?"

Apart from the inanity of the remark to someone actually standing before her, it was of course a rebuke, as most nights I *was* at the play.

"Leave us," I told Clermont.

She looked at her mistress, who turned the better to see me. "Whatever is the matter?" she demanded. "Not *another* execution?"

And this most private matter – supposing that was the reason for my visit – aired before a servant. I began to lose my temper, which I found easier to do when in Belle's company than at any other time.

"Out," I said.

Still she hesitated, and I was for seizing her and heaving her bodily from the room when my wife, no doubt understanding something of what was passing through my mind from my expression, said, "You'd best go, Mrs Clermont. But stay close."

The creature bowed her head, ignored me altogether, and left the room, closing the door behind her.

"And why should she stay close?" I inquired.

"Because I shall need her again, when you have said whatever you have to say."

"I am not going to *say* anything," I told her. "I have come here to do."

Her head jerked. "Byron," she said. "My lord. . . ."

"Do you know how long it is since I have had a woman?"

She flushed. "I really do not care to inquire too deeply into a man's habits, my lord. I know how long it is since you have . . ." she hesitated, "had me."

"And there is the truth of it. Oh, Belle, Belle. . . ." I held her shoulders, lifted her from her stool, took her in my arms, kissed her

265

mouth most passionately, loving even the feel of the swollen belly between us. "Belle, I do love you, Belle. I love you more than I can say. I love you, love you, *love* you. I'm sorry for my moods. God, could I only discover a pot of gold at the foot of some rainbow; you'd discover in me the best and happiest of men. Say you forgive me."

"Of course I forgive you," she gasped. "And I love you too, Byron. But you know we cannot . . . well . . . in my condition. . . ."

"The devil with your condition," I said, half carrying her, half pushing her towards the bed. "I'll put no weight on your belly. I promise."

"You'll harm the child," she begged, pushing against me.

"I'll not touch the child," I said. "Not even with my seed." Her thighs touched the bed, and she sat down, and a moment later was rolled on her side, while I was scooping her nightgown about her waist. "Do you not remember our wedding night?" I whispered into her ear. "I entered you then, by an alternative passage. Oh, Belle, Belle. . . ."

Perhaps I had done better to keep silent. It seemed as if for the first time she understood the enormity of what had happened on that night already eight months in the past. She gave a gasp, and thrust backwards with her elbows. But even winded as I was I was persisting, my breeches already around my ankles, cocker jammed against those delightful mounds, alone of her attributes unchanged by her condition, while my fingers went before to reopen that hallowed passageway. Then she screamed.

The noise echoed about the room, burst against my eardrums. Yet was I so consumed with passion I would have ridden even that, had I not been interrupted by the banging of the door. The foul Clermont was again in our midst.

FRIENDS AND ENEMIES

I was so totally surprised, at once by Belle's caterwauling and by the interruption, that for a moment I could only goggle at her, while my amatory efforts insensibly subsided. Belle took this opportunity to escape my clutches and indeed the bed, pregnant as she was.

"Help me," she gasped, presumably to the Clermont, who promptly started forward.

I reached my knees, quite forgetting my own nakedness. "Out," I commanded. "Get out."

She hesitated. "I'll do no such thing."

"You'd defy me?" I reached the floor.

She stood her ground. "My mistress called for help. I'll stay until she bids me leave."

Belle during this exchange was sobbing quietly to herself in a corner. But she was not so distraught she was not listening, for now she sat up. "Don't leave me, Clermont. Don't leave me."

"Nor shall I, my lady," the dragon's deputy declared, folding her arms. "You should be ashamed of yourself, my lord, assaulting a poor pregnant woman, and in such an obscene manner."

I by this time was recovering from my earlier confusion, and beginning to feel extremely angry. "Belle," I said. "This creature leaves this room. Either you command her to, or I will throw her out."

Belle raised her head. Her face had settled into that monumental firmness I had recognised even before our marriage. "She will not leave," she said. "Clermont will not leave my side until after I am delivered, and. . . ." But she bit off the fatal words which I do believe she had been about to utter. "And if you throw her out, then you had best set about me as well."

"Hum," remarked Mrs Clermont, arms still folded.

I gazed at them in impotent anger, but I have never been a man inclined to violence towards women, alas. Thus I merely stalked from the room, determined to seek my pleasures where I chose that night.

And encountered Fletcher in the hall. "Fetch my carriage," I growled, supposing he had been summoned by the din.

"Indeed, my lord," he said. "But my lord, there is a man here."

A remarkably inane statement. "What man?" I demanded. "And where?"

"I am here, my lord," remarked a somewhat uncultured voice from the foot of the stairs. "Name of Bruton, my lord." He was an average enough fellow, dressed neatly but not richly, and carried his beaver in his hand. But in his other hand he also carried a paper. "An order from the court, my lord," he said, almost apologetically. "I'm to remain."

Throughout my life my troubles have never come singly. At the very moment when my wife decided not to grant me the use of her body – an event I had never supposed remotely possible – the one thing I had *always* feared had come to pass: A bailiff had been placed in my house.

Yet I preserved the calm of my voice. "How many?"

"There are five executions, my lord," he said. "But some more are to come, I believe."

I turned away, reached my own rooms in a dream, allowed Fletcher to dress me, went out, passing and repassing that accursed closed door where my wife remained closeted with her nurse, and gained the sanctuary of the Green Room at the Drury. The play was on, and the place was deserted. I poured myself a glass and sat down, staring in front of me. I drained my glass and poured myself another, and found Douglas Kinnaird standing at my shoulder.

"There's no miscarriage?"

Good Douglas, immediately recognising my state of catastrophe.

I raised my head. "Lady Byron is well enough. Douglas, I've been done. Five executions have been granted against me, and there are more to come."

He poured a glass for himself, sat beside me. "Are things as bad as that? I had no idea. You must find Hanson, and immediately."

"Do you not suppose he knows?"

"And has done nothing about it?"

I shrugged. "He does his best, I do believe."

"Then it is a damned poor best," he declared. "Byron, *I'll* see what can be done. Were I not so damnably strapped myself . . . there's no risk they'll sell you out?"

I shook my head. "The fellow is merely there to insure I do not run for it. But think of it. My wife is close to her confinement. And a bailiff's lout camps on the floor below. I suppose I shall go mad."

He rested his hand on my shoulder. "If my estimation of Belle is sound, she'll take it in her stride. After all, old fellow, Newstead must sell eventually. Something must be sorted out about Rochdale. Wentworth's estate must be probated. It can only be temporary."

It was not something I could discuss. It was only something I could attempt to alleviate. For while I was looking at Douglas's stricken countenance, the play had ended, and the room was suddenly filled, with actors and actresses, and their admirers, all clustering round to discover what was amiss.

"His lordship is unwell," Douglas explained.

"My dear Lord Byron," Kean exclaimed, sitting beside me. "A colic?"

"A melancholy," Douglas said.

"A man with a pregnant wife," Kean said, smiling. "It will pass, my lord. And surely we have the very remedy. Why, there is not a girl here would not be honoured to alleviate your lordship's misery. Would you not agree, Susan?"

Unbelievable as it may be, I had to this moment been utterly faithful to my wife. Which should go some distance towards proving that I am by nature a *dull* fellow, as I have always claimed, who wishes only to be managed by a sensible woman. Had Belle but been able to recognise that simple fact, and at the same time been able to overcome her amatory scruples, what a happy marriage we should have had.

But this height she had been unable to scale, and there I was, evicted from my nuptial bed, on the verge, it appeared, of being evicted from my very home, my mind inflamed at once with anger and with fear of the future and with wine, and surrounded by a bevy of delightful damsels, even if the majority of them did not in any way measure up to my ideals of female beauty as suggested by Haidee or by Liz.

Yet there was one, the very young woman Kean was at that moment addressing, who was a cut above the rest, at least in looks. Her name was Susan Boyce, and I would have been less than a man had I not already noticed her, for she was tall, and slender, and possessed an abundance of pale brown hair which fluttered delightfully as she moved. She was not truly beautiful, but her features were enhanced by her vivacity, for she was ever the brightest and most cheerful of the actresses. She was not one of the leading ladies of the company, but did well enough in good supporting roles to make one suppose a future lay before her in her chosen profession, a direction in which I, of course, could certainly assist. Thus she was ever prepared to smile upon me, and in fact was doing so now.

I sound cynical, because I am, certainly about women. They have been the bane of my existence, and had I at any stage of my existence been able to do without the delicious creatures I would have been a happier man. But there it is. With me woman is a *vice*. Even as I hate them collectively, I adore them individually.

Thus I allowed my desires to come to my rescue, and for a week at least found a shabby happiness. But at the end of that time was once again plunged into despair as I returned home one evening and discovered that in my absence my sister had arrived.

My relationship with Guss throughout this year had not been of the best. Of course I knew this was a temporary state of affairs; what was more upsetting was that, however much I was the younger brother, I was the acknowledged head of our family, the one person above all others to whom she could turn for help whenever she needed it, as indeed she had done nearly two years before. It was quite unbearable for me to have to receive her in a house which possessed a bailiff camping in the kitchen, with every possession under a writ of execution.

Humiliating as this was, there was worse to come. I avoided her to the best of my ability, but eventually she knocked on the door of my study, and there was naught I could do but admit her.

"Would you like me to leave?" she asked.

"My dear Guss," I said. "You are always welcome under my roof."

"You do not act it."

"I have a great deal on my mind, as you may have observed."

"I had to come."

"Is George misbehaving, as usual?"

"Not in the least. Belle sent for me."

I frowned at her. "Belle asked you to come here?"

"She is terribly afraid."

"If they sell us up, well then, we shall have to move. It would probably be the best thing, however humiliating. I may point out that I told her this was likely to happen, a year ago, and invited her to postpone the wedding until Newstead could be sold, and she refused. So now she must grin and bear it."

"She is not the least afraid of your financial affairs. She is afraid of *you*." She sat down, pulled the chair close. "She tells me your moods are positively demoniac."

I sighed. "I was not aware of it. Nor will you be. She exaggerates. She sees everything from her own point of view. I cannot pay her the attention I would wish. I am busy, she is pregnant, and so we are both preoccupied, in different directions."

Guss's turn to sigh. "She says you are taking laudanum."

"Quite correct. I suffer acutely from dyspepsia, which in turn leads to irritation and depression. I am trying to write. I doubt you understand what is involved. I know she does not."

"You could attempt to explain."

"It should not be necessary." I got up. "Use your imagination, if you can. I write. I create. I conjure up visions from inside my own mind, and set them down on paper, in rhyme. I know all my friends, I know you, think it is merely a gift, and a hobby. I feel the Muse upon me, and I sit down and dash off a few lines which everyone is anxious to read. Do you really suppose it is as simple as that? Do you really suppose I would enjoy the success I do by merely indulging a hobby?"

"Byron . . ." she began.

"You asked for an explanation. Do me the courtesy of listening."

She bit her lip and tears started to her eyes; certainly I had not so addressed her before.

"I am fortunate, or cursed," I went on, "by having that gift, certainly. But what is it? An urge to write. It is not a heaven-sent amanuensis who turns my thoughts into verse. *I* have to do that. I have to take a nebulous idea, delightful to dream about as I lie half awake in bed, and turn it into some sense, and some words. But there is more. The gift creates the idea, the atmosphere in which the idea can germinate. Once it has done that it is all left to me. But yet is it *there*, as you might accumulate an unwanted child. You conceived in a moment of the most delicious, abandoned passion. But once it is done, you cannot go back. You must bear the child through months of pain and discomfort, and even then you are not done. You must live with your creation, even at a distance of twenty years and more, when perhaps you have almost forgotten it, and it once again knocks on your door, because it is *yours*, and the world will never let you forget it."

271

I paused, having run out of breath, and she found a kerchief and wiped her eyes.

"I did not know," she said. "As you say, I supposed poetry was a gift and an amusement. You have told me so often enough. Now you make it sound like a drug, a disease, eating away at your mind. I wonder you do not abandon it altogether."

Abandon poetry. Why did I not, indeed? Why had I not, five years ago, and saved myself all this misery? But then . . . "What would I have?" I asked. "What would I be? And do not speak of politics. I know now that I lack the stomach for that miserable business."

"And what *are* you?" she cried.

I shrugged. "Well, as to that, my dearest Sis, I am a man who loves, even if his love is unrequited."

"Byron."

"But I am also a man of some genius, so I am told. There is something to be proud of."

"At what cost? You are also a man whose moods are so irrational as to cause doubts about his sanity. Why else do you suppose Belle has sent for me? She fears for your mind."

My immediate reaction was to laugh, and I did so. After all, I knew better than anyone that I was not the least mad. Which but goes to show how ignorant we are of the forces that operate around us, and hold us in their thrall, whether we would or no.

"Do *you* suppose I am mad?" I asked.

"Of course I do not, Byron. But I *know* you. Belle is still very much of a stranger. She is afraid of you. I suppose because of her pregnancy. She is very young. But I am sure that beneath it all, she loves you. And will love you more as time goes by."

"Let us hope she also practises showing it, at least to me." I held her hands, kissed them. "I would that others would show their love for me, as well."

"Byron. . . ." She tugged, and after a moment I let her go.

"I must go to the theatre."

"Could you not stay home, for just one evening? Belle would so appreciate it."

"But she has you for company, my dearest Sis." I was being cruel, and I knew it. But my anger remained, even feeding upon my liaison with Susan, for truth to tell she was a most confoundedly boring girl, and at the same time had adopted the habit of giving herself the most outrageous airs in the Green Room.

Guss refused to take offence. "At least say a word to her, Byron. She tells me you have not spoken to her this week."

"Has she told you why?"

She flushed. "Not in as many words. She spoke of sexual lust. . . ."

"As if it were some crawling disease, I have no doubt at all."

"She is pregnant, Byron. Close to delivery. She is terrified. We are all terrified at those moments. If you could but smile at her. . . ."

"She brings her misfortunes on herself," I said, and left. But my mood was more savage than ever. And rendered more so by the continuing events of the evening. For Susan was as usual waiting for me in the Green Room, delivering a perfect spate of recriminations because I had not visited her the previous night. In fact I had entirely forgotten whether I had or not, so befuddled had I been with drink, and I took immediate steps to place myself in the same happy frame of mind as soon as possible this evening again. She retired in tears, less at my mood, I am sure – she was becoming used to them – than at being humiliated in front of her fellow actresses, and I departed to Kinnaird's, where I drank some more and recollect becoming involved in a bitter argument – quarrel would be a better word – with Alexander Rae. (i)

It was after midnight before I made my way home. It is difficult to be certain of one's emotions when one's brain is fuddled, but the fact is that Augusta's words had been swirling around my brain all evening, helping to increase my irritability. Am I a bad man? The question had been asked of me before, but never before had I asked it of myself. I am sure I am not. I was sure then I was not. I swear that when I returned home from Kinnaird's on that fateful November morning, I had half determined to do as Augusta had begged me, and attempt a reconciliation.

I did not even take off my hat and greatcoat, but went up the stairs, tried her door, and discovered it was locked. Some of my good humour began to dissipate. I knocked, and heard movement within. "Who is it?"

"It is I, my dearest Pippin," I said.

There was a moment's hesitation. "You've been drinking," she accused.

273

"I have taken a glass of port, certainly. Dearest, if you do not unlock this door, I shall break it down."

The key turned immediately, to suggest she had been waiting on the far side. Her face peered at me. "Byron. My lord. . . ."

Gently I pushed the door inwards; she went with it. "Can I not even address my wife, save by means of an embassy?"

"If I could be sure. . . ."

"Of my mood?" I closed the door behind me. "I am a gentle person, Belle. You of all people should know that."

"Gentle?" She retired across the room and sat on her bed, drawing her robe closer about herself.

"Gentle," I insisted. "And there is no need to take on that protective attitude. I'll not harm you. I'll not even touch you. I shall stand here, and invite you to come to me, and kiss me, as passionately or as tenderly as you wish. There." I anchored myself in the centre of the floor, and thrust my hands into my greatcoat pockets. She continued to stare at me. "My dear Belle," I said. "Will you not even grant me that small favour? Do you suppose, in that tortured mind of yours, that I have come here to assault you?"

She continued to stare at me, and I felt my charity disappearing into anger. My fingers curled themselves into fists, and as they did so, insensibly curled themselves about the butts of my pistols. To my utter consternation there was suddenly a tremendous explosion, followed immediately by a ghastly singeing smell, the whole shrouded in a quite ear-splitting shriek from my wife.

Pandemonium broke out. The door was flung inwards, and we were joined by Augusta and half the servants, it seemed, not to mention the despicable bailiff, Bruton. I of course could pay them very little attention at that moment, for my trousers seemed to be on fire, and I was concerned with seizing the ewer from the washstand and emptying it down my leg. They similarly ignored me as they clustered round my lady, who was repeating, "Oh, my God, oh, my God, oh, my God," over and over again.

"A shot," the bailiff declared, very importantly.

"You can smell it," someone else said.

"My lord?" This Fletcher.

"Oh, Byron, what have you *done*?"

This Guss, and I was by now able to take my part in the conversation. "Out," I shouted. "Get out of my wife's bedroom."

The chattering ceased, and they began to filter through the door.

"Don't leave me," Belle gasped. "For God's sake don't leave me."

Augusta hesitated, and I shrugged. "You may remain."

The door closed, and there was a moment's silence. I took off my coat.

"What happened?" Guss begged.

"My lord fired a pistol," Belle said, leaving target and motive to her imagination.

"I did not *fire* a pistol," I said. "My pistol went off by accident."

"You came in here with a loaded pistol in your hand," Belle insisted.

"I did not. I came in here with my coat on, as you can see, and there was a loaded pistol in my pocket. There always is. I have another one." And I bent to pick up the coat, but was checked by another shriek.

"Do *you* suppose I fired at my wife?" I demanded of Guss.

"Well. . . ." She hesitated, and I became very angry indeed.

"I understand," I said. "I am utterly condemned. Well, then, I am guilty, obviously. What would you have me do?"

Guss licked her lips. "I am sure Lady Byron would accept an apology."

I gazed at my wife, and she gazed at me. I could see her face taking on that rigidly pious expression I had come to know and to fear. I wanted to laugh at the sheer farce of the whole thing. Instead I indulged in some farce of my own, crossed the room, watching her expression change to terror as I approached, watching her mouth open as she meditated an appeal to Guss, and then close again as I knelt before her, rested my head on her knee, and apologised most abjectly for all the misery I had caused her.

"Why, Byron," she said, laying her hand on my head. "My own dear, dear lord, of course I shall be happy to forgive you, supposing I can truly believe you mean what you say."

"Oh, I do, I do," I moaned.

"Well, then, my lord, I shall say nothing more of the matter. Neither shall anyone else. I swear it. You are forgiven."

At which I pushed myself to my feet. The absolute effrontery of it.

"Byron?" She frowned at my expression.

I smiled at her. "Was that not easy? To obtain your forgiveness? Truly, madam, the machinations of your entire sex never fail to amuse me." I picked up my coat. "I bid you good night."

*　　*　　*

275

My own estimation is that it was from that night my wife decided to end our marriage. Certain it is that from that night she sought all manner of absurd reasons to account for any action of mine. Now, I will be the first to admit that I am something of an eccentric. Circumstances have made me so. My health is ever uncertain. I am given to bouts of extreme depression, surely a concomitant of my recurring tertians, which can only be alleviated by strong liquors. My weight, given the indulgence of two square meals in twenty-four hours, tends to increase alarmingly, and can only be combated by drastic purges. My digestion is a constant cause of concern, inflicting upon me such pain that I must have recourse to laudanum in order to live a normal life. None of these, surely, are evidences of any mental disorder whatsoever. (ii)

I am a poet. I need time to contemplate, to think, to compose, to reflect upon my compositions. Time in which there must be absolute quiet. A poet's wife should understand these matters. And when she forces her company upon her husband, who may be in the throes of creation while afflicted by any of the disorders listed above, she must expect his replies to be a little brusque. Not that I recall ever addressing her more severely than to say, "You are in my way," and this on a single occasion. No evidence here of deep-seated malevolence.

I am self indulgent. It is in my nature. It is my habit to live with a dash few other men attempt. My hobbies in this direction are innocent. One of them is to knock the tops off my soda water bottles with a poker. Belle was aware of this, and had not previously complained. Yet on the night she gave birth to our Ada, during which I, in my mental anguish, sat in my study below her bedroom and endeavoured to relieve my spirits, she concluded or says she did, that I was throwing the bottles against the ceiling to drive her to distraction. I will but ask, about whose state of mind does that raise considerations?

I am a man of letters. It behoves me to understand what is going on in the world of letters. That I should read a book such as *Justine* is entirely natural. (iii) It is an obscene work, and that I should choose not to display it upon my shelf, but instead keep it in a drawer, is again but natural. Certainly it is not evidence of sexual derangement. But what are we to say of the mind of a wife who will take advantage of her husband's absence to introduce a doctor into the house and with him search her dear lord's room and possessions, and wave the offending work on high, and cry, I am married to a perverted devil?

And I am a man. My passions run strong, my desires are not easily to be assuaged. Robbed of all possibility of conjugal bliss with my wife, not even admitted through her door, I must seek my pleasures elsewhere. Driven to irritation by her mindless piety, and once again suffering physical agony, I might shout to her the name of my mistress, even indicate that I received more satisfaction in *that* bed than ever in hers. I might even, when in my cups – she says I did – threaten to bring Susan into my own house for my greater gratification; and assuredly this *must* have been in my cups, for surely I have already indicated that desire for *her* was so rapidly replaced by boredom that the thought of actually living with her was impossible. But again, this is no source of derangement, rather the reverse. Yet these were the evidences that my wife was storing away in her tight little brain, to hurl in my face the moment she regained her strength.

Yet such was the exquisite deceit with which she concealed her true feelings, I suspected nothing of this. Indeed for the rest of this year I was the most contented, even the most delighted of men. My child was born, and christened Augusta Ada, the first name for obvious reasons, the second because it had already been used in my family. She was a healthy, charming child, and I have no doubt still is, and grows more so with every day. And her mother also survived in the full bloom of health. And even smiled upon me.

But I was apparently in the course of preparing another terrible sin against our marriage. All in an attempt to save it. For four more executions had been secured against me, and we were in real danger of having our home sold out from beneath us. It was at once to save Belle and the babe from the awful embarrassment of this terrible fate, as much as to endeavour to save some money, that I suggested it would be best for her to take Ada up to Seaham, accepting the invitation extended by her mother some time before. I could not go. Not only was it essential for me to remain near Hanson and attempt to prod him into some financial action, but the very suggestion that I might be leaving London would have brought about the one thing we both dreaded. This was obvious to both of us, as I supposed, and was accepted by Belle, again as I supposed.

Thus we spent our first Christmas together, as it was our last, in apparent conjugal bliss, and for my part, as I have stated, I was perfectly contented. I had in fact already taken steps to break off my liaison with Susan Boyce, and was looking forward to resuming relations with my wife, whenever she felt herself able. At the same time I would be lying did I pretend I was not greatly relieved at the prospect of removing her from London. It promised a breath of fresh air, in which I should once again be my own man, and at the end of which, I hoped, I should be able to bring her back to a solvent home, where my moods and my uncertainties would be a thing of the past. No doubt some of this relief from time to time revealed itself to her.

And then consider, it is well known that I am a man who loathes scenes. Of any sort, but partings are to me anathema. I was therefore acutely embarrassed when on the night of 14 January 1816, all preparations being made, Belle and Ada attended me in the parlour to say farewell. I had little to say myself, and at last could only kiss the babe, and remark, "I wonder when we three shall meet again?"

Her reply should have warned me of the doom hanging over me. But it seemed perfectly in character. "In heaven, I would hope," she said, and left the room. When I arose next morning, she was gone. And yet, a letter which arrived within a few days was written in the most affectionate terms, as was mine to her. I continued to write her, and was only vaguely concerned when, after a fortnight, hers to me ceased. This was unlike Belle, and I began to worry lest she or the babe had been taken ill. Augusta had by this time returned to keep house for me, but also accompanying her was the detestable George, and I mean my cousin, George Anson Byron, not the equally detestable George Leigh. Truth to tell, in my then mood of mingled relief at being left to myself, combined with sudden concern at the cessation of Belle's letters, I was not the best of hosts, particularly when I observed this pair, my only two near relations in all the world, the one the sister I had set above all other women, and the other the man who would be my heir unless I could produce a son, regarding me as if I were a sorely afflicted fellow, and *whispering* together when they felt I was not aware of it.

In fact George Byron I would have found irritating in the best of circumstances. He was a confoundedly, pompously prating fellow, who could turn any conversation into an implied criticism. I had my pleasure at his expense, by behaving as outrageously as I knew, at least in conversation, all innocent of how they were noting everything which could be discovered to my disadvantage. But nothing which occurred during those few days prepared me for the bombshell which was about to be dropped into my lap.

It was doubly unexpected because soon after her departure, Belle had written me begging me to join them at Kirkby Mallory, where she had gone instead of Seaham, as soon as possible, whenever I could escape my creditors. This of course I had not even considered at first; I had no intention of locking myself away in the company of the dragon and rambling Ralph. But as the days passed with no further communication from my wife, I decided at last that I would have to go, if only to discover the truth of what was happening, being quite bemused by Guss's and George's secret mutterings. I had actually ordered the carriage to be waiting for me on 2 February, and this despite the fact that we were in the middle of enduring one of the coldest winters on record, when a messenger arrived for me, with a letter. I took it without great concern, although I frowned slightly when I discovered that it was written by Sir Ralph himself, and yet despatched from within London. Here was another mystery to pile upon the existing ones.

But the contents of the letter was the greatest mystery of all. For in it Sir Ralph accused me of using his daughter with continued and inhuman cruelty, and declared that in the circumstances it was necessary for our respective lawyers to meet in order to prepare a legal separation.

CLAIRE

I was so bemused by this remarkable epistle it was some time before I
could bring myself to reply. And then it was in the most formal terms,
as I had to confess my total ignorance of the enormities I was supposed
to have committed. My last letter from Belle, admittedly some weeks
before, had contained nothing but endearments and entreaties for me
to hurry to Kirkby Mallory. I now addressed to her another letter in
which I begged her to explain her father's meaning.

To this I obtained no reply. But even worse than her silence was the
attitude of everyone around me, not least my own sister. Everyone
regarded me with either pity or with loathing, as if I were suffering
from some ghastly disease. Even Lady Melbourne, who came to call,
added to my misery. She swept into my house, stared around her in
that imperious fashion of hers, which sent my dog cowering into a
corner, and announced rather than questioned: "Byron, where is
Annabella?"

"At Kirkby, I understand."

"There is a rumour sweeping London that you have
separated."

"There may well be," I temporised. "We are at this moment
separated, as you can see for yourself."

She bent upon me one of her most severe stares. "Do you love her,
Byron?"

"Dearly." Nor do I believe I was exaggerating, at that moment. It is
an odd aspect of human behaviour that we only realise how much we
desire something after it has been removed from our grasp.

"Well, then, go after her. Fetch her back here. Do not allow these
rumours to grow." She went to the door. "You will know why better
than anyone."

With which sinister remark she left me. "For God's sake," I cried to
Augusta. "Tell me what they are saying."

"I do not *know* what they are saying," she insisted. "But we are both damned. I have no doubt of it."

A piece of entirely feminine contradiction which left me more bemused than ever. My state of mind was only exacerbated by a reply I finally extracted from Belle, two replies to be exact, I having written her again to beg for some intimation, in her own hand, as to her place in this lamentable business. As usual she wrote a great deal, but only one sentence mattered, and it was utterly damning:

"After seriously and dispassionately reviewing the misery that I have experienced almost without an interval from the day of my marriage, I have finally determined upon the measure of a separation, which my father was authorised to communicate to you and carry into effect."

Once again I was quite bemused, and could do nothing more than write another letter, appealing to her better nature, asking indeed, if she had *never* been happy for a moment in my company. I could only assume that during the preceding couple of weeks she had been so worked upon by her mother and the detestable Clermont as to paint an entirely false picture of her life with me. But once again she chose not to reply.

My confusion, my sense of isolation in the midst of so much apparent gossip, grew. I declare I was on the way to going out of my mind, when Hobby came to my rescue, as he has done so often. Although in this case it might have been better to let me wallow in my misery.

The ostensible reason for his visit was to bring me the first copies of *The Siege of Corinth* and *Parisina*, the two works on which I had laboured during my year of wedded bliss. Murray was as usual very pleased with his subscription, and anticipated as good a sale for these as for *The Corsair*, or perhaps a better one, my name being once again the talk of London. I must confess I turned the pages with scant interest – one of Belle's strictures in her alarming letters had been on my preoccupation with such a puerile hobby as verse – and my dear friend was moved to remark, "You are not looking well."

"I am not well. I am besieged by indigestion and by jaundice, and by confusion and misery most of all. What do you make of this?" I gave him Belle's letter, which after a moment's hesitation he read.

"If I could only understand," I continued. "How terrible I am supposed to have been. I swear I know many a worse husband than I."

"Nothing has been communicated to you?"

"What you hold there. Milbanke's letter. And a request for my lawyer to get together with his to arrange terms of settlement. This I have ignored. I shall continue to ignore it until I hear from Belle herself that our marriage is at an end."

He gave me an old-fashioned look, and laid the letter on the table. "You would not describe this letter as requesting a separation?"

"Oh, for God's sake, I know that is what it *says*. But it gives no reasons. I know, and she knows, that our marriage was not one long misery. She is being dictated to by Judith. I know that. Let her give me one concrete *fact* which made her life such a misery."

Hobby commenced pulling his nose, which was already long enough, God knows.

"Out with it," I cried.

"Well . . . you have heard *nothing*?"

"No one will speak to me, except in the most general terms."

"Hm."

"Hobby," I begged, "if you are my friend, you'll tell me what is being said."

"Well," he said again. "I am sure everything is untrue. . . ."

"Then at least allow me to deny it."

"You will be very angry."

"I will not. I swear it."

"Well. . . ." Once again he pulled his long suffering proboscis. "Lady Byron has claimed that you are mad."

I stared at him.

"There were things, well. . . ." The poor fellow commenced to go very red in the face. "She says you are given to the most terrible nightmares, during which you rush around the house waving sword and pistols."

"And that is proof of being mad? So I have nightmares. It is the laudanum."

"She says you tried to murder her."

"*Murder* her?"

"By firing at her with a pistol while she lay in bed carrying your child."

"For God's sake. Everyone knows that was an accident. The pistol was in my pocket – you know I always carry a weapon – and it went off by accident. Murder her? I damn near shot myself in the leg."

"I'm sure that is the truth of the matter," he agreed. "But I suppose, in her distraught state, she put a different complexion upon it."

"*Her* distraught state. I thought I was the one accused of madness. There has got to be more."

"Well, she says you secretly indulged in obscene literature."

I frowned at him. At that time I had no idea my bureau had been searched. "What obscene literature?"

"Something by de Sade."

"*Justine*. Have you never read *Justine*?"

"Ahem. Well, yes, of course I have. But I wouldn't leave it lying around in front of ladies. Especially my wife."

"I did not leave it lying around. I kept it in a drawer in my desk. It is still there. The wretched girl has been hunting through my belongings. Mad, am I?" I found myself beginning to get angry. "Well, let her bring that one against me. We shall see about that."

Hobby was looking truly distressed. "She has already put the matter to her lawyers, and been advised that there are no grounds for separation, on account of madness."

"Well, then. . . ." I frowned at him. "How do *you* know this?"

"It was . . . ah . . . conveyed to me."

"In order that you might convey it to me." I found myself frowning again. "Then where is the to-do?"

Hobhouse got up, began to pace the room, hands tucked under the skirts of his coat. He was starting to remind me of a lawyer himself. "Thus advised, Lady Byron produced some fresh evidence which she supposed might necessitate a separation."

"Fresh evidence? What fresh evidence?"

"Well, it is of a delicate nature."

"Between you and me, Hobby?"

"I am sure you know of what I speak, Byron," he said, somewhat severely. "And you may believe me that I would far rather *not* speak of it at all. Neither would anyone else."

"Yet my wife appears to have done so."

"To her lawyers, in the strictest confidence."

"Who promptly spoke to you, in the strictest confidence. Just as they have told their wives in the strictest confidence and their wives will have told their best friends, in the strictest confidence. Thus all London will know of it, in the strictest confidence. I am the only person who does *not* know of it."

He paused in his perambulation. "You mean that?"

"I have no idea at all of what she is speaking."

He sat down beside me, glanced at the door. He looked at his hands, which had twined together, then took out a handkerchief and wiped his neck. His face was so crimson I feared he might have a stroke. "Whatever can be the matter?"

He sighed, and licked his lips. "She accuses . . . well, there were rumours . . . of course I took no heed of them, and well, I would take no heed of them now . . . well. . . ."

"Hobby," I said gently, "you are gabbling like the maniac I am supposed to be. My wife accuses me of what?"

"Of attempting to . . . well . . . my God, Byron. You must know what I mean."

I stared at him, while an awful suspicion crossed my mind. But would she, could she, could any woman, much less Annabella Milbanke, so confess to the secrets of the marriage bed? My thoughts must have revealed themselves on my face, for he sighed.

"Belle has accused me of sodomy?"

"My God." He seemed to be speaking to himself.

"And you believe her?"

"I will believe anything you tell me to be the truth," the poor fellow lied, for knowing me as well as he did, how could he possibly have had any doubts?

"But everyone else believes her."

"Well, as I say, she has told only her lawyers."

"Yet all London knows of it."

"I did not say that. I do not think so. I was thinking of the other matter. . . ."

"The other matter? What other matter?" The room seemed to be reeling around me.

"Well . . . my God, Byron, I but repeat what has been said."

"I understand that, my dear fellow. But at least tell me *what* has been said."

"Lady Byron. . . ." His voice sank almost to a whisper. "Lady Byron accuses you of incest with Mrs Leigh."

Once again I felt I was sinking beneath the blow. For as I have already stated, it never occurred to me that anyone could see through our guilty secret.

"And where are her grounds for *that*?" My voice seemed that of a stranger, and came from very far away.

284

"She . . ." Hobby was chewing his lip. "She speaks of your constantly hugging your sister."

"Should a man not embrace his sister?"

"Of your lying one night on that settee, and inviting them both to kiss you, to see who could most delight you, and giving the award of best to Mrs Leigh." Once again his cheeks were pink.

"I was drunk." Indeed I could hardly recall the incident. "For God's sake, it was a game. God save me from humourless women."

"All women are humourless," Hobby remarked, revealing an insight into the fair sex he had not previously suggested.

"And there are her reasons for suspicion?"

Once again he blushed. "Not altogether. She says . . . she says she heard you laughing at Mrs Leigh, and saying, 'I know you wear drawers.' "

Once again when drunk. God damn my weakness for alcohol. Yet I found my anger returning.

"And on those childish suppositions she will condemn me?" I said, getting up. "Well, let her do her damndest. I'll meet then fair and square, head on. We shall see."

Hobhouse was sighing to himself. "There is more."

"There cannot be, more than what you have already told me."

"More weight to her words, Byron. Caro Lamb. . . ."

I turned to face him, my heart turned to stone. "Yes?"

"She has written your wife, repeating tales you told her, she says, of your love for young boys, of your . . . your method of loving them. My God, Byron, but you nested with a viper there."

"Go on." Because clearly he was not finished.

"And she has written of seeing a letter, showed her by you, from an unnamed love, but which she clearly recognised to be Mrs Leigh."

I stared at him. God, I thought, to have Caro and Belle in the same sack, ready for immersion. How they would squeal. And how I would love to hear them squeal. "Surely you are not finished?"

"Have I not said enough? Byron, you are done for."

"The devil I am. I'll fight them. By God, I'll fight them. It is all a blackmail plot. Surely you can see that, Hobby? She means to frighten me into granting her a separation. She means to frighten me into giving up my daughter. No doubt she means to frighten me into giving up my estate as well. Well, she is welcome to my debts, but I'll see her damned before I'll surrender so tamely."

"Byron. . . ." Once again that fatal hesitation which warned me of another impending disaster.

"What now?"

"The fact is, dear friend, you fight here with more than a mere wife. The word is already out, as you say, of what she accuses you. You have enemies. You should know that. You have ploughed too pretty a path through London society these last four years not to have enemies. They say Eldon and Harrowby spit blood whenever your name is mentioned. They say even Holland wishes you were safely across the water."

"Across the water?"

His flush deepened. "'Tis a suggestion. Holland at the least is an honourable man. He knows your game is up. Should you stay and make a fight of it, they will bring you down, deeper than you can imagine possible. If necessary they will bring false witnesses against you. But will they have to? Suppose they send to Malta? They will do so if they have to. They think you are dangerous, Byron. They see in you another George Gordon,(i) and they remember that he has got to be a distant cousin. Fight them, Byron, and they may yet bring you to a gallows."

For sodomy is a hanging offence. I sat down, utterly crushed by the weight of catastrophe which was bearing on my shoulders.

"But agree to a separation," Hobhouse said, "and all will be well. Holland gives you his word. He will act as intermediary himself, and your estates will be safe. Grant your wife a separation, and take yourself back where you have always longed to be."

"Confess my crimes by default, you mean," I said bitterly. "And then take myself into perpetual exile, perpetual obloquy."

"You were happier there than ever here. Your friends will still know where to find you. Leave the arrangements to Douglas and I. We shall see to everything. I only wish I could come with you, but I cannot at this moment. Yet I *will* come to you, Byron. I swear it."

Did ever a man have a truer friend? Or a more honest one. For when I raised my head to look him in the eyes, his face a cloud beyond my tears, he sighed and said, "There is no alternative. Believe me. No alternative at all."

So there it was, out in the open at last. My wife wittingly or unwittingly, had turned herself into an agent of my destruction, as appointed by those social and political enemies I had accumulated during my years of fame. It was this last fact that settled the matter. Belle alone, backed by her family, backed by the inalienable secrets of marriage which she had chosen to let slip, I would have fought. Against a government which had proved its ruthless reactionary nature time and again I knew I was powerless, in England. But I knew too that my pen, once removed from Tory reach, would prove as sharp a sword as anything they could bring against me, and I determined that it should be so.

Thus I *appeared* to surrender. And as I had suspected, by doing so turned all the allegations against me into fact, in the eyes of the vulgar horde. Now it was truly a time to discern one's friends standing out very clear from one's enemies. Hanson remained superficially loyal; Douglas Kinnaird and Hobby, Tom Moore and Sam Rogers and Scrope Davies, these I could count upon.

Guss returned to her true colours, once the calamity had actually descended upon us. She had been terrified by the allegations, by the suggestions, by the fear of the unknown. Once the unknown became the known, she squared her shoulders and revealed herself to be a true Byron, even if she was the one who would have to remain and face her accusers. I begged her to accompany me into exile, but it was not to be; her first loyalty had to remain with her feckless husband and her prodigious progeny. She was again big with child. (ii) But during those last weeks in England she remained at my side, accompanied me wherever I went, let the world know that she was my sister.

Wherever I went. For here again it was a case of seeing very clearly who enjoyed the company of Byron, and who had merely touted to the poet and the rake. The invitations which had clustered like autumn leaves on my doormat ceased. The letters which had bombarded me ceased. Even Lady Melbourne ceased. Caro did not cease. Having betrayed me, she now commenced a siege to assure me that she had not. I can only suppose she decided, on learning of my impending exile, that she was the person best suited to accompany me.

Yet friends remained. Lady Jersey, rising head and shoulders above all around her as she had always done, invited me to her Spring ball, and I went, Guss on my arm, Hobby at my side. Milady was graciousness herself. Not so her guests, who to a man, or more especially to a woman, cut us dead, including my detestable cousin-in-law, George Anson's wife, no doubt already considering me driven to suicide and herself lady of the manor. But there was one notable exception. Dear Meg Mercer Elphinstone abandoned her escort to cross the room to us, kiss Guss on the cheek, and present her own to my lips. "Oh, Byron, Byron," she whispered. "If you had married *me*, none of this would have happened."

How right she was. If my adoration for Lady Melbourne has now entirely dissipated into contempt, it is mainly because she turned me away from that one port where I could have survived any storm in safety.

As might have been expected, my literary fame remained as high as ever, or even rose. People who might never have read poetry in their lives now sought out my works to discover the truth about this monster living in their midst. I continued to be inundated with epistles from would-be writers, seeking my approbation or criticism, and by implication, my help in placing their work. Most was of very poor quality, nor was I in the mood to be charitable. Yet one at the least I regret. It was a packet from a young man named Robert Smith, who had commenced what it pleased him to call an epic poem, a long collection of couplets in the most rabid doggerel, concerning the adventures of Saint George, striding along through time with a scant regard for history or politics. To be sure it was an amusing little work, but I could see no value in it, and was forced to write and tell him so. Imagine my dismay when I received a communication from his mother, a fortnight later, informing me that the silly lad, on receipt of my reply, had proceeded to drown himself. I could only send my sympathies, and reflect that if his mental condition was so precarious in any event, he could never had stood the strain of literary acclaim.

But the entire episode was just one more *gloom* in the general gloom which surrounded me that March. I was desperate to snap my fingers and find myself across the Channel, but there was so much to be done, however diligently Hobby worked at my affairs, for of course he had to proceed in secret as more and more executions were being granted, and the suggestion that I was leaving England for good would have brought the entire crew down on my head. But I was equally desperate, while waiting, for some light relief. It is to this fact alone that I attribute the next load of calamity I pulled down on my shoulders.

It began as usual with a letter. Now, as I have intimated, I was in the habit of receiving dozens of letters every week, from various people all around the country, but in the main from young girls – at least, I suppose they were from young girls – who had managed to convince themselves that they had fallen in love with me through the medium of my poetry. Most were content to leave it at that, praying for a note from me or a lock of my hair – that I have managed to avoid baldness is one of nature's minor miracles – although some few hinted they would like a meeting with me, and one or two, such as the Swiss girl I mentioned a few chapters ago, actually achieved their desire.

But the operative word in all of this had ever been "hint". What then was I to make of a letter which indicated, in the most explicit terms, that its writer was prepared to throw herself upon my mercy? And claiming to be a creature formed entirely by reading my poetry. The whole thing smacked slightly of derangement, and I thought it best not to reply at all, only to receive a further note, in the same writing although again unsigned save for an incomprehensible initial, asking if she could call at seven that same evening – it was a Sunday – as she had business of "peculiar importance" to discuss. This time, poor weak vessel that I am, and cursed with curiosity, I agreed to see her.

And, I admit it freely, was intrigued. She was no beauty. Indeed, Claire Clairmont must be one of the *plainest* women I have ever encountered, with a large, somewhat moonlike face, redeemed only by the spirit in her brown eyes, which suggested a surprising intelligence in one so young, for she was only seventeen. Fool that I am, not to have clung to my so oft repeated resolution never to consort with *intelligent* women, save they be twice my age.

She did, however, possess a most ample figure, again for so young a girl, and this pleased me, as such delights have always done, and God willing, will always do. But what was really interesting about her was her background, for she was the illegitimate daughter of William Godwin, a somewhat scurrilous philosopher whose first wife, Mary Wollstonecraft, had been a vehement proponent of "rights" for women, whatever such things may be, and had even written a book called *Vindication of the Rights of Women*. Godwin had imbibed at this fountain, and in his own works had sought to propagate such ideals as free love. Well, I am all in favour of free love, but part of the delight of it is its very illicitness, and I am against bringing these things out into the cold light of print for the vulgar masses to devour and misunderstand.

Now I already possessed a vicarious acquaintance with Godwin, for his writings had been totally unsuccessful, and it had been suggested to me, by whom I forget, that if I would not accept payment from Murray for my own work, I might allow some of it to be granted to this weak vessel. To this I had agreed, splitting the payment for *The*

Bride of Abydos between the philosopher and Maturin, much to Murray's disgust. But in fact it turned out that Godwin was one of those dull fellows who lack the moral courage to practise what they preach. For all his trumpetings, when his own daughter Mary decided to elope with a married man, he produced all the thunder of your typical outraged father, and expelled her from the house. Now the young Lothario was actually a poet, or I should say, a would-be poet – for so far as I know he has published only one work, something called *Queen Mab*, which survived without any notice whatsoever from the public – by name of Percy Shelley. In recent years I have come to know Shelley well, to like him a great deal, and indeed, I can prophesy for him some slight success in the future if he can so far disturb his own domestic bliss to get down to any proper work. (iii) At that time I had of course never heard of the fellow.

The point of this story is that, Mary Wollstonecraft having died some eighteen years ago, Godwin had remarried, or at least cohabited, with a lady named Clairmont, and Claire was a daughter of this second liaison. Brought up in such a heady atmosphere, conceiving that Shelley was an impossibly romantic figure, she had elected to leave together with the happy couple, and had spent the better part of the past year in following them about Switzerland. Now they had returned to England, they had set up house as a *ménage à trois*, but as may be expected, Mary had not exactly welcomed the attentions of her half sister, and she had been forced to return to her father's home in Skinner Street, to what welcome I really would not care to say.

All of this she told me on our first couple of meetings, discussing her affairs with a quite frightening frankness. From which it will be gathered that I agreed to see her again. The truth is, she pretended she was writing a novel, on which she wished my opinion, and she also wished my opinion on Shelley, and brought me *Queen Mab* to read, and indeed I found it very fine. Following which she even brought along her sister Mary to meet me, another young woman of distinct character and same pretensions to beauty, but entirely caught up in her love for Shelley. (iv) I suspect Claire was attempting to show her that she too could accumulate a poet, and a far more famous one. But I repeat I was not in the least sexually attracted to her. God knows I scarce had the time during those tumultuous weeks to be sexually attracted to anyone. And yet I could not shake her off. I tried passing her on to Douglas Kinnaird, but she would have none of it, and indeed she began to be as regular a visitor to my home as Caro had once been to my apartment. Nor did it seem to worry her that her reputation, in visiting London's best-known roué who was separated from his wife, would be irretrievably ruined. And as time went by I almost welcomed her appearances. She promised some form of continuity in my shattered life, for the Shelleys were already considering a return to Switzerland, and as I had been refused entry into France by the returning Bourbon reactionaries – how my reputation as a dangerous revolutionary had spread abroad, and all on account of a few speeches and the company I kept, with never a shot fired in anger – I was beginning to consider Switzerland as my best possible refuge. To have friends already waiting for me there seemed a delightful prospect.

During this time I never touched the girl. But she was *there*, in all her buxom femininity, while I survived, as best I could, the disasters which were being piled around me, including even the auction of my library, and culminating eventually in the signing of the actual deed of separation. This was in early April, only one factor in the disaster which was to follow. Spring has always found me at my best, as winter has always been my worst period. In addition, Guss, her time very near, had been forced to return to Six Mile Bottom, and Hobby was totally occupied with obtaining me the necessary funds to depart. While on top of all, the actual conclusion of this lamentable business had a most peculiar effect upon my senses. I conceived myself as the loneliest and best-hated figure in the kingdom – I swear I was *hissed* whenever I walked abroad – but at the same time at a stroke the entire burden of being a peer of the realm, of being married, of being a social lion, of being *respectable* – and this is a considerable weight – had been torn from my shoulders and I felt a sense of freedom, a sense of defiance of form and convention, of heaven itself, a desire only to *live*, whatever life was left to me. In short, for the first time in my life, I felt utterly free, to be as good or as wicked as I wished. And in such circumstances, how can goodness hope to compete?

I was in such a mood when Claire invited me to take her into the country for a night.

She had of course been manoeuvring in this direction for some time, regardless of my total disinterest. And her appeal was couched in very pretty terms. "I do not expect *you* to love *me*," she said time and again. "But *I* love *you*. I adore you. I desire only to serve you. In every possible way. And if to spend a night with you would relieve some of the misery that clusters around you, then I am more than willing."

What man could resist such a *sacrifice*? And of course I was not so disinterested as all that. I could perceive that it would not *be* a sacrifice. Indeed, any doubts I may have felt upon the subject were very rapidly dispelled when I discovered that not only had she chosen the inn for our assignation, she had even reserved the necessary accommodation.

Alas, it is not my fate to take my pleasures without paying for them. I enjoyed that night with Claire. But it was the circumstances more than the woman. I had already seen sufficient of her to know that she possessed in greater abundance than most that wretched self centredness which is the curse of her sex. For all her protestations of the most utter love for me, I knew this to be false. She was in love with the concept of Claire Clairmont being loved by Lord Byron. My problems, my affairs meant nothing to her except they were taken in that context. Nor did the greater events which were happening in the world around us have the slightest interest for her. In short, she was too like my wife for me ever to desire more than a passing liaison.

But that night I was passionate, and the results of my passion are invariable. I am now the father of her child, and this when I would as willingly never see her again. See how my crosses follow me around, clinging to my shoulders?

Ah well, it may turn out for the best. In Claire's child I may obtain some compensation for the pain of never seeing my own sweet Ada. Even in extremity, I have never ceased to be the optimist.

At the time, of course, I was unaware that in severing my links with the problems of the past I was but creating an entirely fresh set of problems for the future. Claire indeed, soon after our night together, departed to rejoin the Shelleys who were leaving for the continent. I was to follow in quick succession. Hobby had arranged everything, his *pièce de résistance*, as I was to spend my future time travelling, being a great coach, built on the lines of Bonaparte's own equipage, which contained a bed, and a bath, and even a small library, so that wherever I went I should be in the greatest possible comfort.

But of course this cost a great deal on money, as it cost money to fit me out and money to provide me with a suitable income during my travels. So there at the end was I back to where I had been at the beginning of my adult life, most confoundedly strapped, and hounded from pillar to post by my eager creditors. Indeed they moved into my Piccadilly residence within hours of my moving out, and we were lucky to escape Dover without being caught.

In Dover I received a hero's welcome. Or at least the welcome we are told used to be given to prominent villains at the moment of their hanging. Crowds, mainly women, lined the streets to watch me as I walked down to the waiting barge. Truly I suspect they were looking for a devil's cloven hoof – in which they were not disappointed to be sure – and for an insupportable bulge in my breeches – in which they *were* disappointed – but from my point of view, in my new mood, I enjoyed every moment of it.

Then I was aboard, and saying farewell to England. For ever? I doubt it. Times change, and people with them. I shall return, in the fullness of time. Of this I am certain, if only to disturb the equanimity of the viper who calls herself my wife. But for the present, why, I am easy. Here in Venice I live the life I was meant to live. Perhaps I have indulged too extravagantly. But why should I not, when I have no respectability left to live up to? So I am fat, and I am lecherous, and I write whatever takes my fancy – and am still read most avidly by that very nation which cast me out – and I am visited from time to time by my friends, and were I in better health I might even call myself happy.

And have I no regrets? A million. Were I to list them all I should need another volume. Most of all I regret the constant solace of a lovely and loving woman's arms. I have known too many, in recent months. The Italian woman is a splendid creature. But there is no *substance* to her mind. To find a lady, who would give up all for me as Caro once wished to do, ah, but there is a dream. I am damned by that class, however much they wish to entertain me and stare at me and whisper about me behind their fans. And so I say, the clap upon you all, good ladies, as you have foisted it upon me too often. You have placed me in this squalid bog, and here I shall remain, and sink, until not a trace of me is left. Save a memory, a whisper, upon an occasional lip. Ah, Lord Byron. What a man he *might* have been.

BOOK THE THIRD

THE WANDERER AGAIN

We left England on the morning of 25 April 1816. I had four in my party, Willie Fletcher, of course, Robert Rushton, whom I had extracted from Newstead, the infamous Polidori (i) – I felt a doctor to be necessary because I really was in a most uncertain state of health – and a Swiss named Berger, as my destination was that country. At least unofficially. My true intention was Venice.

Behind me at Dover I left Hobhouse and Scrope Davies.

From that day to this I have never returned, nor do I expect to do so for a good many years yet.

I left England in that continued state of euphoria which I now recognise as being very close to hysteria. I felt like a schoolboy let out at the end of term. All of my problems, and they were enormous, seemed irrelevant beside the one fact of having escaped the stifling cloud of criticism in which I had been for too long surrounded. I wanted to sing and dance, had I been able. More important, I wanted to write. And more important than any of these things, I was determined to indulge my every desire. A short life and a merry one was my motto.

And so I came to Switzerland, and met Shelley.

I had no idea that this was about to happen. We arrived outside Geneva, at Déjean's Hotel Angleterre, on the evening of 25 May, and I sought only my bed. Indeed I was so exhausted I scribbled my age as a hundred years old, much to the annoyance of old Jacques Déjean, who himself welcomed us. But next morning, there was a note for me from Claire, announcing that she was already in residence, and asking me to inform her whenever we could meet. I was instructed to address her in care of Shelley, for she did not "wish to appear either in love or curious".

Silly girl. If, in the last desperate days of London, I had found the thought that she also would be in Switzerland some relief, now that I was actually free of those encumbrances I really had no wish to resume that unwilling liaison. Besides, I had a great deal to do. I found Switzerland a delightful place. There were mountains, such as I had not seen since leaving Greece, and then the lake lying at their foot, and prosperous contented people, with an age old tradition of *freedom*, at least of thought, for I was standing on the very ground which had sheltered Rousseau and allowed his genius to flower. Thoughts of Venice disappeared, and I sought instead a villa I could rent for the summer.

So Polidori and I took a *calèche* into Geneva, visited various estate agents, and were at last directed to a place I had already selected as being ideal for my purpose, the Villa Diodati, which was situated on the south shore of the lake and roughly opposite the hotel. We did not immediately cross the lake, as to tell the truth the rent, twenty-five louis a month, seemed somewhat steep; I was determined to live within my limited means. Nor was the place as large, from a description, as I had supposed. I therefore chose to think about it, and returned to Déjean's, where I discovered two more notes from Claire. It was now that she revealed for the first time her somewhat querulous nature, reminding me that she had been waiting for me here a whole fortnight, and had still had no word, and positively demanding that I climb to the top of the hotel that very night at half past seven; she would be waiting to show me to her room.

Her tone was so very desperate I decided to humour her, and that evening made my way up the stairs and into the darkened recesses of the upper floors, where to be sure she was, all rustling silk, a sound I never could resist. She positively threw herself upon me, and it was all I could do to gain the shelter of her bedchamber before she was discarding gown and petticoats, and fumbling at my own clothes, the while mumbling, "I have the most stupendous news, my dearest Byron."

"You are to marry," I suggested, partly in jest to be sure, but partly because of my innate optimism.

"Oh, Byron," she said, releasing me to sit on the bed, heavy breasts sunk on plump belly, plump belly sunk on to plump thighs. "Don't you love me at all?"

"I doubt I love anybody," I said. "At this moment."

She seized my hand. "Well, you will love *me*, when you hear what I have to say. Byron, I am pregnant. I know it."

I could only stare at her in horror.

"Your child, Byron. Your child."

"How can you be sure?"

Her turn to stare, while her face went crimson, and then she swung her hand, actually attempting to slap my face, an indignity I had never before experienced. Nor did I then. My boxing training came to my aid and I intercepted the blow.

"I meant that you are pregnant," I hastily lied.

"A woman knows these things," she said, beginning to cry. "As to the other, how could you? Do you think I am a whore?"

I refrained from pointing out that her behaviour in pursuing me had not exactly been that of a lady; I had far too much on my mind.

"We must see what must be done," I said.

"Oh, yes, Byron," she said, warming against me.

"There are ways . . . I will consult Polidori. At least we have caught the matter sufficiently early." I looked at her belly, which seemed no larger than usual.

She released me. "Whatever do you mean?"

"Well . . . you cannot mean to have the child?"

Once again a flood of tears. "Oh, *Byron*. Of course I mean to have the child. It will be *your* child. A Byron."

"There are more than enough of those to go round at the moment. Claire, be sensible. I cannot marry you, as you well know."

"I know that. I do not care. I just wish to be with you, the mother of your children. Ours will be one of the great romances in all history. Byron, I will work for you and sew for you and cook for you, and I will bear as many children as you desire."

What catastrophe. "My dear Claire," I said. "If there is one thing on which I am absolutely determined, it is that I shall never again have any *permanent* relations with any woman."

"Byron."

I got up. Clearly this was a matter which had to be settled as rapidly as possible. "It is not as if I have ever pretended to love you."

"Byron."

"I do *not* love you," I insisted. "This heart of mine is incapable of love. Now, or at any moment in the future."

"Byron," she sobbed. "I do not care whether you love me or not. I love you. I will bear your child, even if you send me from your side for ever. Just love me tonight, Byron. Just one more time."

*   *   *

Here was a fine situation. But what could a fellow do? There I was, sitting on a bed with a naked woman clinging to my arm, intent upon one thing. And she carried my child. I obliged her, and left her happy enough, and returned to my own bed in a very sad state of mind.

But it seemed to me that her condition was entirely her problem. She had besieged me. She had been the instigator of every midnight tumble. I had never in any way attempted to deceive her regarding my own feelings. And I had offered to attend the matter of her abortion, and to pay the costs as well. If she was determined to become a mother, then certainly I could not stop her.

But I was not at all sure I wanted to see her again. Next day Polidori and I rowed across to look at the villa, and I was delighted with it, especially the view out over the lake, which was one of the finest I have ever seen. To my chagrin I now learned that it had been promised to an English family for the next three years. In a fine fit of anger I made my way back to the hotel, to encounter, standing on the shore to greet us, Claire, and her half sister Mary, whom I remembered from our London meeting, and the very oddest fellow I had ever seen, for he was well over six feet tall, and with it very thin, so that he seemed to droop rather than stand. In addition his cheeks had the flush of the consumptive, the more increased at this moment because of his obvious shyness at meeting me.

But the face itself was very fine, not handsome to be sure, but possessing a nobility of feature which suggested an equal nobility of thought. I knew immediately that I was going to like him.

As indeed I did, and I am flattered to imagine that he liked me equally, although I doubt he ever truly understood me. Our relationship was of course from the very start handicapped by being built around Claire. She saw to our introductions, and made it quite plain that if I intended to be Shelley's friend then I must continue to be her lover. But in fact this I was prepared to endure, reflecting that it could not continue for a very long while, and indeed she was useful as more than a bed-warmer, for she was prepared to work for me, and happily settled down to copying out my manuscript.

For I was working again. At a third canto of *Childe Harold*, so much had my lost youth regained possession of my senses. Once again I was a wanderer, exiled from my native land. I was also, for the first time in years, in the mood to look back over the events of my youth, and it was now I wrote *The Dream*, recalling the best of poor Mary Ann Chaworth. Now in a purely artistic sense these efforts may be regarded as a retrograde step, but it was a necessary interlude, for even as I wrote I felt within me the stirrings of something big, something *immense*, certainly induced by the surroundings in which I existed, the mountains and the lakes, but equally, I admit without hesitation, a result of my walks and my talks and my sails with Percy Bysshe.

For once his shyness evaporated, and it did very rapidly the moment our exchanges turned from inanities to matters of substance, he was a most entrancing conversationalist. His mind roamed over every conceivable subject, and in fact sought heights to which I was not prepared to ascend. Within a few days we became the closest of friends – I called him Shiloh, and he called me Albé, from my constant reminiscences of Albania – and I began to enjoy my life as I had not done for some time. For I even managed to secure the Villa Diodati, by making a fresh approach, and moved myself in with my entourage, the Shelleys being settled not far distant at Montalegre. I bought myself a little boat, and together Shiloh and I explored the lake, and thereby inspired one of my best *Byronic* poems, *The Prisoner of Chillon*. But I doubt there is anyone who can visit these gloomy dungeons, the more hideous because of the stark beauty with which the castle is surrounded, without wishing to rush into verse. My surprise is that Shelley never did so.

But as I have suggested, he moved on an altogether more sublime plane than I, although he indicated that on my part it was entirely for want of ambition. "I see you, my dear lord," he said, "as the great epic poet of our age. Milton, returned once again to breathe our air, and exhale the blessed images which shall make him forever famous."

"Milton? Me? To write like Milton, one must be inspired by God, and I fear my inspiration comes from a much hotter place."

He smiled at my attempt at humour, as he always did. "You underestimate yourself. And besides, I do not suggest you should write about the Deity. But you have at hand a subject equally important, if you'll excuse a slight blasphemy. Have we not, in our own lives witnessed the greatest, the most earthshaking event in all history? However hard the Castlereaghs and the Metternichs may try, you know and I know, my lord, the entire world knows, that the society of 1788 can never wholly return, that mankind has taken a giant step forward, that our children and our children's children will benefit from the horrors as well as the accomplishments of the French. And you, my dear lord, you are here to record those events for ever, in your deathless verse. You lived through it. You can recall the emotions and the despairs of those tumultuous years. And you have the gift, the genius, the ability, and the determination, to undertake such a mammoth task." He seized my hand. "I can think of no other."

There was flattery for you. But the French Revolution? A great canvas, to be sure, but one requiring so much work and research as almost to be a serious historical undertaking. That was not, and is not, and probably never will be, for me. I must let my imagination flow. It cannot be constrained within pre-ordained boundaries.

But our friendship grew. He was the very best of company, as was his Mary, whom I soon discerned to be a charming girl. With their dilution I was even content to be with Claire, for a while. The four of us were inseparable, and our minds ranged over a variety of subjects, not all of which were as sterile as Shiloh's suggestions for my epic. It was at one of our evening gatherings that *Frankenstein* was born, for while we sat before the fire with the wind howling down from the mountains, we decided that we would each commence a ghost story. I'm afraid Shiloh, Claire and myself accomplished very little, although I certainly scribbled a word or two, but Mary got down to work and produced her melancholy masterpiece which I am happy to think received its just acclaim in due course.

My mind was taken with a new idea, a new departure. Write an epic, my friend had suggested, and I was in an epic-writing mood. But it was to be an epic born of me, of my love of freedom, of my love for the great mountains which surrounded us, and of my own fatal opposition it seemed to the forces of nature, to the very Deity Himself. Thus *Manfred* came to be, and when he stood on his lonely crag and shouted his defiance at God and man alike, I was uttering my own determined thoughts.

It is not, of course, to be supposed that that summer of 1816 was one of unalloyed happiness. For it was now that Caro chose to appal the literary public with her novel *Glenarvon*. I heard of this epic work of denigration long before I read it, nor was I in any hurry to do so, as I could not conceive that any woman would so display her secret emotions for the vulgar horde to examine. In the event my very worst fears were realised, save that the hero, Glenarvon, clearly intended to be me, seemed a very poor likeness. But only to *me*. Everyone else would suppose he was a perfect portrait of the most heartless rake who ever walked the face of this earth.

But the principal source of dissatisfaction in that summer was of course Claire.

As I have attempted to explain, I humoured the girl during my first couple of months in Switzerland. She was there, she was a part of the Shelley *ménage*, and she made her body available to me. She also copied out some of my verses and she was to be the mother of my child. Despite my growing dislike of her as a *person*, all of these things made for a bond. But it was one easily loosened.

For of course as her belly began to swell she became progressively less attractive, and progressively more ill-tempered and demanding, as women will. But from her point of view, probably the worst aspect of the situation was that intellectually she was at the bottom of our elevated scale. Our conversations, in which Mary often enough joined, flowed around her head like water closing over a drowning man. She could not comprehend, her own sallies or attempts at profundity were greeted with smiles on our part, and her descent into perpetual ill temper was completed by our praise of Mary's book, while Claire's attempts were truly puerile. She became a nuisance rather than a pleasure to be with, and I began to avoid her, and intimated that she was not really welcome at my villa.

I had other sources of irritation. Polidari proved no less impossible, with his similar assumptions of mental powers he did not possess, and with his quick-tempered response to anyone he presumed sought to denigrate him. I finally decided to let him go, and we parted, although on remarkably good terms.

Then there was continuing disturbing news from England, from Guss – her letters were a catalogue of vague fears – and because of a suggestion that my daughter might soon be sent abroad for her education. A child not yet one year old? I was horrified, the more so because it could only be part of a deep plan to make sure I never again gained access to her, no matter what might happen to Belle. But how to make my feelings understood at so great a distance, with so much uncertainty in the mails? I finally sent my letters home by Rushton, who truth to tell had not turned out to be the companion I had hoped.

So there I was, at the end, reduced as usual to the faithful Willie and no other, and happy to be so. Besides, in the latter half of August who should arrive to visit but Hobby and Scrope. They should have come sooner, but they had dallied in France to visit poor old Brummell, who was ekeing out a miserable existence in Calais. (ii) But their delay was fortunate for them. They reached Diodati on 26 August, and the day before Claire had called to say farewell before returning to England to have her babe. I must confess I refused to see her, for her manner was now so unchangingly bitter and self pitying that her company was unbearable. I had made every possible provision I could for the child. Claire obviously could not undertake the burden of its upbringing, and Shelley had objected, most strenuously to my first idea, that it should be placed with Guss; he had confoundedly strong ideas on parenthood and family life, and was convinced that every child needed the company of at least one of its parents for the first seven years of its life. (iii) So I had yielded, and as soon as Claire's could leave her breast it was to come and live with me. Think of it, in my haphazard establishment? Surely she could ask no more. Certainly I was not prepared to listen.

And to have Scrope and Hobby with me was a delight. How we talked, and walked, and drank, and *laughed*, because this was a commodity that had been sadly lacking in my recent friends. Shiloh might be the best fellow in the world, and a conversationalist fit to be set beside dear Sheridan, who died this autumn, of drink I have no doubt at all, but he took a confoundedly *serious* view of life and the problems thereto, and was wont to frown upon my lightheartedness whenever I was in the mood.

My spirits therefore revived, I could even look forward to the unpleasant business of packing up once again as my tenancy of the villa came to an end. At the beginning of October, Scrope having already departed, Hobby and I took our places in my carriage to cross the Alps, into Italy.

For this had always been my destination. If I had lingered in Switzerland, it had been on account of the scenery. But there was no *history* in Switzerland, no feeling that one was moving in the midst of great events. It was not a part of the great Mediterranean amphitheatre which stretches from Greece to Spain, and where our civilisation found its birth, and which now strives desperately to regain its earlier freedom.

Thoughts like this had indeed been brought home to me by a visit I received, while at Diodati, from two brothers, Nicolas and Francis Karvellas, who hailed from Zante, the southernmost of the Ionian islands, and were just completing their studies at the University of Padua.

Their company would have been welcome at any time, for their conversation recalled to me all the sunlit delights of Greece, all the adventures and optimisms of my youth. But there was more. In guarded terms they were already beginning to speak of that revolt into which I have now decided to throw my entire being. (iv) It had not yet begun. It was in fact several years from beginning. But the *urge* was there, and the secret meetings were already taking place, and they were *aglow* with that fervour which always overtakes the conspirator.

Some of their enthusiasm communicated itself to me, eager as I always am to support the underdog. It seemed to me then that the whole world was poised to follow the French example and throw off its masters, hopefully while avoiding the excesses and the mistakes of Robespierre and Danton. Shelley was convinced that an English revolution was just around the corner, here were the Greeks beginning to *plan* theirs, while no one could doubt that in the northern provinces of Italy the hand of the Austrians lay too heavy to be endured. In these circumstances, how could I sit quietly by in Switzerland, with so many great things to be accomplished? Thus the Alps, the Simplon Pass, to be exact, and thus, after a brief spell in Milan, where I was lionised by the literati there, we went on to Venice. (v)

Ah, Venice. Here is the most sublime of cities, and I have visited Rome. But Rome is dead history; the very city is dead. Venice still lives, and breathes, with every surge of the tide. As we made our way over the causeway towards the distant cluster of islands I fell in love, and for the first time since leaving Greece, with a *place*, an idea, an atmosphere. Alas for poor Byron. Before I could put these great plans into effect it was necessary for me to discover somewhere to live. We had spent our first days in the city at an hotel, but this life was not for me. I was too much the centre of attraction, too liable to be interrupted at any hour of the day or night. Of course such attention was flattering, but I had had enough of that in London, and I was here to work, and hopefully at more than just poetry. So I determined to find myself a more secluded abode, and it was in pursuit of this that in the early part of November I took myself down to the Frezzeria, an alley off the Piazza San Marco, and discovered a small draper's shop, outside which was a sign depicting a stag but sadly in need of painting; hanging from this sign was another, indicating that there were rooms to let above the shop.

"You do not wish to try there, my lord," said my gondolier, who was acting as my guide. "That Segati, he is an unfortunate fellow."

"I will look at the rooms," I decided, and pushed open the door, to discover not the man I had expected, but a young woman, remarkably small and slight, but possessing a wealth of soft dark brown hair, and a most entrancing face, the features also small and slight, but most delightfully formed, the eyes huge and dark and lively.

But I had seen pretty faces before. To me the ultimate call to beauty always lies in the voice, and this one was perfectly charming, low and melodious, as she said, "My lord?" Thus informing me that she knew who I was. "What can you wish in this poor shop?"

"You have rooms to let," I said.

"My lord?" Her eyebrows arched, delightfully. "*You* would live here?"

"I seek quiet," I explained. "I need quiet, to think. Sometimes to write."

"Of course, my lord," she said. "I understand."

"Providing of course, that my landlord, and my landlady, are congenial to me."

Faint colour appeared in those olive cheeks. "It shall be our pleasure, my lord. My husband is at present out, but I will be pleased to show you the apartment."

I nodded, and she walked in front of me, through a door in the rear of the shop, and up a flight of stairs, skirts daintily gathered in her hand to reveal that her ankles were every bit as attractive as her face.

We reached a landing, and she opened the necessary doors. The accommodation seemed adequate. There was a bedchamber for me, and one for Willie, and there was a sitting-room for me, and even space for a study. It was surprisingly clean, and certainly quiet. There was no spare bedroom for Hobby, but I did not really wish him in here with me in any event, in view of my suddenly formed plans, and of course he was not staying in Venice but was soon to end his visit.

"These will do admirably," I said. "What is the rent?"

"Well, my lord," she replied without hesitation. "Would twenty francs a day be too much?"

Which revealed that she was very much the mistress of her own home, whoever her husband and whatever her youth, for I was sure she was scarce more than twenty.

"Not in the least," I said. "I will take the apartment for two months, to begin with, and we shall see how we get on."

"Of course, my lord," she said. "You understand that I shall do everything that may be required to make you welcome."

I discovered the door to the bedchamber, in which we were standing, had managed to close itself. Can there ever have been a case of more immediate attraction and understanding, of what we both wished, of what we both would have?

"Well," I said. "I should like to know your name."

"It is Marianna, my lord."

I stood beside her. "And your husband will be pleased to have me as a tenant?"

"My husband, my lord," she assured me, "will be pleased at anything that pleases me."

I cupped her chin in my hand, and turned her face upwards. "You are a fortunate woman, Marianna."

"Not so, my lord. It is my fortune to make others fortunate."

Her lips were parted. I kissed them, and dreams of greatness flew out of the window.

A GENTLEMAN OF LEISURE

Here was contentment, after too many years of frantic scurrying. Marianna and I cemented our desire for each other there and then, and I discovered myself to be as deeply in love as at any moment in my life. She was an absolute delight, for her figure, if small, was decidedly voluptuous, and she *squirmed* with desire, in a manner quite foreign to any Englishwoman I had ever met, without exception. For where Caro had always been too conscious that she was being outrageous, and Liz had required her elaborate play-acting to reach her true heights, for Marianna it was the most natural thing in the world, perhaps the only natural thing in the world. She was a creature born for love, and intent upon making the most of it.

Thus I settled into a truly domestic bliss. For Signor Segati did not even have to be deceived. In Italy they arrange these things differently to us. I had not yet encountered the elaborate etiquette of becoming a *cavaliere serviente*, as I was to discover a year or so later, but at this lower level of society the rigmarole was the same. I was Marianna's *friend*, and as such was recognised by her husband. What we did in private was never subjected to inquiry, however much it might have been subjected to speculation. And in public I was of course the soul of propriety. It seemed to me that I had found the best of all possible worlds, in that I had a wife, but she was somebody else's burden, and I had a home, which was not my responsibility, and I was living in the very finest city in Europe.

Hobby was of course scandalised. He found himself lodgings at some distance, and we began to see less of each other.

But as I have intimated, Venice was for me a paradise. Because it was unique. In London, your gentleman is required to walk, as often as he rides or takes a carriage. For a man with a deformed foot it is perpetual agony, physical as well as mental. In Venice no one walked at all, save to and from his gondola. No one rode either, and my passion for horses caused quite a stir. I kept four, over on the Lido, where I was wont to go for a gallop in the mornings, and was the sensation of the city, for there was not another mount for miles.

It may well be asked, in view of the constantly recurring theme of this Memoir, how I afforded these little luxuries. Ah, but I was a changed man to the ruined creature who had fled from Dover. To accomplish that retreat at all I had been forced to have recourse to promissory notes, and on these I had raised £2,500, which had been sufficient to see me on my way. But once having fled, and become the victim of every foul rumour that could be supposed, I could no longer see any reason for preserving my noble disdain for filthy lucre, and when Murray, on reading the third canto of *Childe Harold* and deciding it was far and away the best thing I had ever written, offered me £1,500 for the copyright, I accepted with alacrity. Thrown upon my own resources, I would at last permit my pen to keep me in the style to which I had become accustomed.

Which is not to say that I was not still deep in the financial mire. But a few weeks in Venice convinced me that I had found my spiritual home, besides which that *tight* little island in which I had been born could offer me nothing but misery. So once again I attacked the problem of selling Newstead and turning myself into a wealthy man in the best sense. This would obviously be no easier than it had been in the past, but suddenly it was far less important. I was accumulating no more debts, the existing ones would eventually be paid by the proceeds of the sale, whenever it happened, and in the meantime I had discovered that I could live quite comfortably from the efforts of my brain and my pen, and the reassurance was enormous.

Enjoyment was the key word in my vocabulary. I allowed myself to be inveigled into Venetian society, by way of the Countess Albrizzi, who if well past her first youth was as *energetic* as ever in her pursuit of the famous and the fortunate, and made a dead set at me.(i) Alas for dear Isabella, while for a woman in her mid forties she was splendidly endowed, and while no one could doubt her intellect or her wealth, I had determined that never again, so long as I lived, would I allow myself to become entangled with anyone even remotely to be called a lady. I had tried them all, and they had brought me nothing but misery, whereas the dark eyes, the delicious breasts, the slithery thighs of my darling Marianna brought me nothing but happiness, and promised no alternative in the future.

Nor was I confined to Marianna. For there is a delightful custom in Roman Catholic countries, that, as during the long weeks of Lent they permit themselves not the slightest indulgence or levity, for the few days immediately preceding this austere festival they permit themselves *every* indulgence. This colossal party is known as Carnival, and continues entirely without abatement for some two days and nights, and during it all things are possible. Your chaste maiden, your faithful wife, your elderly senator, your ardent youth, your middle-aged spinster and your crabbed clerk all don strange disguises and not quite disguising masks, and sally forth into the streets, to catch and be caught, to love and be loved, to commit every moral sin they can think of, sure in the certainty that a simple confession followed by several weeks of abstinence in every direction will earn them forgiveness.

Well, I did not subscribe to such views, but I certainly subscribed to such a point of view. No doubt I was in any event damned, but I would enjoy myself as much as any certain-to-be-saved Christian, and in February of 1817 I declare I cut a swathe through the centre of Venice that left them reeling. I would not be exaggerating when I claim that I laid better than fifty females in two days, and nights, and that I satisfied every one.

Alas, such a course of successful fornication is liable to leave a man reeling as well. Remarkably I was not at this time clapped, but my resistance was rendered very weak by the end of it, and I collapsed into bed with a fever. Which left me so low in spirit that I contemplated suicide, and if that was short lived, certainly I began to consider an ultimate conversion to Roman Catholicism, and only turned back from this course by remembering it was what Walter Scott had in fact prophesied I should do, and why should I elevate that old hack into a seer?

When I had recovered from this attack, which apparently afflicts most residents of Venice during the spring and early summer, Hobby and I departed on a tour down to Rome, which neither of us had ever before visited, and from whence he continued to Naples. But I was missing the arms of Marianna.

My return, at the end of May, was however attended by a considerable shock, for Marianna herself had been laid low by fever, and had only just recovered. Much as I loved Venice, the thought of again being attacked, and besides, as the weather grew hot the canals commenced to give off the most frightful stench which added to my discomfort, influenced me in doing as all wealthy Venetians, and removing myself from the city itself for the summer. I travelled seven miles inland, to a pleasant little village called La Mira, where I had taken a six months' lease on the Villa Foscarini, situated on the road from Padua, which involved a certain amount of dust, but this could be resisted by keeping those windows closed, and withal it was large, if unattractively square, and had an English garden at the back, which was delightful. But best of all, it allowed me to keep my horses on the premises, and go for a daily ride, just as it allowed me once again to keep animals, and I have ever felt lonely without a few pets about the house.

In addition I now had the space to entertain guests, and almost the first to arrive was dear old Monk Lewis, one of the most soporific of men, but for this very reason he suited my mood at La Mira. And when he was joined by Hobby, my contentment was complete. Here was the perfect existence, for I rose late, went for a gallop or into Venice for a swim in the Adriatic, returned home to an evening of conversation, and then secluded myself in my study for a night of composition. Nor were my physical needs neglected, for Marianna moved in with me, as apparently it was quite in order for her to do – we were even visited from time to time by Segati – and between conversation and composition there was invariably time for a brief *connection*. And when, later on, Douglas Kinnaird arrived with his wife in the middle of their honeymoon, I felt life could never be so contented. Had I but had Guss at my side, I would have proclaimed myself the happiest of men. Alas, however much I begged her in every letter, and however much she bewailed her fate, left in England to face the unceasing gossip, her sense of duty to husband and family remained stronger than her love.

Thus I spent my second *happy* summer in a row, despite the constant rumble of Byronic misdemeanours from England. For Murray had from the start received *Manfred* as a man might accept a smoking box of gunpowder. His fears had even aroused *my* fears, but I had refused to make alterations or to withdraw the work, and he had at last published it. To a perfect howl of execration from the newspapers, who discovered it run through and through with the theme of incest. Which indeed it was. But at a distance of two thousand miles from London I was not concerned to write anything that did not interest my entire being. And the public bought, as they are wont to do when a work is scurrilously attacked. While I laboured contentedly at the fourth canto of *Childe Harold*.

But soon enough the even tenor of my life was disrupted, as usual. Certain it is that I am the most docile of men, who wishes nothing more than to be left alone to pursue his pleasures in peace. But certain it also is, or was at that time, that I could not for long be satisfied by a single woman. Because at that time I had not yet discovered the *perfect* woman. Marianna, delightful as she was, fell into the same category as all the others I had known; she knew what she liked, and she wished nothing more than to indulge her own particular pleasures, which were straightforward enough. Now, the mere act of flirting with a strange woman, of making advances to her, of being allowed, eventually to kiss hand and then lips, of slowly uncovering her charms and then investigating them, this is the stuff on which the entire liaison between the sexes is founded. A woman's breast may be a woman's breast, but to hold a *strange* woman's breast is always a thrill.

Remarkably, women do not appear to desire this variety of partner. They may spend some time in searching for the ideal man, and often enough, of course, he is not their husband, particularly in countries where a female's virginity on her wedding night is a matter of great importance. But once the man who can satisfy them is found, they are perfectly happy to sleep with him, and be brought to orgasm by him, and no one else, and in the same way as the first time he accomplished it, time after time after time. I am of course speaking of the vulgar horde, not of the Countess Teresa. But then, to my sorrow, the vulgar horde was all I had ever known.

It so happened that that summer of 1817 was one of drought, with all its attendant hardship to a peasant community, and as lord of La Mira I had, from time to time, done what I could to alleviate the more extreme cases of suffering brought to my attention. This is simple enough to accomplish in Italy, where everyone is so poor and everything is so cheap that the distribution of a few pence seems the utmost in generosity. Thus it was that one afternoon Hobby and I were walking our horses along the Brenta when we passed a group of peasants, and noticed two of the women as the prettiest we had seen for some time. One was about average height, with the superb features of the true Italian, and the great dark eyes, and the wealth of flowing dark brown hair which I had come to expect, but on her everything seemed far finer than I had recently observed. What then can I say of the other, who possessed all of these attributes but in addition was the tallest young woman I had ever seen?

312

It was this latter-day Juno who called out to us, no doubt having observed our interest. "Why do not you, my lord, who relieve others, relieve us also?"

Well, there was only one reply to that. I said, "My darling girl, you are too beautiful to require charity."

"Indeed?" she remarked, placing her hands on her hips. "If you saw my hut and my food, you would not make that mistake."

She smiled as she spoke, revealing a most splendid set of teeth, and suggesting that she was by no means as unhappy as she had indicated, and so we gave them a wave and continued on our way.

And thought nothing more of the incident, at least to each other, although I know that that evening as Marianna lay squirming in my arms I found myself wondering what sort of a body so splendidly grenadierlike a girl would possess. But then, a few days later, we encountered the pair again, and this time they were alone, rather than encumbered with their fellows, and we stopped for a chat, and even dismounted the better to make their acquaintance. And discovered they were cousins, the smaller one, whose name I quite forget, being unmarried, and therefore, as I immediately knew, unavailable for anything more than a mild flirtation, so confoundedly do these women protect their pre-marital virginity, so that Hobby, who was obviously attracted, was doomed to a very *sterile* affair. But the other, my Zenobia, was named Margarita Cogni, Cogni being the name of her husband. And she improved the closer I got, so that when she indicated she knew of a ruined chapel not far from where we were, which she was certain would interest so great a lord as myself, I but mounted her behind me, and bade her show me this wonder. Hobby I left to his own devices.

The chapel certainly existed, and certainly had fallen into a state of disrepair, an example indeed of the increasing poverty of this once fair land under the heavy hand of the Habsburgs. The roof was gone, and horses had been stabled in the pews; it had clearly been in this condition since at some time during the wars it had been subjected to gunfire. Yet was it quiet, and peaceful, and there was sufficient straw to separate a body from the crumbled stone of the floor. And Margarita, having spread her cloak upon this bedding, regarded me with a delightfully intent look, even as I felt somewhat like a lamb discovered in a tiger's lair, for she was definitely taller than I was, and not a great deal less broad, and had an almost leonine quality about her.

313

Which was but enhanced by her total self confidence. "You will love me, milord," she asserted. "Because I am beautiful."

I did not argue. Nor could I argue, as she removed her gown and her single shift. Here was beauty on a quite remarkable scale, high, square shoulders, magnificent breasts, so large that both my hands were needed to encompass one, thrusting nipples in the purest red brown, swelling rib cage, flat belly – for all her age, which was twenty-two, and her several years of married life, she had never been a mother – wide thighs, long, powerful legs, while there to be explored was a positively Amazonian forest which promised all manner of untold delights even if a prudent man might have doubted his ability to find his way back to civilisation after once plunging into those dense thickets.

But my immediate reaction, I must confess, having children much on my mind at the time – of which more later – was that could I impregnate her where her husband had so clearly failed, what an Amazon or what a Hero I would most certainly produce.

Meanwhile there were more pressing matters closer at hand. "And I shall love you," she asserted with equal determination, "because you are also beautiful."

Saying which she fell to undressing me herself, stroking my flesh with fingers which if gentle enough at that moment undoubtedly possessed a remarkable strength, and finally discovering cocker with a *growl* of the uttermost joy, whereupon she hugged me against her, spread her legs, and introduced him to the depths of the *matto grosso* without any further introduction, and while we were still standing.

In such circumstances all doubts as to my health disappeared in an instant, and I was spent an instant later, Margarita having brought her legs back together once she was satisfied I was where I should be, and if my back was a trifle exhausted at the muscular effort required for this, to me, unique frolic, I could safely say that never had I been quite so satisfied.

Not that I was anything near satisfying her. I do believe that she had managed an orgasm at the same time as I, for she broke out in the most delicious fine sweat which I have observed is always a sign of female ecstasy – and male too for that matter – but one was not likely to satisfy so overwhelming a creature, nor was she disposed to be satisfied with one of mine. The entire rest of the afternoon was consumed in an immense tumble, during which it seemed that every woman I had ever known had come together into one immortal being bent on extracting every last ounce of sexual endeavour from my frame. When at last she tore herself away from me, still unsatisfied but being under the necessity of preparing her husband's dinner, I was so enervated that on my return to La Mira I was forced to have recourse to that most feminine of excuses, and escape from Marianna under plea of a headache. Not that I was actually lying.

Poor Hobby of course had been totally unsuccessful in his attempts to enjoy a similar experience, as I could have told him.

But I had no intention of forgoing a repeat performance. This time it was necessary to make my escape from my villa at night, when everyone and most particularly Marianna was asleep. But Margarita was even more *consuming* in the small hours, and so I undertook a regular series of jungle explorations, with of course the inevitable result, for while all women have only one real hobby, derogatory gossip, the women of a small country village indulge this pleasure more than most, having little else to do with their evenings. Here was a likely calamity. I first became aware of it when, riding with Marianna, we happened to pass the Cogni and some of her friends on the road, much as Hobby and I had first encountered them. To my total consternation Marianna promptly reined her horse and delivered a most biting verbal assault on the habits of loose women who spent their leisure trying to seduce visiting gentlemen. I anticipated assault and murder, but Margarita merely drew herself up and said, in very even tones, "You are not his wife; I am not his wife. You are his *donna*; I am his *donna*. Your husband is a cuckold, and mine is another. For the rest, what right have you to reproach me? If he prefers what is mine to what is yours, is it my fault?"

Which caused Marianna to retreat in some confusion. Not that we had entirely escaped the murder and mayhem. That came later, when we were home, and my beloved hurled a pair of scissors at me.

But of course all of this indicated that another idyll was coming to an end; much as I enjoyed Marianna she did not compare with the hungry attention of Margarita. With this in mind I determined to rent myself a second villa, as at La Mira I was too closely overlooked by her friends. Hobby and I finally located a comparable establishment at Este, and this I duly leased, although I had no intention of moving down there until forced. I did not actually contemplate a break with Marianna at this time, and my old lodgings in the Frezzaria were there for me to occupy over the winter.

315

Conversation and dalliance apart, my summer was busily enough occupied. In receiving endless letters from Claire, some loving and most recriminatory – one of the most attractive aspects of Margarita was that although as intelligent as anyone, she could neither read nor write – telling me about the progress of our babe, which had turned out to be a daughter, and which the Shelleys had named Alba. This I did not like at all, and I chose instead the Italian name Allegra, and why not, as Italy was to be the little girl's home? But the cause of our immediate epistolary conflict was an idea I had confided to Shelley that it would be best for all concerned, and mostly the child and myself, if I placed her in a suitable convent. This aroused a storm of protest, from mother as well as Shiloh. I would not of course write Claire direct – that would have involved me in far too great a risk of attracting her back to disturb my peace, and what a picture that suggests, Marianna and Claire hurling knives at each other while Margarita cheers them on from the stalls – but I defended my plan as best I could to Shelley, and received the impression that he was cooling towards me. But his entire life was governed by his remarkable attitude towards children, any children, but most especially his own.

Another source of irritation was Murray's attitude to my work, and indeed it was about now that we began that process of estrangement which eventually led me to seek another publisher. Now I have done my utmost, in this work, to be fair to all those who have attempted to rob me and cheat me and generally do me down. And publishers as a whole are of course the most parsimonious of men; I do believe that apart from a natural desire to make a profit, they are genuinely convinced that an author will only produce his best work when on the point of starvation, which is certainly an error, at least as regards me. *I* do my best work when I can sit back with a bottle of expensive wine at my elbow, having completed a rich meal, a good cigar in my mouth, and can contemplate the beauties of nature and of humanity and allow my mind to roll into splendid verses and even more splendid concepts.

However, owing to my circumstances, I had never pressed the point. During my years in England, it may be recalled, I had presented Dallas or other worthy literary causes such as Godwin or Coleridge or Maturin, with whatever Murray had chosen to offer me for my work, and when I at last decided to be sensible and accept payment for the fruits of my midnight labours, and he had offered me £1,500 for the third canto of *Childe Harold* I had been perfectly content, not being at

that time aware what was being paid for other and much less successful works. Now he set about complaining and bewailing that *Manfred*
was as like as not liable to have him prosecuted for obscenity and
blasphemy and lese-majesty and everything he could think of, and
regretting he had purchased it at all, this while the copies were selling
faster then he could print them. On top of all this I discovered from
darling Irish Tom that he had actually been paid £3,000 for his latest
effort, *Lalla Rookh*. I was dumbfounded, and then enraged. The
fourth canto of *Childe Harold* was very nearly completed, no one, least
of all Murray, could argue against the rapture with which the third
canto had been received, and so I attached a price tag of £2,500.

He pretended to be horrified at so mercenary an attitude in one he
had always taken to be a gentleman writing poetry for his own
pleasure. But I would not yield an inch. For on a sudden, I no longer
needed the money. On 10 December 1817, I received the news that
my old schoolfellow Tom Wildman had actually paid £94,500 for
Newstead.

My feelings can only be imagined. After more than ten years of
financial misery, I was at last free of my burdens. Immediately I wrote
Hanson listing all my outstanding debts, or at least all that I could
remember, some of them dating back to those earliest ventures of
mine into London society, and begging that they be discharged without further delay.

But these were only the slightest of the burdens which I felt lifting
from my back. My mind could again roam the possibilities of the
world, and plan instead of merely dreaming. I have always enjoyed
travel, the challenge of new lands. Now I considered throwing the
dust of Europe, of the entire Old World, from my boots, and emigrat-
ing to the untainted air of America. In my new-found energy I was
working as I had never done before. *Childe Harold*, Canto Four, was
already copied and ready for despatch, by Hobby, who was returning
to England at the beginning of the year. But while this work had been
prepared for the press I had been attempting something new, a poetic
exercise in an entirely different metre and in an entirely different
mood, humorously sardonic rather than sardonically bitter. My plot
was based upon a story told me by Signor Segati, no less, which just
goes to show from what unlikely sources it is possible to obtain poetic
material. I called the work *Beppo*, and inspired by my new-found
fortune, rushed at it, and actually finished it in early January. Which

was just as well, for the Carnival was once more upon us, and this year I was prepared to throw myself into the celebrations with twice as much energy as before.

In this decision I was assisted not only by the natural *joie de vivre* which comes from just having completed a lengthy composition, and by my new-found feeling of freedom, and by my experience of the previous year, which served to whet my appetite for another round of amatory jousting, but also and perhaps mainly by a desire to free myself of the cloying attentions of my darling Marianna.

For her jealousy of me had grown quite alarmingly since my meeting Margarita. I was not to be restrained from visiting my lioness, whenever I felt the need for a complete satiation of the senses, and Marianna soon realised this, but she vented her anger upon me in a peculiarly feminine way, by attempting to make me jealous in turn through indulging in the most outrageous flirtations with the most ridiculous people. And succeeding, I am loathe to admit. I was not at that time contemplating an end to our liaison; I was in every way too comfortable in my various situations, with her in close attendance. But I wished to flap my wings, and I did, with enormous success, cutting another swathe through the centre of Venetian womanhood for very nearly a week before collapsing in utter exhaustion at the end of it. And discovering, at the end of *another* week, that I was to suffer for it in the usual manner, as for the second time in my life I was clapped. (ii)

Consider me then, an exile from my homeland, separated from all that I held dear – for Hobby had started upon his return journey just before the commencement of Carnival, having no room in his stiff conscience for such wild carryings on – and yet constantly before their eyes by virtue of my poetry, for letters from Guss as well as others convince me that Belle read everything printed under my name or even supposed to have been written by me, whether truly or not, with the greatest attention; beleaguered certainly by the continued machinations of my wife, who was as determined as ever to keep my daughter from me for as long as possible – and successfully as she has managed to do so on a total basis up to the moment in which I am writing these lines – and who in addition seemed to be poisoning as much air as possible with her hints as to my married misdemeanours – if I can be any judge through the meanderings of Guss's letters, full of veiled suggestions that we had joint cause for fear, as if I could possibly have anything to fear securely tucked away in Italy; suddenly freed

318

from the awful financial restrictions I had known for too long; comfortably situated with three lodging places, one for winter and the others for summer; surrounded by my dogs and my horses and my other pets; served by my faithful Fletcher in domestic matters, by my even more faithful Marianna in sexual matters, with Margarita waiting at La Mira for whenever I decided to take a ride into the country; with all of *common* Venice equally waiting for my attentions should I decide to bestow them; with all of noble Venice at the least interested in having me at their *conversazioni*, but suffering at the moment a certain reserve towards the entire fair sex on account of the unwelcome attention given to me by one of their number; and finally, having arrived, on 22 January 1818, at that dreadful age when a man is no longer a youth, but is not yet shrouded in the protective *greyness* of age, properly buttressed with sufficient wealth and titillating memory to enable him to face the onset of illness and death with equanimity, and is therefore forced to look forward to a wearying twenty odd years while these goals are attained.

There was the complete Byron on that hallowed, that immortal, that never-to-be-forgotten day. It was my birthday, and therefore, feeling as physically low as I was, and I was, for in addition to the discomfort surrounding cocker I was again suffering from that dreadful tertian which has haunted me on and off throughout my life, I nevertheless felt obliged to take myself to Madame Albrizzi's, for how may a man pass his birthday in the sombre solitude of his own room?

And there, while, I must repeat, in this mood of melancholy introspection, I met the woman placed on earth by a discerning Deity to make me happy.

TERESA – THE FIRST PART

Romanticists would have it that in all the world there is only one woman for each man, and vice versa, and that when the pair meet there is an instant rapport between them, an instant understanding that their search is over, that they are arrived safe to port.

I can only say that, in my case at the least, this is the most arrant rubbish. Circumstances may have conspired to make it so. I was, as I have indicated, gloomily aware that evening that my youth had fled, for ever. I had slept with so many women I could scarce remember the majority of them apart. I was exhausted with the excesses of the Carnival, and feeling distinctly misogynous as a result of the discomfort poor cocker was enduring. And yet . . . it was very late in the evening, and I had earlier met one of the prettiest women I could recall, although her name I *cannot* recall at this moment. Then I was introduced to the Countess Teresa Guiccioli.

She was not beautiful, in the sense that Liz or Guss were beautiful. She was short, and was certainly voluptuous; possibly she was a trifle plump. Her face was very lovely, but with rounded rather than the classic contours which make up beauty. Her hair *was* beautiful, a mass of the most magnificent red gold, and she had the splendid dark eyes which is the birthright of the Italian. She was also very young, just eighteen. And of course, her voice was her greatest delight of all, low and gentle, nor have I often heard it raised, for all the many crises through which we have passed together. Of course her true beauty was hidden, for that lies within her, and indeed has only ever been revealed to me. But not at that moment.

And yet, weary as I was, sated as I was, I offered her my arm to go inside to view the bust of Helen of Troy by Canova, the Albrizzi's most celebrated piece of bric-à-brac. So I certainly felt *something* on the instant.

But she refused. For it seems I made even less an impression upon her than she upon me. Again there were extenuating circumstances. She was on the third day of her honeymoon, and if, as is the misfortune of most well-born Italian girls, she was wedded to a man old enough to be her grandfather, she was still at that moment determined to be a dutiful and loving wife. She had also completed a long journey that very day in order to reach Venice in time for the end of the Carnival, and was, she later told me, exhausted. But the fact is, as she has also told me since, I did not register upon her brain at all, nor did she remember my name, and next day was quite amazed to learn that she had been talking with the infamous English lord.

But whether either of us knew it or not, the moment had come, and gone, and however little we might understand it, our lives were from that moment altered, on my part certainly for the better.

But it took me a long time *to* know it. I was, in fact, entering one of those periods of upheaval and change which have always been anathema to me. For of course, now that my financial problems were behind me I was forced to consider my position as a father. I wrote Shiloh asking him to send Allegra to me, and I also began looking around for a more suitable Venetian residence.

This was not only because I wished a little more size, and to be a little more my own man. Marianna and I had reached the end of our romance. It had lasted better than a year, and as affairs go that is very good indeed. Of course, looking back, I now know what had happened. At the time I was at a loss to explain the situation. I merely knew, very soon after that night of my thirtieth birthday, that we had run our course. And so I leased the Palazzo Mocenigo, and departed the Frezzaria for ever.

But I was also on the way to dropping out of the Albrizzi *conversazioni*. This was partly because I discovered that my dear hostess was compiling a book concerning her impressions of the various famous men she had met, and I dislike being regarded merely as material for a reminiscence, but more it was because I now made the acquaintance of the Countess Marina Querini Benzoni, the Albrizzi's great social rival, another middle-aged matron who threw herself at me with an even greater determination.

The Benzoni was in fact considerably more attractive than the Albrizzi, although her *conversazioni* were not quite in the same class. But she had had an unforgettable youth, in which she had embraced the principles of the Revolution with unnecessary ardour, in the eyes of her compatriots, and was reputed once to have danced the

321

carmagnole while in a half naked condition. Certainly she was inclined towards displaying her charms, which even in her middle fifties remained considerable. She encouraged me to call at all hours of the day and night, and the first time I ventured to do so was taken so entirely by surprise (?) that she entered the room where I was seated naked as the day she had been born.

Shades of Lady M. Alas, poor Lady M. This was the year she died, and I learned of it with a pang, for all that since my separation from Belle we had exchanged not a word nor a line.

But this was what the Benzoni wished, and I was in a mood to indulge any and every woman who flashed her eyes at me, much less her tits. I had recovered from my misfortune, and we romped together there and then on the sofa.

But the glamorous countess was, and could be, only one of the myriad women who at this time filled my life. Loving with complete abandon had become as much a way of my existence as sleeping, or eating, or drinking, or indeed composing. I had settled into a routine, as I am prone to do, and on the amatory front it was indeed sterile.

I pretended I had all the company I wished, surrounding myself with my horses, two monkeys, a fox as well as my dear old mastiff Mutz, whom I had accumulated almost the moment I settled in Italy, as well as my lady friends, as well as a host of faithful servants, headed by Willie, of course, but including my dear Tita,(i) huge and black-bearded and ferocious in appearance, although the gentlest of men, who has certainly proved every bit as loyal as Fletcher, and I was unutterably lonely.

I listened to the praises being sung for the publication of *Beppo*, even if there were those who wondered if it had really been written by me, so different in style was it from *Childe Harold*, and I smiled indulgently at Hobby's carelessness in embroiling himself with the assembled forces of the Italian literati on account of the notes he had attached to the fourth canto of *Childe Harold*. And found myself confoundedly bored.

I could conceive several reasons for my discontent, all without perceiving the true one. On the one hand, there was the imminent arrival of Allegra, which was naturally preceded by a spate of letters from Claire, varying as usual from the desperately loving to the angrily condemning. These I ignored, but Shiloh was also at his most critical as he approached, for he was actually bringing the child.

* * *

When she finally came, I was overjoyed, because she was an absolutely charming little thing, and beautiful with it, a true Byron. I looked forward then to a lifetime of happiness with my darling daughter as the pillar of my old age, but of course it really was not sensible to have a two year old in such a *ménage* as mine, and despite protests from beyond the Alps I put her to board with a family called Hoppner, he being the British consul in Venice, and madame being a Swiss of undoubted probity – well, she disapproved of me for a start, which can be no bad character reference – and already a mother several times over. This seemed to me to be an ideal compromise for the time being, as I could see her whenever I chose, and she could not see me *unless* I chose.

But another and more deep-seated cause for discontent was a sudden reappraisal I found myself making of all my work. *Childe Harold* had by now become very much a hack affair. It earned me a large part of my income, and could be kept going for some considerable time, I had no doubt. But I no longer *enjoyed* writing it. *Manfred* had been a bitter outpouring. But having outpoured, I no longer even felt bitter. I felt like writing another *Beppo*, but that subject matter had been so light and inconsequential I really did not feel I could devote my talents to so slight a cause. I wished to write about *me* – which writer does not? – but on a scale far transcending the feeble reflections of the Childe. It was in this mood that I began the first part of these Memoirs. But even this was not sufficiently satisfying. For here I am recalling. There is no creation to it. I am bound by what I did, and even more, I am bound by the things about which I would like to write, but did *not* do.

It was in this mood of sombre reflection that one night, sitting in my study and listening to the call of a gondolier as he made his way past my palace, idly flicking through my accumulations of first drafts and letters and accounts, I once again came across those strange adventures of St George, compiled by the poor lad whose brain had been unable to sustain my criticism.

I turned the pages, and yet again could find no merit in the poem. But the *idea*. Not for St George, of course. There was an unlikely vehicle for the thoughts of a wicked lord. But to take a character, famous the world over, and fit myself inside his skin, and allow him to roam, where and as he chose, to consider everything I wished, to argue anything I wished, to indulge everything I wished, to *reveal* everything I wished. There could be only one hero for such an epic journey

323

through time and space and mind. And, I reassured my conscience, as Master Smith was dead, and his poem forgotten, I was stealing nothing of value.

I settled down to write, and discovered my pen flying over the page. I was away, and happy, in a mood I swear I had not known since, so many years previously, I had first commenced *Childe Harold's Pilgrimage*, with the Albanian mountains brooding over my shoulder and Hobby fretting at my feet. At last I could offer my own opinions on all those who had brought me down, and needless to say, at the head of *that* list I set my wife. Well, she entirely deserved her fate.

I excoriated her character under the guise of my hero's mother, wife of Don José:

> Her favourite science was the mathematical,
> Her noblest virtue was her magnanimity,
> Her wit (she sometimes tried to wit) was Attic all,
> Her serious sayings darkened to sublimity;
> In short, in all things she was fairly what I call
> A Prodigy – her morning's dress was dimity,
> Her evening silk, or, in the summer, muslin,
> And other stuffs, with which I won't stay puzzling.

And exposed for all the world to see the truth about our separation:

> Don José and the Donna Inez led
> For some time an unhappy sort of life,
> Wishing each other, not divorced, but dead;
> They lived respectably as man and wife,
> Their conduct was exceedingly well-bred,
> And gave no outward signs of inward strife,
> Until at length the smothered fire broke out,
> And put the business past all kind of doubt.

> For Inez called some druggists, and physicians,
> And tried to prove her loving lord was *mad*,
> But as he had some lucid intermissions,
> She next decided he was only *bad*;
> Yet when they asked her for her depositions,
> No sort of explanation could be had,
> Save that her duty both to man and God
> Required this conduct – which seemed very odd.

324

She kept a journal, where his faults were noted,
And opened certain trunks of books and letters,
All which might, if occasion served, be quoted;
And then she had all Seville for abettors,
Besides her good old grandmother (who doted);
The hearers of her case became repeaters,
Then advocates, inquisitors, and judges,
Some for amusement, others for old grudges.

And then this best and meekest woman bore
With such serenity her husband's woes,
Just as the Spartan ladies did of yore,
Who saw their spouses killed, and nobly chose
Never to say a word about them more –
Calmly she heard each calumny that rose,
And saw *his* agonies with such sublimity,
That all the world exclaimed, "What magnanimity."

Truly I have never enjoyed myself so much as writing that first canto. But as may be imagined it was not well received by Murray. Indeed he pretended to be horrified, and not only by my somewhat clearly defined allusions to my various enemies. For I saw no reason to conceal my opinions on politics or religion or anything else. His protests were indeed so vehement even I had second thoughts. Changes I would not make, but I did agree to delay publication, although I requested a limited edition of fifty copies to be printed, for circulation amongst my friends.

But this mood of apprehension, I am happy to say, soon passed. I pressed the issue, and *Don Juan* eventually saw the light of day, to the amazement of my friends, the dismay of my enemies, and the entire delight of the reading public.

Don Juan was not the only work on which I was at this time labouring. For I will confess that much as I enjoyed it, much as I felt in my bones that here at last was my Muse following the correct, perhaps the only path for me, I still had doubts. *Beppo* had been dismissed as an idle fantasy on the part of a once great poet. What *would* be said of my entire departure into the realms of satire, something I had not attempted since my vehement youth? And so I laboured at other, more serious works, *Mazeppa* and my *Ode on Venice*, while returning always to my true love.

From which it will be seen that I was not idle, and indeed what with love-making, swimming against Mengaldo,(ii) riding, entertaining, and allowing myself a certain period in which to sleep, I really did not have a moment in which to sit back and reflect. Which is probably just as well, for I was at that time of a man's life when reflection can lead to the gravest of consequences. But my existence was additionally complicated at this time, firstly by the appearance of Hanson, who finally – and unbelievably – arrived in Venice, accompanied by his son Newton, bringing the necessary papers for me to sign in order to complete the Newstead sale. In my ignorance I concluded this was the end of the matter – in the event it turned out to be the end of Hanson as my attorney. For on his return to England he presented, in addition to all my other outstanding debts, a personal account in the neighbourhood of £15,000. I was horrified, and asked Douglas to see to the whole business with the result that *he* became my man of affairs – to my great benefit – refused to pay Hanson a penny until the bill was itemised, which the dear old dishonest soul could hardly do, settled my other debts, and invested the residue in the Funds, which guaranteed me an income of £3,300 per annum, or some three times what I was currently spending, all this in addition to whatever I could earn by my pen.

But a second cause for upheaval that summer was the appearance in Venice of the Shelleys, in the most tragic of circumstances, for their daughter Clara was dying and indeed passed away soon after their arrival, leaving them both desolate, although Shiloh did his best to be his old self, and read my drafts, and agreed with me that *Don Juan* was my finest effort. And thirdly, I was bedevilled by the sudden eruption of the Fornarina, as I called my dear Margarita.

We had now been lovers for very nearly a year, and I was well satisfied. However much I exhausted myself and appeared to sate my desires in Venice, as I have recounted I was in reality doing no more than preparing myself for a later bout of amatory intercourse. But with Margarita I more nearly approached satiation than with any other. The very fury of her love-making left me exhausted, the determination with which she climaxed again and again and again, and indeed tried to do the same for me, with fingers or lips when mere vaginal grasp proved insufficient, drove all other carnal thoughts, all other carnal desires from my mind.

But at least a part of her attraction was the fact that she was not in my continual company, that I sought her when I wanted her, and was not forced to endure her when I did not. Imagine my dismay when one evening she suddenly appeared at the Mocenigo, announcing that she had quarrelled with her husband and would return no more. It was very late, and I was indeed just settling down to my midnight composition, which but complicated the matter, for when I attempted to explain that really this would not do at all, she said she would sleep in the street outside, that she dared not return for the brute of a *becco ettico*, which means consumptive cuckold and was her own description, would certainly beat her. As if there was a man alive would dare lift his hand to my tigress.

Weak vessel that I am, I permitted her to remain, although I am afraid *Don Juan* made no progress whatsoever that night. And next day, as I had feared and expected, Signor Cogni duly arrived. Margarita refused to leave, however, and he departed, briefly, and returned with the support of the police. Even the Fornarina could not resist so much force, and she was duly removed before the Commissary, where she was commanded to return to her husband, but this was no more than a palliative, and within a week she had again run away and was once again installed in the Mocenigo, from which I found it quite impossible to shift her. For how may a man really dismiss a woman who will bare her breast and more and wrap herself around him like Eden's fabled serpent, at the same time entertaining him with delightful expressions of love and devotion? Not this man, to be sure.

I appealed to Madame Benzoni, who agreed to take her under her protection, but this in turn proved a mistake, for Margarita suddenly saw herself becoming a great lady, with all the airs and fancies that went with it, and in addition the tantrums, and when Margarita decided to throw a tantrum it made a mockery of anything I had ever known, and reduced Caro to kindergarten stuff. Her strength was fully equal to that of any man, and she fought with a ferocity few men could equal.

These misfortunes are of course to a certain extent admirable, and certainly my love for her would not have diminished on that account, but no woman should ever allow herself to appear ridiculous, for it is the lowest degree to which the sex can descend. Margarita made this mistake by determining, reasonably enough, I suppose, to shed her peasant garb, in which she looked the fine animal she was, for the clothes of a lady, and in particular, a hat on which she had set her heart, decorated with feathers, and sufficient to make *anyone* look foolish but

327

mounted on top of the leonine beauty of my beloved it turned the entire world into a pantomime.

In addition to this absurd behaviour, she took to intercepting all my mail, opening and scanning the letters, for she was well on the way to committing another unpardonable sin, that of learning to read and write. And yet, I suffered her for too long. She was not wholly without virtue, apart from her amatory prowess. She brought a much needed order and honesty into my domestic affairs, and I must confess that my household expenses halved while she was managing my kitchen.

And that she loved me cannot be denied. Especially I remember one night when I was returning from the Lido and we were overtaken by a sudden Bora howling out of the Dalmatian mountains.(iii) My gondola was shipping water, my gondoliers were crying upon the saints to preserve them, their hats and mine were blown away, we were surrounded by nothing but leaping water and imminent peril, until we came into the Mocenigo landing, to see my beloved standing there, long hair streaming in the wind, clothes soaked by the rain, great eyes burning holes in the darkness, and not at all in a good humour at seeing me returned safe and sound, but beside herself with anger at the thought that I had risked my life unnecessarily. It was all I could do to stop her beating the unhappy boatmen.

Yet in the end she had to go. It was becoming quite impossible to do any work with her in the house. I told her all of this quietly enough, and was rewarded with a series of threats, but then she left, peaceably, to my great relief. I was ever the optimist. The next day there was a sudden crash, and she was in my midst, having quite literally walked through a glass door that led from the hall below to the staircase. While I goggled at her in amazement, she seized the knife that was in my hand, I being at dinner at the time, and in removing it cut my thumb, but only slightly. I had to call my gondoliers to see her out, but this also proved a mistake, for a moment later there was a very loud noise, and on running downstairs I discovered that she had thrown herself into the canal.

She was recovered, and sent home. She returned several more times, but she was herself realising that our liaison was at an end. I was sorry to see her go, but relieved as well. And in many ways it was fitting that so *vital* a spirit should have been my very last serious amour. For there it was. After some twenty years of battering at heartless femininity in an unavailing effort to find a woman who would love me as I wished to be loved, and on the point of giving up the quest for ever, that Holy Grail was about to be displayed before me in all its glory.

I, of course, remained in total ignorance of the blessing that was about to befall me. But I knew that idle affairs were no longer for me. I was become an altogether more serious man or, as I put it in the end of the first canto of *Don Juan*:

> But now at thirty years my hair is grey –
> (I wonder what it will be like at forty?
> I thought of a peruke the other day –)
> My heart is not much greener; and, in short, I
> Have squandered my whole summer while 't was May . . .
> No more – no more – Oh, never more, my heart,
> Canst thou be my sole world, my universe.

Thus it will be understood that the next time I visited Madame Benzoni's salon I was in no mood at all for female dalliance. But it was here that for the second time I met the Countess Guiccioli.

I was actually accompanied by Scott, (iv) and we entered the salon about midnight. We were thus just taking our seats when other guests began to arrive after the theatre, and amongst them was Teresa.

She looked absolutely magnificent, for if she was again very tired – once more her husband had insisted upon her attending a *conversazione* at the conclusion of a long journey – she was dressed entirely in black, both her mother and her elder sister having recently died. I happened to be looking directly at the doorway when she entered, and she happened to be looking straight in front of her, and so our eyes met for a moment, and held each other's, for a moment. I did not then remember ever seeing her before, and in fact I was so disturbed by the uncommon directness in her gaze, emanating from those glorious eyes, that I felt some confusion and actually was the first to look away, while when the Benzoni bustled across and wished to introduce me to the young lady, I quite determinedly declined.

But both Scott and the fair Benzoni pressed the matter, and at last I allowed myself to be escorted across the room, where Benzoni, still holding me by the hand, said, "Countess Guiccioli, allow me to present Lord Byron, a Peer of England and its greatest poet."

Well, I could not help smiling at such unashamed flattery, and Teresa smiled as well, redoubling her beauty.

"My lord," she said. "But we have met before. A year ago almost to this very day."

I stared at her in amazement and consternation, and then recalled her myself. "But of course, Countess," I said. "I wondered if you would remember me."

"How could I forget *you*, my lord," she said, and I discovered that the Benzoni had dutifully disappeared from beside us.

"Shall we sit down?" I invited, and she settled beside me with that rustle of silk and taffeta I so much enjoy. "You have a *palazzo* in Venice?"

"Alas, no, my lord. My husband . . ." and with her gaze she indicated an unpleasant looking fellow, at least three times her age, who was conversing on the far side of the room, "maintains his house in Ravenna."

"Ravenna," I cried. "I mean to go there, and soon."

She smiled at me. "Dante," she said. (v)

"Oh, and Francesca," I insisted. (vi)

"And more besides." A moment later we were engaged in a thorough dissertation on almost every Italian poet of renown. I was at once amazed and delighted that so young a woman, she was only just nineteen, I later discovered, could possess so thorough a knowledge of literature, and could converse on it with such a lack of affectation and such genuine enthusiasm.

But alas, only a few moments later the Count appeared above us, smiling to be sure. "You have forgotten, my dear Teresa," he said. "We have been here much longer than five minutes. You see, my lord," he said, thus informing me that he had not been as disinterested in our conversation as he had appeared, as he had taken the trouble to ascertain my identity, "my little wife is very tired, and made me promise I would spend no longer than five minutes at this *conversazione*. You'll excuse us."

"Of course, Count." I hastily stood up.

He nodded, and rather strangely, without another word, turned and marched across the room towards the entrance where a posse of servants was waiting with coats and capes and hats.

"I should like to see you again," I said, before I really meant to.

"My lord," she said, and flushed.

"To continue our conversation. Nothing more. I give you my word."

She raised her eyes to meet my gaze, the flush slowly fading. For a moment we looked into each other's eyes, and I believe that moment really sealed the whole affair. For me, certainly. For here was youth, as I had never known it before, and beauty, and *completeness* of character, by which I mean that while no one could doubt the underlying seriousness of her personality, she was yet willing to match humour and wits with anyone, and withal education and intelligence to boot. I might have looked my entire life to find her, and oh how I wished I had found her six years before.

As for Teresa, she later told me that she fell in love with me the moment our eyes met, on her first entering the room. So now she said, "In that case, my lord, it shall be my pleasure. My husband sleeps in the afternoons." She gave me her hand to kiss, and went to join him.

Of course I did not suppose myself in love with her. Love was an emotion of the past. I am speaking of the romantic state. I fully intended to *love* her, certainly, because she was a delightful and surely innocent girl, even after a year of marriage. How could such an old dry stick as Guiccioli ever have given her a moment's pleasure?

Thus all unwittingly I went to my fate. But what a delightful fate it has turned out to be.

Next afternoon, as soon as dinner was finished, I despatched Tita with a note, and betook myself to my casino on the Lido, there to wait in some impatience. But back came the faithful fellow only a little while after, and there she was, becomingly concealed beneath a shawl, giving me her hand to be escorted on to the landing.

A moment later we were alone. "My dear Countess," I said, kissing her hand. "You have made me the happiest of men."

"Poetry," she remarked. "My lord is a man of his word?"

"Indeed I am." Matters had already been arranged, and on the table in front of the settee to which I escorted her there waited a bottle of best claret and two glasses. I poured, and touched her fingers as she took the glass. "But that will not prevent me beseeching you to release me from my vow."

She smiled at me. "Yet you will not be angry when I refuse?"

"Will you refuse?"

She raised her glass. "Let us drink a toast, my lord; that we may both attain everything in this life that we most desire."

I was utterly confounded. But I drank quickly enough. And reached for her, and discovered that she had risen, and had walked to the window to look at the sparkling waters. "Poetry," she said. "I should like to read yours, my lord. Alas, I do not read English. Are you not translated into Italian?"

"French?"

"Ah. I will see what I can do about obtaining a copy. Would you sign it for me?"

"I would be honoured to do so."

I had remained sitting, and now she came back to me. "I cannot stay very long. My husband will soon awake."

"And wish you at his side. How my heart envies him, Countess. How I wish I could understand how you come to be married to. . . ."

"To such a charming, and wealthy, and powerful man," she said, softly. "I am a very fortunate young woman, my lord."

"Oh, indeed. I have heard he has been married before."

"Twice," she said, and gave a delightful little laugh. "I am the mother of a large family, most of them older than myself. And now . . ." she checked, and a shadow crossed her face. My heart descended to my boots, as she observed by a glance at my face. "These things are never certain."

Sending my spirits bounding again. And not just because of her reassurance. It was her *attitude* attracted me. For every woman I had ever met, not excepting my own dear Guss, or perhaps my own dear Guss most of all, had always assumed that to miss a single period involved instant catastrophe. Here was the first *optimistic* female I had ever known.

She extended her hand. "And now, my lord, I must return."

I kissed her fingers. How adorable they tasted. "May I see you again?"

"I am sure you would be bored."

"By you, Countess?" I straightened, still holding her hand. "I would but beg to be released from my vow." I watched her expression, and had a flash of instinctive genius. "Tomorrow?"

Still she gazed at me for some seconds, then once again that radiant smile broke through. "Tomorrow," she said, and gently pulled her fingers free.

TERESA – THE SECOND PART

I awaited the morrow with considerable impatience. There was something about this girl that warned me she was entirely out of the ordinary; but what a fascinating prospect that opened up. Gone were all my fears and my resolutions, never again to consort with intelligence or learning or gentle birth. Teresa had all three in abundance. Gone was my resolution to avoid red hair like the plague; Teresa's was like a brilliant sunrise. Gone were my fears of meddling in Latin domesticity – and Count Guiccioli was by all accounts a very *sinister* gentleman. His two first wives had apparently died exactly when it was convenient for him to have them buried.

And gone, most of all, although I did not then realise it, was my most important resolution of all, never to love again. For Teresa *was* something entirely out of the ordinary.

She came, as before, by my gondolier, wearing the same shawl if a different gown, and remarked, on stepping ashore, and to my total amazement, "We shall have to change our method, my lord. I fear two days of this are all my circumstances will permit."

It might have been Margarita speaking, save that here was a girl of nineteen. I was so overcome I could not reply, but merely held her hand as I escorted her inside, and there turned to her, and found her in my arms.

Her lips were moist and warm. She told me later she had been biting them on her journey, and not for fear or embarrassment, but from a desire to make them the more attractive to me. My fingers slipped on her shoulders, and encountered buttons and ties and straps, and her face was away, and she was looking at me from a distance of only a few inches, while my heart sank as I discerned in her the usual feminine coquetry. How mistaken I was.

"No ado, my lord? No wine?"

"If you knew how I have waited for this moment."

"As I also, my lord. I have no doubt you can, and will, make me the happiest woman in the world. As I shall attempt to do to you in turn. But I would know your intentions. Your *love*."

I found my fingers insensibly slipping from her flesh, and went to the table to pour some wine. Her directness was certainly refreshing, if alarming. And much to my gratification, cocker, however he resented being put off, remained as stiff as ever before in his life. Her scent, her clothes, and above all her voice, had accomplished that much.

"Well," I said. "As to love, my sweet Countess, I am old and withered at that game, as you can no doubt see for yourself. My intentions are to love you, certainly, and to the very best of my ability, but how far that will take us I cannot say. I am married, you are married, I am considerably older than you, I am a man of ruined reputation, as you surely know by now. . . ."

"And I am pregnant," she said, each word a dagger thrust into my heart.

I gave her a glass, drank my own. "Then *I* am damned." Fortunately, I allowed just a trace of question to creep into my voice.

"No man is damned, my lord," she said. "Providing he reveals proper atonement upon his deathbed."

"But. . . ."

"I but wished you to understand the circumstances, that should you love me, too deeply, you will be forced to endure a certain separation over the next few months."

A nineteen-year-old girl, warning the wicked Lord Byron that he might love too deeply.

"But if your love can prove of sufficient constancy to endure such a separation, why, then, I see no reason why we should not be the happiest of couples."

Saying which the darling girl began to undress.

I was by now in a state of total bemusement, which was in no way alleviated by the beauty which unfolded before me, for if my first estimate of Teresa, that she was a trifle plump, proved to have been perfectly accurate, this in no way detracted from her attractiveness. Rather the reverse. She had the fullness of an exactly ripe plum, added to which her skin had a quality like satin, and *rippled* when I touched it, although I was almost afraid to allow myself this liberty, so flawless was her complexion.

334

Almost. "Teresa," I said, hardly knowing where to begin. "Teresa, you are the most lovely thing I have ever seen."

She kissed my mouth, and waited while my hands stroked her back and gradually found themselves around her bottom. Then I felt her breath on my neck. "Scarce so beautiful as you, my lord," she whispered. "Although I have naught to judge by, save expectation."

"My dear, sweet child," I said, releasing her long enough to undress, in which I was assisted by her own fingers. "I feel an utter villain. You are so lovely, so young, so chaste."

"So loving, my Byron," she said. "So loving. May I touch?"

Once again, what utter joy. To have such a question, asked so gently, so shyly, and yet with such determination. And if her skin was like satin, her fingers were like velvet. Almost I felt myself warming to Guiccioli, if he had so well taught her the arts of love.

"You will think me wanton," she said, slipping to her knees beside me the better to see, to feel, to caress, to kiss.

"I think you are a dream come true," I said.

"And will you still love me when you are spent?" Revealing a knowledge of male mentality scarce to be allowed in a nineteen year old.

"I will love you for ever, my Teresa," I promised. Well, I would have said those words anyway, at such a moment. And I would have meant them, at such a moment. But even as I spoke, I knew my *moments* were a thing of the past. I *would* love this girl for ever, providing only she was revealing her true self to me, and would never change. As if Teresa could ever change.

She did not immediately reply, her lips being occupied to my utmost delight, but she knew too when I had had all that was possible without a hiatus, and rested her head on my thigh. "And have you naught to do to me, my lord?"

"Oh, Teresa." I scooped her from the floor, and set her on my lap. "To touch you is to creep through the door of heaven."

She rested her finger on my lips. "No blasphemy, Byron. Not even from you. To touch me is to make me happy. And you as well, I hope. Touch me, Byron. Touch me. *Explore* me, Byron. I have dreamed of this all night."

Explore me. I had explored before. I could remember exploring Caroline Cameron, and Caro Lamb, and Liz Harley, whenever she would keep still, and my own darling Guss. I could remember attempting to explore my wife. All had been delicious womanhood.

335

And yet, was there such a thing as delicious womanhood, save the woman be my Teresa? I could hold a breast in my hand, or on my hand, for they were too large to be encompassed. I could touch a pink nipple with my tongue, and feel it harden on the instant. I could rest my head on the fullness of her belly, and hear the soft murmur from within. I could sift the glory of her love forest, dark brown and eager, and almost cry out in my anguish that so much had passed me by until it was so late.

As if it can ever be too late, for man and woman. For if they meet, at last, the *pair* who are so ordained from the beginning of time, it matters not the least whether they are about to die within an hour. That moment makes up for all they have missed before, all, indeed, that they have enjoyed before, and fully atones for anything they might miss in the future.

And still my cup of happiness was not overflowed. For when we had dallied sufficiently, and I would rest her on her back, she smiled at me and said, "Will you not use the other, my lord? It is best, at any time, but doubly so, now."

I misunderstood her, even as my heart soared and I near choked with joy. To be *invited* . . . but I did not know the paradise for which I was being prepared. She rolled on her face, and took our weight on her elbows and her knees, but yet reached behind herself to guide me, giving a little gurgle of amusement as I sought my *usual* path, the only one I then knew. "I am not so sterile, dear Byron," she said, and a moment later I had been brought to book in the most heavenly position I had ever known, and one it had never crossed my mind to attempt, wherein I was trapped in her own sweet cavern, to her greatest pleasure, for being on my knees I could mount so much more forceful a thrust, and yet was I enjoying that unforgettable delight of her buttocks squirming into my groin. I came, and she came, in an explosion of the most perfect mutual pleasure, and I knew then that it was quite impossible for me ever to wish to bed another woman.

"I have told my husband," murmured my adorable girl, she having rolled over to lie in my arms.

I sat up, my mind spinning.

"Well, you see, we cannot continue to meet like this," she explained, raising herself on her elbow, an entrancing sight. "Someone would be sure to find out, and it would get back to the Count."

I scratched my head. "So to prevent that you have told him." I already could hear the daggers being unsheathed in every dark alley Venice possessed.

"He is perfectly agreeable."

Some more head scratching. "I must confess I do not understand this society at all."

She gave a peal of laughter. "Oh, Byron, my Byron. Indeed you do not. I have not told him that. I have told him that I like you very much, that you seem to like me, and that I would like to have you as my *amico*. My *cavaliere serviente*."

Now this arrangement I had heard of, it being common enough amongst the Italian nobility. I had indeed poked fun at it in *Beppo*. The custom enabled a young married woman to enjoy the constant companionship of a young unmarried man, to escort her wherever she wished, and even to call upon her at her home. And perhaps occasionally kiss her hand? No more to be sure, in the eyes of the world, even though in the *heart* of the world a vastly different state of affairs was accepted. Teresa had therefore taken the best possible steps to legalise our affair, and even to legalise such obvious signs of affection as must pass between us, for a *cavaliere serviente* was expected to worship his *amico*, provided he did it with proper decorum. Yet I hesitated. The whole business smacked too much of foppery to be attractive. As Teresa quickly saw.

"My lord." She seized my hand. "You do not wish to be my *amico*?"

"More than anything else in the world, my darling," I assured her. "I but fear such an arrangement may interfere with our mutual pleasures."

"Silly love," she said, and kissed me on the chin. "It will redouble them. We are to discuss poetry together, that my mind may be suitably broadened. And where can we possibly do that but in the privacy of my boudoir? Now, it will not be possible for us to lock any doors, but it may well happen that entirely by chance you call more often than not when my husband is either out or sleeping."

"By chance?"

She smiled that irresistible smile. "Her name is Fanny Silvestrini, and she is a governess in the Count's household. She is my dearest friend, and will do anything for me. Besides, she adores intrigue. Say you will honour me, Byron."

I could do no more than agree, however reluctantly. And entered into a giddy whirl of the utmost delight, tempered with some very serious reflections. For as Teresa had revealed herself to be to me, so she was. Beneath that demure and petite frame there lurked an irresistible spirit, which knew exactly what it wished, and determined that it would have what it wished. Which left me in a highly dangerous position. I was entirely accepted as the Countess's *cavaliere*. I was expected to escort her everywhere, even when Guiccioli was in attendance, and I was expected to call at her house regularly enough, when protected by the eagle eye of the fair Fanny, who was herself the mistress of the Count's man of affairs, Lega Zambelli, so that we were able to disport ourselves as we chose. And I may say that it was now I truly realised that in Teresa I had discovered a twin soul, in that she was never satisfied with continuing as we had last finished, but eagerly sought new experiences and delights, which left *me* in the position I had always decried, for having tasted the delights of her *favourite* sport, I could think of no possible way of *improving* our liaison.

This was all very splendid, but there was another side to Teresa's coin, a madcap disregard for convention or gossip which would have done myself credit. Custom had demanded she enlist her lover as her *cavaliere*, and to this extent had she followed custom. But custom also demanded that in public we behave with the utmost propriety, and this she very rapidly abandoned altogether. She would hold my hand and kiss my cheek, regardless of who was present and what a fluttering of fans was thereby caused. She would talk with me and no other at every *conversazione*, and when we were even temporarily separated, her gaze followed me around the room as if we could communicate from afar, as indeed we could, for a simple meeting of the eyes passed a sufficient message.

To my remonstrances she returned only a confident smile. "My husband is uninterested in my amusements, Byron," she said. "And we have so little time."

We had less time than she supposed, for only ten days after our first unforgettable meeting in my *casino* she one night tumbled into my box at the opera, eyes red with tears, seized both my hands, and cried, "Byron. I am to leave for Ravenna. The day after tomorrow."

I was horrified, and less at what she had to say than at her appearing in my box rather than me in hers, another convention. Not that Teresa noticed. "He is so . . . so secretive," she wailed. "He has said not a word, until now, and now. . . ."

"We have been indiscreet," I pointed out, gallantly sharing the blame. "And he *is* your husband."

"You must come to Ravenna. Promise me, Byron. Swear it."

Ravenna? A place I had always intended to visit, to be sure. But not to beard an already sinister count in his den. And yet, what could a fellow do? "As soon as I can make the necessary arrangements."

"I shall wait for you, day and night. And Fanny will be there. Write to me in her care. Oh, Byron, Byron, I am desolate."

While I, to be frank, was a trifle relieved. The previous ten days had been the happiest of my life, make no mistake about that. But they had also seen the development of our affair into something quite out of the ordinary, and I could not yet accustom myself to the idea that I was taking on something permanent. I had supposed those youthful effulgences behind me for ever. A separation was essential, I considered, in order that we might each reconsider our position, truly evaluate our relationship, decide whether we really wished nothing more than each other. For I knew in my heart that with such a *committed* soul as Teresa it must eventually come to that.

Next day we bade each other a formal farewell, as it was in public, with Guiccioli himself present, and then I was left to my own devices, a state of affairs I had anticipated, but which I soon discovered was unbearably lonely in the absence of my entrancing charmer. I tried work, the second canto of *Don Juan*, in which I took my hero from his native Spain on a voyage through the Mediterranean, in the course of which he was shipwrecked and rescued by . . . Haidee, the first time I had truly used her – for Leila was but a poor copy. But even here I found myself describing not the dream I had known for a brief moment so long ago, but rather the dream who had just left my side:

> Her hair, I said, was auburn; but her eyes
> Were black as death, their lashes the same hue,
> Of downcast length, in whose silk shadow lies
> Deepest attraction; for when to the view
> Forth from its raven fringe the full glance flies,
> Ne'er with such force the swiftest arrow flew;
> 'Tis as the snake late coiled, who pours his length,
> And hurls at once his venom and his strength.

Her brow was white and low, her cheek's pure dye
Like twilight rosy still with the set sun;
Short upper lip – sweet lips! that make us sigh
Ever to have seen such; for she was one
Fit for the model of a statuary.

Which sufficiently explains my ambiguous frame of mind. But writing was poor substitute for the real thing, and besides, with Teresa gone, I was again surrounded with irritations, letters from Hobby on the one hand warning me against continuing this affair – I had written him in a fine flush after our second meeting – and on the other hoping that the second canto would not be as indecent as the first – what effrontery – while even more annoying was the addition of my name and reputation to Polidori's tale *The Vampyre*, which admittedly he had stolen from my idea on that fateful Swiss evening with the Shelleys which had seen the birth of *Frankenstein*, and was now told in a style not remotely like my own.

But the fact was I knew I was lost, and my very last efforts at resisting my fate were ended by a frantic letter from Ravenna informing me that my darling was very ill.

So there it was. The Palazzo Mocenigo was packed up – no small event, as it involved my menagerie as well as my books as well as myself – and my great carriage was greased and set to horses, and I rumbled south across the Romagna plain, to begin the merriest chase ever a man was led.

Teresa was certainly ill. Not only was she suffering from a tertian, but she had also had a miscarriage. In the circumstances I was regarded as important a medicine as Peruvian bark, and was admitted even to her bedchamber.(i) Soon she recovered, and I was able to take her riding, while together we commenced an exploration of Dante, which once again necessitated my spending long hours in her home, and had the great pleasure, soon enough, of cuckolding the Count under his very roof, and in the most perfect safety, for if we dared bolt no doors, Teresa was now surrounded by an army of the most faithful servants, ranging from Fanny down to a little Negro pageboy, who kept watch by relays and informed us in ample time of the return or the awakening of his master.

Yet I was not happy, except when actually in Teresa's arms. The whole thing smacked too much of the ridiculous, to which was added the dangerous, for that Guiccioli was capable of being vicious was not to be doubted. In my desperate love I even proposed an elopement, knowing full well that it was impossible; Teresa might feel no duty at all to her husband, but she could not neglect her family – for her to elope would have been to damn for ever the hopes of her still unmarried younger sisters. And of course my daily calls at his palace left the good people of Ravenna in no doubt as to what was going on; soon scurrilous lampoons were being printed about the fellow's horns. These, Teresa assured me, he ignored, but clearly he did not, for soon enough he was off again, to visit some property of his in the Romagna, and Teresa, being once again restored to health must necessarily follow her lord. And her other lord? Why, he must pack up and return to his carriage, and betake himself to Bologna as well, feeling the most perfect fool, yet quite unable to prevent himself. At least I made the best of a bad job, and had the Hoppners send Allegra to be with me. She was now four years old, and a perfectly beautiful child, while her intelligence was startling. I looked upon her as the sure support of my old age.

Well, not even Guiccioli could overlook so faithful an *amico*, and he now attempted to make the best of a bad job. He asked me first of all to use my influence – all English milords abroad are supposed to have the entire government at the snap of their fingers – to have him appointed English vice-consul in Ravenna. This was in fact less to obtain something from me than to protect himself, for he was well aware that his activities as a potential revolutionary were being investigated by the Austrians, and there was no telling when they might bring pressure to bear upon his papal overlord, (ii) and of course an English consul was immune from arrest. It was in fact at this time that I once again became interested in the Italian underground, and not entirely through a desire to remain on good terms with the Count. For I now learned that the Gambas, father and son – Teresa's father and brother – were deeply involved, and I certainly wished to be on good terms with *them*, a task which promised to be immensely difficult, as Pietro Gamba, my darling's younger brother, had already been writing to his sister protesting against her friendship with so notorious a rake as myself.

I forwarded the Count's request to Murray and asked him to do what he could – which was absolutely nothing – but then the Count proposed that I should lend him some money, and he already a most wealthy man. But then of course so was I, now, my days of debt-ridden poverty only a sad memory. In addition to my steady income from the Funds, Douglas had squeezed £1,500 out of Murray for the first two cantos of *Don Juán* and another £500 for *Mazeppa* and a couple of other trifles. I truly had more money than I knew what to do with. But lending the Guiccioli seemed to me a very good way of surrendering to blackmail, and this request I was obliged to refuse.

Instantly the fellow turned very ugly, ranted and raved and blamed Teresa for influencing me against him. Once again we reached crisis level, and once again Teresa solved it in her own way, by having an immediate recurrence of her horrid tertian. Guiccioli was alarmed, acceded without demur to her doctor's charge that she be returned to Ravenna, but being unable to go himself – I suspect that this sudden decision to take himself to Bologna may have been less to do with me than with the activities of the Austrian secret police – had no better recourse than to agree that I should escort his wife, these trifling duties being an accepted part of the obligations of your true *cavaliere serviente*.

Here was the most perfect bliss. Allegra of course accompanied us, and we made the ideal picture of a contented married family, Papa, his beautiful young bride, and his equally beautiful young daughter. We were happy, and happier yet when I decided to break our journey at La Mira, whence I had abandoned so much of my furniture and books and pets. Teresa was enchanted, as we left Allegra playing in the care of the servants, and strolled through the garden, hand in hand. "Oh, Byron," she said. "That it should never end."

"The cry of lovers from the beginning of time."

"And why should we not be different?" she demanded. "We *are* different. You are you and I am me. We do not belong to the common herd. Were there ever lovers like us, my Byron? Could there be?"

"Probably not."

"Well, then, Byron. . . ." She seized my arm. "You asked me, once to elope with you. And I, so foolishly, refused. Byron, I would change my mind. Where is it you wish to go? Switzerland? South America? The United States? You have but to say, and I will accompany you to the ends of the earth."

Oh, happy thought. But I was growing old, and sober, and therefore losing all of my youthful wisdom. For it is a mistake to assume, as does the world, that greying hair necessarily brings knowledge and understanding. We are born with knowledge and understanding, and it is only the cloying civilisation with which we are surrounded and encumbered from our earliest days that clouds our judgement. Old age too often adds nothing but pessimism, which is no basis for a considered decision.

"And what of the disgrace to your family, to your name, to your as yet unmarried sisters?"

She sighed, and rested her head on my shoulder. "You are right, as always, my dear Byron. You are right. But at least let us make the most of these stolen days."

Which we did. That evening we continued on our way to Venice, and stayed at the Mocenigo, while my darling wrote the Count and explained that she was slowly recovering from her illness and that we were considering continuing up to Lake Como where she would convalesce. In fact we soon moved back out to La Mira, where we spent a week of utter happiness, sleeping the entire night in each other's arms, awakening sated and sweating and utterly in love. There was no possibility of tiring of Teresa. There was no possibility of being tired in her company. Did I lie on my back in exhaustion she yet would *explore* me, with teeth and tongue as much as with finger or lip. Her beauty and her passion flowed around me like the waters of a warm bath, and I was happy.

And when we did manage to tear ourselves away from our private world, there was Allegra to delight us, and friends to visit us, for it was now that Moore came out to see me, and was entertained by me as I showed him the sights of Venice. Irish Tom could not help but fall in love with Teresa himself, and we had a riotous time, for all that he pretended to be shocked at the picture I presented. And why? I had allowed myself to put on weight – never a difficult task for me – and I had not bothered, I had not had the time, to have my hair cut as often as I wished, with the result that it hung on my shoulders, while I had even added a small moustache, as Teresa liked such adornments, but truly I had never felt better in my life, nor could he decry my obvious health.

It was now that I gave him the first part of these Memoirs. Tom had indeed fallen upon hard times, been forced to leave England one step ahead of his creditors, like so many of my friends – Scrope Davies had had to join the unhappy band of exiles – and was existing in Paris. I offered him my recollections of my youth and my fame and my marriage, on the clear understanding that the material could never be used until after my death, and therefore might have to lie in his strongbox for a very long time. On the other hand, I thought – and was proved right – that Murray or some other publisher might be

343

willing to advance a considerable sum of money now, against the certainty of having such a scurrilous bestseller at some future date. Tom was delighted, although a shade less so when he had read the manuscript, as he began to wonder if publication would not have to wait until after *his* death as well.

But he took it, and brought to a close the very happiest period of my life, to that point. For it was only a day or two after my old friend had betaken himself back to France that the Count appeared at my door.

"My dear Lord Byron," he said, as polite as ever. "May I inquire after the health of my wife?"

"My dear Count," I said, "I think it can be said that she is fully recovered."

"And where do you suppose she may be found?"

"Why, I. . . ." I was considering the matter, and feeling exceedingly grateful for the presence of the formidable Tita, when my darling herself put an end to speculation.

"Why, I am here, my dear," she said, appearing behind us. "Where did you expect to find me?"

She had delayed sufficiently to dress herself, which was the only possible blessing that I could discover. I braced myself for instant action.

"Where indeed," the Count agreed, still the last word in mildness. "And looking at your best my sweet, as milord has just informed me. So, as I am on my way back to Ravenna, if you would care to accompany me. . . ."

"To Ravenna?"

"Where else?"

"You will have to give us sufficient time to pack, and milord has his arrangements to make."

"Milord. Ah. Yes. The fact is, my sweet, milord, I have been requested to request *you*, milord, to remain in Venice."

"Eh?" I was too surprised by the entire conversation to offer much of an opinion.

Not so Teresa. "Requested? And by whom, may I ask?"

"By your own dear father, my sweet." Slowly it began to dawn on me, as these amazing exchanges continued, that the truth of the matter was that Count Guiccioli, for all his age and his experience and his sinister reputation, was *afraid* of the little girl who happened to be his wife. I did not know whether to be afraid myself or to jump for joy.

"I don't believe a word of it," Teresa remarked.

"Count Gamba is alarmed by the rumours which persist in following you, my sweet. Now I, I have the utmost confidence, both in you, my sweet, and in your . . . ah, your *amico*. Milord is an English gentleman, and were he to assure me, on his word, that nothing improper had ever taken place between you, I would accept his word without demur." He glanced at my crimson cheeks, and allowed himself a smile. "But then, it would be improper of *me* to make such a request. No, no, I must keep my faith in you, milord, my own secret. Count Gamba has not had the pleasure of knowing you, and thinks of you merely as a *man*."

"I don't believe a word of it," Teresa repeated. "And I repeat, we will need time to pack."

"*We* shall send for your things, my sweet," Guiccioli said, "as I, and you, are leaving now. There is much to discuss."

"What can there be to discuss?"

"Well." He glanced at me. "It has been suggested to me that I take steps to put my house in better order. To this end I have compiled a list of rules, which I consider my wife should follow."

"Indeed?"

"I have them here. You'll excuse this domestic matter, milord." He produced a sheet of parchment. "It is a long list, and I'll not bore you with every detail. An example, perhaps. . . ." Again a quick glance in my direction. "Let her busy herself with those household matters which are within her competence. Let her offer suggestions and ask for advice, but not give orders. After our drive together, in the early part of the evening, reading aloud as before dinner, then together to the theatre, then conversation and to supper and bed together."

"Ha." Teresa walked across the room, very smoothly and quietly, and sat herself at a small desk in the corner.

"Whatever are you doing?" her husband inquired.

"Answering your list with one of my own," she said. "We may exchange them, and follow them. Let me see." Her pen flew over the paper. "I require the right to get up whenever I like. Of my toilet I will not speak. In domestic matters to be absolute mistress of all that is within a lady's province. To dine together as usual, but to spend the time of your rest as I please, even if it were in pulling the donkey's tail. But no concession on your part would be sufficient to make me live peacefully with you, should you refuse two essentials."

"And what may they be?" He was commencing to go very red in

the face, and I was beginning to wonder if I should send Tita for my sword and pistols.

The pen was busy again. "A horse, with everything necessary for riding. The right to receive, without discrimination, any visitor who may come."

"Madame," said the Count, "all these things are for discussion. You will leave immediately."

"I will not," she said. "I am not ready to go."

"Madame."

"Sir."

"My dear Count," I said. "My *dear* Countess. This is clearly a matter requiring much discussion. My dear Count, will you not accept a bed under my roof, for a day or so, while it is considered?"

"Considered?" he shouted.

"Considered," Teresa said quite firmly, smiling at me. "I am sure Lord Byron's plan is best."

In fact my plan turned out to be very much for the worst, as for the rest of the week Teresa and her husband conducted a running battle in my house, in which I was also very much in the firing line, aware that however verbal the exchanges might at the moment be, they could without warning descend to something far more primitive, in which I would have to be even more involved. After several days, during which my nerves were worn to a frazzle, I at last persuaded Teresa to return to Ravenna with her husband, and leave it to me to follow in my own good time. I was, not unnaturally, by now beginning to have serious doubts as to whether any woman, even Teresa, was worth so much disorganisation and continuous crisis, and I really wished to get on with a little work.

She accepted my admonition, tearfully, and they departed. I breathed a long sigh of relief, and rushed into the comfortable existence of *Don Juan*, taking my hero and his delicious Haidee back to the sunlit shores of Greece, a dream indeed I had, with Teresa at my side. She had said she would come. But overhanging us like a shroud would be the world's disapproval, and I had seen too much of the effects of that on poor Shelley. Besides, I was not sure . . . not sure . . . never sure, even of Teresa. So confused were my thoughts I even contemplated a return to England, whatever the reception I was liable to receive. However, I was prevented from taking so drastic a step by the ill health of Allegra, who developed a most hacking cough.

As if I needed to be sure, where Teresa was concerned. For within a month there came a frantic call from Guiccioli, supported by one from Gamba himself. Teresa was taken desperately ill, and without my presence it was feared that she would die. Never again could she be allowed to live without her *amico*. In fact, Guiccioli offered me the second floor of his own *palazzo*, as a permanent residence, with my own beloved darling just a thin layer of wood away. Thus was my fate sealed, into the very happiest of caskets.

5

TERESA – THE THIRD PART

Can a more ridiculous situation possibly be imagined? On the very night of my arrival in Ravenna a great ball was held at the home of Teresa's uncle, the Marchese Cavalli, to which I received a special invitation. And Teresa hung on my arm the whole night, declining the pleasures of the dance, as she knew I was not able. Thus was it announced to the entire world that I was in residence. And still the Count *appeared* not to care.

So I once again settled into a very pleasant routine, commenced the fourth canto of *Don Juan*, and allowed myself to be amused by the scrape that dear Hobby had managed to get himself into, having written a pamphlet against the government which was regarded as seditious, with the result that my oldest friend found himself in gaol. Certainly a fate which would have been mine had I remained in England, but why any human being should live in that unpleasant climate, surrounded by unpleasant people and unpleasanter laws, given half the chance to abandon it for ever for warmer and less straitlaced climes, remains to me an utter mystery.

My pleasure at this time was interrupted only by the constant bombardment I received from Claire, who had learned that Allegra was once again being boarded out – well, I could hardly have her with me in the circumstances of Ravenna – and was threatening all manner of action, of which kidnapping our daughter was only the least, and by increasing concern for my finances. It is remarkable how, when one *owes*, the possession of money is a happy dream, but how, when one is *owed*, it suddenly becomes a nightmare. Supposing Shelley right in his estimation that England was ripe for revolt, I concluded that the Funds was no place for my fortune, and tried to convince Kinnaird that I would prefer an Irish mortgage. He was against this, and I became engaged in another long distance argument. But I survived as best I could, and continued to enjoy the unparalleled pleasures of Teresa's

348

boudoir. Poor Byron. Whenever Paradise approaches it is always stolen, and therefore not to be enjoyed with impunity. I suppose our long and successful exercise in the art of clandestine cuckoldry had made both Teresa and myself careless, but there came the day when as I nestled upon that delightful flesh, we suddenly discovered the Count standing at our bedside.

There is no more difficult position in which a man may find himself. It is impossible to be dignified when in the midst of the act of love; it is impossible to be aggressive when naked and one's opponent is clothed; it is impossible to be angry when one is clearly in the wrong; it is impossible to be afraid because of the presence of the lady; and it is a grave mistake to attempt to be humorous.

I do not very well recall *what* I said or did. Fortunately, Teresa suffered no such inhibitions. She sat up, I having rolled away, did not waste any time in attempting to cover her body, and positively *seethed* with angry energy.

"Wretch," she cried. "Am I entitled to no privacy?"

"Privacy?" he retorted. "In order to fornicate?"

Will it be believed that I had never before actually heard the word used? But I was busy pulling on my breeches.

"Ha," Teresa remarked. "A woman has her needs."

"And is it not her husband's duty to satisfy them?"

I buckled my belt, and began to feel somewhat more in control of myself.

"*Your* duty?" Teresa demanded. "When you are able."

"I am able now. Now," he bellowed. "Now."

Teresa glanced at me. My God, I thought; she is about to ask me to defend her. Against her own husband? Fortunately I had no sword, or even a stiletto with me.

But as usual I underestimated my darling. She knew as well as I how much we were in the wrong, and that only one thing could possibly placate the Count at this moment.

"Will you leave us, Byron?" she asked, very politely.

My turn to hesitate. "Leave you? Will he not beat you?"

"Him? He will not raise a finger to me. Let us only hope that he is able to raise *something*. Go. I will see you soon."

I could do no more than obey this remarkable woman, but I spent an unfortunate hour, until a knock on my door had me hurrying to open it, to discover the Count.

"Milord," he said, polite as ever. "May I come in?"

I stood back.

"It is time you and I had a discussion," he suggested.

"As you wish." Clearly I was about to be challenged to a duel. Well, if I had choice of weapons and could therefore avoid the dagger, I felt I need not fear him.

But as usual I entirely misunderstood the Italian way. "I very much fear," the Count said apologetically, "that I must forbid you to visit my wife again. Or indeed, to enter my part of the house."

"You wish me to leave Ravenna?"

"My dear sir," he said. "Of course not. I do not even wish you to vacate these rooms. You are my honoured guest. But my wife, no. There has been too much talk as it is, and now, well, that things have come into the open, so to speak, there is no other decision can be made."

"And Teresa?"

"My wife's feelings do not come into it at all. But if you wish, I will persuade her, when she is in a better humour, to write you a farewell letter. Come, come, milord, you have had the best of all possible worlds for nearly two years. Do not let us have any unpleasantness."

Another impossible situation. For how could I, a peer of the realm and even more important, a gentleman, react badly to so courteous and polite a proposal, especially when it was based upon such inalienable right. "Well," I began, when with a gentle rustle of skirts, Teresa joined us.

"What is he saying to you?"

"I. . . ."

"I am forbidding Lord Byron the use of my house," Guiccioli explained, still speaking most quietly. "And your company. Just as I am forbidding you his. Kindly return to your bedroom."

"I shall not," she said. "I am instructing my father to write to the Pope requesting an annulment of our marriage."

The Count goggled at her. Well, I was doing the same thing.

"Annulment? On what grounds?"

"Grounds? Ha. Consistent and inhuman ill-treatment. Virtual imprisonment. And perverted sexual desires."

Some more goggling. But he was in no position to utter a word of protest, for Teresa later told me that he had been unable to complete the act in the normal way, owing no doubt to a combination of age and anxiety, and her fingers also proving of no avail, had been forced to handle himself to relief, while using his free hand to caress her body. Now, as to whether or not this constitutes perversion I would not care to say, as I imagine it must, at some time or other in their lives, convict almost every man over fifty and quite a few under that age. But it certainly seemed to carry Teresa's point, for after a very short while the Pope granted a separation, while I could only consider with amazement the twists and turns of fortune, that after being so treated by my own wife, I should be a supporting witness of my mistress doing the same to her husband. Truly the events of life are such as to convince a man that he need only be patient and remain alive and reasonably healthy for all things to come right in the end.

Not that they immediately came right for Teresa and I. While the claim and counter claim for the separation was continuing we were not allowed to see each other, and she had to remain living in her husband's house and indeed granting him conjugal rights. I was alarmed for her safety, and sent her my own cook to make sure she was not poisoned. But the Count, however much of a rascal he may have been, was not so stupid as to murder his wife while the Papal authorities were looking into his affairs. Indeed he supposed he was certain to win his case, not being aware that I had taken the trouble to make a friend of the secretary of the local cardinal legate, a fellow named Alborghetti, and with his persuasion at the official elbow, Teresa was granted her wish.

But it was a wish bedevilled by protocol. The Pope was willing to allow her a legal separation from her husband, because of his ill-treatment, but not in order that she could move in with me. Indeed she was required to return to her father's house, and was expressly commanded to see me only in the presence of others. Here was a damning blow, especially as I was not the most popular man in the world with the Gambas, entirely I may say on reputation, as none of that family had ever taken the trouble to meet me.

In addition to these strictures, there was the matter of Teresa's allowance from the Count, which was fixed at a hundred escudi a month, or very roughly £1,000 a year. In my pragmatic English fashion I assumed that the main part of the family resistance to my calling was fear of losing this not inconsiderable sum, and I wrote to them proposing that I should be responsible for my darling's keep rather than her superannuated husband. And was rebuffed, not least by Teresa herself, for she was determined never to be a burden to me. As if such a situation could ever have arisen.

So there we were, two lovers as thoroughly separated as any in history, our situation made the more absurd by the fact that while she moved *out* of her husband's home, I remained *in*, in my second floor apartment. It was a trying time, complicated by Allegra's continuing ill health, and I could only partly alleviate the situation by work. This year I completed *Marino Faliero*, but I fear it was not one of my best works.

I was additionally distracted by the reception given to the first two cantos of *Don Juan*, which Murray finally summoned the courage to publish. This time even the vulgar reading public affected to be shocked, and sales fell. I even received a letter from Harriette Wilson, who I had actually met once – so she says for I cannot remember – on the occasion of that Watier's ball when Caro and her green tights had caused such a sensation; this good lady took me to task for lowering my character and abilities to write such obscene rubbish.(i) All in all it seemed as if all my troubles were once again arising to overwhelm me, and once again my thoughts turned to countries as yet untrammelled by Pope or by custom.

I was as usual being impatient and underestimating the determination of my darling. Very soon an invitation arrived from Count Gamba himself, for me to call in order to witness from his garden – the finest in the province – the eclipse of the sun. This I did, was greeted most graciously, allowed to sit beside Teresa during the uncanny occurrence, and best of all, allowed a few moments alone with her before departing. I could do nothing more than fold her in my arms and shower kisses on her lips, but she assured me that only patience was required, as my manner and wit and charm had made a profound impression upon her father and even more important upon her grandmother, and that our future happiness could only be a matter of time.

And as usual she was entirely correct, but made so in a manner I am sure she had not considered or even suspected. For a few days later her brother, Count Pietro Gamba, came to call.

Pietro was actually brought by his father, Rugiero, who it seemed had been so completely captivated by me he wished his son also to reappraise the situation. And in fact I liked the lad enormously from our very first meeting. He was only a year younger than Teresa, scarcely taller, almost as handsome, but better than any of these, he was on *fire* with enthusiasm and anxiety. And was, for those reasons, a highly dangerous conspirator, as he had hardly been with me more than a few minutes when he began an indoctrination assault.

"Consider Spain, my dear Byron," he said. "There, there things are happening. There we are at last seeing the power of the people" – I am happy to say that like me, he assumed the people would always be led by men of noble birth – "when they are aroused."

He was referring, of course, to the fact that the iniquitous Ferdinand, who on his return to Spain had revoked the constitution promulgated by the Cortes in his absence as Napoleon's "guest", had recently been forced by the rebelling Spaniards to reinstitute that charter of freedom.

"And now Naples," Pietro continued. "Ah, Naples will lead the way. Naples has always led the way. And where Naples leads, all Italy will follow. And the Romagna will be amongst the first."

"You would fight the Pope, who will certainly be assisted by the Austrians?" I inquired. "You will need men."

"We have them."

"And courage."

His eyes flashed at me. "Do you doubt that, milord?"

"Not for a moment. But courage will be of no avail without arms."

"We have them. We are getting them."

"And none of those three, men, or courage, or arms, will be of the slightest use without organisation."

"We have that too," he said, lowering his voice. "Will you join us?"

There was something about him, about his enthusiasm, that attracted me enormously. Besides, he was Teresa's brother. And he was appealing to all the almost submerged instincts which had made me what I am. And that the whole Romagna was on the verge of an eruption could not be denied. Almost every night was punctuated by a pistol shot down some alleyway, and woe betide any Austrian official or soldier who found himself alone in these secluded places.

"You may count on me," I said. And thereby entered a new chapter of my life, for within a week I was initiated into the Carbonari. I will not, indeed I dare not, reveal even in a Memoir the exact ceremony, but it was *awful* in its binding solemnity, and made me feel that the event upon which we all waited was soon to be upon us, for as I wrote to Murray, "Depend upon it, there will be savage work, if once they begin here. The French courage proceeds from vanity, the German from phlegm, the Turkish from fanaticism and opium, the Spanish from pride, the English from coolness, the Dutch from obstinacy, the Russian from insensibility, but the Italian from *anger*, so you'll see that they will spare nothing."

In fact I was made a Capo or chief in the organisation, or at least a branch of it, as we were divided into three groups, the *Protettrice*, or Protectress, which was the controlling body, the *Speranza*, or Hope, composed chiefly of young students, who were our intellectual branch, and the *Turba*, or Mob, composed of all the rest. It was here that I received my command, my section being named *Cacciatori Americani*, or American Hunters, which was a sufficiently explanatory a name. In this respect I made contacts and purchased arms, and soon had some two hundred muskets stored in my rooms.

I also of course once more attracted the attention of the authorities, who began to tamper with my mail, as I could easily see, and also to have me followed. But I knew they would never dare interfere with an English milord, and went my way in complete confidence. At the same time, such is the nature of civil strife, I found myself often at odds with my own fellow conspirators, as on the night there was a sudden burst of gunfire outside the Guiccioli *palazzo* and on running down the stairs I discovered an Austrian officer, in uniform, lying there shot through the head.

I am a civilised man. What could I do but summon Willie and Tita and have them carry him inside and endeavour to alleviate at once his pain and his misery, to no avail, as he shortly expired. But there were those who criticised this action on the grounds that no Austrian was worth saving, even for a few minutes. Civil war is undoubtedly the most terrible of conflicts, as I have discovered only too well more recently. In view of the amount of financial support I was able to bring to the Romagna rebels, however, my position in their councils could not really be tampered with.

In the meantime, life endeavoured to continue, despite the endless poetry of politics. Both in an endeavour to be near Teresa, and in order to remove Allegra from the August heat of the city, as her health showed no signs of improving, I had been hunting for a country villa, and now I found one, very close to Filetto, where the Casa Gamba was situated, which allowed me to make more regular calls upon my beloved. But our relationship continued to be unsatisfactory, as gone, apparently for ever, were the delicious hours we could spend entirely in each other's company doing the one thing we both loved best, and this naturally led to a certain amount of irritation and even jealousy, she of Allegra, me of anyone who went to call.

In addition I had my usual irritations in the form of letters from Claire, beseeching and bewailing and threatening, to which was added a complication when the Hoppners started a rumour that she had recently had another child, by Shelley. I must say this did neither surprise me nor concern me greatly; after all she had lived with him for years, and if the *ménage à trois* had centred around me I should have kept both Mary and Claire going with the greatest of ease. But Shelley himself was terribly upset about the entire matter, and seemed to blame me because, on receipt of the incriminating letter from Frau Hoppner, I had merely replied in the above vein, thus tacitly implying that I believed her. Truly, for so talented a man, and he was talented, have no doubt about that, his attitude to life was remarkably childish. He was equally concerned about the death of Keats, that apology for a poet dying in Rome this year, and criticised a few lines I scribbled regarding the event. But I had never hidden my opinion of Keats's poetry, and Shiloh had known this when first we had become friends.

Then this summer I also once again found myself over-closely connected with English events publicly, as it was now that our new King Prinny decided to sue his wife for divorce on the grounds of adultery, which, when it involves a queen, is also treason, so that I was asked, as an erstwhile friend of the unhappy princess, to do my best to procure evidence of her innocence – it was, alas, far easier to procure evidence of her guilt – and privately, as I felt in duty bound to write my beloved wife and inform her that I had given my Memoirs to Moore, inviting her to read them and offer her comments. This she declined to do, replying instead that if I attempted such a course she would reveal *all* herself, a very mystifying threat.

I also worked, on the fifth canto of *Don Juan* and on a new venture, *Sardanapalus*, which seemed to me entirely in the mood for my present circumstances. For the wheels of revolution were slowly turning. In Naples the country appeared, from our reports, to be in full revolt. Well, I had never been to Naples, but I knew enough of Neapolitan history not to believe anything of their staying power, and so when our executive committee had its meeting and the young bloods, led by Pietro, clamoured for an immediate uprising in support, and his father counselled rather a waiting game, to make sure the rumours truly could be believed, I found myself supporting the older and wiser heads. Harsh words were spoken, but no one dared accuse us of cowardice, nor will in retrospect, I trust, in view of everything that has happened since, and we carried the day.

But soon enough the news was confirmed, and with it, the news that an Austrian army was being mobilised to go to the support of the beleaguered monarchy. Here was clearly our opportunity to strike a decisive blow. "For depend upon it," I said, "they must march through the Romagna. But let us begin a concerted revolt as they approach our borders, and attack them from all sides. They will fall back across the Po, the Neapolitans will triumph, and all Italy will rise in a single flame overnight."

"There is genius," Pietro cried, climbing upon the table to wave his sword in the air. "Are we united?"

"Yes," they shouted, making a nonsense of the secrecy that was supposed to attend our meeting.

"Then it only remains to organise our venture," Count Gamba said, and began issuing the necessary orders to our various local commanders, to be ready to mobilise their men the moment news arrived that the Austrians had crossed the Po. I took myself home in a fine fettle of excitement, summoned Tita and Willie and told them that men would be coming for our secret store of arms and ammunition, that we were about to strike a blow for liberty which would result in our victory or our death, and retired to my study to write far into the night. Now was a time to shrug off all the years of sloth and dissipation, to recall the leonine youth who had faced the eleven Terrible Turks or who had had the Tory majority in the Lords seething with impotent anger as I tore their infamous schemes to the winds. I reminded myself that I was still young, well, not yet thirty-three, that I was the lover of a magnificent woman who would undoubtedly accompany me to greatness, that this moment was what I had waited for all my life, that glory lay just around the corner. I felt elevated, triumphant, almost unable to restrain myself, but eventually slept, to be awakened by a banging on my door which had me leaping up, seizing sword and pistols and coat and hat, gazing at Pietro as he staggered into my midst, hatless himself and gasping for breath.

"They have crossed the Po?" I shouted.

He nodded, and sank into a chair.

I slapped him on the shoulder. "Then come on. Now is no time for being tired."

"They crossed the Po," he muttered. "Two days ago."

"Eh?"

"They are here already," he said. "Our cause is finished. They are arresting us now. Everyone."

We had been totally outwitted, and our cause was lost, for the time being. In fact, we were so crushed that arrests were kept to a minimum, and in our immediate circle only Tita, my faithful gondolier, was actually incarcerated, this being as close as the authorities dare come to troubling me. But we did not *know* what they would dare, and in the circumstances, expecting the worst, I did not see how I could keep Allegra with me any longer. I was by now fairly fed up with the sanctimonious Hoppners, or rather the sanctimonious Frau Hoppner, for Hoppner himself was a good fellow, and besides, they were talking about sending the child to Switzerland for her education. I wished her to grow up into a warm-blooded and warm-hearted Italian, if possible, a copy perhaps of Teresa, and so I opted for the convent at Bagnacavallo, a place highly recommended by the Gambas, and at which the nuns and the accommodation sufficiently impressed me when I went there on a visit. Claire was of course wild with outrage, but it was the only sensible thing for me to do. That it turned out tragically is a cross I shall have to bear to my grave, but try as I might I cannot in my heart find any cause for self reproach.

For if the authorities would not trouble *me*, they could reach me through my friends, the principal of whom were of course the Gambas themselves. Rugiero and Pietro were not actually arrested, but sentence of banishment from the Romagna was soon pronounced. Here was a fine to-do, as by the terms of her separation agreement Teresa was bound to remain under her father's care.

"I will not go," she declared. "I will not, I will not, I will not. I would rather kill myself than be separated from you, Byron."

"Well . . ." Rugiero commenced pulling his beard.

"Be assured, my dear Count, that I shall follow you the moment you are suitably settled," I promised him. "But there is no point in uprooting myself until you *are* settled, and are sure of asylum in some reasonable state. I am a poet. I must write to live. I cannot write while traipsing about the countryside."

"I will not leave Ravenna without you," Teresa repeated. And we all knew her too well to doubt her words.

"Well . . ." Rugiero said.

"Surely in these most unusual of circumstances, my dear Count," I said, "Teresa is right. No one is going to arrest *her*. It would be far more dangerous for her health to be shunted from pillar to post behind you. No one could argue against her staying here until you have secured a permanent establishment, and sent for her. I will make her care my most important task."

He sighed, and raised his eyes to heaven. "And the Pope's decree?"

"I will talk with Alborghetti, and explain the circumstances to him," I promised. "The Pope will not trouble you. And if he does, why, then I shall carry all of us into Switzerland, where Popes are but a name in the distance."

"I will not leave Ravenna without Byron," Teresa declared, and the matter was settled, so that at last, after close to a year, we were united again in the same bed and in each other's arms. What bliss it was, for those few short weeks, even if I had my time taken up with attempting to secure the freedom of Tita – which I did eventually manage – and with writing, for on completing *Sardanapalus* I launched myself into *Cain*, and even compiled a play, *The Two Foscari*, all the while that *Don Juan* continued on his adventures.

But these were about to come to an abrupt halt. It may be remembered that Teresa had long expressed a wish to read my work, and in fact I had managed to secure her French editions of some of my earlier poems, which she had pronounced very fine. Now, all unknown to myself, she obtained a French copy of the first two cantos of *Don Juan*, and read it in a single night, coming to breakfast the next morning in a most serious frame of mind.

"Byron," she said. "I could not believe it. Such indecency. Such obscenity. Such blasphemy."

"I write what I believe," I said.

"You do not," she objected. "*I* cannot believe that. I know you *feel* that way often enough, but that is a passing mood, caused by the unhappy circumstances of your life. This . . ." she indicated the book with a gesture of contempt, ". . . is not the real Byron. It cannot be. My lord, I most earnestly beseech you, and beg you, and command you, write no more of this carnal rubbish."

What could a fellow do, even if I was convinced that she was wrong, that indeed *Don Juan* is far less obscene than Pope; it is merely the age that is changed? And happily I was eventually able to reverse her decision. But I am anticipating. For the moment I buried the poor fellow away in the recesses of my mind, and confined myself to more mundane matters.

Principal amongst which was her own affairs. For the Gambas were being chased from pillar to post, and Teresa was half out of her mind with worry. I even tried to help myself, writing the Duchess of Devonshire, an old friend, whom I knew was very well regarded by the Pope and at that time resident in Rome, begging her to intercede on their behalf and enable them to return to Ravenna. (ii) Alas, she was away when my letter arrived, and although eventually I heard from her, a promise to do everything she could, it was to no avail. And in the course of time asylum *was* located, in Pisa.

Now it was time for Teresa to do her duty and return to her paternal roof. As may be expected, she was inclined to refuse, even though everyone in Ravenna, including Guiccioli, was aware that we had been living in my villa in the most open adultery for several weeks past. Nor was the old scoundrel backward in bringing this to the attention of the authorities, and I was warned by Alborghetti that a move was afoot to incarcerate my darling in a convent, and for the rest of her life, in view of her flagrant disregard of papal and moral decree.

Yet even this very real danger might not have persuaded Teresa to remove herself from my side even for a brief while – I am afraid she had imbibed too deeply at the well of rumour and gossip and down-right scandal which surrounded my name and which perhaps had been given added weight by her perusal of *Don Juan*, so that while she was sure of me when she saw me every day, she doubted my fidelity were she removed from my side for even a week – had I not gained, at this most appropriate moment, the very best of allies. For Shelley came to visit.

He and Teresa liked each other at sight, which was remarkable, for *he* had been filled by Claire with tales of how it was Teresa had persuaded me to place Allegra in a convent, and *she* was inclined to dislike all English poets save me. But Shiloh proved a tower of strength. He had actually come to talk to me on behalf of Claire, who was near destitution, of mind as well as person, and to attempt to persuade me to allow her access to Allegra, whom she had not seen since delivering the child to Shiloh himself some years before. I was not really inclined to be lenient towards so importunate a bitch, but I was myself in a sorry state of mind, and besides, I needed Shiloh's assistance. I thus agreed to permit the little girl to spend a week with the Shelleys, while Claire was also with them, on condition that he assisted me in solving my own dilemma. This he did in the very best of ways by assuring Teresa that he would himself find a villa in Pisa, that he would then return here and escort me thence personally, and that the whole thing should be accomplished with the very greatest despatch.

Teresa seemed prepared to trust him where she was not altogether prepared to trust me, and agreed. She and I spent a tearful and fearful but entirely loving evening in saying farewell, and then she was gone, and I was left to make my own preparations.

It must be said at this time that Shiloh had had another ulterior motive in coming to see me. He knew a great deal about my secret hopes and ambitions, and was aware that it had always been a dream of mine to found a journal, whence I could let the world know my feelings on great events and literary matters, and which would also serve as a vehicle for those of my own works which timorous publishers might be afraid to handle. All I needed was a competent hack to assist me in the day to day work. This he had now discovered, my old gaolhouse acquaintance Leigh Hunt, who was by way of being a friend of Shelley's, and who had burdened himself with a wife and a perfect tribe of children at a very time when his own earnings were non-existent. "What a fine thing it would be, my dear lord," Shiloh said, "if you were to invite him to join you in Pisa, and together you were to launch that magazine of which you have often spoken."

"It is an interesting project, certainly," I agreed.

"There would be, I'm afraid . . . well, he is absolutely without funds."

"I would be prepared to pay his passage."

"I knew you would, my dear lord. And perhaps. . . ."

"An advance to defray his immediate expenses. Yes. Yes, that will be all right." For what I remembered of Hunt I rather liked. I had not, at that time, met his brood, nor was I aware that he had ideas on child upbringing roughly similar to Shiloh's, or I would have run a mile before allowing him to disturb my equanimity. But at the time I was entirely enthusiastic. "If you could arrange it, my dear Shiloh, I would be most pleased. And you may tell him that the entire profits of the magazine would be his, at least until such time as it and he are fully established. Do you think that is fair?"

"Fair," cried the good fellow. "It is downright generous. Oh, I shall tell him. And, now to find you a house in Pisa."

And so it was that I brushed the dust of Ravenna for ever from my feet.

In fact, all of eastern Italy saw me no more. I had already given up the Palazzo Mocenigo, and my country villas outside Venice. Now I packed up all of my gear for my move to the west, and this was no mean undertaking. Consider my menagerie; I have always had an inordinate liking for animals, they are so much more faithful than human beings, and I have but to settle myself for the briefest spell in one place to have them accumulating around me. Thus, in addition to my vast retinue of servants, it was necessary to provide transport for ten horses, eight very large dogs, a monkey, five cats, an eagle, a crow, a falcon, five peacocks, and two guinea hens, and I may add that every one of these lived in the house as a member of my establishment, and I would have them treated no other way. Nor was this my entire complement, for I decided to leave my goat, who had a broken leg, a rather ugly peasant type dog, two of my monkeys, who were grown old and ill-tempered, my badger, who was equally ill-tempered and had to be kept on a chain, and my Egyptian crane, who would eat only fish and was a confounded nuisance. I do not of course mean that I abandoned these creatures to starve, but I placed them in the care of my banker, Pellegrino Ghigi, who was also to see to any wants of Allegra until I was sufficiently settled in Pisa for her to join me. But what in a large way alleviated both the pangs and the problems of my removal was the adherence to my cause of Lega Gambelli, who was the Count's steward, but abandoned that post to serve me, and has proved a most faithful and efficient – at times too efficient – friend.

In fact my journey itself was sufficiently interesting, for the very afternoon I left Ravenna, as I was entering Bologna, whom should I observe approaching me in another equipage but Clare. Imagine, after all these years. The somewhat disagreeable circumstances of our last meeting were instantly forgotten, both carriages pulled to a halt, and we stared into each other's face, his changed not at all, mine undoubtedly having undergone a considerable alteration. What a flood tide of event and experience had flowed past my head since our school days, and no doubt, on a lesser scale, past his as well. And I do declare that he was pleased to see me. We could spend no more than five minutes together, as he was bound for Rome, but we squeezed hands, and agreed to meet again in the spring.

And *then* who should I encounter but dear old Rogers, indeed, we travelled for some time in company together, reminiscing for the most part, but quarrelling for the rest. Every night as we finished our after-supper wine there was a most tremendous difference of opinion, about various matters, but next morning we had mutually agreed to forget it all, and continue upon our amicable way.

And so I came to Pisa, and once again the arms of my beloved.

And settled, for a brief while, into one of the very pleasantest periods of my life. Shiloh had secured for me a large, rambling place called the Casa Lanfranchi, and here I could spread myself and my household to my heart's content. Here too, I was only a stone's throw from the Gamba villa, which meant that I could call upon Teresa whenever I chose, and yet, as she could not by convention call upon me, I was able to preserve that privacy, that *seclusion*, which from time to time is so necessary for a writer. For Teresa herself had mellowed with age and experience – she was still no more than two and twenty, poor child – was less anxious to shock convention and propriety, and if, once we gained the intimacy of her bed, she was as deliciously *carnal* as I had ever known her, for the rest she was as contentedly placid as if she had been my wife. Had my own dear soulmate died – oh, happy thought – I would certainly have married her had she herself been free, and been the most contented of men. As it was, as I have said, for that brief year I *was* the happiest of men, with all the advantages of marriage and none of the drawbacks.

And thus all of the advantages of determined bachelorhood, as well. For Shiloh had accumulated around him a circle of *English*, or at least, *British*, admirers and intellectuals, and of this last breed there are very few indeed. We had the most splendid dinners, at Lanfranchi, of course, for I was the only one with the least pretensions to wealth, seating perhaps as many as six at a time, Shiloh and I, of course, Williams the soldier, (iii) Medwin, who quite openly declared his intention to Boswellise me (iv) – but I could hardly take offence at that– Tighe, (v) and eventually that rascal Trelawny. (vi)

Actually, I liked Trelawny better than any of the others, although, or perhaps because, I alone refused to believe his quite absurb tales of his youth, how he had been in the Navy, and kidnapped by pirates, and appeared to have fought his way, singlehanded, from one end of the Mediterranean to the other. He assisted this wild romance with his flashing eyes and his flowing beard, but I could not help but wonder if he had not, before his arrival in Pisa and knowing that he was going to meet me, absorbed *The Corsair* and *Lara* and *The Gaiour* and even *Childe Harold's Pilgrimage* in order to present to me a composite picture of all my most famous characters.

Picture me then, in the most agreeable of routines, rising late, as I chose, riding out with my friends during the day, more often than not to practise with our pistols at a farmhouse removed some distance from the town – we could not obtain permission to create a range at the Lanfranchi – occasions on which Teresa and Mary Shelley, who rapidly became very good friends, accompanied us, dining well into the afternoon, calling upon my own dear love in the cool of the evening, leaving her towards midnight, and returning to my study to labour into the small hours.

In fact my labour was the only unsatisfactory aspect of my time at Lanfranchi. I did nothing worthwhile. In part this was due to a running and increasing war with Murray. God knows he had made sufficient money out of me to have retired, had he wished. Certainly to support my work with more optimism. But he had been terrified by the critical outcries over *Manfred* and *Don Juan*, which only increased with the publication of *Cain*, and the thought of which positively turned him white with fear when he first saw *A Vision of Judgement*. In fact it was my *Vision* which finally decided us to break, or rather, me to break from him. (vii) He would not publish it, and sent me letters trying to convince me that I was writing too much, that the public was tired of me, and that it would be better to confine myself to one poem every other year or so. Well, I no longer needed the money, to be sure. But how may a writer not write? I informed him that I would be publishing elsewhere, and entered into negotiations with John Hunt, Leigh's brother, who became, and remains, my publisher. But this step would have been necessary even had I never written the *Vision*. For the real cause of my unsatisfactory output this year was that I *knew* I was wasting my time and my energy and my emotions. My heart lay with Don Juan and his adventures, and when not writing him I was not writing. I thus asked Teresa to release me from my promise, and she, sweet girl, after some thought and mental wrestling, agreed. To her my happiness came before anything, and she knew that unless I was happily *working*, I could not be happy at all.

As I have said, I no longer needed to supplement my income from the sales of my poems. For it was at this time that the dragon herself, dear Judith, died. Which meant that at long last the Wentworth estate was released, and my share of Belle's dowry was finally paid. My

363

wealth was immediately doubled, my income soaring to some £6,000 a year, which in Italy at the least made me very much of a millionaire. To be sure there were trifling formalities to be undertaken, mainly that I should add the name Noel to my own, but this I found amusingly pleasing. For consider, instead of signing myself B, I could now sign myself NB. I remember once, in my cups soon after Belle left me, arguing with detestable George Anson on the qualities of greatness, and claiming that I was probably as great a man as Bonaparte, if not greater – I have no doubt at all that he added this to his list of proofs of my mental degeneration – and here I was at last able to use the same initials. I felt quite a thrill of pleasure whenever I found occasion to sign the monogram.

Ah, what happy days. I do believe that summer of 1821 was the very happiest I have *ever* known, and with my penchant for permanency and my incurable optimism I did not see why my condition should ever change. I was still a young man, my health was better than it had been for a long time, I had an adorable and adoring mistress, more than enough money to live on as extravagantly as I chose – it was this year that I ordered myself the building of a hundred foot schooner for my own yacht, and Trelawny undertook to oversee its fitting out – a circle of admiring and interested friends, a comfortable house peopled by devoted servants and equally devoted pets, and if I was separated from my true family, I at the least possessed a lovely and intelligent daughter, who, I was assured by both Ghigi and the Mother Superior at Bagnacavallo, was increasing both of those assets with every day. I could describe myself as the happiest man alive.

Alas, man is not intended for true happiness. It is at best a transient condition, to be enjoyed while it lasts, but he who looks for permanency is a fool, chasing a star. At the very moment that I counted myself eternally suited, Fate was preparing to remind me that I was nothing more than a suspected exile, at the mercy of every authoritarian whim, and more, that I, and all my friends, and worst of all, my darling daughter, were no more than human clay, which could be destroyed in the twinkling of an eye.

OF LIFE AND DEATH

Picture me then, settled into a very contented community as the year 1821 gave way to 1822. I took my pleasures as I chose, looked forward to beginning my literary association with Hunt – to which end I spent a great deal of money on furnishing the ground floor of the Casa Lanfranchi – and did not quibble when it became necessary to forward him ever increasing sums of money to see him on his way, for he was apparently penniless; not that my advances accomplished a great deal, for inclement weather caused him to remain in England for several months after he had been supposed to depart. Teresa and I both sat for busts by Bartolini – and very fine likenesses they were too – which but confirmed the thoroughly domestic life we were enjoying. (i)

Of course there were irritations. It seems impossible for me to live even the quietest of lives without irritations. Southey – not unnaturally, I suppose – took offence at my *Vision*, and wrote a scathing rejoinder, which so annoyed me I sent him a challenge, being quite prepared to return to England to face him, but Hobby and Kinnaird suppressed it in line with their self-appointed jurisdictions as my financial and moral guardians; and Claire remained always a thorn in my side, pricking away with her interminable letters, once again seeking to drive a wedge between Shiloh and myself, and going a long way towards succeeding, while Tighe fell so completely beneath her spell that he avowed I should be horsewhipped. As if he or any man would dare such a game with me. But I was quite used to these annoyances, and was more inclined to be upset because my new schooner turned out to cost £1,000 instead of the £200 Trelawny had first quoted. But she was a very fine vessel. I wished in the first instance to name her *Teresa*, but being dissuaded from this by my darling herself – she no longer desiring to incense the Pope or give her husband additional ammunition for his continuing war – I settled for *Bolivar*, as I have never faltered in my admiration for this hero. Had I

365

known the first service for which she was to be used I might have chosen differently, but, perhaps fortunately, the future is screened from our mortal gaze.

All in all then, I had no more than usual to complain of, and far less than usual in my domestic arrangements. Until we arrived at 24 March 1822, the first of three horridly eventful dates which were to change my whole life, and even one of which occurred in this year.

The day was Sunday, and as usual, we had ridden out to practise with our pistols, I being accompanied by Shiloh, Trelawny, Pietro and Hay. (ii) Again as usual we were attended by Teresa and Mary in my carriage, and they actually left to return to the city just before we did. While we were following, at a very leisurely pace, we encountered Taaffe, (iii) who had been riding with a Turkish friend, and was now walking his mount back to Pisa in order to allow him to cool before stabling. He joined us, and we proceeded, laughing and talking amongst ourselves. As I recall we rode four abreast in the first line, Taaffe being on the left, and therefore next to the ditch, I beside Taaffe, Shiloh beside me, and Trelawny on the far side. Pietro and Hay were behind, and behind them again was Strauss, my courier. Thus we rode, and were almost at the gates when suddenly a horseman charged through us from behind, and at great speed. When I say through us, he actually passed between Taaffe and the ditch, but so violently as to throw Taaffe's horse into the greatest confusion – Taaffe was in any event not the best of horsemen – with the result that the poor animal jostled into mine and nearly unseated me, while Taaffe commenced shouting, "Well, have you ever seen the like of that?"

Indeed I hadn't, and I was inclined to take exception, especially as I could see that the assailant, who was continuing on his way towards the gates, was an officer in the Tuscan Royal Light Horse. I therefore put spur to my mount and chased behind him, followed by all the others save Taaffe, who was still trying to control his horse. We caught the fellow up just outside the gate, racing past the astonished and alarmed ladies in doing so, and Shelley got in front of him and demanded an explanation of his conduct.

"Conduct?" shouted the fellow, all moustaches. "I owe no explanations to anyone save my superiors. Let me through, you foreign bastards. I shall be late for the roll."

"By heaven, sir," Shelley cried, now very excited. "My second shall call on you."

"As you wish."

"And mine," I shouted. "Here is my card, sir."

The fellow took it, glanced at it, and shrugged. "My name is Stefani Masi, and I shall be pleased to meet you, all of you, if you wish."

"My lord," Hay said, tugging at my sleeve. "My lord. . . ."

I shrugged myself free.

"My lord," the good fellow persisted. "This man is but a sergeant."

I gazed at him in dismay. For now I realised that he was, nothing more than a soldier. And I had challenged him. I looked at Pietro, and he, very red in the face and obviously seething as much with embarrassment as with anger, swung his riding crop and caught Masi across the chest. "*Ignorante*," he bellowed.

"You are mad, mad," Masi yelled. He pushed through us and galloped for the gate. "I could cut you all to pieces if I chose. Arrest them," he cried to the guards, who were by now coming out to see the cause of the uproar. "Arrest them all."

"Arrest me, would you?" I cried, having by now become thoroughly angry. "Come on. We shall ride through them."

I once again gave spur, and we charged, my companions behind me. The soldiers formed rank before us, Masi, still mounted, in the centre of their line, busily attempting to draw his sabre, but I was upon them too quickly, scattered them to and fro, and was through, Pietro at my side, galloping down the street and hallooing like madmen.

We reached my villa, where I was amazed to discover that only the two of us had survived the charge. "We must return and rescue our friends," I decided. "Pietro, send Lega for the police. We must be first with our account of this affair. I will fetch swords."

I ran inside, while Pietro went for Lega, and returned with two sword-sticks, only to encounter Strauss, who was bleeding from the mouth and looked in a very serious state indeed, although it turned out that he had only received a severe blow on the chest. "Surrounded," he wailed, spitting blood besides. "Cut down. All gone."

"I am with you, master," Tita said, appearing armed with two sabres. Pietro had by now returned, and we hurried back to our horses. But at this moment the carriage arrived, disgorging Teresa, who was quite hysterical, and could only repeat, "My God, My God," while her father, who had suddenly appeared from nowhere, attempted to comfort her.

"What the devil has happened?" I demanded of Mary.

"I have no idea, save that there has been a fight. You'll help them, Byron?"

"You may rely on it," I cried, mounting.

"I knew you would. Malucelli," called this remarkably cool woman, addressing Teresa's servant, who had been with them on the coach, "you'd best hurry across to Captain Williams and inform him that our dinner this evening is cancelled. Oh, make haste, Byron, do."

"I shall," I said, and gave rein, Tita at my side. Pietro and the others were left behind. But I had barely reached the street when I discovered Masi riding towards me.

"Ha," he shouted, reaching for his sword. "Are you satisfied, Englishman? I have beaten you all."

"Draw on me, if you please," I invited, wheeling my mount to ride beside his and unsheathing my sword-stick, at the sight of which he hurriedly let his own weapon return to its scabbard. "Ha," I said in turn. "You'll give me your name again, you scoundrel."

"Masi," he shouted. "Stefani Masi." While he spoke he came right against me, causing our horses to whinny, and before I realised what he intended, seized my arm to force my blade back into its scabbard as well, and half imprisoning me, so that we continued back towards the Lanfranchi, apparently joined together, and in the midst of a growing crowd.

"Master, master," Tita cried, pushing his own horse between us. "Use my sabre."

"No, no," I said. "Let the fellow go." For I was under the impression that it was Tita holding all three of us. But at that moment, we having reached my *palazzo*, Masi himself released me and gave spur. I have no clear recollection of what happened next, but there was a shout of "No, no," and someone standing on the steps of my house rushed forward with a lance in his hands and thrust up at the unhappy soldier, at the same time shrieking, "I hit him, I hit him."

"My God," Masi screamed, swaying in the saddle. "My God. I am killed." Saying which he threw his hands up as if in prayer, and fell to the ground.

I realised at once that we might be in a serious situation, and hurried into my house to decide on the best possible course of action, and also to tend to my friends, who had by now arrived, for I discovered that Hay had received so vicious a cut across the nose as to be bleeding

368

profusely, although not even he was in such a state as my darling, who was quite prostrate with excitement and fear. I spent some time in trying to comfort her, and then sent her off with Shiloh and Mary to their house, as it was close to our surgeon, Vacca, and also to the Williams's, whom we knew would be anxious on our account. That done I despatched Taaffe to see the Governor of the Province, Viviani, and gave him our account of what had happened. Then I could ride up to the Shelleys to see to Teresa.

It may be imagined that there was a tremendous to-do. We were fortunate in that Masi did not die – who struck the blow it was difficult to decide, as no one would confess, but it was certainly either Pietro or one of the Gamba servants – but he remained grievously ill for a long time. Naturally we put as brave a face on the situation as we could, and rode abroad every day to show our innocence, although we took care to be fully armed on these occasions, for the mob was greatly incensed against us, this Masi having been a confoundedly popular fellow. The authorities insisted upon taking depositions from all of my friends – they did not care to trouble an English milord – and also from our servants, and as I had experienced in Ravenna, used the opportunity to imprison these poor chaps, or to be precise, poor Tita, although he assisted his own downfall by attending his interrogation armed to the teeth, which, accompanied by his black beard, made him look distinctly piratical.

I was of course furious at this, and demanded his release, but it was not immediately forthcoming, and I could only show my contempt for the Tuscan attitude by sending him the best of food while he was incarcerated. But of course the real fact of the matter was that the authorities were setting into motion the necessary machinery to have the Gambas once again sent on their travels, sure that I would necessarily follow my beloved, and that my troublesome friends would also depart. Soon enough the command came for Pietro and his father to take themselves elsewhere, and I could only suggest Genoa. This naturally induced another fit of hysterics from Teresa, but by now she and I, and even old Rugiero, had decided our circumstances were such as to force us to ignore papal and public opinion alike. Teresa moved into the Lanfranchi to live with me, while her menfolk departed to find another possible residence.

Even Tita was eventually released, although he was ceremonially escorted over the border into Lombardy, and I was forced to maintain him there until things settled down. But of course the event had the effect desired by the Tuscans. Our circle was quite split asunder, mainly because of differences within our own group as to our various behaviour during the affray. In the main these centred on Taaffe, who, having caused the pursuit in the first place, had carefully remained in the background until all the excitement was over. Mary even commenced calling him False-taaffe. But we were dissolving in any event. Hay and Medwin returned to England, the Shelleys went to Spezia, and even I moved out of Pisa for the summer, taking the Villa Dupuy nearer to the coast, where Teresa and I settled down to regain our nerves and our happiness. The weather was good and we might well have accomplished our intention, had we not been interrupted by the second terrible event of this miserable year. On 22 April the news arrived of Allegra's death.

I had of course been aware that my daughter had been unwell, a letter to this effect having arrived from Ghigi only a week or so earlier. It appeared that she was suffering from a slight fever, but I must confess I was not terribly concerned, because everyone living in Venice or in the Romagna suffered from these tertians from time to time, and besides, Ghigi had been quite adamant that the affliction was slight. I was therefore totally unprepared for the shock.

I was sitting at my desk, engaged in composing some more of Don Juan's adventures, when Teresa entered. This in itself was a considerable surprise, as she was well aware how much I need quiet and privacy when writing. But I speedily saw from her expression that something was very wrong.

"Byron," she said. "Lega has this morning received a letter from Signor Ghigi."

I waited. At times like this, does one gain an insight into the future? Or is it merely that every possible catastrophe flashes through one's mind? Certain it is that I knew before she spoke I was about to hear something dreadful.

"It . . . she. . . ." She licked her lips, a very rare gesture, just as her total uncertainty was so unlike her.

"Allegra is worse?"

"Dead," she said, and sat down. "Dead. The fever could not be checked. Oh, Byron. . . ."

For I was still staring at her. In fact the import of what she had said was only slowly sinking through my brain. I know there will be many, it may even have appeared from time to time in this volume to

370

be the case, who will consider that for a father I was remarkably disinterested in my child. But this is untrue. I swear I loved her better than self. But what could I do? My establishment was at once irregular and bachelor. I cannot pretend to be the best of examples to anyone, much less a small girl. I was sure, I am still sure, that placing her in the care of goodly nuns, as is the fate of every well-born Italian girl, invariably with the best of results, was the only thing I could have done. I have heard it said, not to my face but behind my back, that the regime at Bagnacavallo was too spartan to be survived. This is again untrue. The nuns were kind. They were not indulgent, but the best parents are never indulgent. They could not have been more generous in the praises they sang to me of my daughter's intelligence and progress, and I do not for a moment doubt their extreme grief at the disaster which had overtaken them and her.

And I? I know I sat there for some time, gazing at my beloved, while tears rolled down my cheeks. I had long given up any hope of ever being allowed to see Ada again – I doubt I shall, until we are both considerably advanced in years, or unless her mother decides to die and leave us in peace – and it was upon Allegra that I had built all my hopes for the future. Now those hopes were gone, shattered into a million tiny memories, as so many of my hopes have been dismissed. I doubted that life was worth continuing.

Yet life *had* to be continued. Arrangements had to be made for Allegra to be buried. I wished her body sent to England, and this was done. I wished her buried inside my favourite church at Harrow, and this was not done. Unbeknown to me Belle had taken to worshipping there, and was using my pew, so that she would in fact almost have been sitting on Allegra's body. My dear daughter was relegated to the porch, without even a plaque.

There was also Claire to be borne. Her letters to me can only be imagined. If it were possible for the written word to slay then I would have dropped dead on the instant. And in the circumstances I could not even defend myself. The child had been in my care, and she had died. There was nothing more to be said.

And nothing more to be done, save live. Teresa and I had duly removed ourselves to the Villa Dupuy, and it was here, early in June, that I was gratified to receive a visit from Clare, now on his way home. How good it was to see him. How much we had to talk about, to remember. And yet, how *sad* was the entire occasion. I felt strangely as a man is supposed to do when standing on the scaffold, that all my early life was passing before my eyes in review. And at the same time I could discover no confidence in the future. As I said to Teresa when Clare's carriage finally rumbled down our drive, "I shall never see him again." And these were more than mere words.

Yet the future was there, and growing more interesting. It was this summer that I received a visit from George Bancroft, who made me realise for the first time how popular I was in America, and once again aroused my interest in that free if somewhat uncouth society. (iv) But at the same time my interests were being dragged in an exactly opposite direction, for I was concerned with the news from Greece, where the long simmering revolt had suddenly erupted into the most dreadful series of massacres and counter massacres, and where every man of feeling had to take the side of the belatedly awakening Hellenes.

On a more domestic front, things were not so pleasing, if equally exciting. Apart from the launching of my *Bolivar*, with which I was delighted, and which I had armed with four brass cannon to enable her to resist the most virulent pirate, or the average Turkish warship – for my thoughts were already ranging in the direction of an active inter- vention in the war – but which I found to have cost, as I have mentioned, several times the original estimate, and which I now discovered I could hardly berth anywhere along the coast, so unpopu- lar had my name become with the various local governments, my peace was now finally disturbed by the arrival of the Hunt tribe.

This last word is a perfectly accurate delineation of the event, for in addition to Hunt and his wife, there were no fewer than six children. Well, I had been anticipating the event, to be sure; my literary activity had dwindled over the past year, and I trusted that my magazine would be the rejuvenation of my talents. I bestirred myself to see them installed on the ground floor of the Casa Lanfranchi, and looked forward to getting down to work.

But Hunt was a far different man to the careless cockney gaolbird I had dined with in London some years earlier. For one thing, he was completely beneath the wing of his wife, and this good lady was determined to disapprove of me and indeed of everything I stood for, which could not help but cause me to wonder why she had allowed him to accept the partnership in the first place.

Then there were his children, whom he indulged to a point of near mania, encouraged by his wife. Within a week they had converted the floor on which they lived into a pigsty, and were spreading their activities into the entry halls and up the stairs. They wrote on the walls, and tore out the paper; they seemed determined to investigate how every article of furniture I had purchased for them was constructed, by a process of dissection; they tramped muddied feet across my parquet floors; they fought and gamboled with the highest of spirits and voices; they upset my animals and my servants; and when I ventured to remonstrate, when indeed I lost my temper and seized the nearest stick I could find in order to introduce some sanity into my happy home, the dreadful mother rushed to their defence and accused me of being a heartless bully, as she had been warned in England she would find me. I declare that had I not had the Villa Dupuy whence I could escape this constant brawling, I would have gone mad.

But perhaps the worst aspect of the situation was the character of Hunt himself. For I will confess that this I had gravely misjudged, and Shelley, if he had understood it, had not seen fit properly to acquaint me with its intricacies. For here we have a man, of no particular birth, to be sure, and of a fairly radical turn of mind, which caused him to resent those better than himself – mainly me – but at the same time of an almost servile mentality, which equally caused him to fawn upon me, and entreat me never to desert him, while showering me with embarrassing thanks for assisting him in the first place. Thus I never knew where I was with him, for at one moment he would be addressing me as my lord as if he were my steward, and the next as Byron, as if he were my closest friend.

And this uncertainty spread also to his and my work, which was far more annoying. I am acknowledged as the greatest of living poets, well, there is no point in denying the fact, now that, indeed, even *Don Juan* is beginning to find his proper place in the hearts of my readers. Hunt considered that *he* should be acknowledged the greatest of living essayist, an accolade which had not, alas, yet been bestowed upon him. Nor has yet, to my knowledge. Thus he was inclined to vary between the most adulatory praise of my work, however poor it was, and sudden moods of confidence in which he sought to set his puerile prose beside my noble verse. I truly wonder for how long we might have been able to continue in harness, had my life not, for the third time this year, been disrupted in the most ghastly manner. On 11 July Trelawny arrived from Lerici, to tell me that Shelley was missing at sea.

*   *   *

The news was doubly distressing to me, because Shiloh had spent the previous few days visiting at Pisa, endeavouring to keep the peace between Hunt and myself, and to convince me that our projected periodical would actually work. He had come via his own little yacht, which he had had built at the same time as *Bolivar*, and which, out of a compliment to me, he had named *Don Juan*. It was only a half-decked boat, scarce bigger than a ship's tender, but he had always been inordinately fond of sailing, far more so than I, in fact.

His companions on this cruise had been Williams and a young lad, and they had berthed in Leghorn, before coming down to Pisa itself by horse. They had left us to return to their ship on the evening of the seventh, and according to Trelawny, had intended to leave for the short sail up to the Shelley home at Lerici the following morning at dawn. But a thunderstorm had delayed them, and they had not actually set out until noon, when indeed Trelawny in *Bolivar*, for he was virtually living on board my yacht, had accompanied them out as far as the harbour mouth, and had intended sailing all the way with them, the weather being unsettled. But he had been recalled by the harbour authorities, and threatened with all manner of restrictions because he had not officially cleared the port. Such is Italian bureaucracy. Thus the *Don Juan* had put to sea by itself.

With Trelawny was Roberts,(v) who actually went on to the mole to watch the progress of the little vessel, but lost it in a sudden squall which swept across the sea, when he reckoned it was about ten miles distant. This had been two days before, and for the remainder of that time Trelawny and his friend had waited for news, but on discovering that Shiloh and his companions had never reached Lerici, they immediately rode down to Pisa to acquaint me with the situation.

"What of the fishermen?" I demanded, my heart pounding like a bass drum. Somehow the death of even my child had not affected me so much as the *supposition* that so vital a mind, so throbbing a heart, as that of Shiloh's might be lost for ever.

"We have questioned everyone who was out that day," Trelawny assured me. "It was a severe squall, but one *Don Juan* should have been able to weather, properly handled."

"Well then," I said, ever the optimist. "Is it not most likely that they were driven out to sea, perhaps as far as Corsica? They were well provisioned?"

"Oh, indeed," Roberts agreed.

"Of course it is a possibility. And to be hoped for. But none the less we cannot sit here and sweat it out." Trelawny was always the man of action. "Would you, my lord, agree to us using *Bolivar* for a search?"

"Of course. Take her as far as you wish."

He left immediately, and Roberts returned to his inn. I must say my own suggestion greatly relieved me, and I got to bed in a somewhat easier frame of mind, while next day I went into Pisa itself to see the Hunts. But that evening Mary Shelley and Jane Williams appeared, having ridden down from Lerici, although Mary had only recently recovered from a miscarriage. Both women, as may be expected, were in a very dismal frame of mind, and we could only attempt to encourage them with our own hopes. Alas for optimism. On the morning of the sixteenth there arrived a note from Roberts, who had left with Trelawny to continue the search up and down the coast, that two bodies had been washed ashore a few miles north of Viareggio.

Hunt and I left immediately, all personal squabbles forgotten. But the bodies had already been buried in the sand by the authorities, who feared infection. They gave us descriptions of what they looked like, however, and we concluded that one had been the boy, and the other poor Williams.(vi) Of Shiloh there had been no sign, and we were permitted another night of hope before a letter arrived from Trelawny informing us that a third body had come ashore near Viareggio. This also had been immediately buried in quicklime, as it had been in an advanced state of decomposition, but Trelawny had managed to see it first, and had identified a poem in one of the pockets. Shiloh was undoubtedly dead.

We could not, of course, permit the bodies of our friends to remain for ever in unmarked graves on an open beach, and Trelawny immediately began negotiating with the authorities for permission to disinter them, and have them reburied in the Protestant Cemetery in Rome, where indeed Shelley's son William was lying. These negotiations took some time, and it was nearly a month before, his original request having been turned down, he obtained permission only to dig them up and cremate them on the beach.

What a dismal month that was. For my part I was utterly bereft, because Shiloh and I had not been on the best of terms over the preceding year, partly because of Claire's ranting and his own feelings about Allegra's death, and partly because of my obvious uncertainty about the future of my projected partnership with Hunt, the very idea of which was arousing a great deal of opposition amongst my friends in England. But what did these petty differences matter when compared with the death of so vital a spirit? Teresa and I could only do our best to console both Mary and Jane, and I guaranteed Mary all the financial support she might need in removing herself and her furniture back to England.

But we were merely going through the motions of living, until Trelawny's news reached us. Hunt and I once again travelled north, to where Trelawny and Roberts were awaiting us. Trelawny had been very busy, having had constructed an iron box, sitting on four legs, in which the bodies were to be consumed. This travelled by way of the *Bolivar*, which was anchored off the beach. He had also prepared two leaden boxes to hold the bones and the ashes, and these Hunt and I collected in Leghorn on our way up the coast.

We began with Williams. The day was very hot, and our feelings are really indescribable. Hunt and I remained sitting in my carriage while Trelawny and a friend of his, by name Shenley, (vii) superintended the uncovering of the poor fellow's body, and dragged the mutilated and distorted thing across the sand with boathooks. I got down from my carriage to look at it.

"It could be anyone," Hunt said. "How can we know it is Williams?"

I pointed to where the ghastly fleshless skull had fallen back, mouth open to reveal the teeth. I have always been able to identify anyone by their teeth, and those were undoubtedly Williams's. "It is he, all right." But I felt my stomach turn as I looked at the livid and shapeless carcass. "Yet you are right, Hunt," I said. "It could be the body of a sheep, much less a human. Consider, that we shall all resemble that, one day."

The ghastly mess was finally accumulated and placed in the oven, and the fire was lit. It burned fiercely, and we assisted it by throwing in incense, which was very necessary, salt, and sugar and wine. After some minutes, however, I felt I could stand it no longer, and stripped and entered the sea. I swam for some distance, and was then seized with so violent an attack of cramp that I vomited and was in some distress. Fortunately Shenley and Trelawny had come behind me, and they were able to assist me back to the shore, where we found that the body had been almost entirely consumed.

But horrid thought, Shiloh remained.

★   ★   ★

Trelawny spent the night with us in Viareggio, but left early the next morning. We followed an hour later, assuming that by then the dreadful business of digging up the corpse would already have been completed. But he was still searching, the grave having been incorrectly marked. It was a few minutes after our arrival that his spade clanged upon a skull.

I suppose there was very little difference between Shiloh's appearance and that of Williams; all of his clothes, including his linen, had turned black, and the flesh was just a mess of nauseous putridity. But somehow it *seemed* worse, as I could not help but recall the awful energy of my friend, the splendid ideas and conceptions which had issued from those lips, which had emanated from that vanished brain.

Which had been encased inside that huge skull. "Be careful," I begged Trelawny. "To preserve that skull would be a triumph for mankind."

"I shall," he said, and once again sent the spade into the sand, but at the first touch of the blade, or rather the second, the bone splintered and we were left with nothing.

The body was placed in the oven, and the fire was lit. Hunt could not bear to look at it, and remained in the carriage. I certainly could not speak, or even throw on the incense. But Trelawny did enough for all of us, uttering a sort of prayer: "I restore to nature through fire the elements of which this man was composed, earth, air, and water; everything is changed, but not annihilated; he is now a portion of that which he worshipped."

Which was really very fine pagan stuff, and I imagine I said something to that effect, but once again I could not remain still, watching the last of my dear friend, and I betook myself to the sea, this time swimming, without immediate mishap, out to the *Bolivar*, which was anchored perhaps a mile and a half from the shore. When I returned, some time later, the body had been entirely consumed, except for the *heart*, which remained as red and glowing as no doubt it had been in life, and which none of our efforts could destroy. Surely there could be no finer epitaph.

As to what actually happened to the *Don Juan*, it is impossible to say. For a while rumours were current that just before the yacht had been lost to sight in the rain squall another vessel had been seen just astern of her, and there was some talk of piracy, especially as a bag of some fifty gold pieces which was aboard was never found. But I discount this theory. There was no sign of violence to the bodies, and had the yacht been capsized in a sudden squall, as seems most likely, the bag of coin would in any event have sunk to the bottom of the sea.

I only knew for sure that Shelley was dead, and with his death all temptation to allow myself to sink into quiet domesticity with my dear Teresa seemed to vanish.

THE GREAT ADVENTURE

No matter how I fought against the understanding, Italy was finished for me after Shiloh's death. Especially as it came upon Allegra's, and when I was already knowing that discontent which must come to an essentially *active* man when he has been in one situation for too long.

But fight against it I did, for only in Italy, it seemed to me, had I ever known real happiness. My exertions in swimming in the heat of the sun during the cremations left their mark in a severe attack of sunburn and exhaustion which had me prostrate for some days, but as soon as I was well again I threw myself with all my energy into my venture with Hunt, and after some debate, we elected to call our magazine *The Liberal*. I even attempted to interest Moore in contributing, but he would not, and it was left to my fading pen to supply most of the copy.

As if I wished to write, anything, even *Don Juan*. Shiloh's memory hung over my shoulder like a spectre, every word he had uttered, every suggestion he had thrown out. I found there was only one way to rid myself, at least temporarily, of my dread affliction, and to this period of my life can be traced my addiction to gin. But surely it does little harm, and certainly, when my brain has been inspired by the fiery water, I have written some *brilliant* lines.

But it was a visit from Hobby which helped, as it has so often done in the past, to coalesce my thoughts into certainties regarding the path I should follow. For Hobby, dear fellow, having equally splendid memories of our youthful adventures in Greece, had become an even more ardent hellenist than I, and had got himself elected on to a committee of English gentlemen who were determined to assist the descendants of all our favourite heroes of myth and legend to regain their freedom. It was his business to inspire me with a similar fervour. Not that I needed any. But where he was looking for moral support, from my writings, and perhaps financial support, from my wealth, he expected nothing more than that. How he stared at me, as I said, "I shall write, of course, anything that may help the cause. I will offer anything and everything that I can spare, to arm them. But that is not enough for me Hobby. If they will have me, I will go to Greece myself, as a volunteer."

He was delighted, and hurried back to England to have me also elected to the Committee, as well as to convey the good news to the Greek agents in London, for of course I had no intention of attending this war just *as* a volunteer. I wished to serve, to be sure, but in the capacity best suited to my wealth and my talents, and that involved some sort of command.

Meanwhile it was necessary to make provision for Teresa. Not that I told her my plans. I could not envisage, I dared not envisage, her possible reaction. But we were both now anxious to leave Pisa with all its melancholy associations, and so we removed ourselves once again, going first to Lerici, and then taking, for me, the Casa Saluzzo, close to where Count Gamba and Pietro had established themselves. Teresa now returned beneath her father's roof. The truth of the matter was that our mutual fire, from constant conflagration, had burned low. It burned. Make no mistake about that. But after three such tumultuous years as we had known, we were already in the position of an old married couple, and she, most thoughtful of women, was understanding on both how much I needed to live by myself in order to write, and also how my carnal ideas had slipped from their constant high pitch into a smooth running stream which only on occasion whipped itself into wavelets.

In fact my literary career was now again developing. However much I may carp at the uncertainties of Leigh Hunt, I can point no such stricture at his brother John. This noble fellow had dared to publish my *Vision* where Murray had refused, and had suffered prosecution for it. Now he willingly took on the burden of proceeding with *Don Juan*, which I naturally would not permit to appear merely as part of a magazine, even my own magazine, but which must enter the world on its own merits. So once again the name of Byron *launched* itself upon the English public.

There were the usual number of visitors to be coped with as well. Webster suddenly appeared, pursuing, as vainly as ever, some fleeing female, and the while bewailing and putting forth plans to regain his dear Fanny. More important were the Blessingtons, from my point of view. Not as company. The famous lady was not exactly as beautiful as she was reputed to be, (i) and she was more interested in hearing my conversation than in putting forward her own ideas, but after a somewhat stiff beginning we got on famously, and they remained in and around Genoa for some time, with useful results. I bought her favourite horse, Mameluke, at a very exorbitant price. And Blessington, not to be outdone, bought *Bolivar*, at a fraction of what it had cost me to build. But I had no stomach for the yacht any more; she was too closely associated with those dreadful July and August days of the previous summer. Nor was she at all suitable for my Greek expedition, whenever that came about.

For as last year wore on, my plans slowly began to come to fruition. I was visited by Blaquiere and Luriottis, (ii) to ascertain exactly what my plans were, what sort of funds I might be able to supply to their cause, and in what manner I wished to serve. And at this point it may be of interest to recapitulate the course of the strange revolution as it had then proceeded.

Although Hobby and I had both noted, on our visit to Greece in 1809, that there was an undercurrent of growing nationalistic feeling which I, at the least, was sure even then must eventually erupt, I suppose the revolution itself can be traced back to 1814, when Hypsilanti founded the *Philike Hetairia* in Odessa. (iii) This was a secret society very much on the lines of our Italian Carbonari, but unlike my friends, the Greeks were already assured of powerful external support in the form of Russia, which country as we all know has ever had her greedy eyes on Constantinople.

For some six years matters continued in this subterranean way, until in February of 1821 there was an insurrection in Wallachia against Turkish misrule. This was quelled easily enough, but the die had been cast, and on 6 March Hypsilanti proclaimed a revolt in Moldavia and called on the Tsar for aid. Here he discovered how little faith can be put in the clandestine promises of kings. Metternich said no, as he has consistently said no to every national aspiration which could conceivably upset *his* order of things. What a shame he has never had the courage to follow Castlereagh's example and blow out his brains. However, without Russian support Hypsilanti was defeated, and fled across the border into Austria, where he was promptly imprisoned.

But what he had started could not now be stopped, and in the Morea, and some of the Aegean islands, the Greeks rose against their

Turkish overlords. Civil War, as I have already remarked, is never a pretty thing. Hatreds run too deep where opposing factions have lived cheek by jowl perhaps for generations, and from the very start this war of ours has been marked by the most diabolical cruelty. Thus the Greeks, on raising their standard, massacred every Turk, man, woman and child that they could discover, and the Turks responded by hanging the patriarch and murdering every Greek they could find in Constantinople.

But these events had happened before, especially in those unhappy portions of the world ruled by Turkey. What fanned the flames into a full-scale conflict was a belated interference on the part of the Tsar, no doubt suffering from his conscience. On 27 July he presented the Porte with an ultimatum, demanding the restoration of the Christian churches and official protection for Christians. The Turks refused, and Russia prepared for war. But once again Metternich and Castlereagh reminded the poor fellows of the dangers of supporting insurrection, *any* insurrection, and once again the idea was dropped.

But not by the Greeks. On 5 October a Greek force took the main Turkish fortress in the Morea, Tripolitsa, and no fewer than ten thousand Muslims were massacred. After this there was no turning back. On 13 January 1822, a Greek assembly meeting in the ancient theatre of Epidauros, declared independence and drew up a constitution which by its liberality put to shame all the so-called civilised states of Europe.

Now the war became general, and involved even my old friend and would-be lover Ali Pasha. He had long preserved himself in almost total independence of his nominal overlords. Now the Turks seized the opportunity to invade Albania, take Janina, and murder Ali and his family, while in the spring of this year, while we were setting Pisa by its ears in our conflict with the guards, and while my dear daughter was dying in her convent at Bagnacavallo, a Turkish fleet took the island of Chios, where the Greeks had early asserted themselves, and massacred or enslaved *every* person they found. The Greek response was magnificent. On the night of 18 to 19 June Constantine Kanaris, with two fire ships, sailed into the midst of the Turkish fleet and ignited himself. The resulting conflagration took the Turkish flagship and most of its consorts straight down to hell.

Cause and effect. The Turks now launched an army of thirty thousand men on an invasion meant to destroy the Greek cause for ever. My friends could not possibly face such a mighty force, and fell back into the Morea, but the Turks came to a halt before this same dismal swampy village of Missolonghi where I now reside. They arrived in July, while Trelawny and I were searching for Shiloh's body, and sat down before the fortress. A month later, while we were cremating my dearest friend, the gallant Marco Bozzaris led three hundred men on a night raid into the Turkish camp. Marco was slain, but his men put no less than four thousand Turks to flight, and became national heroes on the instant. The Turks fled, the siege was raised, and it seemed that the Greek hour had come.

But alas, life was never so simple. For what did Blaquiere and Luriottis have to tell me? With the country again in their own grasp after so many centuries, the Greek leaders fell to quarrelling amongst themselves, each captain claiming the allegiance of his own men and by right of that limited authority claiming also to dictate to the rest of the nation. Here was my cue. Sending arms and money and moral support was all very well, but if anything was to be accomplished the Greeks needed a leader of international reputation, a man behind whom they could close their ranks.

"I am a poet," I protested.

"You are an English milord, my lord," they argued. "And famous as a believer in liberty. Your poems are known throughout our land. Our people will follow you, where they will follow no other. You have but to go, and all Greece will be yours."

"And will I be given authority?"

"Governor-General, at the very least."

"Purely for the duration of the struggle, of course," Blaquiere said. "But afterwards, why, my lord, Greece will need a king."

There was a heady dish to set before a simple poet. But it remains a magnificent dream, and if even I, from time to time, have despaired of bringing any cohesion to these most disparate of peoples, it is that dream which forces me on. How it would drive Southey *mad*. And what will dear Belle think, to suppose that she might have been queen?

I became aware, even before I set foot in Greece, that I was dealing with the most selfish and grasping people on earth. No doubt I remembered some of these characteristics from my own experiences as a lad, but yet it came as a shock when I was again visited by Nicolo Karvellas, full of enthusiasm for my adherence to the cause, only to discover that his real purpose was to solicit a loan of a hundred guineas for himself. But this was the attitude of everyone connected with this miserable affair. I was the most popular man in the world, so long as my guineas kept coming. Fortunately, thanks to Douglas's efforts, there was no sign of this source of power drying up, and when my election to the committee was confirmed, in May, he was also able to confirm that I would have credits in excess of £8,000, truly a fortune in these parts of the world, to take with me.

So at last the time for dreaming was past, and the time for action had arrived. All was bustle, as I despatched Trelawny to discover a suitable vessel for our expedition – he was of course determined to accompany me – and had my tailors start accumulating for me a sufficient store of uniforms to grace a governor-general, while I indulged, for myself and my immediate companions, the fancy of some helmets, cast in the ancient design, such as Agamemnon himself might have worn, and crowned with nodding plumes. For if display without substance is a mockery, substance enhanced by display doubles its effect and its value, and I was under no doubts that I must impose my will upon those whom I was proposing to lead to freedom.

Alas, before I could even approach that happy state, I must impose my will nearer to home. I had already confided my plans to Pietro, who was also determined to accompany me. I therefore decided to let him break the initial news to Teresa, and awaited in trepidation her arrival.

"I will come with you," she said, very simply.

"Now, my darling, that is quite impossible. At least at this moment."

"Because you will be killed."

"Oh, come now, my darling," I said. "Generals are very seldom killed, and governors-general most seldom of all."

"You will forget all about me."

"Never. I could never do that. You are part of me, Teresa. Do you not understand that?"

She sighed, and sat beside me. "As you are a part of me, Byron. And now you will tear that part asunder. Why? In the name of God, why? Send them money. Write in their support. But why go yourself? You are not a Greek."

Why, indeed? I found it devilishly difficult to put into words. "It is something I must do," I said. "It is something I think I have known I must do for a good many years. Try to understand, my darling. Life has been good to me. It saw to it that I was born a lord, and not content with that it gave me a gift of genius. It gave me beauty, for the most part, and it gave me spirit. And in the course of time it has given me you. And what have I put back into that life? A few poems which so many people, yourself included, consider to be obscene. That is not enough."

"You are become a philosopher," she said. "You were not so when I met you, and loved you." She squeezed my hand. "I loved you the moment I entered the Benzonis' salon, that night. I knew then that I could love no other. I love you still. But you have changed."

"*You* have changed me. By giving me so much happiness, and so much peace, you have made me think, about myself, about my place in the world, perhaps about my place in history." I made myself smile. "I fear I am merely growing old. But you are all to me, my darling. You have but to forbid me to go and I shall stay."

"Forbid you to go," she said. "How simple to say. How impossible to do. You have made your case, Byron. This is something you feel you must do. How can a mere woman stand in your way?"

"You will be well here until my return. And it shall not be long, I promise you."

She gazed at me for some seconds. "It will not be long," she said, half to herself. "I will return to Ravenna."

"To Guiccioli?"

"To my husband," she said. "I cannot live alone. You are taking Pietro, and Papa has grown old and withdrawn. I will return to my husband."

"And when I come back?"

"When you come back, Byron, oh, my Byron, or when you decide to send for me, I shall be there. If I have to wait for ever, I shall be there, my own sweet lord."

As she will be, I have no doubt at all. But from the moment of her permission, all my life was concerned with making ready to leave.

With Barry's aid, (iv) Trelawny had secured a real tub of a vessel, but known appropriately enough as *Hercules*, and on to this we loaded our supplies. While this was going on I was endeavouring to make suitable financial arrangements for those servants I was leaving behind, for Hunt, and also for Mary, whom I regarded very much as a charge on my purse. It was now however that we had a lamentable quarrel, which arose entirely out of a difference I had with Hunt, needless to say over money, he being of an opinion that in charging off to Greece I was leaving him in the lurch. How few people understand that their own puny lives count as nothing in the great onward march of humanity. But Hunt and I soon squared our differences, whereas Mary, who had taken Hunt's side, she feeling very much responsible for the fate of that miserable family, as it had been Shelley's idea in the first place that they should come to Pisa, continued to regard me with hostility, despite Teresa's best efforts to heal the breach.

It grieved me to part from any of our circle except on the best of terms, but duty was calling. The *Hercules* was loaded, and our departure was fixed for 13 July, but on that day as fortune would have it there was no wind at all, so that I was permitted to return to the shore and spend another last glorious night in the arms of my beloved. In fact, by a continuous succession either of calms or of storms our departure was held up for some considerable time, leaving me a prey to the most melancholy reflections as I wandered through the Casa Saluzzo, or endeavoured to pass my time in reading, when not actually with Teresa. But at last on the fifteenth we weighed, several ships' boats from the visiting American fleet assisting us from the harbour, and although it took us five days even to reach Leghorn, twenty miles away, we were finally launched upon my greatest adventure.

And what did I feel, as we sailed so slowly past the coast I had come to know so well, the coast where Shelley had been washed ashore, the coast on which my own weeping darling was watching us fade into the distance? The coast to which I would return no more? I had the strangest premonition. And yet, not so strange, for should I return to Italy, it will be to Ravenna to regain my darling. Or, as is more likely, should I rise to triumph in Grecian circles, then I shall send for her to come to me. Tuscany and Genoa have no very happy memories, on due reflection.

And did I not fear the future? I have never truly done that. I do not do so now, when things are very much worse. Then I was full of optimism, full of certainty that I had but to dare to do. And if I feel less confident now, from time to time, it is undoubtedly entirely because of this dreadful tertian which persists in dogging my footsteps. I will be well again when the rains cease. Summer was ever my best time. And then, once again, I have but to *dare*, as I have always done, and I shall succeed. Depend upon it.

My spirits improved enormously once we were actually underway, even if at every port where we stopped there was a perfect army of Greeks, all claiming to have the ear of Mavrocordato, (v) or the mysterious Odysseus (vi) in the Morea, all anxious to receive money on behalf of their supposed patrons, and all equally anxious to receive a token of my esteem for themselves. They all had to be gently but firmly turned away, but there could be no doubt that everyone in Greece, and that included the Turks, knew that I was on my way. I felt almost like a Messiah.

Our party consisted, apart from myself, of Trelawny, Pietro, a Dr Bruno, as I felt the need of a personal physician, and Constantine Skilitzy, (vii) to whom I had promised a passage back to his homeland. In addition there were our servants, including Willie and Tita, five horses, four of mine and one belonging to Trelawny, and two dogs, my old bulldog Moretto, and a magnificent, and enormous, New-foundland by name of Lyon, who had been given to me earlier that year by Edward Le Mesurier. (viii) So it will be seen that we were equipped for every eventuality.

I would not have it supposed that I rushed into this adventure with the blind passion of an inexperienced youth. Serve with and for the Greeks I was determined to do, and it was equally obvious that depending upon news in Italy, and delivered by whoever happened to arrive there, with whichever interest he happened to support, was no way to wage a successful campaign. But my intention was to approach the whole business very carefully, and to this end we made for Cephalonia in the Ionian islands, these having been granted a British protectorate instead of a French one by the terms of the Treaty of Vienna.

Here we were sure of a welcome, and indeed we found the resident, Charles Napier, the very soul of helpful sympathy. (ix) In his support of the Greek cause he even managed to embarrass his employers, our pusillanimous government as usual choosing to sit on the fence until it was too late.

It was actually on the night of 2 August, last year, that we made the port of Argostoli, and received a royal welcome. And immediately became even more aware of the difficulties facing us, for Blaquiere had not waited for our arrival, but had departed no one knew where, various representatives of various chieftains were waiting to see me on behalf of their leaders, and the island was swarming with refugees from the mainland, for the most part Suliotes, those wild mountain men whom I remembered so splendidly from the past. These at the least I was glad to see, and I immediately enrolled sixty odd of them into a personal bodyguard, a service they seemed more than happy to perform. Of course even then I recognised that their lack of discipline might eventually prove a hazard, but I supposed – ever the optimist – that during our wait I would be able to beat them into some sort of military routine. That they were splendid fighting men could not be doubted for a moment.

And the wait was clearly going to be a long one. I despatched messengers in search of Mavrocordato and anyone else we could think of, informing them that I was actually within sight of their shores and desired only to be informed where I was likely to do the most good. Then I could sit back and explore these ancient places, Ithaca where Odysseus – the real Odysseus – had held sway, and all the other ancient ruins. But it was during this enforced waiting period that I suffered a most painful, in every sense, experience.

It actually happened following our visit to Ithaca, which lies only a few miles distant from Cephalonia. We crossed in an open boat, and explored the island, afterwards being well entertained, in particular with lashings of Ithacan wine, in which I imbibed perhaps a trifle too freely. That evening I was aware of a terrible headache, and try as I might, even in the dead of night, I could not cool my body or my mind. The result was that next morning – as we were not due to return to Cephalonia until afternoon – I spent swimming, despite the heat of the sun. I know now this was very careless of me; it seems that since my immersion during Shelley's cremation I can no longer stand the combination of salt water and semi-tropical sunshine. Another sign of age, I suppose.

In any event, I remember the journey back to the larger island as if it were a dream, and after landing my mind goes quite blank as to what happened, until I awoke the following morning to find myself sleeping on the floor. I can only repeat what I was told by my friends, that upon us reaching the monastery where we were staying, I insulted the monks who greeted us, shouting and screaming, in the main that my brain was on fire, and refusing all attempts to comfort me, eventually going so far as to barricade myself in my room while apparently I raved like a madman. Eventually I had to be assaulted as if I were indeed a dangerous lunatic, and put to bed with drugs and soporifics, and at last collapsed upon the litter bed in the corner, leaving Hamilton Browne to sleep in my own more comfortable one.(x)

I could do nothing more than apologise to the good ecclesiastics, and take my leave, a prey to the most serious considerations. I could not doubt that I had behaved very badly, nor that I had had some sort of fit. But why? The Ithacan wine? The effects of the sun and the sea? Or was I becoming a victim of some dread and unknown disease, which might have been lurking in my system ever since birth? I felt no ill effects, to be sure, other than extreme weariness, but alas, have recently suffered another such attack, which left me feeling even more debilitated. I confess that I sometimes frighten myself.

Meanwhile the dreary waiting business went on, and soon enough the lease of the *Hercules* ran out and she was forced to depart for other tasks, forcing me in turn to take up permanent residence ashore. But this was welcome enough after the cramped weeks on shipboard, and I found myself a very pleasant villa at Metaxata, where I passed the time in writing, and receiving letters – not all of them pleasant, to be sure, as it was now that I learned for the first time of Ada's illness – and in disputing with the local Methodist minister, a man called Kennedy, regarding the various uses and abuses of religion. Some of these debates were fairly public, to the amusement of all, myself included, but *excluding* the pious parson. He was a good fellow, but so confoundedly serious that he was very easy to take advantage of. He even wished to dispute, quite honestly, as to Juan's religion.

But not all of my companions, alas, were so patient as I. Trelawny in particular was his usual bounding ball of activity, reproached me bitterly for sitting on my backside when I could be up and doing, and finally took himself and Browne off to the Morea in search of action. Although I have no doubt that his real reason was the approach of the best season for shooting. Indeed his later letters confirmed this. But these impetuous friends were soon replaced by others, for it was now that Leicester Stanhope appeared. I would have preferred the return of Trelawny. For here was another of those confoundedly serious-minded fellows who can never see a bush for carefully counting the blades of grass beneath. My only relief was provided by the discovery of a true *friend*, in the person of a lad, Lukas Chalandritsanos, a fugitive from the mainland, together with his mother and two sisters, all of whom I was happy to assist. But Lukas was someone apart. Although only fifteen he had seen his share of fighting with the famous Colocotronis,(xi) and had killed his Turk. He was in addition one of those splendidly *pretty* boys – he reminded me of dear forgotten Nikky – and he desired only to serve. Did I, in his company, regain the fiery impulses of my youth? Have I? Well, perhaps from time to time I vouchsafe him a warm embrace. And perhaps I hope, and feel, and even know, that in the course of time he may become as precious to me as Nikky ever was, but for the moment, why I am engaged in fighting a war, and fighting disease, and I have little time or desire for love-making.

For even my patience eventually wore thin. By last December it was clear that I had obtained all the information I was going to, I had received the wildest promises of support and acclaim from the various Greek leaders, and even from other western adventurers like myself, notably a fellow called Hastings, who dreams of creating a fleet to match the Turks, (xii) financed by my cash, of course, and I had finally even received a *carte blanche* from the Greek Committee in London to go where I saw fit and to do as I thought best. Thus I determined to launch myself into the struggle itself. But the Morea, with its comparative tranquillity, if we except the internecine squabbling of the chieftains, was not for me. I determined upon Missolonghi, the centre of that resistance which had broken the Turkish advance, and a place sadly lacking a leader since the death of Bozzaris.

Which is not to say that transferring myself from Cephalonia to the mainland was a simple matter of decision. The channels between were heavily patrolled by Turkish vessels, and although Mavrocordato wrote that he was sending two Greek warships to escort me, I had had such promises before and elected not to wait for their dubious arrival. I therefore hired two vessels, a light, fast little boat called a *mistico*, in which I proposed to travel myself, and a larger bombard for the horses and our heavy gear. These ships were actually made ready in twelve hours, and on 29 December we put to sea. Pietro took command of the bombard's expedition, while I took with me Bruno and Willie, Lyon and Lukas. Lega, Tita, a Negro serving lad left behind by Trelawny, and the rest of the servants, went with Pietro.

I declare that actually setting forth for Greece was probably the most *inspiring* moment of my life. The air was crisp and cool, visibility was so sharp we could make out the distant shores perfectly clearly without the aid of a glass, the sea was calm, although heavy cloud to the north warned us that this fortunate state of affairs might not last, and above all, after the delay and the dishonesty with which I had been surrounded, I was on my way, to glory or to the grave. I burst into song as we rowed out to my little craft, quite amazing those English residents who came to bid us farewell, as they had seen very little of me except gloom over the preceding weeks.

We did not head immediately for the Gulf of Patras, whence our destination lay, but instead made south for Zante, both to throw any lurking Turk off the scent and also to obtain additional credits from my agent, Hancock. Once armed with an extra eight thousand dollars, which brought my total reserves, in cash and credits, up to near fifty thousand, enough to, just for example, maintain a force of some fifteen hundred Suliotes armed and ready for upwards of a year, we set off again at six of the evening, with a fair wind astern, and every expectation of entering the Gulf in the small hours and making our harbour safely by daybreak. Pietro and the bombard kept us company for a while, and we were all in the very best of spirits, our sailors singing, and ourselves hallooing from boat to boat and firing our pistols as darkness fell. But as the evening drew on my faster *mistico* gathered speed, and by midnight we were alone on the waters. It was the last day of 1823. We looked forward to meeting again on the first day of 1824, in Missolonghi.

Life is not that simple. We sailed on through the darkness, our captain sure in the direction indicated by his compass, when suddenly, it would have been about two in the morning, a large vessel appeared out of the gloom dead ahead.

"Mavrocordato's warship," I cried. "Oh, happy omen."

"It is a Turk, milord," the captain rejoined. "I beg you to keep your voice down."

Well, I was about to call him a pessimistic dog, when there came a hail across the water. "What ship is that?" and the words were Turkish.

I must say our captain promptly revealed a most welcome amount of nerve and decision. "Harden those sheets," he said, without ever raising his voice above a whisper, at the same time putting down the helm so that we turned away from our enemy. "Pray, milord," he suggested. "If your dog should bark. . . ."

I stroked Lyon's ears, and he settled his great head on my lap. Once again the hail came across the water, but by now the Turk was almost lost to sight, and we knew we were safe.

For the moment. Soon the wind freshened, and we bounded along, but with the increasing waves our captain, so brave a few minutes before, was reluctant to venture amongst the shoals off the coast, and so reduced sail to await dawn, which came at half past six, when a most discouraging sight met our eyes. Far astern of us a large Turkish vessel, no doubt our friend of the previous night, was in full sail

391

behind the bombard. Worse, from our point of view, there were no Greek ships to be seen in the Gulf, save a lone fisherman, and he was desperately signalling us to keep away, for behind him, and patrolling the gulf itself, was another Turkish warship.

Once again we turned away from danger, and made our way into a little creek, where I landed Lukas and another Greek lad, as they would certainly be in the greatest danger should we be captured – my papers indicated I was merely sailing from one Ionian island to another – gave them a letter for Stanhope, and told them to make their way across country to the safety of the town. We ourselves put to sea again, the Turk in hot pursuit. But he could not match our shallow draft, and we dodged from creek to creek until at last, exhausted but exhilarated, we came safe to the little harbour of Dragomestre, where we were protected by a couple of cannon. I was on Greek soil at last.

It was another couple of days before I actually reached Missolonghi itself, as the Turkish men-of-war were still out, and I was reluctant to abandon the *mistico*, with its precious cargo of dollars, and go overland. But eventually Mavrocordato sent a couple of gunboats down to help, and we reached the town. To find the bombard also arrived, but after even more hair-raising adventures. For the Turk had actually caught them, and summoned Pietro and the captain on board. With death by hanging apparently imminent, Pietro had dropped his incriminating papers overboard, including my journal. Well, I have never been very fortunate with journals.

But it so happened that when they were taken before the Turkish captain, he recognised Pietro's companion as the man who had saved him from drowning some years earlier – now, would any fiction writer dare create such a remarkable coincidence? – and instead of hanging them he merely made them accompany him into Patras, where Pietro managed to convince the authorities that they were innocent of any desire to help the Greeks, and they were released.

Thus for our simple overnight voyage. It was but a foretaste of the difficulties and delays I have experienced ever since coming here. For what did I find? The town as miserable and damp as I remembered it, added to which it has scarce stopped raining for a day since my arrival. The Greeks in a state of total demoralisation from long inactivity and lack of support; the Suliotes about to mutiny for lack of pay; the defences crumbling; the leaders divided, as usual; the small band of Europeans, and our foreign legion consisted of men from almost every country, the largest contingent being German, near desperate with frustration.

But against this must be set the almost hysterical welcome I received. I might have been accompanied by ten thousand British grenadiers, an artillery regiment, and escorted by half a dozen ships of the line. The entire town turned out to cheer me and attempt to touch me, the garrison fired off a twenty-one gun salute, such as only a ruling prince might expect, and truly for a brief moment I knew the soaring exhilaration that Napoleon must have become so familiar with.

For a brief while. Then the sterner realities of the situation removed any suggestion of euphoria. Well, I set to work immediately, and have accomplished a great deal. The Suliotes were re-enrolled under my banner, with guarantees of pay. I set men, and women, to working on rebuilding our defences. I opted for an early assault on the Turks in Lepanto or Prevesa. And immediately encountered opposition. These places were strongly defended, and we had no field artillery. It became necessary to wait, how these people do love to wait, on the arrival of a promised rocket company from England.

On the credit side of the situation, I liked Mavrocordato enormously, and discovered in him one of the very few Greeks I could trust, nor have I found any reason to change my mind. And then, of course, soon after my arrival news came that Rochdale had finally been sold, for £11,000. Imagine. Twenty-six years ago Mama and I had set out from Aberdeen in search of my fortune, with the gold of Rochdale and its immensely rich coal deposits beckoning like a beacon. Worth a hundred thousand, Hanson had said in his airy way. And now it had fetched a mere eleven. And when I no longer needed a penny of it, for my personal fortune. I immediately requested it made available for the Greeks.

But my own portion was one of unending labour. It is apparently necessary to lead the Greeks by example. Certain it is they are not to be merely commanded. I declare no Negro slave has ever worked as hard as I these past weeks. Yet I found time to take my daily ride, and even to advance Juan's adventures a stage further, in company with his sweet Adeline.(xiii) But the weather has been unfailingly bad, and I early began to feel – following repeated soakings by the rain – the onset of the tertian which is now beleaguering me. I swear that even my optimism began to suffer, and I was preparing to sink into a slough of despond, when I was restored by the arrival of Parry.

* * *

For a man exposed for some weeks to the conversation of the sanc-timonious Stanhope, Parry was like a breath of fresh air. Here is no gentleman, to be sure. But here is a practical soldier, who has been able to point out the most of our mistakes, even those of mine, and who has the incisive mind that is able to slice through a problem and expose the core.

Alas, welcome as he has been, he brought with him no artillery train, merely the wherewithal and the knowledge to make a rocket battery, and this he undertook immediately. I was not for waiting any longer, however. The Suliotes, to the number of some three thousand men, assured me that they would follow me to the gates of Constan-tinople, if I commanded them, and I certainly intended to lead them against the walls of Lepanto, for our spies informed us that the garrison there was in a very bad state, and ready to surrender at the first blast of our trumpets.

So our plans were put into action; I rode forth to lead my barbaric horde – and discovered not three thousand, but a bare three hundred, and so was forced to return to my house in some dejection. But this incident is only typical of the war as a whole, and I have come to realise that much as I would like to startle my friends out of their lethargy by some bold act, it is necessary to disperse that lethargy first, and *then* proceed with boldness. To this end I have despatched messengers to Trelawny and his friends in the Morea, asking them to meet me for a conference, whence I shall attempt to unite our forces, and hopefully with the support of Parry's battery, begin our long delayed assault on the Turks. But for the time being I must wait, on word from Trelawny, on Parry's progress, on some abatement of this intermin-able rain, and on an improvement in my own health.

For I must confess that I am beginning to become a little worried, and, dare I confess it even to my Memoirs, a little frightened. I have had another fit, such as afflicted me on my return from Ithaca. Once again my mind blacked out, and once again my friends, and these are a different set of friends, who knew nothing of my earlier seizure, tell me that I was all but unmanageable during its course.

To be sure I was granted sufficient cause, as it arose from the most serious crisis I have had to face since arriving in this misbegotten spot. It was on 17 February, I think, that a Turkish vessel ran aground at the entrance of the narrow channel through the lagoons which lead up to the town. Instantly all was excitement as we prepared to launch an attack upon the stranded ship. I was not allowed to go, by Bruno, as I was running a temperature – in consequence of a soaking I had received a day or two earlier while exercising my Suliotes – and indeed the assault, in my absence, did not turn out as well as we had hoped, as before the guns and stores could be taken off the Turk, three more men-of-war appeared, and Parry was forced to set fire to his prize. Yet it was a triumph, and left everybody in a highly excitable state.

Now, as may have been gathered, the forces in the town were divided into three definite sections. The Suliotes, who swaggered about the place armed to the teeth and talking of all the great deeds they had done, which was not altogether a lie, as many of them had served with Bozzaris, and were going to do, which was a less likely prospect; the Greeks, who were terrified of their wild guests; and the Europeans, to whom I had given most of the positions of responsibility, and who regarded Greek and Suliote alike with contempt.

Thus it was that on the night following the destruction of the Turkish brig one of the Suliotes, named Yiotes, and a famous man who had been at Bozzaris's side when the hero had been killed, determined to take Bozzaris's little son to look at the rocket battery, growing behind the walls of the Arsenal. The German sentry very properly refused him admission, whereupon Yiotes and he came to blows, a scuffle which was interrupted by the arrival of the officer of the day, Lieutenant Sass, a Swede. The quarrel immediately spread to these two, and Sass was unwise enough to draw his sword. Instantly Yiotes also reached for his weapons, which consisted of a dagger and a pistol. In the ensuing fight, while Yiotes was wounded, he managed not only to almost sever Sass's arm, but also shot him through the head. Yiotes made his escape, Sass was taken upstairs, but died almost immediately.

At this time I was lying in bed absolutely wracked with fever. I could scarce hold a cup, so much was my hand shaking. And now suddenly the entire town was called to arms, and people came rushing into my room, shouting that the Suliotes were out in all their thousands, screaming death to all Europeans, and determined to sack the town.

"We are lost," Parry cried, even he beginning to lose his head. "They will not be restrained."

"Help me up," I said.

"You cannot leave your bed, milord," Bruno protested.

"I must and I can," I declared, forcing myself up. "Help me dress."

They assisted me, and a few minutes later I was able to stagger down the stairs and into a crowd of frightened Europeans, while beyond the gates to my house there was a most tremendous hubbub.

"Be quiet," I shouted. "Only determination will stop this becoming a riot. Mr Parry, you'll have those cannon dragged over here and point them at the gate. Gentlemen, you'll prime your weapons and take your places here, behind the cannon. Now, Pietro, when I give the word, throw open the gate."

"You'll not go out to them, Byron."

"I must. It is the only way." I walked forward, as stiffly as I could in my weakened condition, adjusted my sword and my pistols, straightened my helmet, and nodded to Pietro. He pulled the bolt, and I stepped into the street, to face several hundred howling Albanians. But at the sight of me they somewhat quietened their shouting.

"What do you here?" I demanded.

"Vengeance," they called. "Vengeance."

"Against whom? Yiotes has not been killed. It is my man who has been killed. Suppose I demand vengeance against you?"

That quietened them even more, and I took the opportunity to step aside and show them at once the cannon, and the waiting gunners, and my people drawn up behind, armed and ready.

"You seek to assault me?" I shouted. "Your benefactor? The man who will lead you to victory over the Turk? By God, I will have discipline or I will have death. Make one move forward, nay, continue to stand there but a moment longer, and I will command my men to fire into you."

A risky moment. Parry later considered I should have given them a few minutes to disperse. But my blood was up, and in my feverish state I truly cared not whether I lived or died. And my fervour carried the day. Within a minute they were drifting off, back to their billets, and the crisis was over.

That crisis. My own came later that night. I had triumphed over human obstacles. I had proved my qualities to lead this motley band, to bend them to my will. And I could not control my own weaknesses. Twice in six months. Will it happen again? And when? In the midst of battle? In the midst of an important conference?

Perhaps when I am about to be crowned king of this nation? There is a dreadful thought.

Great news. Since I wrote the above, things have taken a definite turn for the better. Letters have arrived. From Trelawny, saying that the

Morean chieftains are willing to meet me at Salona. From Hobby, informing me that I have become quite a hero in England. There is a turn up for the book. I wonder what Belle makes of it all? And another informing me that the Turks have set a price on my head, and will surely execute me if they can catch me. But they will have a merry chase, I can promise you. Once again my patience, and my determination, is bringing me through all the perils that beset me. English support is building. Hobby is talking of coming out himself. And once I meet this Odysseus, depend upon it I shall make him follow me as eagerly as Mavrocordato. Besides, summer is coming. In summer all things are possible.

In summer I shall be rid of this fever. It was ever so, and so it shall be again.

EPILOGUE

Byron's fever grew worse. For a good deal of March and April he was not entirely sane, although he certainly had his lucid moments, as his letter to Augusta shows. But by 15 April he knew he was dying, and his friends, led by Parry, began to make plans to get him away from the fever-laden swamps of Missolonghi and back to Zante. It was too late. At six o'clock on the evening of 18 April, after spending much of the day in rambling delirium, he said, very quietly, "I want to sleep now," and closed his eyes. Almost exactly twenty-four hours later, he died, without again speaking or opening his eyes.

An autopsy was performed, but no satisfactory cause of death was ever established. That it was mainly malaria seems certain; fits are indeed a malarial symptom. The body was sent home to England, but was refused burial in Westminster Abbey, and was eventually interred in the family vault at Hucknall, his coffin being laid, as no doubt he would have wished, on top of that containing the Wicked Lord.

On 17 May, in the parlour of Murray's house, which was also his publishing house, and in the presence of Murray himself, Hobhouse, Moore, Wilmot Horton, representing Augusta Leigh, and Colonel Doyle, representing Lady Byron, the fair copy of the first two parts of these Memoirs was burned. Moore alone dissented.

On 9 May 1832, Turkey recognised the independence of Greece.

Willie Fletcher, faithful to the end, accompanied his master's body on its last journey back to England. He was given an annuity by Hobhouse, but later fell on hard times through attempting to partner Lega Zambelli in an unsuccessful macaroni factory.

Lady Byron (Belle) was to die in 1860 at the age of 68. She became increasingly interested in religion as she grew older, and increasingly aghast at the experiences she had undergone during her brief marriage.

Ada Byron was married on 8 July 1835, to William, 8th Lord King, who was later created Earl of Lovelace. She died of cancer, on 27 November 1852, aged only thirty-six, the same as her father.

Caroline Lamb's mind broke altogether soon after Byron's death, and she lived the last few years of her life in seclusion at Brocket. She died in March 1828.

Augusta Leigh lived until 12 October 1851, amidst ever increasing debts and family problems, but perhaps with *decreasing* guilt as to her immortal love affair.

Elizabeth Medora Leigh had a miserable existence, mainly through debt and love affairs, just like her father, until she died in 1849, at the age of thirty-five.

Teresa Guiccioli, following the death of her husband, eventually married, at the age of forty-five, the Marquis de Boissy, perhaps the richest man in France. She died in 1873, a memorable old lady, who to the very end enjoyed recalling her few years with her adorable Byron.

FOOTNOTES

THE LETTER

i   Guss was Byron's nickname for his sister, the Hon. Augusta Leigh.
ii Bleeding was the only remedy Byron's doctors in Greece could suggest for his malaria. It was probably the worst of all treatments.
iii James Hunt, brother of Byron's one-time literary colleague Leigh Hunt, replaced the House of Murray as Byron's publisher soon before the start of the Grecian adventure.
iv Augusta and Teresa did in fact meet, eight years after Byron's death, when Teresa visited England in 1832.
v   Byron's pet name for Percy Shelley.
vi Colonel Leicester Stanhope was a representative of the Greek Committee who was in Missolonghi when Byron died. He did not approve of Byron's immorality.
vii William Parry was an artillery expert sent to Missolonghi to form a battery for Byron's use.
viii Edward John Trelawny was an adventurer who attached himself to Byron's star.
ix Count Pietro Gamba was a younger brother of Byron's mistress, Teresa Guiccioli.
x   It was Byron's intention that his sister should be provided for out of his estate, but this was largely defeated by the machinations of Lady Bryon.
xi The Pharaohs made a habit of marrying their sisters.
xii This was Byron's symbol for a kiss whenever he wrote to Augusta.

BOOK THE FIRST
CHAPTER 1

i   Captain Jack Byron died, actually in Chantilly, on 2 August 1791.
ii The Norman ancestors of Lord Byron spelled their name de Burun.
iii William, 5th Lord Byron, known as the "Wicked Lord".
iv John Byron, known as Foulweather Jack, from the number of storms at sea he encountered during his career in the Navy.

v   Amelia, Baroness Conyers, who was the wife of the Marquess of Carmarthen, later 5th Duke of Leeds.

vi   This was Sir William Gordon, third son of George, Earl of Huntley by his second wife Princess Annabella Stuart, daughter of James I of Scotland.

vii   One Gordon ancestor forced a King's messenger to eat his own letter.

viii   These words were written probably in 1818, two years after Byron separated from his wife in circumstances of extreme bitterness.

ix   Richard Brinsley Sheridan, the leading orator of his day.

x   Admiral Lord Nelson.

xi   Byron was a confirmed and vehement Whig.

xii   Gentleman John Jackson, champion boxer of England from 1797 to 1803, when he retired undefeated.

xiii   Byron had not yet met Teresa Guiccioli, whose hair was also red, and who brought him greater happiness than anyone save Augusta.

CHAPTER 2

i   Not long after this portion of the Memoir was written, Byron finally broke with Hanson, and entrusted his affairs to his friend Douglas Kinnaird.

ii   Zeluco was an anti-hero, whose father had also died while he was a boy, and who was compelled to behave outrageously by forces beyond his control.

iii   Frances Byron, eldest sister of Mad Jack, married General Charles Leigh and was the mother of that George Leigh who was to marry his cousin, Augusta. She lived, as Byron has related, in Chantilly with her brother for some time after he had fled his wife, and the evidence of Mad Jack's letters to her after she had returned to England strongly suggest an incestuous relationship, a possibility which seems to have occurred to Byron, although he could not possibly have read the letters.

iv   George Leigh, referred to in the previous note, was to become a hussar officer and, for a while, a favourite of the Prince Regent. He was a compulsive gambler, and lived from one debt to the next.

v   Juliana Elizabeth Byron, the cousin with whom William Byron, son of the Wicked Lord, eloped and was as a result disinherited. Her second husband was Sir Robert Wilmot. We can only surmise her feelings on meeting the boy who had become the 6th Lord, for had her first husband not quarrelled with his father, or had her son, the William Byron killed in Corsica, lived, *she* would have been the dominant figure in the family.

vi   Robert John Wilmot, Juliana's son by her second marriage, who was born in 1784.

vii   Augusta Barbara Charlotte Byron, younger sister to Mad Jack, Frances and Juliana, who married Vice Admiral Christopher Parker.

viii   Sir Peter Parker, killed in action in 1814.

ix   Margaret Parker, the beautiful cousin to whom Byron wrote his first verses, and who was to die at a tragically early age after a fall from a horse.

x   Sophia Byron, youngest of all Mad Jack's sisters, who never married.

xi   George Anson Byron, born in 1789, the year after George Gordon, the son of Mad Jack's brother, also named George Anson, who had died in 1793. Cousin George was to succeed Byron as 7th Lord.

xii   Robert Charles Dallas, brother of Henrietta Dallas whom the first George Anson Byron had married. He had literary aspirations, and Byron was to see a lot of him in later years.

xiii   Julia Byron, George Anson's sister.

xiv   Augusta Mary Byron, Byron's half sister, daughter of Amelia Conyers.

xv   The duel had been caused by a disagreement over methods of curing game, and had indeed been irregular, in that the two antagonists had been locked in a darkened room, from which only William Byron emerged alive. He was actually tried for murder before the House of Lords, but escaped with a conviction for manslaughter.

xvi   William Pitt, then Prime Minister.

xvii   King George III.

xviii   At this point four pages of the manuscript are missing. These would appear to deal with Byron's years at Dr Glennie's school in Dulwich, the attempts of the London doctors to find a cure for his foot, and more important, his own account of his first meeting with the Earl of Carlisle. We have Hanson's evidence that Byron did not take to the nobleman who was to be his guardian. The missing pages also seem to cover his confiding to Hanson the truth of his relationship with May Gray, to the effect that the lawyer eventually persuaded Mrs Byron to send the girl back to Scotland.

xix   Edward Noel Long, later to become a close friend.

xx   Byron's memory is playing him false here, for it was in the summer of 1802, in his *second* year at Harrow, that Mrs Byron took him to Bath. He himself corrects the mistake without noticing it, in Chapter 3.

CHAPTER 3

i   See note in previous chapter.

ii   Elizabeth Pigot, one of Byron's most faithful female friends, although their relationship was entirely platonic. He actually met her for the first time the following year, as she lived in Southwell.

iii   Byron is a little unjust here, as there is extant a letter from Mealey to Hanson, written at this time, complaining that Byron gave a dinner party, at Mealey's house, for all of his servants, an occasion for which Mealey had to foot the bill.

iv   Mary Ann's name was Chaworth. Her mother had married a second time.

CHAPTER 4

i   Henry Angelo was the leading fencing master of the day who shared rooms with Jackson the prizefighter at 13 Bond Street.

ii   George John West, 5th Earl of Delawarr. He died in 1815.

iii Colonel Thomas Wildman, who was to purchase Newstead Abbey from Byron.

iv John Fitzgibbon, 2nd Earl of Clare (1792–1851). His father had been Lord Chancellor of Ireland (described alternately as the basest of men and the greatest of Irish patriots), and Clare had succeeded to the title the year before he went to Harrow.

v While Byron was at Dr Glennie's school in Dulwich, Mrs Byron had fallen in love with a French dancing master, and had even considered eloping with him. It is possible Byron refers to this unfortunate episode, which did nothing to raise his mother in his estimation, in the missing four pages from Chapter 2.

vi Byron later wrote a poem called *The Dream* which describes his emotions for Mary Ann Chaworth and for Annesley itself.

vii Zanga is a character in Young's tragedy, *The Revenge*, who speaks an oration over the body of his friend Alonso. The play was at this time running in London, and Byron had seen the great actor Kemble in the role.

viii The regular series of matches between Eton and Harrow which continues today did not commence until 1818.

ix The MCC remains the premier cricket club in the world, as Lord's Cricket Ground is still regarded as the headquarters of cricket.

x Byron's estimate of his own prowess in this match does not tally with the figures given in the records, which indicate that his scores were actually seven and two. It is possible that he refers to the number of runs added to the score, by *both* batsmen, while he was at the wickets.

xi Members of the nobility wore distinctive gowns at the universities, much more elaborate and made from richer materials than the commoners.

xii The cost involved in Byron's first visit to a brothel suggests that it was a very good establishment.

xiii Thyrza was the wife of Cain, in Gessner's *Abel* which Byron read as a boy.

CHAPTER 5

i Charles Skinner Matthews. His tragic and ghastly death a few years later made a deep impression on Byron. See Chapter 10.

ii John Cam Hobhouse (Cam was his mother's maiden name) (1786–1869), later Baron Broughton, was Byron's closest friend, despite the complete antithesis of their characters, and despite Byron's frequent irritation with his friend's moralising.

iii Douglas William James Kinnaird (1788–1830) was the fifth son of the 7th Baron Kinnaird. He remained a close and faithful friend of Byron's and took over the management of his affairs when finally Byron and Hanson parted company. This did not take place until after the events recalled in the first two books of this work, but Byron's finances immediately improved and he became a wealthy man.

iv Edward Law, Earl of Ellenborough (1790–1871), later Governor-General of India, was to have every bit as disastrous a marriage as Byron himself. His second wife was Jane Digby, the most beautiful and the most notorious woman of her time. He divorced her after she had run away with Prince Schwartzenberg, and she worked her way eastward, and through a succession of lovers, before finally marrying a Syrian sheikh.

v William George Spencer Cavendish, 6th Duke of Devonshire (1790–1858), a man of great literary tastes whose library was to become one of the finest in England.

vi The Treaty of Tilsit, between Napoleon and Alexander I of Russia, was signed on a raft in the middle of the River Niemen in June 1807.

vii Cornelian is a species of chalcedony which has a peculiar reddish tint.

viii The printer's name was John Ridge.

ix Some of the lines were particularly scathing in their reference to the Earl of Carlisle, Byron's guardian.

x Joseph Manton owned London's leading shooting gallery.

CHAPTER 6

i William Gifford (1756–1826) was a poet whose attacks upon some of his contemporaries were even more violent than Byron's. He was also a Tory, but Byron remained an admirer of his work throughout his life, perhaps because a few years later he recommended *Childe Harold* to Murray.

ii Thomas Campbell (1777–1844) was a very popular poet of his time. Byron admired him for holding a point of view similar to his own; he also attempted to emulate Pope, and wrote verses to "Caroline".

iii Robert Southey (1774–1843) had not yet become Poet Laureate, but Byron bore a lifelong antipathy to him, which is surprising because in their youthful lives they were very similar, Southey having been expelled from Westminster School and having undertaken a journey to Portugal which inspired some of his best work.

iv William Wordsworth (1770–1850) had, after a liberal youth, become an opponent of all liberal thought, sufficient to earn the dislike of Byron.

v Thomas Moore (1779–1852), poet, and Admiralty Registrar in Bermuda, a post he administered by proxy. He was for a while, following the publication of *Childe Harold*, a close friend of Byron's.

vi Sir Walter Scott (1771–1832) had just achieved critical fame with the publication of *Marmion*, although his great years still lay in the future. He was always an admirer of Byron's poetry, and the two men became good friends a few years later.

vii In 1817 Byron's greatest work, *Don Juan*, was still to be written.

viii Tom Cribb (1781–1848) had defeated Jem Belcher for the boxing championship of England in 1807. He was not to retire until 1821.

ix Arius (d. AD 336) was a Greek ecclesiastic at Alexandria who taught that Christ was a separate and inferior deity to God (Arianism), a belief which at one time enjoyed wide support. According to Gibbon his bowels burst open while he was seated on a privy.

x Rochdale was not actually sold, for just over £11,000, until just before Byron's death.

   xi   Hewson Clarke (1787–1832), miscellaneous writer, editor of the *Scourge*.

  xii   Byron is here referring to the Earl of Carlisle.

 xiii   John Scott, 1st Earl of Eldon (1751–1838), Lord Chancellor almost continuously from 1801 to 1827. He was the son of a coal merchant, which would not have endeared him to the always class-conscious Byron.

 xiv   *Tom Thumb* was at this time playing in London.

  xv   Charles John, 9th Lord Falkland.

 xvi   Christina, Lady Falkland.

xvii   Byron is as usual being less than just to his mother. Amazingly, despite her knowledge of his extravagance and of his insolvency, she *was* prepared to allow him the use of her money, only supposing she could guarantee for herself a sufficient income on which to live.

xviii   The Reverend Francis Hodgson (1781–1852), later Provost of Eton.

 xix   James Wedderburn Webster, who periodically appears in Byron's narrative.

  xx   King Henry VIII.

 xxi   Scrope Berdmore Davies (1783–1852), a highly unlikely Fellow of King's College, Cambridge, was, as Byron indicates, one of London's leading gamblers and dandies. He became a close friend of Byron's and it was due to his dilatoriness in delivering proofs to the printer that the other recent discovery of Byronic material was made.

xxii   Robert Rushton, with whom there is some evidence that Byron had a homosexual affair, although he does not refer to it here. Certainly he took great care of the boy for the rest of his life.

CHAPTER 7

   i   A previous William Kidd (1645–1701) had been England's best-known pirate.

  ii   William Beckford (1760–1844), extremely wealthy man of letters whose Gothic novel *Vathek* had been published in 1782. He had been forced to leave England following homosexual accusations.

 iii   John William Ward, 1st Earl of Dudley (1781–1833), who later boasted that he had robbed Byron over the sale of these saddles.

 iv   John Hookham Frere (1769–1846), English diplomat, who later was one of the founders of the *Quarterly Review*.

  v   Maria Agustin, the girl who had inspired the Spanish under Palafox to defend Saragossa successfully against an overwhelming French army, in the previous year. Byron included her exploits in *Childe Harold*. Saragossa was to capitulate, after another siege, in this same year of 1809.

 vi   Puerta Santa Maria.

vii   In modern bullfights the horses are protected by heavy blankets made of matting, which saves *them* from the worst horrors of the sport.

viii   Richard Colley, 1st Marquis Wellesley (1760–1842), elder brother of the Duke of Wellington.

 ix   Byron is here referring to the Battle of Talavera, fought on 28 July 1809 between the French armies of Marshal Victor and King Joseph Bonaparte, and an Anglo-Spanish army commanded by Sir Arthur Wellesley, later Duke of

Wellington, and General Garcia de la Cuesta. The battle was tactically a draw, but strategically an allied victory, as the French retreated. Cuesta became a national hero, but he was so incensed at Wellesley's refusal to pursue that he withdrew the Spanish contingent from the army.

x   Sir Alexander John Ball (1757–1809) was, as Byron states, one of Nelson's favourite captains. His apparent failure in hospitality must have been at least partly due to his fading health, as he died in this same year. It is recorded that he was adored by the Maltese he governed.

xi   Ali Pasha (1741–1822), known as the Lion of Jannina, a Turkish governor who had made himself virtually independent. He was to be assassinated by order of the Sultan.

xii   Thomas Bruce, 7th Earl of Elgin and 11th Earl of Kinkardine, had arranged, while the British Ambassador to Turkey, for the removal of the best preserved of the Acropolis marbles to the British Museum, an act of vandalism hardly credible today. The work had commenced in 1803, and by the time of Byron's visit to Athems was very nearly completed.

CHAPTER 8

i   This was of course some considerable time before the researches of Schliemann. Jacob Bryant (1718–1804) was an antiquarian scholar who delighted in disproving all the legends of history, not excepting the Old Testament.

ii   Sir Stratford Canning (1786–1880), Viscount Stratford de Redcliffe, first cousin of George Canning, a noted Middle Eastern diplomat later to be known as "the Great Elchi". He was to become ambassador at Constantinople during the years preceding the Crimean War, and indeed it was his sympathy with the Turks which largely led to British involvement in the struggle.

iii   It is interesting to contrast Byron's innate patriotism, especially when his own standing is affected, with his often bitter comments against the Tory government which was conducting the war. In fact the Turkish attitude was hardly surprising. Their war with Britain had been ended only the year before, and during it, in 1807, a British fleet *had* forced the narrows, only to withdraw in consequence of suffering heavy casualties.

iv   Byron's pique on this occasion was regarded as poor form by the English colony in Constantinople, yet he was but anticipating the behaviour of the average English nobleman abroad during the great days of empire which were to commence soon after the end of the war with France.

v   A piastre, also known as a *ghurush*, was a Turkish coin representing 1/100th of a Turkish pound. The widow Macri was therefore asking two hundred Turkish pounds for her daughter. As a Turkish pound by no means equalled a pound sterling, this was probably about the same sum of money Byron had paid for Caroline Cameron, although of course in terms of today's money both amounts were considerably greater than their face value.

vi   The Marquis of Sligo, Lord Altamount, had been contemporary with Byron at Cambridge, and an occasional friend of his in London.

vii Byron actually means a monastery, but the word convent was then applied equally to houses for either sex.

CHAPTER 9

i *Gaiour* means, literally, child of a race whose women have no shame, i.e. they leave their faces uncovered.

ii This is the first full explanation of this strange episode ever published. That Byron did rescue a Turkish woman from being drowned for adultery was of course widely known and Lord Sligo later published an account of the affair which Byron agreed was near enough to the truth, but he himself was always, and for him strangely, reluctant to discuss it. That it rebounded against him, as he here confesses, is reason enough.

CHAPTER 10

i This was the story prevalent at the time, but is obviously as untrue as the suggestion that Mrs Byron drank herself to death. In view of the growing references to pain and ill health in her letters to her son, it is extremely probable that she died of some form of cancer.

ii There is no reason to disbelieve Byron's claim that extreme grief drove him to violent action. Compare his behaviour at Shelley's cremation, Book the Third, Chapter 6.

iii After Sir Arthur Wellesley had defeated the French at the Battle of Vimiero, 21 August 1808, he was replaced by a more senior officer, Sir Hew Dalrymple, who instead of taking advantage of the situation, concluded with Marshal Junot the Convention of Cintra, by the terms of which the French army was allowed to evacuate Portugal without hindrance.

iv This is the second time Byron has used this phrase. That he was afraid of being so described seems obvious.

v The unkind reviewer had not been Jeffreys at all, but actually Brougham.

vi Samuel Rogers (1763–1855) was a poet whom Byron had praised in *English Bards and Scotch Reviewers*.

vii At the time Byron was furious that Gifford had been allowed a pre-publication look at the *Pilgrimage*, being afraid that any praise might merely have been a response to his own praise of Gifford in *English Bards*. He was unaware that Gifford was a reader for Murray.

viii There had been a brief truce in 1802.

ix The frame breakers were named after Ned Lud, a half-wit who destroyed a frame in 1779.

x The 1st Earl of Harrowby, formerly Sir Dudley Ryder (1762–1847), at this time Lord President of the Council, a position he was to hold until 1827 when he refused the premiership.

xi In fact Byron's speech was instrumental in having the Bill returned to the Commons with amendments in favour of leniency. The Commons threw out the amendments and the Bill became law in its original brutal form.

xii   The home of Henry Richard Vassall Fox, 3rd Baron Holland (1773–1840), nephew of Charles James Fox, perhaps the leading Whig politician of the day.

xiii   Sarah Sophia Villiers (1785–1867), wife of the 5th Earl of Jersey and daughter of John Fane, 10th Earl of Westmoreland, was for many years London's leading hostess. Her word on dress and manners became almost law, and she once turned the Duke of Wellington away from a reception because he arrived a few minutes late.

xiv   Jane (née Saunders), second wife of the 10th Earl of Westmoreland (d. 1857). She was Lady Jersey's stepmother, although not greatly older.

CHAPTER 11

i   William Lamb, 2nd Viscount Melbourne (1779–1848), who was to be Queen Victoria's first Prime Minister, was fairly widely accepted as being the result of an affair between Lady Melbourne and Lord Egremont. His titular father never acknowledged him as his son.

ii   Caroline Lamb was twenty-seven when she met Byron.

iii   Now the Scottish Office.

iv   Caroline's son, George, was a valetudinarian, who was to die in his early twenties.

v   Lady Caroline Foster married William Lamb's younger brother George (who may have been the son of the Prince Regent). Her mother had been the 1st Viscount Melbourne's mistress. Such were the tangled moral webs of Regency England.

vi   This is the first of the bracketed passages which Byron undoubtedly deleted before giving the manuscript to Moore.

vii   Byron's history is at fault here. Napoleon did not actually cross the Niemen until June.

viii   Rogers is referring to William the Conqueror's stumble when he landed at Pevensey in 1066 to fight the Battle of Hastings.

ix   Anna Isabella Milbanke was the young woman who was to become Lady Byron.

CHAPTER 12

i   Annabella was twenty-one at this meeting.

ii   Sir Godfrey Webster had been Lady Holland's first husband.

iii   Lady Melbourne was actually sixty-three in 1812.

CHAPTER 13

i   Brocket Hall was the Melbourne country seat, in Hertfordshire.

ii   Edward Harley was the 5th Earl of Oxford, a direct descendant of Queen Anne's prime minister. The amours of his wife, Jane Elizabeth (née Scott) were the scandal of even Regency England. Byron was to be her last lover.

iii The Countess of Oxford was actually only just forty when she met Byron.

iv Lord Archibald Hamilton (1770–1827), younger son of the 9th Duke of Hamilton, was a leading proponent of parliamentary reform, and in 1809 had attempted to charge Lord Castlereagh with corruption.

v Margaret Mercer Elphinstone (1788–1867), Viscountess Keith, Baroness Nairn, and after her marriage, Comtesse de Flahault, was the only daughter of Admiral Keith, Viscount Elphinstone, and probably *was* the richest heiress in all England. She several times revealed her fondness for Byron, and almost certainly would have accepted him as a husband. *Had* they married his life would have been quite different, and he would have died a happy and hearty old man. But then, perhaps, he would never have written *Don Juan*, and probably be remembered only as a minor poet.

CHAPTER 14

i John Cartwright (1740–1824) was a Nottinghamshire man who was an old friend of Lady Oxford's sometime tutor, Horn Tooke, and a dedicated political reformer.

ii Charles Stanhope, 3rd Earl Stanhope (1753–1816) was known as Citizen Stanhope, from his determined support of the French Jacobins even after they had been discredited. He was indeed a most dangerous man, in a political sense, for Byron to agree with. He was the father of Lady Hester Stanhope, whom Byron had already met, but was no relation to the Colonel Leicester Stanhope who was to be with Byron in Missolonghi.

iii James Henry Leigh Hunt (1784–1859), essayist and poet. He was later to be associated with Byron in editing *The Liberal*.

iv In this fashion, Byron dismisses probably the most fateful year of his life. For what really brought about his marriage to Miss Milbanke, see Book the Second, Chapter 1.

BOOK THE SECOND
CHAPTER 1

i This is the chapter referred to in the introduction, which is so different in style to any of the others that it seems certain it was written not for publication, even at a later date, but for Byron's own pleasure. It covers the same period of time as the preceding chapter.

ii Anne Louise Germaine de Staël (née Necker), Baronne de Staël-Holstein (1766–1817) daughter of the Swiss banker, enemy of Napoleon, French authoress.

iii Lady Adelaide Forbes, the daughter of Sir Charles Forbes. As he was described as a "Tory of the Tories" he could hardly have welcomed the prospect of Byron as a son-in-law, although he *was* in favour of Catholic emancipation.

iv George Colman the Younger (1762–1836), dramatist, miscellaneous writer and poet, became one of Byron's closest friends during the misery of his marriage. Colman's erotic poem *Don Leon*, written shortly before his death, is supposed to be about Byron.

v Byron's affair with Frances Webster remains a mystery. He spent several weeks with the Websters this summer, but in a letter to Lady Melbourne he claims that he never did more than kiss her, although she appears to have thrown herself at him like most young women of his acquaintance. There is no reason to disbelieve Byron's version. He was startlingly frank about most of his amours – even regarding his own sister – in his correspondence with his beloved Lady M.

Fanny Webster was later to become notorious through an affair with the Duke of Wellington.

vi *The Corsair* was probably the most successful of all Byron's poems. Murray sold 10,000 copies in a single day.

vii The girl's name was Henrietta D'Ussières. She was only one of many young women, akin to the pop fans of today, who besieged Byron with letters and requests for assignations.

viii Remarkably, after his recent protestations about not being a hack, Byron accepted £700 from Murray for *Lara*, the first payment he had ever actually received. Understandably, he does not mention the fact.

ix George Eden, Earl of Auckland (1784–1849), later a Governor-General of India.

CHAPTER 2

i Edmund Kean (1787–1833), actor, became famous after acting Shylock at Drury Lane on 26 January 1814, and was soon recognised as the greatest tragedian of his day. Byron admired him and saw a lot of him during the following two years.

CHAPTER 3

i It is difficult to understand how Byron expected anyone reading a statement like this not to draw the obvious conclusion.

ii Throughout his life Byron believed that it was Mrs Clermont's evil counselling which drove his wife into such persistent enmity. In fact considerable evidence has been unearthed to suggest that the old nurse favoured a reconciliation.

CHAPTER 4

i It is interesting that Byron, now almost at the end of the narrative he was to present to Moore, and after all his earlier prevaricating, brings his relationship with Augusta into the open. It is also noteworthy that he is perfectly explicit about his sexual problems as regards his wife. It is possible that he meant to delete some of these passages, and did not, perhaps through carelessness, more likely because he was in one of his moods of almost maniacal defiance of convention and opinion. Whatever the reason, I would hazard a guess that it is the contents of these three chapters that led to the burning of the entire manuscript, for Augusta and sex apart, his picture of his marriage cannot be considered as particularly damning to Lady Byron. No doubt he is right in suggesting that an older and more experienced woman would have been better able to cope, but it was *his* moods – undoubtedly caused by circumstances Annabella was not prepared to understand, but present none the less – that she would have had to cope *with*.

ii Augusta was also certainly pregnant at this time (see Chapter 6).

iii *Cristabel* was a poem by Samuel Taylor Coleridge (1772–1834). Although the plagiarism was undoubtedly innocent, it must have been the more embarrassing to Byron, as he had recently assisted Coleridge in finding a publisher.

iv Sarah Siddons (1755–1831) née Kemble, the greatest tragic actress of her day.

v William Sotheby (1757–1833), author, to whom Byron had been generous in his *English Bards and Scotch Reviewers*.

vi Charles Robert Maturin (1780–1824), Irish novelist and dramatist, who was recommended to Byron by Scott.

CHAPTER 5

i Alexander Rae was an actor-manager employed by the Drury Lane Theatre.

ii It never seems to have occurred to Byron that his dieting with its accompanying purges, added to his drinking – the effects of which must have been increased when his stomach was empty – was the cause of his chronic indigestion.

iii *Justine* was the title of a novel by the Marquis de Sade. Unfortunately for Byron it is the story of a young woman who preserves her virginity at all costs, mainly because the endless list of men who assault her all prefer sodomy.

CHAPTER 6

i Lord George Gordon (1751–93), third son of the 3rd Duke of Gordon, leader of the so-called Gordon Riots against popery in 1780. No doubt he was related to the Gordons of Gight, but there are 157 branches of the House of Gordon, so he was a very distant cousin.

ii See Chapter 4.

iii These words were of course written in 1818, when Byron and Shelley had only a recent acquaintance.

iv This is an interesting misapprehension of the situation on Byron's part, for although Mary Shelley's love for Shelley cannot be doubted, many eminent authorities have come to the conclusion that she might have welcomed a liaison with Byron.

BOOK THE THIRD
CHAPTER 1

i   John William Polidori (1796–1821) was undoubtedly a man of talent and education. His father had been Alfieri's secretary, and he himself received his medical degree from Edinburgh University at the remarkable age of nineteen. His sister was to marry Gabriele Rossetti and become the mother of the three famous Rossettis. But he was, as Byron records, too arrogant, self opinionated, and quick tempered to be an easy companion, and in Switzerland he once challenged Shelley to a duel over an alleged slight. He had been offered £500 by Murray to keep a journal of Byron's travels, and this is a useful source book. He was also, although Byron does not here mention the fact, to borrow Byron's plot for a ghost story – after the Frankenstein evening – and write it himself. He eventually committed suicide.

ii   Beau Brummell had been forced to flee England with debts of over £50,000 and held the post of English consul in Calais until he died.

iii   Byron's complacency in assuming that Augusta would welcome his child by another woman is remarkable.

iv   These chapters were written late in 1823, when Byron was on the point of departing for mainland Greece.

v   Amongst the "literati" Byron met in Milan was Henri Beyle, who under the pen name of Stendhal was later to become as famous as Byron himself. But he does not appear to have made much of an impression.

CHAPTER 2

i   Contessa Isabella Teotochi d'Albrizzi (1770–1836), Italian writer whose house in Venice was a rendezvous for celebrities.

ii   He had suffered this misfortune while in Athens in 1811.

CHAPTER 3

i   Tita's real name was Giovanni Battista Falcieri, and he began his employment as Byron's gondolier.

ii   Cavaliere Angelo Mengaldo was a soldier of fortune who was Byron's friend for a brief period. He was equally proud of his swimming ability, and once challenged Byron to a race to the Lido. According to Byron, the Italian had to be pulled from the water when exhausted, while he made the journey in comparative comfort, whatever his dissipation.

iii   The Bora is a wind which arises in the Adriatic and can blow with considerable strength.

iv   Alexander Scott, a Scotsman, was another friend of Byron's at this time. It was he who introduced Byron to Mengaldo.

v   Dante lived in Ravenna for the last six years of his life, 1515–21.

vi   *Francesca da Rimini* was a tragedy set in Ravenna.

CHAPTER 4

i   Peruvian bark is nowadays known as quinine, which suggests that Teresa, like Byron himself, was suffering from malaria.

ii   The Romagna, in which Ravenna was situated, was part of the Papal State, unlike Venetia, which was an Austrian province; but the Pope was scarcely less reactionary than the Court of Vienna, and the two governments worked together to suppress Italian liberal thought.

CHAPTER 5

i   Harriette Wilson was Regency England's most famous courtesan, who, according to *her* memoirs, slept with all the leading men of her time, and kept herself in her old age by threatening to publish their names. It was in reply to one such letter from her that the Duke of Wellington answered, "Publish and be damned." However, Byron gives no indication that he was ever one of her clients, not does she so claim, although she certainly wrote him with some regularity.

ii   Elizabeth Cavendish (1758–1824), 5th Duchess of Devonshire. As the widow Elizabeth Foster she was a travelling companion to Georgina, Duchess of Devonshire, probably the most noted beauty of her day (she died in 1806, before Byron had had the opportunity to meet her) and on her death married the Duke. She lived in Italy for many years, and dominated Roman society. Byron's friend Ticknor described her as a female Maecenas. She had been Byron's landlady during his marriage.

iii   Edward Ellerker Williams (1793–1822), retired Indian army officer, who had become one of Shelley's circle at Pisa. He was to perish with his friend in the tragic sea accident. See Chapter 6.

iv   Thomas Medwin (1788–1869), English man of letters, best known as Shelley's biographer, although he did publish *The Conversations of Lord Byron*, the material for which he obtained at the Pisan dinner parties. He was Shelley's cousin.

v   George William Tighe, who had eloped with Lady Montcashel, and was living with her in Pisa.

vi   Edward John Trelawny (1792–1881), described in the DNB as "author and adventurer". He became a close associate of Byron's, both in Italy and later in Greece, although, according to his memoirs, he never liked the poet, and was for years a suitor for the hands of both Mary Shelley and Claire Clairmont.

vii   When King George III died, in 1820, the Laureate, Southey, wrote *A Vision of Judgement*, considering the old man's rapturous reception in Heaven, and by implication, extolling the success of his reign and the achievements of his ministers. Byron replied to this with *The Vision of Judgement*, in which he satirised the earlier work, suggesting that St Peter accepted the old king, and his Laureate, with the greatest reluctance.

CHAPTER 6

i Lorenzo Bartolini (1777–1850), was a noted Tuscan sculptor. He had per formed busts of both Napoleon and Madame de Staël.

ii Captain John Hay was an old friend of Byron's, and had been one of those Byron had bet a hundred guineas that he would never marry. He had come to Pisa on a shooting expedition.

iii John Taaffe Jr, was an Irishman who had been forced to flee England following an affair with a woman in Edinburgh. He had lived in Italy since 1815, and fancied himself equally as a writer – he was engaged in a translation of *The Divine Comedy* – and as a horseman. In both fields Byron held him in contempt.

iv George Bancroft (1800–91), born in Worcester, Massachusetts, was completing his tour before returning to America to become a teacher. His real future lay in history, however, and he was to write a ten volume history of the United States which made him famous.

v Captain Daniel Roberts was on an extended leave from the Royal Navy, and looked forward to a summer's yachting with Byron and Shelley.

vi The third member of the crew of the *Don Juan* was an English boy named Charles Vivian. He was totally neglected in Byron's and Trelawny's grief over the deaths of Williams and Shelley, and was left to moulder in the sand.

vii Captain Shenley was a naval officer.

CHAPTER 7

i The Countess of Blessington (1789–1849), had, as Margaret Power, lived an exciting and scandalous life before marrying, in 1818, Charles John Gardiner, 1st Earl of Blessington. She had not changed her habits, and in addition to her husband, travelled with her *amico*, the Count d'Orsay. She was described as the "most gorgeous" Lady Blessington, but I must agree with Byron that her portrait does not convey such an impression to me.

ii Edward Blaquiere and Andreas Luriottis were agents of the Greek revolutionary leaders.

iii Alexander Hypsilanti (1792–1828), more commonly spelled Ypsilanti, was the leading member of a distinguished Phanariot family who had long been in opposition to Turkish rule.

iv Charles Barry was the Genoa partner of Webb and Company, with whom Byron banked. He played a more important part in organising the Grecian expedition than Byron suggests.

v Alexandros Mavrocordato (1791–1865) was, as Byron suggests, the most disinterested of all the patriot leaders. He was to become Prime Minister of an independent Greece.

vi Odysseus was the adopted name of the leading Morean chieftain. His real identity is unknown.

vii Count Constantine Skilitzy (Schilizzi) was a Greek patriot leader.

viii Edward Le Mesurier was a retired navy lieutenant living in Italy.

ix   Sir Charles James Napier (1782–1853) was one of Britain's most distinguished soldiers, who is famous for his despatch following his conquest of Sind, in Northern India: *Peccavi* (I have sinned).

x   James Hamilton Browne was a Scotsman who had been dismissed his post in the Ionian islands for showing too much sympathy to the Greeks. He actually joined Byron's expedition in Leghorn.

xi   Theodore Colocotronis (more usually spelt with a K) (1770–1843), was to emerge as the leader of the Greek forces in the Morea. His later life was stormy, and he was condemned to death for conspiring against the first king of Greece, Otto, but he was eventually pardoned.

xii   Frank Hastings is, with Byron, the great foreign hero of the Greek Revolution. His likeness is with Byron's in the Garden of Remembrance in Missolonghi.

xiii   The final cantos of *Don Juan* are devoted to his adventures with Lady Adeline Amundeville.